The Wraith

A novel by

T.R. Braxton

MONTEBELLO BOOKS

This book is dedicated to Jumpin' Jack Brax and Kris Kristofferson Krzyzewski, the dual lights of my life. Know that Dr. Victor Von Woobenstein aka Da-Ja-Ba will always be glad to have you around.

Chapter 1- Drowned Men, Dry Land

I

John Rainbird Jeffries regarded his surroundings with electric blue ovals that were not his own.

The brilliant spheres belonged to a blond man with a wiry build and slight drinker's paunch. A greasy sheen coated the man's unruly hair. The stubble on his face promised to birth a sandy beard if not soon exposed to a razor. Dark scars on his left shoulder and right breast held the tale of knife slashes. His right ear stood out from his left, a discolored cauliflower.

The scarred slob wore dingy cotton socks and a pair of boxers that had seen better days. A wreck of a couch served as the squalid throne of a shabby efficiency apartment. There he sat, smoking a joint, eating pizza, and drinking National Bohemian. His relic of a television blared from its place atop a wooden stand that might have been some high school kid's woodshop project. Once he had his fill of pepperoni slices and controlled substances, the sandy haired man climbed into bed.

John Rainbird realized that he knew the scuzzy loser by name - Gregory Rollins. Although he had never known or heard of any such person, he felt dead certain of the identity.

The briny smell of river water and sodden leaves disrupted Gregory's inebriated sleep. John Rainbird continued to inhabit Gregory's consciousness, sharing his thoughts and employing his senses in a flood of imagery. The dual smell grew cloying in intensity. Gregory's concerns about the smell's origin dissipated as he drank in the sight of the nude young woman at the foot of his bed. He rubbed his eyes, thinking that he must be dreaming. The naked figure remained rooted in place. Gregory hoped that the scenario his subconscious had cooked up ended with him getting laid by the stunning apparition.

Her round, pert breasts were as perfect as he had seen. Wide hips angled into strong thighs. A sunken stomach gave the ethereal beauty the appearance of one whom hardly ate. Gregory wondered how voluptuous she would be if she ate a few good meals.

Her face was an unblemished canvas, accented by full lips moist with sexual promise. Gaunt but smooth cheeks framed a thin, slightly rounded nose. Voluminous brown hair rested on her lithe shoulders.

Fierce intelligence filled the girl's eyes. The violent orbs locked onto Gregory's gaze, making him their prisoner.

The fantastic ovals shifted colors, reinforcing Gregory's certainty that he must be dreaming. They cycled from dark green, to dark blue, to deep brown, and back again. Gregory's consciousness fell into the changing pupils as if they were a great pit. He offered no resistance as a current of eerie images swept him along.

A pretty girl of perhaps fifteen years old stood at the shore of the river that passed through his hometown. She stared into the water beneath her, ignoring the whistling night wind that tousled her dark mane of hair. Gregory did not process the girl's resemblance to the nude form standing before his bed. Instead, he thought of the good times he'd had along that very shore, drinking and smoking pot, fucking and getting blowjobs among the trees.

A dry and hideous laugh escaped the girl's up tilted head as Gregory reminisced. The sound reverberated through the darkness like the call of some strange animal. She removed her jacket and tossed it to the dirt before tearing off the rest of her clothing. Not a single shiver escaped her naked flesh as the winter night assailed it. A razor blade appeared in her hand. She dragged the glinting steel across her left wrist before doing the same to her right. She took a running start and leapt from the embankment, leaving rivulets of blood in her wake.

Gregory's mind hurtled to the present. He felt as if he had just ridden the most turbulent coaster at Six Flags after gorging on greasy food. The naked young woman still stood at the foot of his bed. Her luscious lips curled into a mischievous leer. Gregory realized that he shouldn't be able to make out more than her shape, what with all the lights turned off and blackout shades drawn. A distant part of his mind announced that he had urinated on himself, dampening his boxer shorts and thighs. He processed the fact that the girl was lit from within like some giant firefly. That golden glow illuminated his dump of an apartment.

Gregory shut his eyes, keeping them closed while counting to ten. The young woman remained at the foot of his bed when he opened them. She remained naked, her beautiful body exquisite with curves. Her lamp like glow abided. The smell of river water and sodden leaves continued to emanate from her. Her lips remained frozen in a mischievous leer.

"Shit," Gregory said, chuckling. "I got to stop smoking weed before bed."

The young woman emitted a laugh to match that of the girl he'd imagined by the river. Gregory realized that the two figures were one and the same. "It is no dream, Uncle Gregory."

A tripled voice escaped the figure, performing as a ghastly chorus. One of the three voices was the dulcet tone of a teenage girl, matching the gloriously nubile, somewhat underfed body before him. The droning and robotic second voice complemented the disturbing quality of the figure's laughter. The third voice belonged to a little girl who'd been part of Gregory's life some years back. He dated her mother before moving in with them both. The little girl had known him as

Uncle Gregory, but they were no blood relation. As he had many times in the past, he found himself wishing he'd never met the girl or her mother.

Gregory's bladder released once more as the weight of fear settled upon him. "N-no," he stammered. "It c-can't be you."

"Sure it c-can," the figure mocked, its lips stretched into a gaping grin. "What's the matter, Uncle Gregory? Haven't you missed me? Aren't you glad to see me?"

Gregory didn't see the figure climb onto his bed, though he hadn't once looked away. Yet, there she was on top of him, her nude body straddling his sheet covered form. Up close, the smell of briny water and sodden leaves overwhelmed him. He felt compelled to trail his hands over her nude body. He found it wet and slippery, though his eyes thought her dry.

The young woman laughed and swept the sheet aside as Gregory's bladder fired another round.

"Why, Uncle Gregory," the creature teased with its tripled voice, its smile as seductive as it was terrifying. "I do believe you've wet yourself."

"That's alright," she said. Gregory felt her cold and clammy body press against his. "I like water sports. And I still love you." More dry and ghastly laughter escaped her. "You know, I never forgot anything you taught me."

A hand a thousand times stronger than its delicate appearance ripped off Gregory's urine soaked underwear, causing a loud, tearing sound. The same hand began to pleasure him with erotic dexterity.

"I never forgot how to stroke a man's cock. How to use my mouth."

Gregory felt just as helpless to stop his arousal now as he had been when he first knew his visitor. Realizing the depravity of his actions failed to grant him resistance.

Gregory always knew that he deserved a reckoning, even while trapped in the throes of his sick deeds. He now knew that the attack that scarred him years ago was not the end of his punishment.

The young woman's eyes shifted colors faster than before. A tremor rocked Gregory's body as he accepted that the creature astride him was real, not some construct of his tortured imagination. This creature was his erstwhile "niece", but not as he knew her. He awaited the mercy of this young woman, not the other way around. The time had come to face his true reckoning.

"Of all the things you taught me when I was a little girl, there's one I remember best," the young woman said. "How to kiss. Let me show you that I haven't forgotten."

The figure's powerful left hand pulled Gregory's face close while her right hand continued its expert work. Lips as cold and clammy as the rest of her body clamped over his. Gregory felt more resigned than scared as he opened his mouth to accept a wormlike tongue. As it explored him, his mind flooded with visions from his so-called niece's life once he departed it. He beheld her suffering countless hardships. He held no illusion that what he did to her was the root cause of all that befell her.

Gregory again beheld the teenaged girl ending herself in the river that the creature reeked of. He saw something that was and was not her emerge from the water.

Gregory Rollins did not resist as the river's harvest filled his lungs. He did not wish for mercy or even survival. Kissing the girl he loved most wasn't a bad way to die.

II

John Rainbird Jeffries woke to a dark dorm room and the bearish snoring of his roommate. Sweat coated his head and torso. His heart pounded far quicker than its normal pace. He sat up, taking deep breaths in an effort to compose himself.

What a crazy fucking dream, he thought. He switched on his bedside lamp and picked up "The Truth About Chuck Norris" book that he'd left on his nightstand.

He flipped through the book, laughing at the ridiculous jokes such as, "There is no chin under Chuck Norris's beard. There is only another fist. "

John grew calm, reasoning that the dream had to be some weird manifestation of his grief. There was no other explanation for his dead friend appearing as an avenging demon.

III

After six years on the job in Harford County, Detective Mark Ballinger found himself dispatched to the scene of his first homicide in Abingdon. The sprawling county only averaged three murders each year, almost all of which occurred in Edgewood. Detective Ballinger credited the population of section eight transplants from the roughest parts of Baltimore City for Edgewood leading the way. The worst of those government dependents bought city problems such as drugs and gang activity to the verdant suburbs.

Abingdon was far different from Edgewood. The picturesque town was almost 90% white. Well to do and nicely seasoned white at that. There were very few wiggers running around, dying to act like what they thought was "gangsta" because of daily BET overdoses. Just about every residential area in Abingdon was storybook pretty. The house that hosted the dead body Ballinger now examined with his sharp brown eyes was a strong exception.

The shabbiness of the corpse's apartment pegged him as a real loser. His stark naked form lay face up on a bottom of the barrel bed, affirming Ballinger's impression. The recently departed was thin, but a pouch of a belly revealed that he liked his beer.

An old knife scar trailed along the right side of the victim's chest, accompanied by another scar on his left shoulder. Ballinger wondered if his misshapen right ear were suffered in the same attack.

Empty National Bohemian cans littered the dead man's nightstand. More cans decorated the floor in front of the beat up couch.

Cheap drinker, Ballinger thought, cataloging several marijuana roaches in an ashtray on the nightstand. *The better to save money for the weed.* An old pizza box bisected the cans in front of the couch. Baby roaches idled atop the cardboard, their antennae twitching. The squalid apartment's bathroom stood to the rear left of the bed. The tiny kitchenette occupied the right corner.

A pale, portly man with white hair and rounded shoulders slumped against the front door. He had discovered the body when he came to demand rent from the deceased. The way he told it, Mr. Loser Dead Guy had been even later with his payment than usual. Mr. Stuyvesant left several messages, demanding that he pay up. After several days without response, Stuyvesant stormed over, intending to confront his debtor in person.

Mr. Stuyvesant got psyched up after spotting the guy's banged up old Honda Accord parked in the driveway. "I was going to tell him," he said, his lips quivering as he recounted the details of his discovery, "give me what you owe or face eviction. I didn't want to hear any more of his stories."

Stuyvesant let himself in through the door on the old house's porch before banging hard on the apartment entrance to the left of the inside stairs. When the dead guy didn't answer, Stuyvesant got even more worked up and let himself into the apartment. Shock and fear replaced his disgust when he found his debtor dead.

Some young patrol cops showed up after Stuyvesant's 911 call. After confirming Rollins's death, they called for homicide and the coroner.

Ballinger beat the coroner there. He tried to determine the cause of death as he stood over the body. He touched the dead man's arm with plastic gloved fingers. It felt cold and stiff with rigor. The entire corpse had a ghastly, faded pallor. Ballinger figured that the poor guy had been dead for about two days.

The victim reeked of urine. A pair of ripped boxer shorts lay a few feet from the bed. His left hand rested palm up, revealing the dark impression left by another long ago knife slash. There appeared to be dried semen on the right thigh of the deceased. Cheap bedclothes hung off the mattress.

Ballinger balled his right hand into a fist and pressed it against his forehead.

"Fucking disgusting, right?" One of the uniformed officers asked. The kid's hair was as sandy as the victim's, but much more well kempt "Looks like the guy pissed on himself- then jerked off. Or vice versa. Maybe he had a heart attack or something from all the fun."

Ballinger smirked as he read the younger man's badge. "I guess that's why I work homicide and you're a patrolman yet, Officer Harris." He leaned over the body and massaged the victim's lips open. A tiny stream of water spurted out. "I can see exactly how this poor loser died." He straightened up.

Officer Harris arched his eyebrows in anticipation.

I might as well tell him, Ballinger thought. *Though he won't understand how such a thing could be possible any better than I do. Hell, maybe no one will.* "It looks to me like this poor bastard drowned."

IV

Ballinger left his barber's chair and headed straight for the ME's office. He had his reddish-brown hair trimmed every other week, accentuating the perfect trim he gave to his own mustache and goatee whenever he felt the threat of an unruly follicle. This held true even on the rare occasion when he caught a possible murder case. In this particular circumstance, possible was the operative term. *Actually, there are two operative terms*, he thought. *Possible and impossible.* The latter of those two terms loomed large in his mind. What physical appearances would have him assume about the departed Gregory Rollins was impossible.

The water that spurted from the poor guy's lips when Ballinger pried them open was prime evidence of drowning. But where the hell could the guy have drowned? In his bathtub? That claw legged relic wasn't large enough for a grown man to drown in, even if he had somehow knocked himself unconscious while sitting in it. The only way for Rollins to drown in that piece of shit tub was for someone to force his head into the water and hold it there. If that had happened, there would have been evidence of one hell of a struggle.

But there wasn't a single bruise on the guy's body. There was no evidence visible to the naked eye that anyone else had been in his apartment, save for his landlord. By the looks of him, the landlord couldn't beat his way out of a wet paper bag.

So what do we have here, Mark? Ballinger thought as he cruised up route 24.

He took no notice of the naked trees that lined the four lane road. *We got a stiff who somehow managed to drown while lying on his bed, masturbating to orgasm and urinating on himself?*

"That just can't be," he spoke aloud. "Better to stop speculating. The ME's probably figured it out." *After all, that's her job.*

He turned off the road and headed up a hilly driveway flanked by trees. A security booth greeted him at the crest of the path. The huge yellow and black striped lever that stood beyond it blocked unauthorized access.

A husky and russet skinned guard stood within the booth. Ballinger flashed his badge as he said good morning.

"Good morning, Detective." A smile punctuated the sing-song admiration of the guard's voice. He pressed a button that raised the huge lever. "Going to look at a stiff?"

"That's right."

The big man winked. "Best get on the case, then. Have fun."

"I always do," Ballinger said, heading into the parking lot. It was no idle statement. He always felt a special thrill when he was on a case- although not special enough that he would want to work someplace like Baltimore City where people were murdered in the hundreds each year. No, he figured the rarity of the homicides he investigated was what made them so exhilarating. He didn't know if he wanted the type of thrills this case seemed to promise, though. He'd worked as primary to five murder cases during his time as a detective, and this was the first whose circumstances foreshadowed that it might be unsolvable.

Ballinger parked beside the Buick SUV that belonged to the person he needed to see. He opened a glass door and entered an assuming one story brick building that could have passed for an auto insurance office. Only the words- *Harford County Police Department of Forensic Pathology*- imprinted on the glass entry door betrayed the building's true nature.

Moments later, Ballinger stood next to the ME before a metal table. He spent as much time regarding his petite, oaken skinned colleague as he did the unfortunate Mr. Gregory Rollins. Dr. Chandrunkunnel was of Asian Indian heritage and looked to be in the neighborhood of 30. She wore her lustrous, jet black hair in a bun. Her full lips were unadorned by lipstick or gloss. Cerebral glasses combined with her white lab coat to punctuate her portrayal of a full on Poindexter.

Ballinger mused on how hot she might look all dolled up and away from the human meat locker that served as her workplace. *Keep it professional, Mark,* he chided himself.

"So what do you have to tell me, Doc?" he asked. "You know I've been waiting almost a week for this information."

"I completed the autopsy as soon as I could, Detective." Chandrunkunnel's generic American accent belied her exotic appearance. "It isn't my fault that it took so long to locate a next of kin."

"Yeah- Sorry, Doc. I just get a little impatient when I work a case."

Dr. Chandrunkunnel turned to face him. "I would have thought that you savor each case, considering the infrequence of them," she said, smiling.

Ballinger complemented her smile with one of his own. "That's what I like about you, Doc C. You're always handy with the gallows humor." He rubbed his hands together like an excited eight year old. "Now, spill it for me. I just have to know."

Dr. Chandrunkunnel grew serious. "It's just as you expected. His lungs and stomach were full of water. There's no question he drowned."

Ballinger fell silent for a while before asking about the urine and semen.

The ME sighed. "That's where this defies all science. Just as it appears, he urinated on himself, achieved orgasm, and drowned in rapid succession."

Ballinger's eyes bulged. "So, this guy pissed on himself, masturbated, and somehow drowned in bed?"

"It's highly unlikely that he masturbated. There were no traces of semen found on either of his hands."

"But there's no evidence of any sort of struggle. Right?"

Dr. Chandrunkunnel nodded. "No bruising or skin under his fingernails. And no one else's fingerprints on his body."

Ballinger formed a fist with his right hand and pounded it into his left palm, causing a loud smacking noise. "Come on, Doc C! Are you telling me that some boogeyman got this guy off and drowned him in his bed at the same time? All while he pissed on himself? What is this-the Sci-Fi Channel?"

Chandrunkunnel shrugged. "I'm simply telling you what the physical evidence suggests. I have sent samples of the water to the Harford County Environmental Studies Department. At least we should be able to determine where that came from. Other than that, there's nothing more I can tell you, Detective."

Ballinger pounded his left palm again, producing another loud smack. "Fuck me," he groaned.

V

A cavalcade of thoughts swept through Kevin Anderson's mind as he bedded down following a Friday night keg party. His hope to not be hung over for morning basketball practice was foremost among them.

Screw it, he reasoned. *I'll just take a long hot shower and drink a ton of coffee. Besides, I only drank like a ton of beers. I didn't touch any liquor, so I shouldn't be too bad.*

Kevin felt glad that the coming Sunday afternoon game would be played at Comcast Center. It was against Howard University, a black school in nearby D.C. The Terps regularly crushed such lightweights during their non-conference schedule. Kevin hoped that the trend would hold. If it did, he might get his share of garbage time minutes.

Although basketball had been a secondary sport for Kevin in high school, he still thought himself to be very good at it. He'd made Third Team All-Metro as a point guard during his senior season. In high school, he'd always been one of the quickest guards on the floor. The six-two, 190 pound frame he'd graduated Mackenzie High with had been a good size for a guard at that level.

Things were far different at the University of Maryland. Kevin was only big and quick enough to be fourth guard on a Terrapin's team that couldn't carry the jockstraps of the team that won a national championship in 2002. The seven pounds of muscle he added since graduating high school had only served to keep him off the practice squad. In addition to intense strength training, he'd used a rigorous plyometric program to improve his explosive movements. Kevin soon learned that no matter how many box jumps and sprints he did, he'd never be quick enough to keep up with his black teammates. He had played in only four of the Terrapins' first six games. The nine minutes he played in the second half of a blowout win against Farleigh Dickinson University were his longest stint so far. He scored an astounding season high of five points in that game.

What disturbed Kevin most was the fact that the majority of his playing time came against other teams' second strings, yet he still struggled to keep up with whomever he guarded. He wasn't even quick enough to keep pace with second string guards from second hand schools.

Fuck basketball, Kevin thought. *And fuck all these black guys and their super speed and jumping ability. My scholarship is for baseball. Maybe I can't keep up with all those jackrabbits, but chasing them around will surely make me even quicker on the base paths come spring.*

He'd like to see any of his basketball nemeses match him on the diamond. No Iverson impersonator could crush a home run to the opposite field or throw a base runner out at second from the outfield fence, like he could. Yeah, come spring his status in the athletic pecking order on this huge campus would be much improved. Come spring, he'd be the top dog. As top dog, his share of "bitches" would increase exponentially. Sure, he'd hooked up with six different chicks since arriving at campus in August- two brunettes, a natural blond, a bottle blond, a Latina, and one Asian. But he'd managed that just on the chiseled good looks he'd been blessed with, along with endless on line and in person flirting.

Besides, screwing six girls in four months was really nothing to write home about. This wasn't high school. On a campus of 35,000 students free to come and go as they pleased, he should have been nailing at least one new piece every week. Spring would rectify that, though. Kevin was as sure of that as he was sure of the fact that he'd dominate on the college baseball diamond.

Kevin soon drifted into the land of sleep. It was not a quiet place for him. His unconscious mind drummed forth thoughts of something he did to threaten his life of athletic privilege.

The viral humiliation of his ninth grade girlfriend was not something he felt proud of, though he'd been quite pleased with himself when he was 14 years old. He couldn't explain why he had that video uploaded, other than the fact that she had pushed him away. He just didn't feel she had a right to do that – not after he reached below his station to date her. He ignored the fact that she was working class and half black because he really liked her. He'd also ignored the fact that kids called her the knife lady's daughter all through middle school. Kids called her that because her mother went crazy and tried to stab her ex-boyfriend to death. He'd overlooked all of that.

He treated her good, too. He hadn't even pressed her for sex when she said she wanted to stay a virgin. He was more than content with a little oral. After all that Kevin sacrificed to be with her, she had the audacity to make a scene at that Halloween Party. She made him the butt of jokes at school, just because she caught him making out with another girl. What was he supposed to be- a monk? That chick was all over him. Besides- it was a fucking party.

Kevin had recorded the video of the two of them just for fun. It was something he did with all of his hook-ups back then. They didn't need to know that the cute stuffed Teddy Bear he kept within plain view was really a spy camera.

Kevin had always kept his videos private until he uploaded that one. He only wanted to repay the girl for embarrassing him, not ruin her life. He didn't intend for the video to be seen by the entire Mackenzie High student body. Okay, maybe he had. But he didn't expect school administration to get wind of it or everything else that followed.

Sure, it sucked being kicked out of a prestigious school and being ridiculed as some huge slut, but Rebecca should have toughed it out. Maybe she should have moved from Harford County to someplace where she wasn't so recognizable. Even if she had stayed put, things would have died down just as soon as some other kid suffered a huge humiliation. She didn't have to do what she did.

VI

Volcanic anger welled within John Rainbird as he dreamed. He wished that he could do more than imagine Kevin's narcissistic, responsibility shirking thoughts. He wished he could climb into the dorm room where the asshole slept and kick the shit out of him.

Don't be silly, John chided himself. *You couldn't take this guy in a fair fight if you tried.* Kevin had grown several inches taller and built a wall of sinewy muscle in the four years since he and John fought. His arms rippled with coiled strength and a barrel chest pressed against the cotton tank top he slept in. His jaw seemed chiseled by a fine sculptor.

Kevin's roommate slept like the dead, to Kevin's right. His brawny build betrayed him as a fellow athlete.

A large bean bag separated the roommates' beds. Each of their nightstands housed a laptop. A laser printer rested against the rear wall, under the lone window and behind the bean bag. A flat screen HD T.V. sat astride an entertainment center by the door. An IPOD interfaced with a stereo docking system on the shelf directly beneath the T.V. The third shelf housed a Sony Playstation 3, various game disks, and DVDs. Textbooks, binders, and rumpled clothes cluttered the floor.

A fathead of Mark Teixeira in California Angels gear swallowed most of the wall over Kevin's bed. John sensed that Teixeira was the major league baseball player that Kevin most admired. The Maryland native had amassed huge power numbers during the last few seasons. Though he'd never followed baseball, John now knew this.

This is some dream, John thought. He felt like he was playing "Second Life" and Kevin was his avatar.

Chilling cold besieged the room, causing Kevin to awaken. Shivering, he gripped his granite shoulders with his large hands. "What the fuck?" he grumbled.

He processed his surroundings a moment later. His dorm room bore no resemblance to the place he fell asleep in. He sat up in bed, forgetting how cold he was as he took it all in.

Big Jason and his bed no longer rested to his right. In fact, that entire side of the room was gone.

Kevin swiveled his head to check out the rest of the room, but there was no rest of the room anymore. The only man-made object that remained was the bed that a wide eyed Kevin shivered upon.

A thick, cartoon like blue mist replaced the walls and floors. The mist swirled about Kevin in a glacial manner, seeming about as real as one of those moving paintings he'd seen in Chinese restaurants. He chuckled, thinking that he was having some crazy fucking dream.

His right hand passed through a shred of mist when he tried to touch it. He realized that the ethereal blue substance stretched as far as his eyes could see. He also realized that although his bed lay outside, no moon, stars, or animal sounds of the night accompanied it. Only the strange blue substance and the bone chilling cold greeted him.

Kevin stripped off his blanket and reached for bulkier clothes.

What are you-an idiot? He thought, smacking one broad palm against his forehead. *Trying to warm yourself up in some dumb ass dream?*

"It is no dream," a voice as ethereal as the mist itself whispered. The two fold voice combined the pleasant, deliciously feminine tone of a young woman with a droning, robotic tone.

Kevin stood as straight and tall as his considerable height allowed. The crew socks on his feet plunged though the swirling mist, seeming to stand on nothingness.

Kevin feared that he'd crash to the ground like Wile E. Coyote in one of the old Roadrunner cartoons he saw on the Cartoon Network if he dared to look down. He felt even more afraid of the possibility of looking and finding that there was no ground beneath for him to fall to.

"Who's there?" Kevin croaked, speaking against his better instincts. He couldn't have felt any more vulnerable as he stood helpless, clad only in a tank top, mesh shorts, and socks.

"Don't you even recognize my voice?" the droning/coquettish duo responded, sounding louder this time. The question was followed by a cackle that sounded gleeful and mechanized at the same time.

Kevin pivoted in the direction from which the sound came. There was nothing there, save for blue mist that had grown much thicker and more vivid in its' coloring. It seemed as if some giant artist looked down upon the canvas of the dream world. Said giant artist's discerning eye must have told him that the image would benefit from a more generous application of azure paint.

Perhaps that same giant figure had decided to turn up the cold in the freezer that confined Kevin. The chattering of his teeth matched the violence of his shivers. If not for his certainty that he was dreaming, he would have feared the onset of frostbite.

"Don't worry." The voice came from behind him this time. Kevin turned with an athlete's quickness, only to be faced with nothing but more mist. "You won't die from the cold." This time the droning/ feminine voice came from his left. Another ghastly cackle followed. "It wouldn't be any fun for me if you died from the cold."

"Who are you?" Kevin bellowed. Dream or not, he was starting to feel pissed off.

"You really don't remember me?" The voice sounded indignant and robotic at the same time. "I must admit… that really hurts my feelings!" Those last words exploded in a mixture of banshee wail and mechanical roar.

Kevin covered his ears as he staggered backward. He recovered his balance and began jogging in place in an effort to warm himself. "I don't know what you're talking about! How do you expect me to remember you when I can't even see you?"

"Is that all?" The voice taunted, coming from far to Kevin's right. "You only need to see me?" Now the voice came from a few yards to his left. Kevin stopped jogging and turned in that direction.

Something cold and clammy touched his shoulder from behind. He pivoted and beheld a horror he couldn't have imagined.

"Well, now you see me," the voice's owner said.

What Kevin saw turned his insides as cold as his outside. He hoped that he was having a particularly bad nightmare, brought on by guilty feelings that he'd suppressed for years. If what he saw wasn't some nightmare figure conjured by his guilty conscience, then he was about to die in a most unpleasant fashion.

VII

A naked and exquisite young woman stood before Kevin. Her figure was as athletic as it was voluptuous. Skin the color of butter pecan ice cream complemented dark brown, shoulder length hair. Ample round breasts rivaled the succulence of ripe fruit. A taut stomach found its equal in thick, toned thighs. Shapely shoulders crested strong but supple arms.

Despite his fear, Kevin felt pangs of desire stirring within. The girl's intense brown eyes smiled with the rest of her striking face. When she spoke again, the robotic drone departed, leaving only a dulcet, sweetly feminine voice. "You remember me now. Don't you, Kevin?"

Kevin felt a tremendous swelling in his lower region. Unable to speak, he nodded a confirmation.

The beautiful young lady stepped closer, leaning in as if to kiss him. The smell of wet leaves and briny water struck him when she did.

The figure's pleasant smile twisted into something cold and hateful. Kevin tumbled onto his bed as he backed away.

The figure's skin took on a deep blue pallor as Kevin sat astride the bed. Long black scars materialized across its wrists as it held out its arms, seeking an embrace. The scars formed shallow but jagged holes, as if they were the result of a drunken surgeon's scalpel work. Tiny worms plopped from the openings.

An underfed figure replaced the delicious fullness of the body that Kevin first saw. Kevin scrambled over the bed and tried to run, but there was no place to go.

The nightmare creature appeared in front of Kevin at the spot that he'd scrambled to.

"Are you afraid of me, Kevin?" The robotic drone usurped the feminine voice. "Don't be afraid. I only want to show you what I've learned. I know how to do far more than suck a dick now!"

The figure emitted a mechanical cackle as it swept its intended into slender but overpowering arms. The embrace sent numbing cold through Kevin's body-cold that invaded his lungs when he inhaled.

"Let me show you how I can please you."

Kevin could not resist staring into the eyes of the creature that had once been his girlfriend. The burning orbs promised him the secrets of unknown worlds and time beyond time. The burning orbs promised him ecstasy and death.

Kevin did not struggle as the creature's paint blue lips engulfed his. Instead, he opened his mouth wide to accept a flicking serpent of a tongue. An earth shattering orgasm coursed through his body as water filled his lungs.

VIII

John Rainbird Jeffries woke with a start in his dorm room. Once he composed himself, he started to wonder about the dreams he'd been having, particularly the one he'd just awakened from. He didn't like that each of the dreams featured his dead friend returning to take revenge on someone who had wronged her. He was half Maupai and many of his tribe believed that the spirit world sometimes punished the living for their deeds.

John's superstitious side was balanced by the rational worldview of his deceased father. That rationality spurred him to dismiss his dreams as manifestations of his own desire. There was no denying the fact that he'd like to see the people who'd persecuted his friend punished. But in the past four years, he'd grown too pragmatic and mature to do what he'd done before. He wasn't about to assault anyone or engage in any more Indian mysticism. If that mumbo jumbo really worked, his ancestors would not have lost their lands to the Europeans.

John's thoughts turned to the town of Bay Corner. He hated the place because of what it did to his friend. Before her demise, he had made it a point to leave Blessed Earth and explore the town proper as often as he could. After she died, he hated even riding through it on the Havre de Grace High school bus.

John's high school years couldn't pass quickly enough for him. He felt elated to be at the University of Delaware, more than 30 miles from that ass backward little town. He would have preferred to attend college much farther away, but UD was the strongest school to offer him a full academic scholarship.

The school made up for what it lacked in geographical distance by being worlds apart in culture from the place where John grew up. During his first semester at college, John met people from all over the country. The more than

2,000 acres of self-contained campus stood as Mount Everest in contrast to the anthill of the Blessed Earth. Some of his fellow freshman who came from big cities found the campus and surrounding town of Newark to be a bit boring, but John saw the setting as a bold new world. He did not look forward to leaving campus for the upcoming semester break.

When he went home for Thanksgiving the previous week, his only contact with the town proper was passing through it on the way to his girlfriend's house in Havre de Grace. If there were any other way of reaching Brittany without passing through the little backwater, he would have exulted to take it.

John hated many things about Bay Corner, but what he hated most was the fact that the town had birthed Kevin Anderson. John was certain that the silver spoon licking asshole would also soon be home from school for winter break. The bastard would no doubt spend his time off being the arrogant, sexual predator of a rich kid he'd always been.

Yeah, John, he told himself. *That dream was definitely just wishful thinking. The fucking asshole is busy living a life of privilege right now. He probably hardly even thinks about what he did.*

John's grandfather often spoke of the importance of balance. To John's grandfather and other Maupai who embraced traditional beliefs, justice was a principle component of balance. Those who commit heinous offenses must face severe punishment. John didn't see any balance in what happened to his friend or the fact that Kevin Anderson's only real punishment had come in a vivid dream.

IX

David Tremblehorn and Lonny Carpenter were nearing their ninth year as partners in the Prince George's County Police Department, Homicide Division. The job offered plenty of work, with the district averaging 100 murders each year. A large percentage of the killings were drug related. The county had never been as drug heavy as Baltimore or even neighboring D.C., but it had its fair share of dealers and addicts.

Tremblehorn and Carpenter had seen firsthand the results of a number of drug deals gone wrong. They'd also seen the results of street beefs settled with guns and knives. On occasion, they witnessed the results of husbands or wives deciding that their spouses were better off dead. They'd seen many people killed by many methods and for many reasons.

The veteran detectives had never heard of any murder occurring at the University of Maryland College Park. Year after year, top scholars and athletes matriculated at Maryland's flagship public university. The worst trouble to occur there followed the Terrapins basketball team winning the NCAA Division I championship in 2002. Fueled by drunken whimsy and the foolish exuberance of youth, hundreds of students set bonfires around the sprawling campus.

"It's just over the crest of that hill," Tremblehorn said, pointing his right hand toward patrol car lights that flashed ahead of them as he kept his left hand on the steering wheel.

"I got eyes," Carpenter grumbled. "20-20 vision." He used those eyes to observe the great crowd of people gathered on the hillside leading to the crime scene. Word must have spread across the huge campus like wildfire, no doubt transported by cell phone, text, and e-mail.

"So you always say," Tremblehorn said. "Makes me wonder if you're compensating for something."

Carpenter grinned. "I'll measure my dark meat against your red meat any day."

Tremblehorn chuckled. "I hear red meat has more protein than dark meat. Seriously, partner- a murder at College Park? I would've never imagined it."

Carpenter snorted. "You kidding me, Red? Anything is possible in this crazy world. The pendulum swings to all corners of the room, eventually."

Tremblehorn laughed again. "How many times do I have to tell you? Save the mystical talk for the half Indian member of the duo. You stick to what your people do best."

Carpenter raised a brow. "And what's that?"

Tremblehorn grinned. "You know, singing and dancing. Dunking basketballs. Frying chicken."

Carpenter laughed as the unadorned sedan neared the scene. As he expected, the scores of gawkers standing about were all students. "That's so very racist of you."

"Sorry," Tremblehorn said. "Sometimes, I just can't stop my white side from coming out."

He pulled the car into a parking lot the size of a city block. A group of tall buildings stood at each end of the huge lot. Yellow police tape cordoned off the second closest building to the road. Two patrol cars flanked a coroner's van, their lights continuing to flash blue and red. A campus police car rested alongside the patrol car on the right. The line of onlookers that started on the hill approaching the lot terminated at the very edge of the police tape.

Carpenter exited the car first, unfurling his tall, athletic frame. He extended a chocolate mitt to Officer Evans, one of the patrolmen at the scene.

"Ever imagine this scenario at the academy, Lonny?" the ruddy- faced officer asked.

Carpenter shrugged. "Can't say I have - though I'm not exactly shocked."

Evans nodded. "I guess you homicide boys reach the point where nothing surprises you, anymore."

"Not me." Tremblehorn smiled, ambling his stocky frame onto the sidewalk in front of the building. "My partner here's just jaded."

"That's what makes me such a pleasure to work with," Carpenter deadpanned as Tremblehorn and Officer Evans shook hands.

"So give us the rundown," Tremblehorn said.

As Evans led them into the building, Tremblehorn glanced backward at the crowd edging up to the barrier. Two beat cops he didn't know urged them to keep back. Why couldn't the kid have been found on a Monday - when most students had classes? He hoped they could inspect the scene and bag the poor bastard before the local news arrived. He knew the vultures were in flight already, breaking their necks to get there.

Evans told them all he knew as they scaled several flights of stairs. Tremblehorn hated taking the stairs, but walking them left more time to hear the story.

Less than an hour earlier, Evans and his partner, Officer Tripoli, received a radio call for any cars in their sector to get to the College Park campus, Driesell Hall, Unit B21. They rushed over, arriving in less than ten minutes. They discovered the stiff, learning that his roommate woke up and found him that way. The roommate left him alone for a while, figuring he'd had one too many beers last night and was sleeping it off. Then he noticed that the guy's chest did not rise or fall to indicate breathing.

"He told me and Mikey that when we first got here," Evans said. "Big kid. He's with campus police right now. Poor kid was a mess of tears and snot when Tripoli and I got here. You guys seen any Terps basketball so far this season?"

27

"Nope." Tremblehorn shook his head.

Carpenter nodded. "I've seen some."

"The vic is Kevin Anderson. Freshman reserve guard. He's got- he had a full baseball scholarship. He managed to walk on with Coach Williams, too."

"Blond kid?" Carpenter asked, his eyebrows reaching skyward. "Mostly plays in garbage time?"

"Yeah, that's him. When I looked at the poor kid's body, I saw something that my naked eye just can't understand," Evans said. His breathing grew labored as he led the others off the stairwell, into a fourth floor corridor. Carpenter breathed just fine, but only pride kept Tremblehorn from doubling over as he sucked wind.

"I'm in terrible shape," Tremblehorn said.

Evans stopped in front of a rectangular wooden door that had a j-shaped handle similar to the ones common in hospitals. "Maybe the coroner can explain what I saw," he said, "but I can't."

Evans depressed the door handle and stepped inside. Tremblehorn and Carpenter followed, exchanging pleasantries with Officer Tripoli as they entered. While this happened, the balding coroner bent over the bed in the left corner of the room, using his medical glove covered hands to snap digital photos of a recumbent male corpse.

"I guess we'll leave it up to you professionals, now," Tripoli said, as he and Evans left. "I guarantee you this won't be an easy nut to crack."

"What you got, Messier?" Carpenter asked, sidling over to the balding man at the foot of the bed. He measured the stiff with his eyes as he asked. He shot a look at his partner, who stood to his right, a moment later. From the knowing look that Tremblehorn returned, Carpenter assumed that the Indian also thought nothing appeared to be wrong with the body.

"I know what you guys are thinking," Messier spoke with the gravelly tone of a chain smoker. As if to ensure that no one thought he might have come by such a voice naturally, he emitted a hacking cough. "You're wondering why you were called out here when it looks like the poor kid died peacefully in his sleep. You're wondering if maybe he wasn't one of those kids with a bad ticker who doesn't know it until it gives out and the poor soul dies right then and there."

The two detectives said nothing, continuing to observe the body for signs of wrongdoing as Messier spoke.

"You're thinking we'd all like to go so peacefully, only not so young."

Messier fell silent for a moment. From past encounters with the dumpy coroner, the two detectives knew that this was not an invitation to chime in. Messier enjoyed drawing things out almost as much as he liked the sound of his own ruined voice.

"So, why are you gentlemen here?" Messier set the camera down before walking alongside the left edge of the deathbed. Doing so placed his back to a fathead wall hanging of Mark Teixeira in a Rangers uniform. He reached out a stubby, still gloved hand and pushed the victim's left cheek inward. A thumbnail worth of water spurted from the dead mouth.

Messier feasted on the detective's stunned reactions like a vampire on fresh blood. "There's more where that came from." He applied more pressure to the cheek than he had the first time. A miniature geyser spewed forth, coming to rest on the mattress.

"That's right, detectives." The dumpy, balding man smirked. "It seems that young Mr. Anderson drowned to death. I still have to do the autopsy to confirm it, but I've seen enough drowning victims to know that's what we're looking at."

He shrugged, holding his stubby hands palms out toward them. "Now, how that's possible in an otherwise normal looking and perfectly dry dorm room is beyond my pay grade. If I had to wager, I'd bet that you fellows are about to investigate a case for the ages."

Chapter 2- The Teammate and the Failed Mother

I

Jason Hanson's huge hands covered his melon size head as he sobbed like a small child. The comforting hand of a campus policeman on his back did not calm him.

"I can't believe it," he said, rocking in the passenger seat of the campus patrol car. "I can't believe he's gone."

The towering young man was too distraught to notice the campus cop rolling down his windows as Carpenter and Tremblehorn approached the car. Nor did he process the slim, middle aged officer exiting the car to shake each of the detective's hands.

"John Taylor," he said. "I've been working this campus for nineteen years and never heard of anything like this." He motioned toward his sobbing charge. "Poor kid's all yours."

Fifteen minutes or so later, the detectives and their witness shared a table at an off campus coffee shop. Only a few other patrons occupied the quaint space. Carpenter faced Jason from across the table. Tremblehorn sat to Carpenter's right. The young man sipped from a steaming paper cup held in a protective jacket.

"You can start filling us in whenever you're ready, kid," Carpenter said. "We know you just suffered a terrible loss. In fact, we can take you back to campus- come back tomorrow- if you like."

Jason shook his large head. "No way. I don't want to go back there, other than to get my stuff. I'm probably going home for a few days." A slight twang accented a speech pattern that reflected a South Jersey or perhaps Philadelphia upbringing. "I know the end of the semester's almost here, but I can't be in that place. I'll need a new room assignment, for sure."

"Where's home?" Carpenter asked, taking care to keep the expression on his face impassive.

"I've lived in Willingboro- South Jersey, since I was twelve." Jason took another sip of his drink before setting it down. "But my family's from the country- Rocky Mount, North Carolina."

Detective Tremblehorn allowed himself the slightest of smiles. "We'll, I'm sure your country family will be sure to comfort you in these troubling times." He raised his eyebrows. "If you don't mind me saying- you're a big, strong kid. What are you- 6'3"? Maybe 220?"

Jason smiled. "6'4". 226. I'm hoping to add ten more pounds of muscle by the time I'm eligible for the Major League Draft."

"Oh, so you're a ballplayer like Kevin?" Tremblehorn sought to relax the kid with his masterful pretense of ignorance.

Jason nodded. "Yeah. Baseball's my only sport, though. You know what's a trip? Even though I focused solely on the diamond while Kevin devoted time to basketball and baseball, he was still a better baseball player than I am."

Tremblehorn tapped his partner under the table. They could see that young Jason was starting to compose himself. A little longer and he would be able to give reliable answers. Detective Carpenter engaged him in a series of questions about his baseball career. He asked what positions Jason played, what side of the plate he batted from, and how fast he ran from the batter's box to first base. He even asked the kid about his offensive stats as a high school senior. Jason's athletic ego took over during the questioning, just as the detectives expected it to. In a short time, he went from distraught to wearing a huge grin, while bragging and trying to seem humble at the same time.

He was going on about hitting for the cycle in the first round of the New Jersey State high school playoffs when Tremblehorn sprang it on him. "Tell us what happened this morning."

The smile dissipated from Jason's face. All at once, he remembered that he sat in a coffee shop with two homicide detectives, not two members of the Jason Hanson fan club. "May I have another coffee, please?" The voice that had been bursting with expression moments earlier grew hushed and dry.

After a waitress delivered his request, he downed almost half of the black liquid in one draught. Tremblehorn expected the kid to go bug eyed, but an eerie calm overtook him instead.

"When I woke up this morning, I was surprised to see Kevin still there. I knew he had Saturday practice 'cause he'd been grumbling about it before we went out last night. I don't drink at all, but Kevin cut loose and had his share of beer. He's the kind of guy can-could stay up half the night drinking and still be up at the crack of dawn. Some guys are just like that- you know?"

He sighed and took another sip. "So, anyway, when I woke up I saw him just lying there. I thought, 'Fuck.' He actually slept through practice this time. Coach Williams is gonna kill him'." He chuckled and shook his head. "Isn't that sick? I actually thought that. 'Coach Williams is gonna kill him'. Turns out I should've been worried about someone else killing him."

He took a longer sip this time, producing a slurping sound. Fear filled his brown eyes as he shifted them between detectives.

"Anyway, I started yelling across to him, 'Kev, get up, bro. Coach Williams is gonna kick your ass'. Loud as I am, he doesn't stir one inch. I go over to his bed to shake him. That's when I notice his chest isn't rising. I checked his wrist for a pulse and felt nothing. Not only that, but his body was cold. It was cold like he had already been dead for a long time." Jason's eyes grew wide at the horrible memory. "Shit, it was cold like it had been kept in someone's refrigerator."

Both Detectives kept their facial expressions clinical while filing that revelation away for later. They asked the strapping young man a few more questions before driving him back to campus. Having been beaten to the scene by Messier, neither of the detectives had touched the victim's body. In his enthrallment over the victim seeming to have drowned, the ME neglected to mention the unusual temperature of the corpse.

As Tremblehorn drove away from the campus, Carpenter dialed Messier's number on his cellular phone. "It's Carpenter," he said. "You forget to tell us something, Mess?"

"I guess I did." Messier emitted a sound that was a combination of a cough and the world's driest laugh. "I was going to call you guys, but I see you must have found out from the witness already."

Messier confirmed that corpses only grew as cold as the unfortunate Mr. Anderson's after a few days. Yet, according to young Jason, the victim had been alive last night.

Carpenter was the first to break the long silence that ensued after he ended his call with the ME. "Could be we just got sucked into some sci-fi shit, partner." He shook his head. "This is going to be one fucked up investigation."

II

An attractive, bottled blond woman answered the door of a Spartan second story apartment. She wore grey sweatpants and a form hugging t-shirt. The harsh coloring and hard lines of hard drinking trod a path on her face. Voluminous hair hung over both cheeks, hiding the origin of a scar that ended just above the right side of her chin. She measured Detective Ballinger with skeptical eyes, only opening the door after he identified himself and held his badge to the keyhole for inspection.

"Are you Miss Tricia Nealy?" he asked.

She hesitated before nodding. "Yes, I'm Tricia. But, I don't know what you want with me, Detective. I don't get mixed up in nobody's trouble." Her throaty voice marked her as a heavy smoker.

"I wholeheartedly believe that, Miss Nealy," Ballinger said. "I'm not here because you're suspected of any involvement with the case I'm currently investigating. I'm only here to find out if you know of any reason that someone might want to harm the victim."

"Victim?" She gasped, clutching at her breasts. "Oh, God- something's happened to someone I know. Who?"

Detective Ballinger motioned behind her. "I think it would be better if I told you inside."

Tricia stepped out of the doorway, gesturing for him to come in. Ballinger seated himself across from her in her living room, in a chair that matched the imitation red leather couch she perched on.

Ballinger spat the news out without delay, revealing that Tricia's ex-boyfriend had been found dead. She crumbled at the revelation, bawling and tearing at her hair. If she had been an older woman or even a fat, unattractive one, he might have wrapped his arms around her in a gesture of comfort. He didn't feel comfortable doing so with a woman who was a few hairs shorts of smoking hot, despite her bad habits. He offered her a handkerchief instead.

She managed to calm down after an interminable amount of time, using the handkerchief to blow her nose and wipe her tears. "Thank you," she said, offering it back to Ballinger. He declined with a shake of his head.

"Right." She sat it down next to the half-full ashtray that rested on the table before her "You probably don't want it anymore, now that I've used it. What kind of cop carries a handkerchief around, anyway?"

Ballinger smiled, having heard that question a few times before.

Tricia sighed. "I haven't seen Gregory in a couple years." She fished a rubber band out of a sweatpants pocket and used it to tie her hair. Doing so revealed that her scar only ended above her chin. It started just above her right ear, tracing a diagonal to its terminus. She pointed to it. "We broke up not too long after that crazy bitch gave me this. I just couldn't be around him without thinking about that night."

Like her now deceased ex-boyfriend, Tricia had left Bay Corner soon after Emma Saulters assaulted them. She didn't go far- settling in the southern extreme of Harford County- in Joppatowne, just a hop and a skip from Baltimore County.

Ballinger discovered Tricia's connection to the departed Mr. Rollins when he checked into the man's background. The deceased had a history of petty crime, such as small time pot dealing and trading in stolen goods. Ballinger's investigation also revealed the nature of the gruesome scars he bore.

He had been the infamous "Knife Lady's" victim, as had the woman sitting across from the detective at this very moment. Ballinger remembered the violent incident well, because it happened in the town he grew up in. He supposed that being assaulted as Tricia had been was the type of thing that would never leave her. No further explanation of her heavy drinking and smoking was needed.

Tricia crossed one thin leg over the other, rubbing her palms together. "You mind if I have a cigarette?" She reached for the pack of Salem Lights next to the ashtray, not waiting for Ballinger to answer. She already had one lit by the time he shook his head.

"It's fine."

"Thanks." She took several long drags from the cancer stick, causing the fire at its lit end to flicker. A newfound calm washed over her as she exhaled plumes of smoke.

"I always feel so much better after a smoke." She stubbed the lit end out in the ashtray, leaving the cigarette dangling there. "I have to drag them out nowadays, though- with how much they cost and all."

Ballinger leaned forward in his seat. "I know you're very upset right now, but I need you to answer one question. Other than Emma Saulters-when you were involved with Gregory- did you know of anyone who might have reason to harm him?"

Tricia stilled herself, the cigarette having done its work. Her striking hazel eyes looked directly at Ballinger. "No I can't think of anyone who'd want to harm him, other than the crazy bitch who did this," she said, pointing to the scar. "The last I heard, she's supposed to be a model citizen now that she's medicated and in therapy and all. The parole board let me know about her when she got out."

Her eyes widened, threatening to burst from their moorings. "You don't think it could be her – do you? Maybe she came off her meds and…"

"I promise you, that's not possible," Ballinger said, cutting her off. "What was done to your ex-boyfriend could only be done by someone strong enough to overpower him. If he was murdered, it had to be done by a man."

"How was he killed?"

"He was found dead at his apartment, having apparently been drowned." Ballinger omitted the details that would have made his answer sound like science fiction.

Tricia gasped, covering her face. "Oh, God- why would someone want to do that to him?" She looked at the cigarette she had just stubbed out before finding Ballinger's eyes again.

"This all sounds so crazy to me, Detective. The Greg I knew had no reason for anyone sane to try to harm him. He sold a little weed for extra money, but he was always small time." A bitter laugh escaped her. "He could've brought more money home if he'd been anything but small time." Fresh tears brimmed in her eyes. "I'm sorry I can't be of more help, Detective."

Ballinger stood to go. "Don't beat yourself up about it. You told me all you knew."

Tricia lit her cigarette again, sucking on it like a hungry baby at its mother's nipple. "You think he's really been murdered?" she asked. "I suppose he could've drowned himself. He was a broken man after what happened."

Ballinger hooked the fingers of his opposite hands together, in front of his chest. "That is a faint possibility, Miss Nealy. But murder is far more likely. It's my job to find out for sure." He turned toward the front door. "Thank you for your time."

She took another drag of her cigarette as she saw him out. "Well if he has been murdered, I hope you catch the bastard who did it. Gregory was no angel, but he never harmed anyone. He was always sweet to me."

Ballinger left with a promise to do his best. He kept his belief that his best wouldn't be good enough to himself. He had interviewed several people in the wake of Rollins's death, including Rollins's estranged mother. The old woman hadn't seemed too upset about her son's passing. So far, the detective hadn't turned up any leads, or any information that even hinted at a lead. Even if he found a legitimate suspect, he still had to unravel the confounding matter of how anyone could drown a man in his own house without some signs of a violent struggle.

The frustrated detective figured he might as well track down Emma Saulters. Just as he told Tricia, he didn't think it was possible for a woman to be the culprit. Still, he had no better options. He might as well confirm whether the "reborn" Ms. Saulters remained a model citizen or if she'd backslid into the troublesome ways of her past.

III

Ballinger parked his Sedan alongside a flat curb, in front of a homely rancher on Einhurst Road. It had been a good while since he'd come to Bay Corner, as people of his profession served little purpose there. Only two noteworthy incidents of violent crime had occurred within the tiny municipality since the Carter administration.

Back in 1980, Charlie Casserly had gone all Travis Bickle, killing four people and wounding several others. Ballinger was just a child on that dark day, but he learned the story well from older folks as he grew. The most heinous case of Bay Corner violence since then had been perpetrated by the very person Ballinger came to interview.

Ever fastidious about his appearance, the detective adjusted his dark wool suit. The early December weather grew surlier with each passing day, but he refused to wear an overcoat until it was downright nasty outside. Satisfied with his nattiness, he headed up the walkway.

An empty driveway sat to the far left of the property. A large placard stood on a wooden pole to the driveway's immediate right, dug into the center of a garden plot that had died its seasonal death. The colorful sign read "Rebecca's Garden", with the smaller words "We Will Never Forget Her" underneath. Painted flowers wrapped around each painted letter of the sign. Ballinger had no doubt that come spring, a beautiful garden would be cultivated to complement the homemade artwork.

A winter green holiday wreath stood at the highest point of the house's front door. Wind tickled the chimes that hung from the porch light, inspiring them to sing.

Ballinger buzzed the doorbell once and waited. "Coming," a woman's voice called from within. Ballinger soon sat with the owner of that voice, in an understated living room. The center of a large couch that had a chaise longue built into its right side served as his seat. His hostess perched at the end of the chaise longue, her body turned toward him.

Ballinger had sized Emma Saulters at about 5'7" as she invited him to sit. She wore a well maintained mane of light brown hair. Wiry muscle covered her thin frame. Ballinger could tell that she worked out, but not enough to destroy her natural curves. She was a good looking woman, though her eyes told of ages spent in hell. A plastic tag that read "Manager" hung from the right breast of a white blouse that fit her with dignity. Unassuming black slacks and black walking shoes completed her uniform. An oblong scar marred her right palm.

Ballinger sipped from a cup of coffee she had given him. "Let me begin by saying that I appreciate your cooperation, Ms. Saulters."

"No problem." She treated him to a pleasant smile, speaking in a slight drawl. "Although, as I said on the phone- I don't know how much assistance I'll be."

Ballinger nodded. "I understand. Still, with your connection to the victim, I figured it wouldn't hurt to interview you."

Emma studied him with her sharp eyes, as if trying to read his thoughts.

"So long as I'm not a suspect." She chuckled. "I mean I know I tried to kill the bastard before, but that was years ago. I'm nowhere near the same person I was then."

When Ballinger contacted her at work the previous evening, she knew right away what the inquiry was about. She confided that she read the "Aegis" article about the mysterious circumstances of her ex-boyfriend's death.

"I know that," Ballinger said. He placed the coffee cup on a coaster that sat on the end table in front of the couch. "I've spoken to your parole officer, you know. She says you've been a model citizen since you got out. Said she only bothers to check on you because it's required, but she's sure you're solid. She said she was worried you might go off the rails after-"

"After my daughter passed," Emma said, finishing his statement. "Yes, well that actually became my fuel- my inspiration. I spend every day trying to be someone Rebecca would have been proud of. I only wish I could have been that person sooner." A tear welled in her eye. "Things might have been different for her, if I had been."

"I'm sorry to upset you, Ms. Saulters."

Emma made a pained attempt at a smile as she wiped the tear away. "It's okay. I'm easily upset when it comes to my daughter. I wish she was here now."

Ballinger nodded, shifting in his seat. "You know something, Ms. Saulters? You couldn't have murdered Mr. Rollins, even if you were the same as you'd been before. Not in the way that he died."

Curiosity colored Emma's eyes. "What do you mean, Detective?"

Ballinger leaned toward her, searching her pupils as he spoke in a conspiratorial tone. "Can I trust you? I mean if I tell you something the press doesn't know- you'll keep a lid on it?"

Emma unleashed a braying laugh. "Detective, I can assure you that if I never have any contact with the newspapers again, that will be too soon. I got more than my fill of attention from them with the things I've gone through in the past."

Ballinger nodded before clearing his throat. "You remember what it said in the paper about Gregory dying under mysterious circumstances?"

Emma nodded.

"Well, those circumstances aren't mysterious to the Sheriff's Office," Ballinger said. "That's just a line we fed the folks from the local media and "The Sun" to keep them from going bonkers. We discovered the cause of death right away. The victim drowned."

Emma gasped as her eyes performed a dance of stunned realization. "But, wasn't he found lying on his bed?"

Ballinger couldn't help a smile. "That's right, Emma. He was found lying on his bed. What's more, there was no sign of a physical struggle. So, there you have it. No sign of a physical struggle or break-in, yet the victim's lungs were full of water. So you see, Emma. I wouldn't look at you, or any other woman as a suspect, even if I'd heard that you'd been promising to finish what you started before you went to prison. I mean, you are a fit woman, if you don't mind my saying, but..."

"But, I'm no damn Zena Warrior Princess. There's no way I could have overpowered Gregory and drowned him-what in his bathtub?"

Ballinger shrugged. Although he knew the answer to that question, he'd already told the woman more than he should have according to police protocol.

"So then, if you think I couldn't possibly have done it- why bother questioning me, Detective?" Emma asked.

"I guess I just hoped that you might know why someone would want to kill him. So far, I've learned that he had a hard time keeping decent work and was no stranger to selling a little marijuana and other petty crime, but I doubt if he was killed over small potatoes like that. So can you think of a reason why someone would want to kill him?"

Emma fell silent, gripping the edge of the chaise longue with both hands. The corded muscles of her thin forearms pulsed as she squeezed. Ballinger saw that the back of her right hand was scarred, same as the palm.

Pained uncertainty danced across Emma's face. After a few moments, she released her grip and kneeled on the carpeted floor in front of the couch. She bowed her head and murmured a prayer.

Ballinger sat silent, figuring that she was using some sort of calming tactic she'd picked up in AA or another support group.

Emma assumed her previous seat after she finished, taking care to brush off her slacks. "Okay," she murmured, more to herself than Ballinger. "Okay." Her voice gained volume as she made eye contact with him again. "Okay, I'll tell you. I haven't told anyone other than my shrink and my own mother, but I'll tell you."

Ballinger exercised his considerable patience when she fell silent again. Scores of interviews had taught him the value of that skill.

"When I went to prison," Emma began, "everyone thought that I had attacked him just because I was bipolar and needed medication. Sure, that was part of why I got into such a state. But, that wasn't the real reason."

Her eyes bore into the detective's, burning with intensity they had lacked until now. "I tried to kill Gregory because I had every reason to believe he molested my daughter. I only stabbed the poor woman he was living with because she tried to stop me."

Ballinger pondered her revelation in silence before responding. "Were you absolutely certain about that?"

Emma's voice trembled, betraying the anger that threatened to erupt from her. "Detective, one night I discovered that my nine year old daughter had been watching a porno and apparently practicing fellatio on a banana. Shortly after that, I found a treasure trove of pornos in that bastard's toolbox. I broke up with him and put him out of my apartment right then, not wanting to explore the matter any further because I didn't want Rebecca embarrassed. I ended up embarrassing her anyway. "

"Becoming-" she paused to make air quotes, 'the Knife Lady' and all. But, I wasn't going to force Rebecca to deal with everyone knowing she'd been molested. I preferred everyone thinking I was completely off my rocker." She placed a hand on her bosom and took some deep breaths. "Anyway, that could be your- what do they call it- motive, Detective Ballinger. Maybe Gregory did something he had no business doing with someone else's kid. Maybe they decided to fix him and did a better job of it than I did."

"That just might be," Ballinger conceded. He was not humoring her. This new information about the deceased Mr. Rollins made the possibility of him being murdered far more plausible. Emma's revelation had transformed him from small time loser to sick pervert.

Emma hung her head, her eyes finding the carpet. "You know I didn't even talk to Rebecca about what he did to her, not even after I got out of prison. Maybe If I had- she would have been better adjusted. Who knows maybe she would have done things a little differently, not had to go through that whole mess."

44

Ballinger sensed the remainder of the sentiment that this poor woman left unsaid. Maybe Rebecca would still be here. "You think so?"

"She told me as much herself."

Ballinger adjusted his position, now expecting to occupy his current seat for a while longer. His time as a detective had imbued him with the ability to sense when someone needed to unburden themselves by telling a tale.

"Yeah?" He committed to his impromptu role as the audience. "How'd that go?"

IV

Rebecca and her mother walked side by side, along the beautiful promenade of Baltimore's Inner Harbor. Rebecca had caught a train from Aberdeen into Penn Station, taking a cab the rest of the way. She smiled as she recounted the driver talking fresh with her. "He said that in his country, 14 year olds are often married," she said, shaking her head. "I think he should go back to his country, then."

"Amen to that," Emma said, her own smile as sunny as her daughter's. "I guess you'd better get used to that sort of thing. After all, you did inherit my good looks."

Rebecca rubbed her own arms in an attempt to get warm. The cold coming off the harbor water was much stronger than elsewhere on this late fall day. Though she wore only a light jacket in contrast to her daughter's bubble vest and pullover, Emma didn't seem at all bothered by the weather. Rebecca wondered if her mother had gotten that way because there wasn't good heating in prison.

"Course I've lost a little of them, what with how I abused myself in the past," Emma continued.

"You're still pretty, Mom," Rebecca said.

"Thank you." Emma swept her daughter into an embrace. "You're so sweet," she said, looking into the girl's eyes. "Yeah, I guess I'm still pretty, but nothing like I was when I was a young girl. I let myself get scarred, you know? I don't ever want you to get scarred like that."

Powerful emotion welled up in Rebecca at those words, emotion she had no control over. It took her a moment to recognize the feeling as anger. Here was her mother, pretending like everything was all fine between them, when that couldn't be further from the truth. What the hell did Emma mean she didn't want her to get scarred? Couldn't she see that happened a long time ago? Couldn't she see that she was the one who did the scarring? *Between what she did to me and what Uncle Gregory did*, Rebecca thought, *I never had a chance.*

"Rebecca, what's wrong honey?" Emma said, her eyes widening. "Rebecca, why are you crying?" She extended a concerned hand, but Rebecca pushed it away.

"N-no," Rebecca said, her lips quivering. "I don't want you to comfort me. Everything that's happened is because of you. So, I don't want you to comfort me!"

Emma reeled from her daughter's words as if she had been punched. She glanced along the promenade. The few passersby on that cold morning chose to act as if the unfolding drama was none of their concern.

"What's the matter, Mom?" Rebecca seethed. A malevolent glint replaced her tears. "Was I too loud, just then? Afraid I'll make a scene and embarrass you? You should be embarrassed!"

Emma regarded her daughter with sadness. "I should have known this day would come," she said. "I should have been the one to bring it up, but I guess I haven't had the guts."

She stepped forward, her movements deliberate and gentle as she coaxed Rebecca back into her arms.

"I'm sorry, baby. You're right. I should be embarrassed, 'cause I let you down. Your whole life, I let you down."

Rebecca was still for a moment before attempting to twist free of her mother's grip. Emma held fast with prison fashioned muscle and sinew.

"You deserve to tell me all about it," Emma said. Tears streamed down her face, but the tone of her voice remained soothing. "You deserve to heap all kinds of abuses on me- but not here."

She let Rebecca go before pointing to her right. "We don't wanna have that cop rousting us for disturbing the peace."

A harbor cop had stopped within ten yards of them and scoped out the encounter.

The tall officer sat astride a bicycle that stood as strapping and muscular as his own frame, his huge hands gripping the handlebars. No hat adorned his block of a head, but he wore thick gloves and a navy blue jacket that read BPD in yellow letters.

"Everything all right ladies?" He squinted, his square jaw jutting toward them like an image from a 3-D movie. When he said all, it sounded more like *awe.*

"Everything is fine, Officer." Emma flashed her best charming smile. "Just one of those emotional mother daughter moments."

"Don't I know it," the officer said, grinning as if he and Emma had just become co-conspirators. "I got a teenage daughter of my own. You ladies take care."

Huge feet churned the bike's petals as he rode away.

"You see," Emma said, pleading with her eyes as she extended her hand.

Rebecca's eyes smoldered with resentment as she let the offered appendage dangle. Emma swallowed hard as her hand fell to her side. "This is not the place to purge your emotions," she said. "I know what we need to do."

About half an hour later, they exited a taxi cab on Route 40, just into Eastern Baltimore County. "I haven't gotten used to how much more a cab ride costs since I went to prison," Emma grumbled.

She and Rebecca stood in the parking lot of The Pleasure Inn. The quarters beyond it connected in one long, three-tiered structure. Black painted railings led up the stairwells that connected to walkways on each level. Other than the railings, a color best described as Pepto-Bismol pink covered the entire outside of the rooms.

A large overhead sign faced the road. It bore the motel's name, along with the promise of a room with HBO for $39.95 per night.

Emma noticed the sign and snickered. "People definitely come here just for certain kinds of 'pleasure'," she said, speaking more to herself than her daughter. "Not, today though." She turned and sought Rebecca's gaze. Rebecca's cherubic cheeks flushed a deep crimson as she looked away.

Emma paid for the room and sat on the old, cheap bed within. Rebecca sat opposite her mother in a chair that had seen better days.

Emma took a long look at her daughter, who seemed to find the motel room carpet worthy of lengthy examination. Trembling lips accompanied Rebecca's furrowed brow.

Emma sighed. "So, let's have it. Say everything that I deserve to hear."

Rebecca swung her head up with all the violence of a crocodile snagging prey at a water hole, locking onto her mother with soul-boring eyes. Her lips twisted into a sneer that belied their lusciousness.

"So you think it's that simple, huh?" she hissed. "You think you just say 'let's have it.'" Her fingers formed air quotes. "I tell you everything fucked up about yourself that you already know- maybe curse you out-what- maybe even slap you? After that, you tell me how sorry you are- that you know you could never make it up to me. We cry a few buckets of tears together- then on with the healing? Well, it's not that simple, mother. It's not you that I want to talk about. I want to talk about Uncle Gregory."

Emma's eyes attempted to flee her skull as her stomach dropped to her toes.

"That's right." Tears froze at the rim of Rebecca's burning eyes. 'Uncle Gregory. I know you know what he did to me. That's why you went to prison in the first place. But, what you can't know is that I liked it! No, I loved it. Just like I loved him."

"Rebecca, please." Emma's hands flew to her chest as sweat beaded her forehead.

"No!" Rebecca screamed, pounding her fists against her own thighs. "You wanted to hear it. Well, now you're going to hear it all. Uncle Gregory was my first love." She cackled. "That's right. My first boyfriend was a grown man. And you," she said, pointing an accusing finger at Emma, "made it all possible."

"Rebecca, please," Emma gasped, burying her head in her hands.

"I never got over him," Rebecca continued, her tone almost mocking in its' cruelty. "I missed him after you took him out of my life by trying to kill him. He taught me how to kiss, how to suck a cock real good."

"Oh God, no," Emma moaned, causing a creaking sound as she collapsed into a prone position on the mattress. She closed her eyes and covered her ears, as if doing so could free her of the waking nightmare she'd plunged into.

Rebecca dragged her knuckles across her own face to dispose of her brimming tears. Then, she went to her mother, prying Emma's hands from her ears.

"When I got a real boyfriend my age, the most natural thing for me to do was suck him off," she said, stabbing Emma with her words. "So I did that. I went over to his house and sucked him off, 'cause that's how I learned to be from Uncle Gregory. Unfortunately, that didn't work out so well for me."

Rebecca spat out the tale of the ordeal caused by said boyfriend all the while gripping Emma's wrists lest she try to cover her ears. After Rebecca finished, she sat back in the motel room chair, regarding her traumatized mother the way a med school student might regard a cadaver.

Emma trembled like a fault line just prior to an earthquake as she curled into the fetal position. She wailed like a stricken infant, like a dog whose master had died. The motel room bed creaked with each tremor of her body.

"I think I'll call Grandma to take me home, Emma," Rebecca spoke in an uncaring tone, after a few minutes of observing the damage she'd done. Emma did not reply, continuing to wail as Rebecca began the arduous process of dialing the motel room's rotary phone.

V

"I could have died after she confronted me with all of that," Emma said, tears brimming in her eyes. She wiped them away, fighting new ones back. "My mother came to take Rebecca home, then drove back and talked me out of that motel room. God knows I just wanted to make a hiding hole of it, never come out. But, Rebecca called me later that night, told me that she could forgive me now that everything was in the open. It felt good to know that she forgave me. It still does feel good. I haven't quite forgiven myself, though. Not even after all these years."

"Maybe it's time you do," Ballinger said, rising from his seat. "It seems if she could forgive you, you should be able to forgive yourself."

He thanked Emma for being so forthcoming before he departed. Hope filled him as he drove away. He would leave no stone unturned in discovering whether Rollins had engaged in any other sick conduct with kids. Discovering a possible motive was a beautiful thing, though there was still the huge matter of the discovery that the ME had dropped on him the day before.

Chandrunkunnel's usual stilted tone gave way to a leap of excitement when she revealed the source of the water found in Rollins's lungs. It came from the Snake River that traversed the southwestern edge of Havre de Grace and continued through Bay Corner.

More than twenty four hours later, Ballinger still hadn't reconciled that revelation. It was not possible that anyone could have drowned the victim in the Snake River without him offering up any kind of a struggle, moved him more than ten miles to his Abingdon apartment, masturbated him to orgasm and placed him on his bed, all without leaving a shred of physical evidence. Ballinger felt certain that dead guys couldn't have orgasms at all. He waged a mental battle within, forcing himself to stop thinking about the confounding aspects of the case and appreciate the possible motive he now had. He couldn't control the science fiction aspects of the investigation, but he could find out who had reason and means to cause Gregory Rollins's death.

Chapter 3- A Return to Blessed Earth

I

John Rainbird Jeffries awoke to a dorm room in flux. It was Saturday, December 13, 2008- moving out day for both he and his roommate, Earl.

Portly and red haired, Earl hailed from Greensboro, North Carolina. His quiet nature matched John's, meaning that they got along just fine. It wasn't unusual for them to spend hours ensconced in amiable silence within the dorm room.

Earl had a lot more possessions than John. Among those possessions were a twenty-seven inch television, a collection of rock posters, a swanky Macbook laptop, a bean bag chair, an IPOD complete with stereo docking system, just about every video game console, controller, and accessory on the market, a ton of video games, and a treasure trove of DVDs.

That morning, John insisted on helping Earl carry his many possessions out of the dorm and load them into his father's Buick SUV.

"Thank you, John," Earl's father spoke in a slight twang as they finished. He extended a sun weathered paw.

"No problem, Mr. Danvers," John said, shaking like he meant it. "It's my pleasure to help you and Earl out." He didn't mention that Earl was the one true friend he'd made at Delaware.

John's lack of social acquaintances at the university was all his doing. He knew UD (as locals and students called it) as a very open, friendly place. Students of all creeds and colors co-existed without conflict, for the most part. The entire length of Newark, Delaware's Main Street served as a student hang out while school was in session. John committed all the good gathering places to memory within weeks of his matriculation. Doing so helped him achieve his goal of avoiding people.

Opening up and being social seemed an alien concept after everything John had been through. He supposed that he and Earl had to be friendly because they were roommates. Living with someone for three and a half months was not conducive to standoffishness. You had to either really like the guy or not be able to stand him.

John and Earl liked each other plenty. Earl and his dad felt determined to give John a ride to the train station in Wilmington before they left. It took five refusals before they accepted that John wanted to catch the bus in.

"I don't mind at all," John said. "Taking the bus will give me time to think about some things. Besides, I don't want to inconvenience you guys."

Mr. Danvers looked at John as if he'd just said the moon was made of cheese.

"That has to be, without a doubt the silliest thing I've heard you say all morning," he said. "Where Earl and I come from, one good turn deserves another."

John nodded. "It's the same where I'm from." He patted Earl on the shoulder. "So I'll call a favor in from Earl later, if you insist. But I really do prefer catching the DART into Wilmington."

"Alright, J," Earl said. "But you and me both know the DART is slow as molasses."

John chuckled. "That's alright. I'm not in a hurry."

John headed back to the unadorned dorm room after Mr. Danvers drove off. He loaded his paltry amount of clothes into the wheeled suitcase that served as his only piece of luggage and slung his Jansport over his shoulders. The backpack held toiletries, an off brand MP3 player, and some tattered paperback novels. John took what would be his last look at the dorm room for the next five weeks before trudging down the hall and through the lobby.

"Enjoy your winter break, John," Phillip, the RA said, his eyes somehow finding John through an unruly mop of brown hair.

"Thanks, man," John said, stifling the urge to say 'Yeah, right'. He thought of reuniting with Brittany as he waited for the Campus Shuttle to come along. He and Brittany had been an item since his freshman year at Havre de Grace High School. Their relationship had even survived the rough patch that followed Rebecca's death. John felt very fortunate to have Brittany in his life. He had known two truly wonderful young women during his young life. He supposed that made him luckier than most, even though he had lost one of them.

Brittany had come up by train to visit John three times during the fall semester. They had also spent a lot of time together during Thanksgiving break. Those visits were not within shouting distance of enough for John. He smiled at the prospect of satisfying his desire to be with Brittany every day for the next five weeks. Such sunny thoughts were balanced by the dreary prospect of returning to Blessed Earth (the tribal commune John grew up in).

Riding the just short of empty shuttle bus to the DART stop did nothing to derail John's train of thoughts. The 25 minute ride to the Wilmington train station did nothing to interrupt his thought process, either. His happiness about soon seeing Brittany continued to clash with his resentment of returning to his childhood haunts as he boarded the 11 am southbound Amtrak.

John watched the scenery outside his window roll by as the train began its' forty five minute trek to Aberdeen. He did not doubt that his grandfather was already headed to the station. John thought that it would make a lot more sense for the old man to at least get a pre-paid cell phone like he had. That way, John could just call him when the train approached. John shook his head, thinking that such actions were against the Traditionalist views that Wise Eyes swore by. Hell, the old man still didn't have phone service at home. Until John obtained cellular service for himself, his only access to any sort of telephone had been the trio of payphones that stood at the outskirts of Blessed Earth. He had always felt ridiculous, walking a mile just to make a phone call in the 21st Century.

Fear of technology was a big part of the Traditionalist views that the old chief espoused. Oh, Wise Eyes had no problem with driving his rickety old truck to work. But he and other Traditionalists believed that using technology just for pleasure- such as cell phones, video games, and television- corrupted the soul. Recorded music was fine, so long as it was nothing salacious. It seemed that Wise Eyes's Traditionalist views always worked out so that everything he wanted to do was fine, but things that John liked to do were impure.

Fuck purity, John thought as the train made the first of three stops before Aberdeen. He didn't think that Wise Eyes's ideas were hypocritical, just antiquated and inconsistent in their implementation. He felt that if his grandfather insisted on being so wary of technology, the old man should follow that thinking to its logical extremes. He should get rid of the truck and use a horse to get around. He chuckled as he pictured his grandfather blowing a gasket if he ever verbalized such thoughts.

John's thoughts of his grandfather were replaced by thoughts of the frightening dreams that now plagued him as the train rolled along its tracks again. He hadn't mentioned the dreams to Brittany because Rebecca (or some nightmarish manifestation of her) was the central figure in them. He didn't need Brittany thinking that he was obsessing over his long dead friend.

Brittany had been jealous of Rebecca after she died. She had never been vocal about that jealousy, but John sensed the feeling was there. The weird thing was that Brittany hadn't been jealous of Rebecca prior to her death. John had always thought Brittany pretty, but Rebecca had blossomed into the kind of physical beauty that could have led to a career in front of a camera. Still, Brittany hadn't seemed the least bit threatened by John's friendship with Rebecca. It was only after Rebecca's death that John's feelings for her seemed to make Brittany uncomfortable. The way Brittany swallowed her own worries to help him through his grief only made John love her more.

John decided to keep his own counsel, telling himself that the dreams were only manifestations of his grief. In the verging on four years that had passed since Rebecca's death, John learned that he would never get over it. His pain persisted, though it had downgraded from a great, gaping, raw, wound to a haunting but distant buzzing that inhabited the depths of his subconscious as life moved on. *My anxiety about going home for so long probably stirred those thoughts up,* he told himself.

John couldn't rationalize the fact that his dreams seemed to reveal new information. He had known that Rebecca's mother went to jail for attacking an ex-boyfriend, but he hadn't known anything about that boyfriend molesting Rebecca. In addition to revealing things that John couldn't know, the dreams seemed as real as the fuzz on John's chin. He could see 'Uncle Gregory' and that bastard Kevin Anderson living just as his dreams depicted.

A frightening possibility occurred to John. *Maybe,* he thought. *No, that couldn't be. There's no truth in such things. They're just primitive, stupid Indian beliefs. That was just a stupid thing I did when I was only fourteen and full of hurt. If something like that worked, it would have happened before now.*

John dismissed his concern as the countryside continued to roll by. His imagination had gotten way too stirred up, that was all. The first man he dreamed had to be nothing more than a figment of his stressed imagination. Kevin Anderson was real and had hurt Rebecca, so John wished that he could somehow be punished. He didn't want that punishment to happen the way he'd dreamed it, though. He didn't want Rebecca's spirit to return from beyond and take revenge, even if he had tried to make that very thing happen after she died.

John laughed. Yeah, those dreams were just wishful thinking, manifestations of anxiety conspiring with the anger he still felt about what happened to the best friend he'd ever known.

Rebecca's body is in the grave she was buried in, he told himself. *Her spirit has to be in a better place than the one she lived her life in.* He took a deep breath, thinking that he had to get himself together. *I've got to deal with these things better, like I used to. It's up to God to punish those who hurt Rebecca. She isn't coming back in any shape or form. She's not ever coming back.* The train reached shouting distance of the Aberdeen station by the time he managed to convince himself.

II

As they rode from the Aberdeen train station to Blessed Earth, Wise Eyes informed John that the traditional Celebration of Return would be performed in his honor that evening.

"Please, Grandfather," John said. "Can't it be done tomorrow? I would just like to settle in today."

Wise Eyes shook his head, which was covered by a white Stetson with a crow feather tucked in its brim. "The maleen is the Maupai way. If you do not like it danced in your honor, perhaps you should not go away so often."

John started to point out that he'd only left Blessed Earth twice since he'd come to live there as an eight-year old – to leave for college in late August and to return to college after Thanksgiving break. He stilled his tongue, having traveled the road of futile debate with his grandfather many times before. The old man was sure to have a counterpoint for any argument John made and John didn't feel up to matching wits for the entire drive home.

Wise Eyes smiled, causing the creases of his leathered face to stand at attention. "Besides, you only have to receive the dance. It is not as if you have to perform yourself."

The old man spoke as if receiving the dance was a sedentary activity, when in fact it was a lengthy, exhilarating, and exhausting exchange with every tribesman old enough to recite the words of the ceremony. John hadn't thought that he would have to participate in the ceremony only three weeks after the previous one. As Wise Eyes's truck neared the Bay Corner limits, John resigned himself to getting it over with.

"So do you think you did well on your finals?" Wise Eyes asked, saying the last word as if it he had just learned it in a beginner's foreign language course. John supposed the old guy would always treat any concept of Anglo origin as something foreign. From Wise Eyes's perspective, attending college was almost as fantastic an event as undertaking a lunar landing. Still, John appreciated the old man's effort.

"I think I did very well," John said. "The Chemistry exam was a little challenging, but all my other exams seemed like a breeze. I think I might pull all A's for the semester."

Wise Eyes sighed, turning his head to glance at his grandson. "You have always been a great student of books," he said. "You will go far in the white man's world. I only hope that you will not forget all about your tribe when you become successful."

John smirked, thinking, *Here we go, again.* "Please don't start talking that way, Grandfather. I'm only just coming home. Can we keep things light between us?"

The old man chuckled as his eyes returned to the road. "I ask your pardon, Son of My Son. We shall keep things as light as a feather. How is that?"

"That would be wonderful, Father of My Father."

Silence ruled the remainder of the ride. As he had at the train station, John sized his grandfather up. Even in his ripe old age, Wise Eyes cut a regal, almost intimidating presence. His eyes remained as piercing and mysterious as they had always been. His aquiline nose still lent him the bearing of a hawk or some other great bird of prey. The creases on his brick colored face and hands told of many years spent working outdoors.

The blue chambray shirt Wise Eyes wore was tucked into jeans tight enough to outline his package and the sack they balanced on. Two shoulder length silver braids spilled from his Stetson.

John tried not to think about the cowboy boots or the belt with giant buckle that topped off the old man's ensemble. He couldn't figure why the old man insisted on dressing like a character out of an old Western while expressing such disdain for the Anglo world.

John wore a hooded sweatshirt, some baggy jeans, and a pair of black Converse All Stars. A long ponytail corralled his jet black mane of hair. Although the same Maupai blood coursed through their veins, he supposed that he and Wise Eyes couldn't have been more different.

No matter how much he disagreed with the old guy's worldview and clothing choices, John loved Wise Eyes. He felt a bottomless debt of gratitude for the old man taking him in after his parents were killed. Wise Eyes raised John as best he could, without a spouse to help him. John's grandmother had long passed by then, having lost a painful struggle with cancer when John was four years old.

Having to raise John did not excuse Wise Eyes from his duties as Chieftain of Blessed Earth. It was his job to defend the tribe's interest in matters of local and state government, settle quarrels, dispense advice, and lead ceremonies. He also had oversight of the tribe's business endeavors, such as Chesapeake Bay canoe tours, selling tribal food, tribal clothing, and tribal artwork, and mobilizing crews for contracting jobs. As if those responsibilities weren't enough, Wise Eyes worked full time in the construction and building trades. John thought his grandfather was a great man, even if he did tote around a pack of ideas that verged on silly in their antiquity.

None of the Maupai spoke a word to John as he exited Wise Eyes's truck in front of their simple home. Those who saw him only whistled a brief tune as he passed by. John sauntered up the walk into the primitive structure he'd grown up in, knowing that a bigger fuss than he wanted would be made over him later.

Stepping inside the hand-built structure felt like traveling 100 years into the past. John settled onto the threadbare couch that rested in the midst of the planked floor of what served as a front room.

"Make yourself comfortable," Wise Eyes said, walking past his grandson. "I'll start the fire."

Yeah, sure, John thought. He felt just as he had during his first return trip from college- that he could never feel complete comfort with life at Blessed Earth again.

For one thing, everyone on the commune actually got their heat from fireplaces. It was almost two thousand and freaking nine and they used fireplaces. Another thing was that although they all had running water, the archaic plumbing did not allow it to burst forth from the faucet or sink with much vigor. The water in a Maupai residence never ran stronger than a medium spray. John recalled his father telling him that the tribe first received running water in the 1970's, making the grudging switch because of concerns about pollutants in the water they once drew.

A structure that approximated a shower stall stood in the rearmost part of the chieftain's one story home. The tiny washing area within stretched no larger than coat closets found in more modern homes. A toilet worthy of a jailhouse jammed in next to the shower, allowing perhaps a full adult step between the two structures. A tiny sink sat in the near corner. The pipes underneath it stood naked. A mirror just as diminutive stood attached to the portion of the thick cloth enclosure that overlooked the sink. The enclosure and plastic curtains that surrounded the shower were the only things that protected the wash chamber from the elements and potential voyeurism. John found showering in this primitive space to be tolerable during the spring and summer, comfortable even. During fall and winter, he found doing so to be a vile experience that felt far worse for him now that he'd grown accustomed to using indoor facilities.

John shuddered as he thought of the three days he showered there during Thanksgiving break. The wind whistled a cruel tune, while the cold morning air of late autumn penetrated the sheeting. Now that winter rounded the corner, mornings were even colder than those of late November. He imagined his balls shrinking to the size of pebbles when he next used the primitive chamber.

The heat of newborn flames stirred John from his reverie. Wise Eyes handed him a parcel of butcher paper as the lit fireplace did its work. "Dried venison," he said. "It will satisfy you until the maleen. I must go and finalize preparations."

"Thank you, grandfather," John said, watching Wise Eyes depart. He unwrapped the paper, revealing a palm sized pieced of meat. He bit into the jerky like morsel, finding it as delicious as always. *Nicely seasoned*, he thought. *Still, it would be better fresh roasted.* He expected to have some of the roast variety at the feast that would follow the ceremony. The regular eating of deer meat was one definite advantage of life at Blessed Earth.

John thought the worst disadvantage of life at Blessed Earth to be the lack of electricity. The Maupai used battery powered devices, such as radios and flashlights, but no wired electricity. John believed that Wise Eyes and the elders insisted on this because they didn't want to pay any money they earned to BGE. Keeping younger generations in the dark about the ways of the modern world served as an added benefit.

"Ridiculous," John snickered. For the most part, the tribe still used candles and kerosene lamps to light their homes. *Kerosene lamps! In the twenty first century!* John considered it a miracle that none of the young ones or the very old ever started a blaze by breaking a lamp or knocking over a lit candle. Wise Eyes and the other elders drilled the idea of limited flashlight usage into their brethren. After all, flashlights used batteries and batteries cost money.

Home sweet home, John thought. He hoped that once he went out into the world and became a successful scientist, he could return to Blessed Earth and affect change in his people. He yearned to convince the Maupai that adopting some modernity and mixing with the world at large would make their lives better.

Those thoughts were interrupted by thoughts of Brittany. John fished his cell phone from his pocket and dialed her number.

Brittany's line went to voicemail after five rings. "Hi. You've reached Brittany." Her voice sung a sweet melody to his ears. "I'm unavailable to take your call right now. Leave a message and I'll get back to you, if I like you. If I don't, then you're probably a jerk and you'll never hear from me."

John chuckled at that last bit, as he always did. He left a message saying that he was back at Blessed Earth and that they'd meet up some time later.

He finished the last bit of the dried venison as he continued to think of her. He wished he had some water to wash it down with, but he didn't want to drink from the wash chamber sink.

Cheer up, John, he thought. *You'll get through this silly ceremony. Then later on you'll be with her.* He seated himself on a homemade wooden chair, in front of the fireplace. Its pleasant warmth caused his eyelids to grow heavy.

He did not realize that he'd fallen asleep until his grandfather shook him awake. The front room's lone window stood open, revealing the fading sun of early evening.

"It is time you prepare yourself," the old man said.

John sighed, knowing that he could not escape the coming ceremony.

Chapter 4- Notice of Death

As lead investigators into Kevin Anderson's death, Tremblehorn and Carpenter were responsible for notifying his parents. Their trip took them from the Capital Beltway to 95 North to the Aberdeen Throughway to Route 40 East, and then to Bay Corner Road, which flowed into the small town. Tremblehorn traveled each highway at a steady 65 mph, not in any hurry to shred the hearts of the victim's loved ones. The Anderson family lived in a filthy rich area known as Mackenzie Hill. A series of sprawling estates comprised the landscape, each gated with wrought iron at the main road.

Detective Tremblehorn eased the squad car up to Anderson Manor, identifying it by the wrought iron letters that stood atop the gate. A two foot tall lion's head stood to the left of the A in Anderson. Its twin stood to the right of the R in Manor. The watchful eye of a security lens stared from above the call button on the right corner of the gate. Tremblehorn reached his left hand outside the window and depressed the device.

"Who is it?" A stilted female voice crackled from the intercom.

"It's the police, Ma'am. Is this the Anderson residence?"

There was a long pause before the woman's voice crackled an answer. "Yes, it is. But, we have no business with the police."

"Please, let us up Ma'am. We need to have a conversation that should not be had over an intercom."

A loud, lingering buzzing noise was followed by the gate sliding open. The detectives exited the car moments later, being sure that their badges hung in plain view from the lanyards on their necks. A thin, middle aged brunette emerged from the mansion's front door. She took one look at the two detectives and crumbled into a heap of tears. Detective Tremblehorn stepped forward and caught her when she swooned.

"Oh, God," she sighed. "I was just watching Fox News when a crawl went across the scene, saying that a student had been found dead in his dorm room at College Park. I immediately called Kevin on his cell phone, but I didn't get an answer. I tried to tell myself that it was just a coincidence, that it wasn't that unusual for him to miss my calls now that he's off enjoying college life. But now that you all are here, I know. I know!"

The detectives maneuvered the now grieving mother into a great room the size of a basketball court. Mrs. Anderson curled up on Tremblehorn's shoulder like a small girl seeking comfort from her father. She confided that her husband was away on a business trip and that Kevin's younger sisters were out with friends.

"Telling them all will be the hardest part," she said, speaking between sobs.

Carpenter nodded. "Yes, Ma'am." He sat to the distraught women's left, on a grandiose suede couch. "Mrs. Anderson – I can't imagine the pain you feel right now, but we've come here to do more than notify you of Kevin's passing". He took a deep breath. "We have to wait for autopsy results, but we think there's a good chance that your son was murdered."

Tears streaked Mrs. Anderson's eyes as she pulled away from Tremblehorn and turned to face Carpenter. "Murdered- but who? Who would want to murder Kevin?"

Carpenter shrugged. "We were hoping that was something you might be able to help us with. Is there anyone Kevin might've had a conflict with?"

Mrs. Anderson took a moment to wipe her tears before shaking her head. "No. Kevin hasn't had a conflict since- well, since- How much time do you detectives have?"

"All the time you need, Ma'am," Tremblehorn said.

Mrs. Anderson turned and patted him on the hand. "I'll get you all some tea, then. I don't have my housekeeper work on the weekends. I'll get you all some tea, then I'll tell you about the most serious conflict I've ever known Kevin to have."

Chapter 5- Acceptance

I

Four days prior to the detectives' visit to Anderson Manor, John Rainbird Jeffries sat studying his Chemistry text in a study room at the University of Delaware library. He felt nervous about his upcoming exam- the only exam he didn't feel confident about acing. That concern dissipated as his consciousness swam away from the present, leaving him to regard the world through the eyes of a friend he had lost.

II

Tuesday, June 20th, 2004, was a huge day for Rebecca Saulters. On the previous Friday, Mr. Halloran left a message for Rebecca and her grandmother. This was not Mr. Kenneth Halloran, principal of Bay Corner Elementary/ Middle School. It was his brother- Edward Halloran- the principal of Mackenzie High.

Principal Edward Halloran revealed that Mackenzie's Board of Directors considered Rebecca to be a strong candidate for one of that year's Mackenzie scholarships. They always held in person interviews with finalists and their guardians before making their ultimate decision.

Grandma Rose took a half day at the factory so that she could accompany Rebecca. Rebecca squeezed her guardian's hand as they approached the majestic institution. The school's gothic architecture belied the fact that it was not yet twenty years old. It resembled a small castle more than a school building.

Rebecca wore a pristine white blouse and a long black dress skirt, along with the same mules she had worn to her graduation. Grandma Rose wore a flower patterned dress with complementary orange flats.

The pleasant voice of a secretary invited them in after identifying them through the intercom. The double doors of the school's office stood to the left of the long corridor that stretched before them. As they approached the office, a tall black man emerged from within. Except for being maybe two inches shorter and having a large mole on his left cheek, he was the spitting image of his brother.

"Hello." He smiled his brother's Chiclet smile as he extended his hand to Grandma Rose. "I am Edward Halloran, principal of Mackenzie High. You must be Mrs. Saulters."

"Pleased to meet you." Grandma Rose begrudged a smile, grasping his hand. "I'm Rose Saulters, Rebecca's grandmother."

The man nodded, turning his smile toward his potential student. "And you must be Rebecca?" He offered his hand to her. "My brother has told me a lot about you."

Rebecca and her grandmother followed him into a well-lit conference room, where a huge meeting table occupied most of the square footage. Before directing them to their seats, Mr. Halloran introduced them to Mr. Hunter, the Dean of School Affairs. Rebecca had never heard that term before, but she could tell that the heavy set man was at least as important as Mr. Halloran.

Butterflies rampaged in Rebecca's stomach as she and her guardian sat across from the pair of officials. A pitcher of water and two plastic cups sat in the center of the table. Mr. Halloran invited her to drink as she pleased. Although her lips were parched, she dared not out of fear that her anxiety might cause her to lose control of her bladder. Grandma Rose offered her the small comfort of a hand on her knee beneath the table.

"This interview should not take long, ladies," Mr. Halloran began. An austere expression replaced his affable smile. "Rebecca is an outstanding candidate on academic merits alone. And my brother has been campaigning for her ever since he found out that she desired one of the Mackenzie scholarships."

"Yes." Mr. Hunter agreed with a nod, causing his massive jowls to jiggle.

Rebecca suppressed her laughter as she thought that Mr. Hunter looked like a pink, featherless turkey. "What Mr. Halloran says is spot on", the Dean said. "We've already approved Rebecca's admission to our illustrious school. But you all seek more than just admission for Rebecca. You seek for us to fully fund Rebecca's matriculation here."

Grandma Rose scowled. "You make it sound as if we're looking for a handout."

Mr. Hunter's eyes widened. "Oh, no-o." He shook his head. "I wholeheartedly apologize if I seem to imply that. The Mackenzie School and the esteemed family that supports it would never dream of giving anyone a handout. The idea behind our scholarships is to provide financial assistance so that hard working, academically gifted students who might not otherwise be able to pay tuition to our nationally renowned school are not denied its' life changing experience. My meaning is that although academic competence is the single largest consideration in granting our exclusive scholarships, there are other important factors."

"Yes," Mr. Halloran said, taking the verbal baton. "Some of the factors we consider are social in nature. Though Rebecca's academic record is extremely impressive, we are concerned that she did not have any extracurricular activities at Bay Corner School. There were a number of such activities for the middle grades there-a few sports teams, drama, reading, art, and chess clubs just to name a few. Rebecca never participated in any of them. We don't like for our students to be isolated at Mackenzie."

Grandma Rose took a deep breath, seeming to gather herself. Rebecca trusted her not to lose her temper, although it was obvious that she was offended.

"Do you know that Rebecca completed her community service hours at the local soup kitchen?" Grandma Rose said. "Do you know that she continues to volunteer there twice a month, even though she accumulated the required hours last November? How's that for an extracurricular activity?"

Mr. Halloran smiled. "Yes, we're aware of that. Continuing to work with the less fortunate shows great character and willingness to serve the community at large- but what of the school community? We have no knowledge of her participating in extracurricular activities that involved her peers. We like for our students to be close knit here. If Rebecca attends this school, we want her to receive the full benefit of its experience. We wouldn't want her to focus solely on her coursework and otherwise crawl into a shell."

Grandma Rose kept her voice even, though an inferno raged in her eyes. "Rebecca didn't 'crawl' into a shell at Bay Corner School. She was harassed into one. Surely, you know about her mother. Everyone else in this Podunk town does."

Mr. Hunter performed another turkey neck bob. "Yes. We know about her mother."

"But, can you know that that one incident has made her an outcast among her schoolmates for the last three years?" Grandma Rose balled her hands into fists and dug her fingers into her palms. "They - they called her…"

"The Knife Lady's daughter," Rebecca finished the statement. "Can I say something, Grandma?"

Grandma Rose bit her lip. "Sure, baby. Although I'm sure it'll be a colossal waste of breath." She glared at the interviewers. "I thought this was an interview, not an inquisition."

"Mrs. Saulters," Mr. Halloran began, "we did not mean for-"

"It's alright, Mr. Halloran," Rebecca said. She turned to her grandmother. "I meant can I talk to them alone?"

Grandma Rose's eyes expanded like rising yeast. "Rebecca, I don't think…"

"Please, Grandma," Rebecca pleaded. "Please. Just for a few minutes. I promise I'll be alright."

Grandma Rose stared at Rebecca for a long time. Finally, she stood. "Alright, but if these –gentlemen- say anything you don't like, just give a holler. A scholarship isn't worth your dignity. You've already been accepted to Harford Technical. They're a fine school from what I can tell." She marched toward the door. "I'll be just outside."

A wan smile bloomed on Mr. Halloran's lips as he glanced at Rebecca. "Harford Technical is a very good high school."

Rebecca nodded. "Yes. But my first choice is Mackenzie."

"Yes. You made that clear in your application essay. Very elegant and heartfelt writing, by the way."

Rebecca kept her face impassive. "Thank you. Do I really have a chance at getting this scholarship?"

"You have a very good chance," Mr. Hunter answered. "As we were trying to explain to your grandmother, our chief concern is that you will not open yourself up at this school. We don't like it when students isolate themselves socially. Our sense of community, of an extended family as it were, is very important here."

Rebecca smiled. "I'd like to have friends like any other kid. It's just that after what happened with my mother, other kids treated me like some kind of freak. It's hard to live things down in a small town. Especially when you have classes with the same kids, year after year."

"Yes." Mr. Halloran nodded and sighed. "I can't imagine how difficult that's been for you." The affable smile returned as he folded his hands and leaned forward, toward Rebecca. Excitement danced in his voice when he spoke. "The good thing for you, Rebecca, is that less than ten percent of our enrollment hails from Bay Corner."

"I know," Rebecca said. "You accept students from all over Harford County, as well as from Eastern Baltimore County and Baltimore City. That's why I think things will be different for me if I'm granted a scholarship to this school. It will be like a fresh start. I'd like to take part in extracurricular activities, so long as I don't have to worry about kids messing with me on my way home. I could be a good part of this school community, Mr. Hunter and Mr. Halloran. All I need is a chance."

She looked earnestly into their eyes. "Please just give me a chance. No one needs this chance like I do."

The softness in their returned gazes told Rebecca that she had touched them. She knew that her grandmother would consider what she'd done to be begging, but she didn't care. She'd been nothing but a whipping girl for cruel treatment for the past couple of years. Why should she be proud?

Mr. Halloran cleared his throat and strummed his fingers on the table. "I want to thank you for opening up to us like that, Rebecca. That showed a lot of courage."

"No, it didn't," Rebecca said, shaking her head. "Stepping outside of my house every day knowing that I was the least accepted kid in my entire school showed courage. Courage that I'm tired of having to muster."

The two officials said nothing in reply, only regarding her with a mixture of awe and sadness.

"So, can you guys give me a general idea of when the decision will be made?" Rebecca asked.

"I promise you it will be very soon," Mr. Halloran said, flashing his now familiar Chiclet smile. "It will be very soon."

III

Rebecca heard the mailbox clatter shut, interrupting her diligent work on a Sudoko book. She sprang from her seat at the kitchen table, just avoiding knocking over her glass of juice. The contents of the box included a BGE Bill and TV Guide magazine. The third piece of mail was addressed to her- from Mackenzie High School's Board of Directors.

Her heart leapt and did a series of cartwheels. Butterflies amassed and battered her stomach. She placed a hand over a bosom that heaved in anxiety.

"This is it," she said aloud. It had only been two days since her interview. Mr. Halloran hadn't lied about the decision being made very soon. She started to open the envelope before deciding that she couldn't bear to. She felt as excited about the possibility of receiving the scholarship as she felt terrified about the possibility of being denied.

Rebecca wished that her grandmother was with her, instead of at work. That way, she could turn away as the news was read to her. Unfortunately, her grandmother would not be home until after 5. Her toy of a wristwatch confessed that it was only 12:27.

There's no way I can wait that long, she thought. *But I just can't read it to myself.*

The realization that she could get John Rainbird to read it struck her. She put on a cap and her tennis shoes; then hopped on her bike. She wished her friend had a phone at his house so that she could call and arrange a sure meeting. As it was, she'd have to hope she ran into him.

Having stuffed the letter into a pocket of her shorts, she peddled as if competing in the final leg of the Tour De France. She ignored the sweat that spread under her t-shirt and shorts as she braved the humidity of the second official day of summer.

Rebecca continued past the library when she didn't see John's bike outside of it. She didn't slow down until she reached the Nissum Trail. Frustration took hold her when she did not find him there. *He really should have a phone,* she thought. She rode back and forth along the trail until the heat got the better of her. She rested on the large rock that she and John held their first in-depth conversation on.

She wrestled with anxious thoughts as she clutched the letter to her chest. *Maybe I should just stop being a chicken and open the thing myself. No, I can't do that! It will be too terrible if it's bad news. Damn, I wish his tall Native American behind would come along right now.*

She heard the groaning of churning pedals a few minutes later. She smiled as she looked up, thinking that she hadn't even needed a genie or a leprechaun.

John Rainbird smiled, slowing to a stop when he saw her. "What are you doing sitting here by yourself like this?"

"I was hoping you'd come along, dummy."

"Really?" John said, widening his eyes in false shock. "I know you like me and all. But I thought we'd agreed that you wouldn't stalk me." He laughed.

"Shut up," she said, scowling as she removed the letter from her pocket. "I wouldn't have to go through all this if you had some sort of access to a phone."

John sat down beside her. "Tell it to my grandfather." He pointed to the letter. "What's that?"

"A letter from Mackenzie High. I was hoping you'd open it for me."

John clapped as his eyes lit with excitement. "Too nervous to do it yourself, huh?"

Rebecca frowned. "Please don't make fun about it."

"Aww." John squeezed one of her cheeks as he pursed his lips into a mocking pout. "My little squaw is scared. Relax. There's no way they could turn you down."

"Says you." Rebecca held the envelope out. "Now, hurry up and read it. The suspense is killing me."

"Okay." John took the envelope and opened it. "Here goes."

Rebecca closed her eyes and clasped her hands in silent prayer.

"Aren't you supposed to be reading it?" she demanded, after she was done.

"Take it easy, girl. I read it silently."

"Well, read it out loud, dummy!" Her face contorted in annoyance as she shoved him.

"Alright. Alright," John said, regaining his balance after a brief stumble.

He cleared his throat, playing up the drama of the situation. "Dear Rebecca. After much careful consideration and review of your impressive credentials," his voice rose, "we are pleased to offer you a full academic scholarship to Patrick F. Mackenzie Senior High School for the 2004-2005 school year! It is our pleasure to welcome you to the Mackenzie family!"

"Omigod!" Rebecca screamed, exploding from her seat. "Oh, my God!" she jumped up and down, dancing about the path. "Oh, my God! I'm so happy. I'm so happy, John Rainbird!" She launched herself into his arms. "I'm so happy!"

The tall Maupai caught his friend and embraced her. "I'm happy for you, too, Rebecca. I'm happy for you, too. See, life doesn't suck all the time."

Chapter 6- Reunion

Rebecca rose bright and early on Saturday, July 2nd, 2004. Her eagerness inspired the role reversal of her waking her grandmother.

"It's barely 8 o'clock, child," Grandma Rose said, smiling as she paused in front of the bathroom door, still clad in her nightgown. "We're not due to leave for a couple hours."

"I know," Rebecca chirped. "I've been up since six. I didn't sleep much at all."

"That's because you're all anxious about seeing your mother."

"I sure am! You didn't have trouble sleeping?"

"I was doing just fine 'til you woke me," Grandma Rose said, frowning. "Since you're so worked up, why don't you make us a nice breakfast?"

"Okay."

Rebecca whipped up two cheese omelets and four slices of French toast using skills her grandmother taught her. She complemented the hot food with sliced honey dew melon and tall glasses of orange juice.

Grandma Rose dressed herself before sitting down to the spread. She voiced her approval as they ate, remarking that she'd make a cook of Rebecca yet.

They sat on the couch after breakfast, half watching Saturday morning cartoons. Rebecca couldn't stop checking her watch.

"Its ten thirty," she finally chirped. "Shouldn't we be going now?"

Grandma Rose smiled at her granddaughter's impatience. "Alright, Miss Daisy. Alright. Let's go."

Rose Saulters maneuvered her old truck through the town proper, onto the endless length of Route 40 west. Twenty-five miles or so later, the scenery shifted from a sprawling expanse of greenery, roadside businesses, and motels into the cracked and littered streets of East Baltimore. A number of the ubiquitous brick row houses were boarded up or had been stripped to empty shells. Such eyesores were contrasted by construction sites that promised the birth of new architecture. Grandma Rose guided the old Harvester through the neighborhood surrounding Johns Hopkins Hospital, into Downtown Baltimore.

Even on a Saturday, there were far more cars on the road than Rebecca felt accustomed to. They didn't go far without Rebecca seeing people milling about or hurrying along on the multitude of blocks they passed.

"We're almost there," Grandma Rose announced, making a right turn toward Pennsylvania Avenue. Grandma Rose turned left at the next light, under a traffic sign that read Martin Luther King Boulevard.

Rebecca had last been in town when she was 8 years old. Uncle Gregory had talked her mother into a trip to the National Aquarium on a late August day. Though she was now five years older, the sheer size and activity of Baltimore still amazed her. Taking in the sights and sounds of Maryland's largest city eased some of the anxiety she felt about her impending reunion with her mother. That anxiety came rushing back when her grandmother parked in front of their destination.

"That must be it," Grandma Rose said, pointing to a three story row house with a large bay window by its front door. The imposing structure stood at the end of a block of similar structures.

"Come on, child." Grandma Rose climbed out, leading Rebecca up the stairs of the unadorned building. *They probably don't want everyone in the neighborhood to know it's a halfway house,* Rebecca thought.

A tall black woman dressed in a power suit answered the great wooden door a few moments after Grandma Rose knocked on it. Rebecca stood silent as her grandmother made introductions, smiling as she displayed ID and told the woman who they came to visit.

"Just a moment, please," the authoritative looking woman said, after examining the identification. She stepped back into the house, closing the immense door in her wake.

When the door creaked open again, a beaming Emma stepped out. Three generations of Saulters women fell into joyful hugging and kissing. They tore free of each other just long enough for Emma to explain that she wouldn't hear of Rebecca and Rose visiting her in her tiny, bare room.

"I've been cooped up in a tiny room every time I've seen y'all for the past couple of years," she said. "Let's go out somewhere."

"You're allowed to go out?" Grandma Rose asked.

"Sure, Mom. They keep tabs on us and we got a curfew, but the halfway house ain't the Women's Correctional Center."

They headed to the Inner Harbor. Grandma Rose felt miffed about having to pay to park on a lot, an uncommon occurrence in Bay Corner or its surrounding areas. Emma chuckled at her mother's frustration, promising that she'd pay for the parking on the next occasion.

"After all, I am waiting tables now," Emma said. "Funny, I've only been out for a week but I've already been working for four days. Isn't that something?"

They walked along the Harbor promenade, enjoying a fleeting breeze off the water and eating ice cream. Rebecca took care not to stare at the dark scar on her mother's right hand as they walked.

Kids, adults, and teenagers of different creeds and styles of dress milled about. Some were quiet while others were loud. A musclebound man in short shorts and a crop top rollerbladed past. A pair of bicycle cops pedaled at a languid pace, clad in tight shorts of their own. Rebecca hadn't seen anything like that back home.

A large ship rested near a dock a short distance away. Its fancy insignia read "The Bay Lady". Mallard ducks floated in the surrounding water, drifting past the occasional floating trash. A Hard Rock Café, complete with giant hanging guitar stood about 50 yards to the east of where they walked, neighbored by a huge Barnes and Noble bookstore. The cluster of restaurants and retail stores that made up Harbor Place stood just beyond the promenade. The National Aquarium and the Maryland Science Center cast their beautiful shadows on the landscape.

Rebecca's eyes fell on a water taxi making its way across the water.

Emma smiled. "I bet you'd like to get on one of those someday."

"Don't go making promises you might not keep," Grandma Rose warned.

Hurt flashed in Emma's eyes. "I know better than to do that, Mama. I was just asking. I'm a lot different now. You'll see. I wasn't just putting on an act when y'all came to see me. I know I don't deserve for you to believe me yet. But in time, you'll see."

Grandma Rose stared at Emma for several beats, holding her licked clean cone in her right hand. "Well, you certainly seem different," she allowed, her mouth threatening to smile. "I suppose I'll check out some of those stores. Give you two some mother and daughter time."

Grandma Rose headed up the concrete steps that led into Harbor Place.

Emma watched her depart before turning and continuing to walk along the promenade.

Having licked her ice cream down to the sugar cone, she began crunching it. She laughed when Rebecca followed suit.

"You do seem different," Rebecca offered, after finishing the last of her treat.

Emma polished off the last of her own cone before responding. "Good different?"

"Yes."

"Yeah, I guess I am a lot better." Emma placed an arm around her daughter. "Funny what good meds and a little self-awareness can do."

"You've gained some weight, too."

"You trying to say I'm fat?"

Rebecca chuckled. "No, Mom. The last time I saw you, you had gotten too skinny."

Emma dropped her arm and shrugged. "I guess that's true. But what was that-like six months ago?"

"A little more than six months, actually. Right before Christmas."

They passed the docked ship. "Christ, how could I forget that? You having to visit my sorry ass in the cold."

Rebecca shrugged. "I didn't mind. It really hurt me when you told me not to come see you anymore, Mom."

Emma stopped walking, turned Rebecca around and pulled her into an embrace. Rebecca felt corded muscle born from prison workouts. "I'm so sorry, Rebee. That was a hard thing for me to do, but I had to do it."

Tears welled in Rebecca's eyes as she slid from her mother's grasp. "But why? Why did you have to do it?"

Emma's lips quivered. "Because, Rebee." She sighed. "When I found out I would be eligible for parole, I just knew that I had to deny myself the pleasure of seeing you. That way, I'd be sure to be on my best behavior until the review. All I did was work out, work in the laundry, and otherwise keep to myself. The whole time, I thought about getting to see you outside of those bars. I was like a little angel up until I sat before that parole board."

She held her arms out as if she were presenting herself. "That's why I'm standing here now. Don't you see, Rebee? Missing you was my motivation for getting out of that place. It's going to be my motivation for getting out of that halfway house, too. After that, I'll be a much better mother than I was before. As bad as I feel about it, I know that I can't take back any of the screwing up I've done in the past. But, I can be a better mother than I was to you before. I will be a better mother than I was before."

Rebecca embraced her mother then. Tears fled each of their eyes as they held each other. They wiped their faces and retreated into lighter conversation after separating. Emma commented on how pretty her daughter had become.

"You're not a girl, anymore," she said. "You're definitely a young lady now, so act like one. Don't be like I was when I was a teenager."

Rebecca promised that she wouldn't before giving Emma the good news about the Mackenzie scholarship. Emma exulted, promising to get her the best present she could after she had worked for a while. Rebecca told her that wasn't necessary. "I'm happy just to know that you're proud of me," she said.

"Don't do that," Emma said, scowling.

"Don't do what?"

"Don't tell me not to do something for you, especially when you deserve it. Now I want to know, if you could have your choice of gifts from me- what would it be? And don't pick something little because you don't want me spending a lot of money on you. I mean it, Rebecca. Getting into Mackenzie High School is a huge accomplishment that deserves a huge reward. I won't accept you being cheap about what you want."

"Okay, okay." Rebecca smiled as she considered the offer. Her eyes lit up a few moments later. "Well, what I would really like is a new bike. I'm still riding that old thing-." She fell silent, dropping her eyes.

"That Gregory got for you," Emma finished. "It's okay to say so. The past is the past. And I will get you a very nice bike."

"It's okay. You really don't have to."

Emma wagged an index finger. "Uh-uh. What did I just tell you, Rebee?"

"Not to tell you not to do something for me."

"Exactly." Emma hugged Rebecca again, this time accompanying it with a kiss on the cheek. It occurred to Rebecca that her mother had been more affectionate this day than in any of the ten years Rebecca lived before she went to prison. "Now, just give me some time and I'll have a nice bike for you. And it's not because I'm trying to make up for anything. I know I can't make up for how I've failed you. I'm going to do this for you because you deserve it."

The three generation of Saulters women said their goodbyes an hour or so later. Rebecca didn't make a peep as Grandma Rose wheeled the Harvester along 40 East.

"Thinking about your mother?" the silver haired matriarch broke the silence.

"Yes." Rebecca answered in a toneless voice.

"What exactly are you thinking?"

"I'm hoping she'll stay better, like she seems."

"I hope so too, Rebee. I pray to God she will. But if she doesn't, you always have me. You know that I'll always be here for you, don't you?"

"Yes, Grandma." Rebecca smiled as the big road morphed back into the sprawling stretch that encompassed its suburban portion.

Chapter 7- A Promise Kept

I

"Your feet smell like an ass factory," Rebecca teased, pinching her nose as she and John dangled their bare feet off the bank of Snake River. "You'd better cover them up before all the fish start keeling over."

A Cheshire grin spread across John's face as he stood. "Think you're funny- do you? You know there aren't any witnesses out here. I could toss you in the river and no one would ever know."

Rebecca squealed, rising as well. "You know you wouldn't hurt your best friend."

"Oh, so I'm your best friend now?"

"Yup." Rebecca's eyes brimmed with mischief as she backed away from the riverbank. "We're such good friends that I'll hang out with you even though the smell of your feet probably violates environmental laws." Giggling, she turned and ran.

John caught her in three long strides. Rebecca squealed as they tussled and stumbled to the ground. Sprawled on top of her, John stopped smiling and stared into her eyes. His breathing intensified as Rebecca returned his stare. His voluminous, unbraided hair brushed against her lengthy mane. John's dark mass smelled musky, but pleasant. Backing away, he stood and helped her to her feet.

It was a while before either of them spoke. When they did, they discussed staying in contact with each other once school started. Summer had sped by and hanging out with each other wouldn't be so easy once they began attending their respective high schools. Rebecca suggested that they meet each other at the Bay

Corner Library every Thursday after school. John offended her by predicting that the arrangement wouldn't last long.

"Why do you say that?" she asked, frowning. "Why are you being so negative?"

John sighed. "I'm just being realistic. I know that once you get tight with some of those cool Mackenzie kids, you'll forget all about me."

"No. One's. Cool enough. To make me. Forget John Rain-birrrd!" Rebecca belted in an unpracticed, but pleasant singing voice. "Besides, what makes you think Mackenzie kids are so cool? Have you met any?"

"Yeah." He nodded. "I've met you."

"Aw." She hugged him. "That's so sweet."

He made a retching noise. "Eww. You touched me. That's disgusting."

As Rebecca peddled home from their encounter, she wondered why John didn't take advantage while he was on top of her. She knew he was attracted to her. She had kissed him before, when they first got to know each other. *I could tell he liked it*, she thought. *But then, everything went wrong.*

Rebecca decided to push that incident out of her mind, along with what had just happened. John was still a good friend, even if he didn't allow himself to act on wanting more. Rebecca credited his Maupai upbringing for making him that way.

More pressing matters concerned Rebecca, like this being the last weekend before freshman orientation at the Mackenzie School. She felt a mixture of excitement and dread over the big day. She also felt excited about visiting her mother in Baltimore, one day before the big occasion.

The wistful expression that Grandma Rose wore for most of the drive to Baltimore made Rebecca think that something was being kept from her. She never suspected that her mother would deliver on a huge promise.

"You're acting weird, Gran," she said, taking her eyes off the prodigious scenery that the Harvester passed.

"I most certainly am not, young lady," Grandma Rose said, ceasing the whistling she had been doing and breaking into a huge grin. "I most certainly am not."

"Yes, you are."

"No, I am not."

"You always tell me not to lie, Grandma."

"And I'm not lying, Rebecca. I'm simply withholding information."

Rebecca's eyes bulged. "Withholding information? You can't do that, Gran! You have to tell me!"

Stopped at a red light, Grandma Rose glanced at her. "I don't recall any law saying that I have to tell you anything."

"Well, maybe there's no law, but it's really mean to get people all curious about something and then not tell them about it."

The light changed. Grandma Rose chuckled as she stepped on the accelerator.

"So? I've been mean to you before. Doesn't bother me any."

Rebecca fell silent for a few moments, before making what she thought was a great response. "You also always tell me that God doesn't like ugly."

"I certainly do," Grandma Rose said, smiling. "That's why it's a good thing I've still got some looks left. Now hush, Rebee." She resumed her whistling.

Rebecca gave up trying to get anything out of her grandmother, knowing that she'd only get into trouble if she continued her pestering. *It must be some good news,* she thought, watching her unusually cheery guardian. *Maybe Mom's getting released from the halfway house early, just like she got out of jail early.*

II

A thousand watts shone in Emma's eyes when she stepped out of the halfway house. She greeted her mother with a hug and her daughter with a kiss on the forehead.

"You didn't tell her- did you?" she asked, staring at Grandma Rose.

Grandma Rose shook her head. "Nope. Although she tried to interrogate me on the way here."

"Ha-ha!" Emma patted Rebecca on the shoulder. "Tried to get it out of your Gran, huh? You'll enjoy it better as a total surprise. I'll be right back."

She zipped inside before Rebecca could respond. The door creaked open moments later, held by another of the halfway house's residents.

"Thanks, Flo," Emma said to a tall, husky woman with thick, frizzled cornrows. Rebecca's eyes threatened to take orbit as they drank in the sight of the magnificent bike that her mother brought onto the porch.

"Just like I promised, Rebee," Emma said, smiling and enjoying the shocked expression on Rebecca's face. "Been saving for it. Your birthday's coming in a few weeks. So you can consider it a combination early birthday and late graduation present."

"Omigod, Mom!" Rebecca screamed, rushing into her mother's arms. Her excitement would have resulted in the bike clattering to the porch if not for Grandma Rose wheeling it the rest of the way and extending its gleaming kickstand. "Omigod, Mom! I can't believe you did this for me! Thank you, so much! Thank you!"

She peppered her mother with kisses.

"Alright, alright." Emma twisted from her grasp. "Don't love me to death over here. It's nothing you don't deserve."

"I never dreamed you'd get me a bike like this." Rebecca moved in for another hug.

"One more hug." Emma held out her arms. "Then we'll check out your cool new bike."

"You know what kind of bike this is?" she asked, draping an arm around Rebecca's shoulders as they surveyed it.

"Do I?" Rebecca's eyes sparkled as she ran her hands over the beautiful blue and silver frame. "This is a Mongoose Kaldi, Women's Model. A triumph of engineering among commuter bikes. See these things? They aren't just handlebars. They're Revo Twisters. If you want a more precise instrument for angling and turning, you'll have to get a BMX rally bike. Its' got a metal alloy frame, a forged alloy crankset."

She touched or pointed to each feature of the bike as she identified it. "Oversize steel ATB Straight Blade Fork. This seat is a VELO Comfort Design Saddle with super soft foam and dual density base. It has 26 inch wheels, Alex Alley tires and 1.6 Sport Contact tires. Isn't this a 21 speed?"

"That's right." Emma's smile shone as bright as a floodlight's glare. Her mother's and daughter's smiles were just as radiant. "I wasn't sure if I should get you something that goes so fast, but your grandmother assured me that you're a great bike rider."

"Thanks, Grandma Rose." Rebecca hugged her grandmother before hugging her mother again. "I appreciate this so much, Mom. I couldn't have a better present. I'll take good care of it, you'll see! I just hope you didn't spend too much money on it."

"You let me worry about that, Rebee." Emma pinched her daughter's cheek. "How about you give her a spin?"

"Love to!" Rebecca shrieked, undid the kickstand and hauled the sleek cycle down to the sidewalk. She hopped on it and took off down the block.

Rebecca couldn't keep quiet as she and Grandma Rose rode home with the new conveyance in the back of the Harvester. "I really love that bike, Grandma, but I hope Mom didn't break herself buying it. I know those bikes cost more than 300 dollars. I would have been happy with a regular Huffy or Schwinn, as long as it wasn't beat up like the one I've been riding."

"Its bad form to look a gift horse in the mouth, child," Grandma Rose replied. "Besides, your mother may not make a lot of money waiting tables- but it's not like she has to pay rent at the halfway house. Her rent is making curfew every night and staying out of trouble otherwise."

Rebecca thought for a moment. "Still- she can't stay there forever, right? She'll eventually need a place of her own."

"You're right about that. I guess you're figuring she could have saved the money she spent on that bike toward getting herself a place to live when she leaves."

"Yes."

"Well, what I say to that is," Grandma Rose's voice grew louder. "It's not your job to worry about her! Her job is to worry about you and do for you, something she was very poor at before she went away. I say that anything she gives you from this point on is simply a small payment on what she owes you, but can never fully pay. Understand?"

Rebecca knew her grandmother was getting upset, so she decided that it was best to agree. She didn't have the same hard feelings toward her mother that Grandma Rose had. But then, Grandma Rose didn't know the real reason that Emma had stabbed Uncle Gregory and that poor woman.

Rebecca rushed her mind from that, preferring to think of the wonderful present her mother had given her. She didn't dare predict what would happen between them, but she did know that Emma was much better than before. She felt glad that her mother's condition had been diagnosed and that she now received proper treatment and medication. She sighed, thinking that things might have been better a whole lot sooner if only they had known.

Things are better now, though, she thought as she lay in bed that Sunday night. *Mom is better. I have a good new friend and tomorrow is my orientation at a wonderful new school.*

Rebecca couldn't wait for morning to come. She only imagined good things happening to her at Mackenzie High School.

Chapter 8- Orientation

I

Rebecca wore a white blouse and a dark, pleated knee length skirt, along with a pair of low cut Skechers that were patterned like saddle shoes. Looping braids held her dark brown hair, done by her own hand.

Not bad, she thought, checking her appearance in the bathroom mirror. *I think I look pretty decent.*

She felt grateful that Mackenzie High School's uniform policy called for her to wear variations of the same outfit year round. She didn't think style of dress could be ammunition for ridicule when everyone dressed in a similar fashion.

She inhaled a bowl of Cinnamon Toast Crunch before stepping outside. The air on this last Monday morning of August felt warm and pleasant, with a slight breeze.

Rebecca locked the house before wheeling away on her cool new bike. Lacking any kind of portable music player to listen to as she rode, she whistled and hummed her favorite songs. She hoped that her grandmother would do as she asked and get her either a Discman or some sort of generic MP3 player for her birthday. She did not delude herself into thinking she'd get a super expensive I-Pod.

Grandma Rose had spoken of going into work a little late so that she could drop Rebecca off. Rebecca felt relieved to convince her otherwise. This was the first day of high school. She didn't want to be escorted like some little kid. She didn't dare risk anything that might ruin her first legitimate chance for social acceptance in years.

Rebecca maintained an unhurried pace during the four mile bike ride. She used the back of her hand to wipe away the few beads of sweat that stood on her forehead when she reached her destination. Surprise seized her as she saw scores of kids either dropped off or accompanied into the building by adults. She still felt glad that Grandma Rose hadn't brought her. Spotted among a myriad of expensive cars and SUVs, the old Harvester would have consigned her to immediate second class status. *Okay, third class*, she thought. *No- third world.*

She decided that her grandmother's truck must never venture within seeing distance of the school. She secured her bike to the rack near the main entrance and joined the crowd of entering students. Everyone kid and adult she glanced at looked well to do. Everyone smiled with pride. Rebecca smiled with pride also, although her family had nothing approaching the financial status of her peers.

Einhurst Road address or not, ex-convict mom or not, she had earned her way into this prestigious school, just as she would someday earn herself out of Bay Corner and into a better life than the town offered.

Well-dressed faculty with pleasant demeanor stood at different points of the school's first floor corridor. They directed the incoming students and their families to the school auditorium. Rebecca beheld its' magnificence as she entered amidst the pleasant procession. The auditorium's vinyl seats were like those in a movie theatre, only sans cup holders. A center section bisected the left and right sections of seats. Spacious walkways flanked the center section. The front row of each section rested well beyond the stage, leaving room for an orchestra pit. A group of uniformed students filled the pit, safeguarding various instruments. The letters PMH emblazoned their blazers in fancy script. An austere looking middle aged man sat at the outer edge of the young musicians. Huge spotlights overlooked the stage. Smaller but still impressive lights interspersed along the cavernous ceiling, spanning front to rear of the auditorium.

Rebecca marveled at the setting as a staff member ushered her into a seat in the fourth row of the center section. She had only ever known Bay Corner School's auditorium. That was no real auditorium, just a vacant library room packed with folding chairs and used for grade level assemblies.

Rebecca smiled, thinking that although she had yet to receive her class schedule; high school was already a much different experience for her. Comfortable in her seat, she scanned the auditorium for familiar faces. She saw Kimberly Meisner and her parents head toward some seats in the right most section.

Mr. Halloran took several long, majestic strides to the podium after all students and guests were seated. "Good morning, future Patrick F. Mackenzie High class of 2008," he said, his amplified voice carrying as he smiled like a patriarch regarding the gathered and successful fruit of his loins. His voice was satin and steel, as charming as it was commanding. "On behalf of your fellow students and staff, and Mr. McCall, our music director, the distinguished Mackenzie High Band will now welcome you with a musical selection."

Mr. McCall sprung to his feet and set his arms to the dance of conducting. The students segued into a flawless orchestral rendition of Carlos Santana's "Game of Love." Rebecca had never imagined classical instruments playing a contemporary pop song. The pathetic band at Bay Corner School had all it could handle playing notes at all. *These guys are great*, she thought. The violinists even managed to mimic the song's electric guitar solo. When Mr. McCall's dancing arms completed a final flourish and the number concluded, the entire audience gave an unprompted (and very loud) standing ovation. The conductor and his musicians bowed in unison.

Rebecca looked around at her fellow students. They all seemed as excited as she was. Mr. Halloran returned to the podium, exuding calm as he signaled for them all to sit. He waited a few moments for compliance before flashing a thousand megawatts of charm.

"Not a bad little band- is it?" he asked, drawing a smattering of giggles. He cleared his throat after a few seconds of that, prompting seriousness from everyone assembled.

"Here at Mackenzie High," he continued, "we believe that everyone should excel at whatever it is they choose to do. That is why we have chosen each of you. All 102 members of this freshman class managed high levels of academic achievement while also impacting their respective schools and communities in a positive way during their grade school years. All 102 members of this freshman class come from quality families. All 102 members of this freshman class will leave a sterling legacy in the halls of this esteemed institution that will accept nothing less. All 102 members of this freshman class have been recognized as the cream of the crop of incoming 9th graders in the entire state of Maryland! Give yourselves a big round of applause!"

The audience erupted into another joyful chorus. Mr. Halloran's already Grand Canyonesque smile somehow managed to stretch even further. After allowing the audience to carry on for a few seconds, he held his arms out. His palms faced the floor as he moved them up and down, causing a hush to befall the auditorium.

"A select few of you attend this school on Mackenzie family scholarships," Mr. Halloran said. "Others pay tuition. No matter how your attendance here is funded, you still had to meet rigorous qualifications in order to be granted admission. I'm sure most of you are aware that although the Mackenzie School is relatively young, we have achieved monumental success, as have our graduates. Things could not be any other way. After all, the man whose name we bear essentially built this town! Although he passed a few years back, his family's legacy lives on in our students and staff. Similarly, when the Mackenzie School sends graduating seniors out into the world, the legacy of their time here goes with them. Our historical rate of graduating students who matriculate here as freshman is 91 percent. The class of 2003 graduated 94 percent of their entry group. Of those 94 percent, every one of them has been accepted to a four year college and 71 percent of them have been offered full scholarships to those institutions of higher learning!"

He paused with a perfect sense of the dramatic, eliciting a round of impressed clapping before continuing. "But, we at Mackenzie High are not satisfied with that achievement. We believe in always improving, no matter how high our current success level. We think of ourselves as the educational equivalent of Michael Jordan in his prime, always adding something to our game even though we're already the best. You see, at Patrick F. Mackenzie High School, we don't compare ourselves to others. To do so would only make us complacent, as we clearly stand at the proverbial 'head of the class'. No, here at Patrick F. Mackenzie High School, we compare ourselves to ourselves. We compete with ourselves, always pushing ourselves to do better. Here at Patrick F. Mackenzie High School, our school motto is 'No Horizon is unreachable'. So, I challenge you, the Mackenzie High Family challenges you all to reach that seemingly unreachable horizon." He paused, surveying the crowd before continuing. "From your first official day of school tomorrow to your last day here as a senior, we expect nothing less. Our ultimate goal is to have all graduating seniors receive full scholarships to four year universities. I challenge all 102 of you to aggressively pursue that goal. I challenge all of your families to fully support your pursuit of excellence. Is everyone with me?"

Every student and adult exploded to their feet at the shouted question, clapping, cheering, and catcalling. This time Mr. Halloran let them continue, beaming as the passing seconds did nothing to dull their rancor. Rebecca bounced on the balls of her feet while she clapped. She felt blessed and privileged to be a part of this. She couldn't speak for the other 101 freshman, but she felt certain she would obtain a full scholarship to a four year university. In four years, she'd punch her ticket out of Bay Corner. The cost of the trip would be funded by excelling at this wonderful school.

II

After the orientation assembly ended, Rebecca filed out of the auditorium with everyone else. She approached the bike rack out front when a husky voice called her name. She turned around, finding herself greeted by the surprising sight of Kevin Anderson. Another student sidestepped her as she stopped in her tracks. Kevin smiled the dreamy smile of a heartthrob, murmuring something to his family before walking over to her. They remained near the school's entrance, watching him for a moment before falling into their own banter.

"Hi, Rebecca," Kevin said, extending a sinewy hand. Rebecca hesitated before grasping it. Her body tingled at the brief touch.

"Hi, Kevin," she said, feeling as nervous as a yearling. She hadn't expected him to get into Mackenzie, though she did remember that he usually made honor roll at Bay Corner. Still, she suspected that he wasn't there on academic scholarship.

"Good to see you," he said. "I saw Kimberly Meisner in there, too. It's nice to know I'll have at least two old schoolmates at this fancy place."

"Yeah." Rebecca nodded, deciding to speak her mind. "But, it's really only like one. You barely ever spoke to me at Bay Corner. I understand why, though."

Kevin's eyes widened. "Yeah," his husky voice momentarily climbed to a higher pitch, "Because you barely ever spoke to me, Rebecca! You think I'm going to talk to someone who won't even look straight at me?"

Rebecca had to admit that she never made eye contact with Kevin at their old school. Still, she felt skeptical about him approaching her. "Well, you're talking to me now."

"Well, your eyes aren't in the floor, now. Something's different about you."

"Maybe what's different is that you saw how I look in a dress at eighth grade graduation."

Kevin chuckled. "I won't lie. You looked really pretty that day. But, I guess you've always been pretty."

"Thank you." Rebecca blushed, her resolve softening. The glint in Kevin's eyes and the fact that he had stopped her in the first place were signs that he meant what he said. Although she had just stepped out of the school's just north of frigid air conditioning, she felt very warm.

"I think what's changed about you is that you don't seem so timid anymore. You seem like a really cool girl, now." Kevin cleared his throat. "Could I call you?"

"Rebecca," she said. "My family calls me Rebee."

"Rebee." Kevin tried the word out, flashing his charming smile. "That's a really cool nickname. But, I was asking if I could call you on the phone."

Rebecca's eyes bulged as she swallowed hard, struggling to collect herself. "I- uh. I never had a boy ask to call me on the phone before. I don't know how my grandmother would feel about that."

Kevin nodded. "Granny's old fashioned, huh? I understand. Well, what if I give you my number? That way you can call me when you're able."

"Okay!" Rebecca flashed a brief smile that shifted into a frown. "We didn't have to bring any books today. And I don't have a cell phone to save it into."

"Oh." Kevin smiled, holding up an index finger. "Hold on a sec. I'll be right back."

He waltzed over to a woman who must have been his mother. Two girls who must have been Kevin's younger sisters flanked the woman. A man who seemed to be Kevin's father looked in Rebecca's direction. He uttered something that burst the small group into laughter as the woman reached into her purse. "Attaboy, Kev!" the man yelled as Kevin scurried back to Rebecca. He handed her a pen and a small scrap of paper.

Rebecca scrawled the number as Kevin recited it. She folded it as small as possible and tucked it into her blouse pocket. Kevin looked around. "I just realized you're here by yourself. How are you getting home?"

Rebecca shrugged. "My grandmother had to work." She pointed to the bike rack. "I'll ride my bike, just like I rode it here."

Kevin's eyes bulged. "Wow. That's an awesome bike. Look at how it shines."

"Yeah, I just got it," Rebecca said, smiling. Smiling was getting to be second nature around Kevin. "I love it. It was a present from my mom." She watched his face for any change in expression at the mention of her infamous mother. There wasn't.

"Cool." He nodded. "Listen, Rebecca. I don't care about any of that stuff from Bay Corner, you know? That was kid stuff. We're in high school now. A damn good high school at that. We have to leave that middle school crap behind. I think that you're really pretty and really cool. I really hope we can hang out."

He stared into her eyes as he spoke. She blushed a deep crimson, her heart doing all sorts of gymnastics.

Kevin held out his hand as he had when first approaching her. Again, she tingled when she grasped it. "See you, Rebecca," he said, skittering off to rejoin his family.

Rebecca couldn't stop thinking of Kevin's handsome smile as she pedaled home. That dazzling smile blinded her to the wolfish hunger in his eyes.

Chapter 9- New School, New Friends

I

The Tuesday following freshman orientation was the first official day of the 2004-2005 school year. On that day, Rebecca learned that Mackenzie High teachers piled work on from the outset. Textbooks were distributed and homework was assigned in all her major subjects. *Bring it on*, she thought. She intended to pour herself into her studies- to behave as if her life depended on stellar academic achievement- because she believed that it did.

Rebecca was enrolled in the Accelerated and Intensified Academy, one of two academic tracks at Mackenzie. The other track was the Excellence Academy. If the Excellence Academy served as the academic equivalent of a Mercedes, then AIA was a Bentley. There were a total of 18 ninth graders in AIA. Rebecca assumed that most, if not all, of the other 2004 Mackenzie scholarship students had been distributed among them.

Because of the rigor of the AIA curriculum, school administration didn't allow students enrolled in it to participate in extracurricular activities during the first quarter of the school year. They wanted such students to have a few months to adjust to the intensity and volume of the workload.

AIA students existed as their own unit in content area classes, only mixing with other students in elective courses such as PE and Art. Kimberly Meisner was the only one of Rebecca's AIA classmates who lived in Bay Corner. Rebecca had expected Norman Myers to be among the group, but she had been wrong about that. She devoted all of ten seconds to wondering if she had beaten the poor geek out for the scholarship she received.

During the first few days of school, Rebecca and Kimberly said little more than "Hi" and "Bye" to each other. The ice between them thawed on Thursday, when their Accelerated Biology I teacher partnered them to fill out a chromosome chart.

"Hey, Rebecca," Kimberly said, smiling a mechanical smile as she smoothed the chart out on the table.

"Hi, Kimberly," Rebecca said, shooting a quick glance at her partner before directing her focus to the assignment. "Do you mind?" she asked, poising her pencil to fill in some of the blank spaces.

"Go right ahead," Kimberly said, smiling a genuine smile this time. "How about if we each do half?"

"Cool." Rebecca studied the chart, pausing to reference her copy of the guide they had each been given. *Piece of cake*, she thought, finishing her part in no time. "Your turn," she chirped, dropping her pencil and easing the chart toward Kimberly.

Only stopping to glance at her own guide a few times, Kimberly zipped through the rest of the assignment. "All done," she said, giggling as she pushed the chart closer to Rebecca. "So that was like- really easy, right?"

Rebecca smiled. "Yeah. I guess it was."

Kimberly craned her neck to inspect the completed chart. "It's all correct," Rebecca assured her.

Kimberly looked at Rebecca and winked. Her gesture struck Rebecca so funny that she had to cover her mouth to stifle laughter. "I know that," Kimberly whispered. "I want Mrs. Fox to think we're still working on it so we can talk a little. Now, pick up your pencil and do like I'm doing. And stop smiling so much. That'll tip her off."

Rebecca did as instructed, pretending to still be working on the chart.

"How are you ladies progressing?" Mrs. Fox's melodic voice sailed along the flawless acoustics of the classroom. She stood at the promethean board in the front of the room.

"We're okay," Kimberly responded. "We just need a little more time."

When Mrs. Fox looked away, Kimberly whispered to Rebecca. "See. All teachers are the same in that way. As long as you appear to be working, you can get away with a bunch of stuff."

She pointed her pencil to a random spot on the paper. Rebecca nodded her head, as if listening to what her partner was saying about it.

"You're catching on already," Kimberly said, allowing a crack of a smile to emerge on her face. "So listen, Rebecca. I know that we hardly ever talked at Bay Corner. I wasn't a friend to you- but I never picked on you, either. You know that- right?"

Rebecca nodded, wondering that the valedictorian of the Bay Corner School Class of 2004 was getting at.

"I know I could have been much nicer," Kimberly continued, erasing part of the chart she had filled in, only to scrawl the same response that had been there initially. "But the thing is- that's the past now. Eighth grade is kid stuff. This is high school, the best one in the area. We're both in its' best course. Plus, look around. We're among the few students in AIA who haven't been fitted for a custom made retainer."

Taking a quick survey of their classmates, Rebecca couldn't help giggling. A majority of them were Grade A Poindexters.

"You see what I mean, don't you? Anyway, Rebecca, I think it's like Mr. Halloran said at that assembly. We're both the cream of the crop. So since we're both cream of the crop- maybe we should hang out together- unless you like hate me from ignoring you at Bay Corner."

"I don't hate you," Rebecca said, allowing herself a small smile.

First, Kevin, she thought. *Now Kimberly Meisner wants to be my friend? And they're both singing the same song about forgetting about the last three years? Things are better for me already.*

She had acquired more friends during one week at Mackenzie High than she'd managed during the previous three school years at Bay Corner.

II

After school, Kimberly introduced Rebecca to Phyllis Hyman, one of her friends from her well off neighborhood. The tall girl looked a lot like a teenage Naomi Campbell. Her straightened hair fell to her upper back. Rebecca felt certain that a good deal of it was weaved in. *It's very well done, though,* she thought.

"Try not to be put off by Phyllis," Kimberly said, smiling. "She spent her formative years in private schools, so she can come off a little snooty."

"I do not." Phyllis frowned. "In any case, we're all in private school now, aren't we?" She offered a dainty hand to Rebecca. "Pleased to meet you, Rebecca."

"Nice to meet you, too." Rebecca smiled as they shared a brief shake.

"We might all be in private school, but Rebecca and I are in AIA," Kimberly said.

Phyllis frowned. "So, I'll call you girls in ten years when I need a rocket built. Meanwhile, I'll keep going to class with guys who are actually cute."

"Looks like I'm about to have a Bay Corner reunion," a sonorous voice said from behind them, interrupting their conversation. Rebecca knew the speaker even before she and the others turned to face him.

"Case in point," Phyllis said, smirking. "Only this one's no damn good."

"Hello, ladies." Kevin fell in among them, beaming a smile straight from the heavens. "Were you all talking about me?"

"You wish." Kimberly frowned, sighed and rolled her eyes.

"Ah, Kimberly." Kevin placed a hand over his heart. "Such hostility really hurts my heart. Be careful that you don't break it."

"Right." Kimberly's face reddened. "As if it's possible to break something that doesn't work to begin with."

"Oh, Kimberly." Kevin sighed, turning to Rebecca. "Hi, Rebecca." His voice grew as sweet as his smile. "How are you?"

"I'm fine," Rebecca said, barely suppressing a giggle. Kevin extended an open palm toward her. She trailed her fingers along its surface.

"And how are you, my statuesque Nubian goddess?" Kevin sidled up to Phyllis.

Phyllis frowned. "Don't waste your time trying to flatter me."

Kevin shrugged. "Sometimes the truth just sounds like flattery." His winning smile remained plastered on his face as his gaze fell on Rebecca and rested there. "I'm sorry to interrupt you ladies' conversation, but I'd like to speak with Rebecca for just a moment."

He held out his arm for her. She smiled and hooked hers in it. They walked the short distance to the bike rack, where her Mongoose Kaldi rested.

"So, why haven't you called me?" he asked, worming his arm fee and turning to face her.

Rebecca dropped her head in embarrassment. "I haven't had a chance to," she said. "I want to do it when my grandmother's not around. Like I said before, I don't think she really wants me talking to boys."

"Is she always around?" Kevin asked- his frustration visible.

Rebecca nodded. "Unless I can call you right when I get home. She gets home from work around 4."

Kevin sighed. "That's no good. I'm at practice right after school." He checked his Movado wristwatch. "I actually have to be there in a few minutes."

"I'm really sorry, Kevin," Rebecca said. "I promise I'll find a way to call you."

Kevin frowned. "I hope so. I'm really interested in you, Rebecca- but if we can never even talk to each other, what's the use? It's not like we're in any of the same classes."

Kevin glanced at his watch again. "I actually have to get to practice now." One hand trailed along Rebecca's braids, provoking a now familiar tingle. "I'll see you around, okay?"

"Okay." Rebecca sighed, feeling pressure mount her. She knew that if she didn't do something, the dreamiest boy around would soon lose interest in her. After all, he had plenty of other options.

Kevin waved as he passed the other girls. "See you around, Phyllis," he said. "Au revoir, Kimberly."

"Whatever," Kimberly said, dismissing him with the flip of a hand. Phyllis rolled her eyes, not bothering with a verbal response. Rebecca walked her bike over to the other girls as Kevin passed through the entry door.

"You'd better watch yourself with that one," Phyllis warned her.

"Yeah," Kimberly grumbled. "I'd steer clear of that jerk if I were you, Rebecca."

Rebecca's eyes voice climbed an octave. "You think Kevin's a jerk? He is so sweet."

"Don't confuse his looks with his personality," Phyllis said. "And anyone can act nice."

"Yeah," Kimberly agreed. "Unlike you, we actually know him. And I'm warning you, Golden Boy is nothing but lead underneath. All he thinks about is sex, just like other guys. You don't want to get involved with him."

Rebecca changed the subject to something she felt more comfortable talking about. She didn't know what Kimberly and Phyllis had against Kevin, but she decided to judge him on how he treated her. She bid the other girls goodbye a few minutes later. Her mind raced as she peddled home.

She speculated that Kevin and Kimberly may have dated and broken up.

Maybe Kevin had dumped Kimberly. Yes, that was probably it. Then again, maybe not.

Maybe it was presumptuous to assume that. Rebecca certainly had no way of knowing. She confessed to herself that she wasn't exactly in the social loop at her previous school.

Whatever the reason, Rebecca hoped that Kimberly's dislike for Kevin didn't affect her and Kimberly's burgeoning friendship. She sprouted a huge grin, excited by the newness of even having to consider such things.

So this is what its like to have a social life? She thought it was a lot better than being an outcast.

Things had taken a huge turn for the better during the first week of school. No one had called her Knife Girl of Knife Lady's daughter. Kevin Anderson, perhaps the cutest boy she'd ever seen, showed interest in her. Kimberly and Phyllis wanted to be her friends. Before that, the only kid who'd befriended her had been John Rainbird.

Fuck, Rebecca thought. *John Rainbird!*

She had pedaled three blocks past the library before remembering that she was supposed to meet him. She sprinted back toward the little building and secured her bike out front. She breathed easy, glad to see his rickety mount there.

She chided herself for almost forgetting about him.

No matter how many new friends I make, she thought, *I can't forget the one person who was a friend to me when no other kid would even talk to me.*

Rebecca marched inside, expecting to find John among the library's carrel of desktop computers. Instead she found him seated at a reading table, thumbing through a sci-fi magazine.

"Hi, John Rainbird," she said, in the most pleasant tone she could manage.

"Hey, Rebecca," John said, smoothing his dark hair out of his face. Unbraided and untied, it flowed over him like a black waterfall. "How've you been?"

"I've been okay." She plopped down across from him. "I'm surprised you're not at a computer."

"Maybe before I go." He yawned. "I just came here to do my homework and wait for you. I just finished up a few minutes ago."

"You tired?"

"Hell, yes," he groaned. "You know classes start at 7:10 at Havre de Grace? I have to get up early as hell and ride my bike over to Chesapeake Grove Road by 6:30. If I miss that bus, I have to ride my bike 10 miles to school."

"That sucks." Rebecca reached across the table, gliding a hand over his knuckles.

"Why doesn't your grandfather drive you?"

"Yeah, right." John smirked. "I told you he doesn't want me going to school with 'Anglos' at all. Besides- being seen getting out of his relic of a truck would have even worse social repercussions than having to mount that shitty bike on the back of the bus before I get on."

"I feel the same way about my grandmother's old Harvester," Rebecca said, giggling.

John set the magazine down and stared at her. "Oh, I get the feeling it wouldn't matter with you."

"What do you mean by that?" Rebecca squeaked, drawing a warning "ahem" from the elderly librarian.

John smirked as he leaned toward her. "I mean look at you, Rebecca. You're on your way. All cleaned up in your school colors. You look really pretty." He pronounced the last word as if it were profanity, causing Rebecca's face to tighten. "You're in another world now. You'll see. I bet you'll even be popular at Mackenzie High. You're not a loser anymore. Not on the outside looking in, like me. I'm stuck sharing classes with a bunch of idiots. I'm stuck in Loserville."

He laughed, his voice softening when he spoke again. "Listen to how bitter I sound. I'm sorry. That wasn't fair to you at all. It's not your fault I didn't get into Mackenzie or Harford Tech."

"I'm sorry you don't like it at Havre de Grace."

"Believe me, you wouldn't like it either. The suck fest starts as soon as I load my shitty bike on the rack. If the bike thing isn't conspicuous enough, there's these ratty clothes and the fact that I'm half-Indian -which is just plain Indian as far as they can see- even if they've been taught to say Native American. Can't say I blame 'em. The most any of those kids have ever seen of the Maupai is on those stupid canoe tours we run. The way my grandfather's got us all living isn't much different than some fucking cave dwellers, you know? So even though nobody's really messed with me yet, I know I'm a big spectacle to other kids. They probably wonder if I can kill a bear with my bare hands or something."

"Can you?" Rebecca asked, smiling.

John burst into uproarious laughter. "Good one, Rebecca. Good one."

His mirth drew the librarian's attention. "Young man," she began.

"I know, Ma'am." John continued to cackle as he stood. "If I can't keep the noise level down, I'll have to leave." Still laughing, he gathered his books. "Okay, I'm going."

Rebecca smiled as she joined him outside. "I wasn't ready to leave yet, silly. I just got here."

John chuckled. "Well, you should have thought of that before you made me laugh like that." He sobered up, gazing at her for a few beats before wrapped his arms around her and squeezing. "I'm going to miss our friendship, Rebecca."

"What the hell is that supposed to mean?"

"I mean it's been really nice. But no way can our friendship last."

Rebecca grew angry. "Stop talking like that, John Rainbird. Why are you being weird?"

John shrugged. "I'm not being weird, Rebecca. I'm just being realistic. You're making new friends at Mackenzie, aren't you?"

"Yes," Rebecca admitted, feeling her first ever tinge of guilt about that development.

"And I bet those new friends aren't Indian and don't live on the outskirts of civilization," John said. "I bet they have real bathrooms and showers in their houses. I bet they don't have to feed fireplaces to keep warm and light candles or use flashlights or kerosene lamps to see at night. I bet they're pretty or handsome and all neat looking like you are now. I bet they have telephones, cell phones, you know actual technological methods of corresponding with you. Why are you going to keep looking for me around town, then? Why put forth so much effort just to hang with me?"

Tears welled in Rebecca's eyes. "Because you were there for me, that's why! You were there for me when everyone else treated me like some freak. You're a good friend to me, John Rainbird."

"Don't cry, Rebecca," John said, the bitterness in his previous tone wilted. "I am a good friend to you- like you are to me. I really care about you. There's an old Maupai saying I like. Translated into English it means 'The beauty of this world is not ours to hold captive.' I don't want to hold you captive, Rebecca. You have a good life ahead of you."

"So, now you believe in that crap?" Rebecca seethed. "What happened to you believing that stuff was all just stupid campfire stories?"

"There is wisdom to be found even in stupid campfire stories." John planted a soft kiss on her forehead. "It's been a pleasure to make your acquaintance, Rebecca Saulters."

Rebecca threw her arms around him, holding him with all her might. "No," she howled. "No. I won't allow it. Do you understand me? I won't accept it. I've never had a friend like you and I want to keep you as my friend. I don't believe in that Maupai stuff. I want to keep you captive."

John laughed. "You are keeping me captive, right now."

"Just like I want to." Rebecca giggled.

John sighed. "What am I to do with you?"

"Stay my friend."

"Alright. I'll do that. I guess I was trying to save myself the pain of when you decide you have no more time for me."

Rebecca released him and stood back, staring into his eyes. "That's not going to happen."

John shrugged. "I doubt that you're right about that, but I guess I'm not too proud to make myself available to you as long as you have time for me."

"I'll always have time for you."

John forced a smile as he rested a hand on Rebecca's shoulder. "It will be nice if that turns out to be true. Don't you have schoolwork to do?"

Rebecca nodded. "Mmm-hmm."

John chuckled. "Well, let's see if the librarian will allow me back in so I can keep you some company."

"Oh, wait," Rebecca said, hoping that she wasn't about to seem like a total jerk, but unable to help herself. "Check out my new bike before we go back in."

Chapter 10- A Promise to Grandma

Rebecca's 14th birthday fell on September 6th, 2004, the Sunday before Labor Day. She woke up that morning with butterflies in her stomach, happy to be a year older and thinking about what she must summon the courage to do.

She and her grandmother went to brunch at the Denny's in Edgewood after attending a 10 am church service. While they were there, Grandma Rose excused herself to go out to the old Harvester. She held a colorful gift bag when she returned.

"Here's your present," she said, handing it over. Rebecca hurried to remove purple wrapping from the crescent shaped item inside. She yelped, "Thank you, Grandma! You got me an MP3 player. Just like I wanted."

The cheaper Phillips model was nowhere near as glamorous as an IPod, but Rebecca was glad to have any MP3 player.

"Did you think I would get you a poodle instead?" Grandma Rose quipped. "Happy birthday, Rebee."

"Thank you so much, Grandma." Rebecca crossed the table to hug the older woman and kiss her cheek. "The only thing that could make this birthday better would be if Mom was here."

Grandma Rose sighed. "You know she had to work a double, Rebee. At least she called."

Rebecca shrugged. "Yeah." She smiled. "She's doing real good, Isn't she?"

Grandma Rose nodded. "Yes, your mother's doing a lot better. So long as she keeps to her medicine, her meetings, and keeps busy. I do think the 'Knife Lady' will stay gone for good."

"You think maybe, after she's done with the halfway house, she might come stay with us?"

Grandma Rose ran her right hand through her silver hair as she stared into Rebecca's eyes. "I don't think that would be a good idea, Rebecca."

"Why not?"

"Well, think about it. We're all doing pretty well right now- right? Your mother's stable for the first time in her adult life. You're at a wonderful new school where no one cares about the baggage her actions dumped at your feet. And I'm on my way to a happy retirement. We're all in a good place right now. I think it's best to keep things that way."

"You don't want me to be around Mom every day?" Rebecca blurted.

Grandma Rose's face hardened. "No, I guess I don't. I think I've done pretty well raising you up to this point and I trust myself to finish the job more than I trust her. I can't help it if the truth isn't always pretty." She reached a concerned hand across the table, patting one of her granddaughter's.

"I guess you're right," Rebecca admitted, breaking a few seconds of uncomfortable silence. "She was never a good mother, the whole time I was a little kid. And she's just getting herself straightened out. Maybe she couldn't handle more than just visiting with me." She sighed and placed a hand to her forehead. "I'd rather not live with her than have her end up like she was before. Have you guys talked about it?"

Grandma Rose nodded. "She agrees with me."

"I guess that's best, then. Gran- you know I'm 14 now –right?"

Grandma Rose eyed her with curiosity. "I just gave you your present- didn't I?"

Rebecca giggled. "I know you *know* I'm 14. But do you know what that means?"

Grandma Rose grimaced. "What does it mean, Rebee?"

"It means I'm in high school, and I finally have some friends. And maybe I'm starting to get interested in boys. It means that for the first time I have the chance to actually have a social life!"

Grandma Rose frowned. "I should have known this was coming. I'm not allowing you to date yet, Rebecca."

Rebecca giggled. "I know that. There's something else I'd like though."

They came to an agreement right there, over their All American skillet meals.

Grandma Rose granted Rebecca reasonable phone privileges, but only after all schoolwork was done and not after 9 pm. After Rebecca explained who Kevin was, Grandma expressed doubt of his interest before seeing how she looked in her graduation dress. Rebecca remembered thinking that, too, but she didn't dare voice her agreement.

"Just be sure all you do is talk," Grandma Rose warned. "Don't let me catch you sneaking around with any boys, Rebecca. I won't have you end up like your mother."

Rebecca frowned. "I'm not my mother, Grandma."

Grandma Rose looked at her long and hard. "No, I don't guess you are. But you wouldn't have to be your mother to let some sweet talking young man throw you off the path you've laid out for yourself."

Rebecca leaned forward and looked her guardian square in the eyes. "I promise you, Grandma. I promise myself. Nothing's going to stop me from busting out of Bay Corner and having a successful life. Nothing!"

Rebecca felt more certain of the truth in those words than any words she had ever spoken. Leaving Bay Corner and living a life far different from her mother, or even her grandmother, meant everything to her. She knew she wouldn't be able to stomach falling short of that.

Chapter 11 - The Game Begins

Rebecca saw Kevin after school the day after Labor Day. He acted like he'd just won a million dollar jackpot when she promised to call him that evening, pumping his fist and hugging her. "Man, that's something nice to look forward to," he said.

Rebecca looked forward to it, too, despite Kimberly and Phyllis urging her to avoid him. She completed her homework prior to exhausting the better part of an hour in summoning the courage to dial Kevin's number. The phone rang through to his voicemail. Rebecca stammered a message, asking him to call back if he could, but not after 9. He didn't call.

Rebecca tossed and turned that night, thinking that Kevin might have returned the call if her phone curfew wasn't so early. She refused to submit to her dread that he might have lost interest in her.

Why would a heartthrob like Kevin like the Knife Lady's Daughter, anyway? A wicked little voice asked. *Maybe he's just come to his senses.*

No, Rebecca rebuffed the doubting creature. *I'm not the Knife Lady's Daughter, anymore. That's the past. Kevin really does like me. I'll find out why he didn't call tomorrow. It's no big deal.*

But she didn't see Kevin the next day. They seemed to cross each other's path several times a day before then, despite not sharing any classes. If nothing else, they were sure to see each other in front of school after dismissal. Now he was nowhere to be found.

Rebecca decided that not running into Kevin was a disappointing coincidence. It took all of the restraint she could muster to resist calling him that night. No one needed to tell her that she shouldn't be the only one making an effort, no matter how much she liked a boy.

She next saw Kevin in the hallway on Thursday after leaving English class. He greeted her with a cursory wave and kept walking.

"What's up with that?" she grumbled, glaring in his wake. For the first time, she considered that Kimberly and Phyllis might be right about him.

"He's just playing the game, girl," Kimberly said, striding down the hall with her. "All boys do. Your dreamboat just happens to be better at it than most."

"Well, I don't like that game," Rebecca said.

"He'll probably call you tonight or tomorrow," Kimberly said. "Making you wait after exchanging numbers is like guy law. They like for us to feel like they could take us or leave us."

Rebecca frowned. "Well, if he's going to act like that, I'll leave him."

"That's the spirit!" Kimberly's voice soared as she slapped Rebecca's palm. "You'll be better off if you do."

Rebecca once more thought that her new friend protested too much. Still, Kimberly proved right about the timing of Kevin's call. Rebecca was on the phone with her when his number appeared on her caller ID.

"That's lover boy, isn't it?" Kimberly asked when Rebecca clicked back over.

"Yes." Rebecca wondered if she sounded as excited as she felt. She hoped that Kimberly wouldn't try to put a damper on things.

"Alright, girl," Kimberly said. "I'll see you in school tomorrow. Just remember what we talked about."

"I do," Rebecca said, before clicking back to Kevin. "Hey," she chirped, hoping that she didn't sound goofy.

"Hey. What's up, Rebecca? Was that your buddy, Kimberly?"

"What makes you think it was Kimberly?"

"I just thought- I mean I always see you guys together. I thought maybe you were BFFs."

Rebecca chuckled. "We're in like all the same classes, Kevin."

"You are?" Kevin sounded surprised. "I hope she hasn't been saying bad things about me."

"Why would she say bad things about you?" Rebecca asked, growing suspicious.

"She hasn't told you? Kimberly and I used to go out."

Rebecca nodded, her suspicion confirmed. "You guys used to go out? No, she didn't tell me that. So what happened?"

"It was just a middle school thing." Kevin sounded so nonchalant that Rebecca pictured him shrugging. "We just didn't get along very well after a while. Your friend's kind of pushy, in case you haven't noticed."

Rebecca giggled. "Yeah. I've noticed."

"So, has she said anything bad about me?"

"Only that you're like totally obsessed with sex."

Kevin's voice cracked. "She said that about me? Man, she must really be bitter."

"So, are you saying that isn't true?"

"I'm not saying one way or the other. I guess you'll just have to find out for yourself, Rebecca Saulters."

Rebecca giggled. "I guess I will have to find out for myself, Kevin Anderson."

The subject of their conversation switched to how cool their new school was before shifting into a discussion of their favorite music. Grandma Rose called Rebecca from the phone just as Kevin confided that he liked listening to System of a Down while working out.

"Bye, Kevin," Rebecca said, trying to sound sweet. "I'll see you tomorrow."

"I can't wait," Kevin said.

Now he's Mr. Nice Guy, again, Rebecca thought, replacing the cordless phone in its docking bay. She wanted to tell someone about their conversation, but she didn't want to give Kimberly or Phyllis a chance to bad mouth Kevin again. Anyway, she was a little pissed at Kimberly for not telling her about having dated Kevin.

Oh, well, she thought. *Nobody's perfect. Kimberly is still a good friend. But Kevin's a nice guy, no matter what she says. He's nice, cool, and cute enough to be in the movies or model or something.*

Chapter 12 - Losing John Rainbird

I

An unexpected roadblock kept Rebecca from her Thursday meeting with John Rainbird.

Mr. Radisson, the Expanded Ancient Civilizations I teacher assigned a group research presentation due for submission the following Friday. Rebecca, Kimberly, a gangly boy named John Stevens, and a bespectacled girl named Eloise Mclaughlin were assigned to work together. They had to gather and present information about the duties and importance of various Egyptian governmental positions during the Middle Kingdom. Kimberly suggested that Rebecca come to her house after school to get started.

"I have my own computer, All-in-One, and High Speed Internet," she said, as they walked to their next class.

"Come on, it'll be fun. We'll show those two freaks that we can get at least as much accomplished as they can."

"I don't know," Rebecca said. "My grandmother's used to me being at home or the library when she comes home from work."

"Well, maybe it's time your grandmother got used to you doing other things," Kimberly said, sidestepping a horse playing boy who almost ran into her. "Watch it, you jerk! God! Boys are so immature."

She watched the offending party continue up the hall before turning back to Rebecca. "It's not like you're doing anything wrong. We're just trying to get our work done. My mom will take you home, no problem."

"There's something else I'm supposed to do after school," Rebecca said, unable to resist the merits of Kimberly's idea. She didn't mention John Rainbird, opting to keep that part of her life from Kimberly just as she kept it from her grandmother.

"Whatever it is, it can't be more important than getting your schoolwork done," Kimberly said. "You should call your grandmother at lunch time."

Rebecca spent much of the next class considering what to do. She decided that if John Rainbird was a true friend, he'd understand. Excelling at her schoolwork took precedence over everything. When the lunch bell rang, she walked to the main office and asked if she could use the phone. She called the factory and asked for her grandmother, telling the operator the bold faced lie that it was an emergency. She waited several minutes for Grandma Rose to reach the phone before explaining the situation to her.

"That does not qualify as an emergency, Rebecca," Grandma Rose said. "Do you know hard it is for someone to get to the phone in this factory? Let me explain one last time. An emergency is if you're hurt or in trouble. Don't call about anything like that again! Understand?"

"Yes, Grandma Rose," Rebecca said, using her meekest voice. "But can I go?"

Grandma Rose sighed. "I don't like the suddenness of this," she said. "And I want to talk to the other girl's mother and meet her when she drops you off. Any funny business and I won't give you another chance for a long while. Understand?"

Saying that she did, Rebecca thanked her grandmother with enthusiasm before hanging up. She spent the rest of the day feeling torn. She felt sure that she'd enjoy hanging out at Kimberly's house. Kimberly's family had money, so their house had to be pretty nice.

She wished she could contact John Rainbird so that he wouldn't wait around too long for her. She assured herself that she would make it up to him as soon as possible. She hoped he wouldn't be too angry with her.

Rebecca went ahead to Kimberly's awesome house on Rivera Road, where they managed a blazing start on the project. Kimberly's immense bedroom housed every technological amenity she mentioned to Rebecca. Her friend also had a walk-in closet and her own bathroom.

A huge lawn, pool, and grandiose backyard patio highlighted the perimeter of the house. Kimberly's pretty, stylish, and very cool mom dropped Rebecca home after she and Rebecca finished for the day. Mrs. Meisner left Grandma Rose smiling after they met.

"Mrs. Meisner seems really nice for someone so well to do," Grandma Rose admitted.

Rebecca's pleasure with everything going so well was balanced by the guilt of blowing off John Rainbird. As cool a friend as Kimberly was, in many ways John Rainbird was even cooler.

Though it was not their scheduled meeting day, she went looking for him on her bike after volunteering at the soup kitchen that Saturday. She did not find him at the library or on the Nissum Trail.

"Why can't he have a phone?" she whined, feeling sad as she peddled home.

II

For Rebecca, the days leading to the following Thursday crawled along at a snail's pace. She passed the time by completing tons of schoolwork (particularly Mr. Radisson's project), sharing a Saturday lunch with her mother, tackling household chores, socializing with her new girlfriends, and flirting and giggling with Kevin.

"Your grandma says you're starting to like boys," Emma said, during lunch. A slight tremor in her voice betrayed her nervousness. "I'm not going to act like I don't know what that leads to. Promise me- you'll be smart and be careful. I don't want you to end up like me."

I could never end up like you, Rebecca thought. *For one thing, I'm not bipolar.*

"I promise I will be smart and careful, when that time comes, Mom," she said. She giggled. "Don't worry. I don't intend for that to be anytime, soon."

"I'm glad to hear it." Emma smiled, the nervous tremor having departed her voice.

Rebecca appreciated her mother caring enough to give advice, even though she felt that Emma's track record didn't qualify her to do so with any real merit.

When that Thursday came, Rebecca spent a good portion of the school day wishing for time to speed forward. Instead of indulging her habit of idling outside of school with Kimberly and Phyllis after the final bell ring, she told them she had to go and zoomed off toward the library.

Rebecca felt a mixture of disappointment, hurt, and anger as she stood outside of the designated meeting place. She directed that anger at herself and the only person to befriend her when no one else did. She remembered how John Rainbird talked the last time she saw him. He seemed to believe that crap he said about not wanting to hold her back. Maybe he'd just been waiting for her not to show up one time, so he could have an excuse to avoid her. Maybe he'd made some new friends and felt like he no longer had any time for her. She didn't know the exact reasons for him not being there, but she knew that his absence caused the tears that streamed down her cheeks. She wiped her face before peddling home with a heavy heart.

Chapter 13 - Rebecca and Kimberly

As September sprinted toward October, Rebecca continued to throw herself into her studies and newfound social life. She and Kevin talked often on the phone, lingering together after school as well. Contrary to Kimberly's claim, he didn't seem the least bit concerned about sex. The only physical contact he sought were hugs or kisses on the cheek.

Rebecca pointed Kevin's behavior out to Kimberly, having grown tired of her acting annoyed when he came around.

"Maybe he's changed," Rebecca said, stopping herself from completing the statement with "since you guys went out." If Kimberly didn't want to reveal that she and Kevin had gone out, then Rebecca wouldn't spill that she knew about it.

"Maybe he's acting like he's changed," Kimberly said, "but I still think you shouldn't trust him."

Kimberly was a good friend, despite her disapproval of Rebecca's involvement with Kevin. She stayed at Rebecca's house during the last weekend of September. Though she came from the second wealthiest neighborhood in Bay Corner, Kimberly seemed content within the humble lodgings of Grandma Rose's rancher.

She and Rebecca stayed up late her first night there, watching DVDs and eating popcorn. Rebecca placed her twin mattress on the floor when bedtime arrived.

"Will you be comfortable on that?" Kimberly asked, watching Rebecca lay on the box spring.

"I'll be fine, Kimberly," Rebecca said, smiling. "I just want you to be comfortable."

"Okay," Kimberly said, her eyes doubtful as she settled onto the mattress. "But tomorrow night, I'm sleeping on the box spring."

"I can't let you do that."

Kimberly slid a pink sleep mask over her eyes. "Either you let me sleep on the box spring or I'll sleep right on the floor."

Rebecca laughed. "Alright," she relented. "If you insist on torturing yourself, I guess I can't stop you."

Once they made themselves comfortable, Rebecca said, "There's something I have to do in the morning. You can come if you like."

Kimberly smiled at her friend as she propped herself up on one elbow. "Of course, I'm going to come with you. What do you have to do?"

They left the soup kitchen at mid-morning, having helped the other volunteers serve scores of homeless people.

"That wasn't so bad," Rebecca said, beginning the walk home with a purpose. "Was it?"

"No, it wasn't." A sheepish expression covered Kimberly's face as she kept pace with her friend. "I had no idea there were so many homeless people in Bay Corner."

Rebecca shrugged. "They're not all from Bay Corner. People come there from different parts of Harford County. It's a really good soup kitchen."

Kimberly smiled as she slung an arm around Rebecca's shoulders. "You're a really good person, Rebecca."

That afternoon, Rebecca and Kimberly set out for the Bay Corner library, to work on an English assignment. Before Kimberly came over, Rebecca gave fair warning that she didn't have the internet or a computer at home.

"If I need to look something up or type it, I always go to the library," Rebecca said.

Kimberly shrugged. "So, I'll go with you."

Rebecca laughed. "You probably don't even know your way around a public library. You have all of the stuff you need at home."

"And when you come to stay over my house-we'll use all that stuff. But when in Rome…"

Rebecca smiled. "Do as Romans do."

They walked to the library because Kimberly didn't have a bike. If Kimberly could sacrifice far better surroundings to hang with her, then Rebecca could forego her beloved bike for once.

A familiar, but unwelcome voice called from behind as they neared their destination, bringing an abrupt end to their pleasant girl talk.

"Well, well, well. Is that the Knife Lady's Daughter?"

Rebecca turned to see Pamela Lawson, Veronica Myers, and Shanae Edwards form the vertices of a triangle, about thirty yards away. She had hoped to never see them again, but there they stood. Unlike Rebecca and Kimberly, none of them wore knapsacks. One of Veronica's bear paws strangled a twenty ounce bottle of Cherry Coke.

"It's hard to tell." Shanae joined Pamela in her ribbing, grinning like a hyena over a felled carcass. "I mean, the chick kind of looks like her, except for the fact that this one seems to have actually bathed."

"Why don't you guys leave her alone?" Kimberly hissed.

"What's it to you, Miss Valedictorian? Little Suzy Perfect. I'm surprised to even see you hanging around with this freak. I'm surprised to see you off Rivera Road."

"Maybe she's doing community outreach," Pamela quipped. She and her cohorts pealed laughter. "Maybe it's help a freak day."

"If I wanted to do community outreach, I'd hang out with you losers," Kimberly snarled. Her face flushed red with anger.

"Who the fuck do you think you're talking to?" Veronica roared. Rebecca girded herself, disliking her and Kimberly's chances if a fight started.

"I'm talking to you, you fat loser." Kimberly's eyes flashed malice as she pointed at the big girl. "You're such a loser that you can't even see that girls like Pamela and Shanae only keep you around to do their dirty work. Oh, well. Maybe it's good practice for when you grow up to be a bouncer or a female wrestler. That's about the only way you'll ever get out of this town."

Veronica hurled her soda to the ground, sending its contents rushing out like an oil slick. "I'll beat your skinny ass." Her hands formed meaty fists, brown fingers digging into her pink palms. She looked like an angry bull set to charge a matador.

"Have you forgotten who my father is, fatty?" Kimberly asked, wearing a predatory smile. Her father served as a prominent member of the Town Council. "If you ever even think about touching me or my friend, I'll have your elephantine ass charged with assault."

To Rebecca's amazement, the big bully took two cautious steps back. Menace dissipated from Veronica's face, replaced by confusion.

Rebecca found Pamela and Shanae to be just as deflated.

Kimberly wagged her finger at the three erstwhile bullies. "Now, this is what's going to happen," she said. "The three of you are going to leave Rebecca the hell alone. You are going to find someone else to indulge your sadistic tendencies with. I would suggest you try some poor soul who's been sentenced to the hell of a high school you all attend. But you will leave Rebecca alone. You will realize that your days of tormenting her ended at eighth grade graduation last June. You have nothing else to say to her, at least not until the day comes when you welcome her to whatever fast food place you happen to be working in and ask if you may take her order."

Triumph painted Kimberly's face as she observed her vanquished challengers. Her predatory smile downgraded to a garden variety smirk as she turned her back on the terrible trio. "Come on, Rebecca. We have actual school work to do. Our school's not going to issue us a diploma in four years just to be rid of us."

Feeling as stunned as her former tormentors did, Rebecca did as Kimberly instructed. Her shoulders tensed as she walked. She listened for footfalls to alert her that Pamela's gang had decided to attack. To her amazement and relief, that sound never came.

"Take it easy, Rebecca," Kimberly said, smiling as they approached the library's entrance. "What- did you think they'd come after us? They're just bullying cowards. They realize we're above them on the food chain now."

Rebecca smiled. "Yeah, I guess so."

"Nothing to guess." Kimberly threw an arm around her friend. "I just trained that pack of dogs for you."

She laughed. "And when I say dogs, I mean bitches. Isn't it good to be my friend?"

No, it's wonderful, Rebecca thought. *It's wonderful being your friend.*

Lots of things are wonderful in my life now. It's wonderful attending Mackenzie. It's wonderful seeing Kevin. And it's wonderful that my mother is turning her life around.

The only thing that wasn't wonderful in Rebecca's life was losing contact with John Rainbird. After a number of futile efforts, she gave up looking for him. Disappointed in losing his friendship, she only hoped that he was getting along alright.

She knew that she was getting along better than she ever had. Youthful folly convinced her that all of her hard times were over.

Chapter 14 - Rebecca and Kevin

I

"Hey, Rebecca," Kevin said, smiling and wrapping an arm around Rebecca's waist. "You know we've been talking and hanging out for more than a month now- right?"

Rebecca nodded as she strolled alongside him in front of the school. Kimberly and Phyllis seemed displeased as they waited for her by the school's front doors. Rebecca hoped that they wouldn't waste any more of their breath or her time trying to convince her to avoid Kevin. "It's been exactly six weeks."

"Has it?" Kevin chuckled, planting a kiss on her cheek. "I guess time flies when you're having fun. Anyway- I don't think we've ever made it official, so I'd like to now."

He stopped walking and positioned himself in front of her, holding her gaze with his striking blue eyes. "I want you to be my girlfriend."

Rebecca squealed with delight, hugging and squeezing him. "So, I guess you're cool with that?" he asked.

"Of course I'm cool with that, silly." She squeezed even harder. "I thought you'd never ask!"

They continued as they had been for a few days before Kevin started to complain, saying that he wasn't satisfied with being her boyfriend and only seeing her around school. An upset Rebecca reminded him that her grandmother wouldn't allow her to date yet.

"So sneak around," he said. "Get your friends to cover for you."

Rebecca followed Kevin's suggestion, starting to work on Kimberly the next day in study hall.

"Are you coming to my Halloween Party?" Kimberly asked, keeping her voice a whisper. "You think your grandmother will let you?"

"I think so." Rebecca smiled. "She trusts your mom and all. Hey- I need you to do a favor for me."

Kimberly looked up from her Biology textbook. "What kind of favor?"

"I need you to cover for me, so I can meet Kevin outside of school."

Kimberly's face became a mask of hostility. "Ready to give it up now, huh?"

"What?"

"You heard me. You're ready to give it up to lover boy, now. Aren't you? And you want me to help."

Rebecca looked around to see if the study hall proctor had homed in on their conversation. Mrs. Liebowitz was helping another student across the room.

"Why are you acting like that?" Rebecca demanded, struggling to maintain her whisper. "I just want to spend some time alone with my boyfriend. You're my friend. You're supposed to help me. It's not my fault if things didn't work out when you two were together. Maybe you guys just weren't compatible. Anyway, you need to let it go. That was just middle school stuff."

Kimberly didn't respond right away, only watching Rebecca with hurt in her eyes. When she did speak, her voice was soft and measured. "So he told you. I bet he didn't tell you everything, though."

Rebecca leaned in close. "What's 'everything'?"

"What are you girls talking about?" Mrs. Liebowitz's shrill voice echoed through the large room.

"We're just talking about our biology work," Rebecca lied, keeping her voice even as she made eye contact with the teacher.

"Be sure you limit your conversation to that topic," Mrs. Liebowitz said, wagging an index finger that looked as if it had never seen the sun.

Rebecca waited for Mrs. Liebowitz's attention to retreat elsewhere. "What's 'everything'?"

Instead of answering the question, Kimberly said, "Do you think that everything that happened to you in school the last couple of years was just 'middle school stuff'?" She made air quotes as she said the last few words.

Rebecca's face turned beet red. "Why would you bring that up? Damn, Kimberly. Are you my friend or not?"

Kimberly shook her head, the way Grandma Rose often did when someone did something she found to be stupid or ridiculous. "Yes, I'm your friend," Kimberly grumbled. "I'm your friend, so I'll do it. I'll lie for you. I just hope you like how it works out."

They had their scheme all worked out by the following Monday. That evening, Rebecca asked her grandmother if she could go to Kimberly's house to study after school the next day. Grandma Rose gave her approval so long as Mrs. Meisner gave Rebecca a ride home.

Kimberly told Rebecca that Mrs. Meisner always arrived home between 6:30 and 7:00. Kimberly and Kevin lived only a mile from each other. That meant that Rebecca could sneak over to Kevin's before leaving for Kimberly's house. Mrs. Meisner would assume that she'd been there all along.

After school on the appointed day, Kevin asked if he could pedal Rebecca to his house on her bike. She squeezed behind him on the Mongoose's sturdy seat and wrapped her arms around his lean waist. He had to peddle from an upright position to leave enough room for both of them. The ease with which he did so impressed his passenger.

Kevin's family lived in what could only be described as a mansion. It wasn't anywhere near the size of the Playboy Mansion Rebecca had once seen on T.V., but it was large enough to swallow Grandma Rose's house and several others like it. Kevin led her around the rear of the property, after keying in a combination to allow them through the black wrought iron gate that read "Anderson Manor". A large outdoor pool stood about fifty yards beyond the main house. Rebecca's host led her to the pool house that stood just beyond it, walking with her bike all the while.

The pool house was one large, open room. Rebecca estimated it as the size of her grandmother's living room and dining room combined.

Kevin owned a mahogany computer desk large enough to seat two people with ease. A top of the line laptop, All-in-One, digital camera, and camcorder rested on it. In the center of Kevin's domain sat a plush couch, along with a coffee table and opposite facing, matching loveseat. A home entertainment system framed the leftmost wall, topped by a large flat screen T.V. The entertainment system's shelves were lined with electronic entertainment and DVDs.

Typical teenaged boy's posters- sports stars, musicians, and hot women wearing next to nothing- dressed the pool house walls. Those things were contrasted by the plush teddy bears that sat on the top shelf of the entertainment center. The shining eyes of the bears told Rebecca that Kevin still possessed some of the sweetness of a young boy.

A king sized bed reigned over its fiefdom at the rear of the structure. A white painted door stood a few steps to its' right. Rebecca assumed that it led to a bathroom. A tall refrigerator stood a short distance to the bed's left. A steel-framed microwave glistened next to the refrigerator, resting on a wheeled stand.

Rebecca smiled. "Wow. If I were you, I'd never want to leave here."

Kevin led her to the couch and settled in next to her, pecking her on the lips.

"If I could keep you here with me, I'd try not to."

"Aww," Rebecca crooned. She pulled his face to hers, initiating a deep kiss.

She slid her tongue into his mouth, exploring it like an anteater probing for its lunch. Kevin responded with equal vigor, exploring her body with his hands. They lay down on the couch, him on top of her. Both of their faces flushed as their breathing intensified. An unmistakable bulge announced Kevin's arousal, poking Rebecca through the crotch of his khakis.

"I'm so hard," he gasped. "You got me so turned on."

"I meant what I said before," Rebecca responded, "about not having sex." She'd told him that she didn't intend to have sex anytime soon- at least not until she graduated high school.

Kevin let loose a huge sigh and sat up. Rebecca smiled and touched his arm.

"But there is something that I will do for you," she said.

Though she'd been out of practice for four years, Rebecca found that using her mouth on someone was like riding a bike. Once a person learned the skill, they never lost it. It only took a short time for her to demonstrate perfect technique, even after such a long absence. She brought her beau to an explosive orgasm within a few minutes.

Kevin leaned back on the couch, looking sated and amazed as Rebecca wiped her face with a paper towel that she tore from the roll next to the microwave.

"How'd you get so good at that?" Kevin asked as she sat beside him.

Rebecca's eyes narrowed as her voice dropped into a near whisper. "I'll never tell you that," she said. "I will never tell you that."

II

A few days before Kimberly's Halloween party, Rebecca cajoled her friend into covering for her while she snuck over to Kevin's again. On that occasion, she and Kevin did everything short of sexual intercourse before she satisfied him with her mouth again.

Rebecca didn't mind using her oral skills on Kevin in lieu of sex, but she worried that she wouldn't be able to sneak over very often. Her grandmother was too smart to believe that she and Kimberly were assigned to do projects together every time she turned around. If Rebecca went to the well too often, Grandma Rose would look further into it.

Rebecca wanted to keep Kevin satisfied, but there was no way she would risk her grandmother finding out that she was sneaking around with a boy. The first thing Grandma Rose would think was that Rebecca was turning out like her mother.

Which isn't true, Rebecca thought. *I'm not bipolar. And I only do oral. You can't get pregnant from that.*

On the day of the party, Rebecca saw a side of Kevin that made her stop caring about satisfying him. This was after she had done much cajoling and pleading just to convince Kimberly to invite him and a few of his jock friends.

Rebecca asked Grandma Rose to drop her off at Kimberly's early, so that she could join the host and Phyllis in making final preparations. The three girls admired each other's outfits as they set up. Kimberly was dressed as a Viking maiden, complete with a faux horned helmet. Phyllis was dolled up like Cleopatra, lashes, wig, and all. Rebecca's hands and face were painted a pasty white and her hair was tied back. False spectacles and a dark lightning bolt painted in the middle of her forehead completed her Harry Potter look.

The first guests rang Kimberly's doorbell just after 7. From then on, teenagers arrived in a steady trickle. There were about twenty costumed Mackenzie students present by the time Kevin made his appearance. He came dressed as a police officer, complete with fake badge and cuffs, rubber nightstick, and toy pistol.

Three of Kevin's jock buddies accompanied him. Tory Mims came dressed as a cave man, his usual braided hair plucked out to its' full wild plumage. A rudimentary toga showed off his sinewy shoulders, one of which he draped a huge rubber club over. The toga tapered into dark jeans which were complemented by a pair of the latest Air Jordans.

Ryan Jennings seemed to be dressed as a baseball player from hell. His droopy jersey, uniform pants, and cleats were offset by menacing face paint. The fourth of the bunch, Michael Ealy, wore a dashing suit and blond hair slicked back in an approximation of either a seedy lawyer or Wall Street trader.

"It took you guys long enough to get here," Kimberly said, scowling as she let them in. Her gaze fell on Kevin as she spoke. "I was starting to think that Rebecca had wasted her time begging me to invite you."

Kevin smiled. "I bet you were just holding your breath for my arrival."

He looked past her, to Rebecca.

"I must be turning gay, 'cause I think I'm in love with Harry Potter," he chuckled, raising his voice to be heard over the Alicia Keys song that blared from the stereo.

"You're so crazy, Officer Anderson," Rebecca said, giving him a big hug.

"At your service, Mr. Potter. I'm here to protect and serve."

All of the furniture rested against the far wall of Kimberly's large living room, creating a makeshift dance floor/ mingling area. A short riser linked the living room and dining room. A pair of tables rested against the rear wall there. One held various bottles of soda and plastic cups, along with a huge punch bowl. The other held metal trays of assorted munchies. The arrangement of the two rooms created plenty of space for guests to roam.

Kevin danced with Rebecca for a few songs, his feet light and his movements rhythmic. Rebecca felt wonderful until she took a bathroom break. When she returned, she found him dancing suggestively with some shapely girl she didn't know. The girl was dressed as a pornographic approximation of Snow White, her boobs threatening to burst free of her too tight costume.

Not wanting to seem jealous, Rebecca chose not to intervene, believing that it was just harmless dancing.

"You see how he is?" Phyllis buzzed in her ear, appearing at her side.

"He's just dancing," Rebecca said, turning to face her friend.

Phyllis rolled her eyes, false lashes and all. "Yeah, he's just 'dancing'. Rubbing his nuts on Tracy Caldwell's ass. That girl's a slut if there ever was one. You better watch your so-called boyfriend."

"He's not my so-called boyfriend," Rebecca said. "He's my actual boyfriend, and I trust him."

Phyllis snickered at that. She then turned and hollered across the room to Kimberly. "You'd better watch your guests, Helga! Your mother won't like it if she comes downstairs and sees all this bumping and grinding!"

While Kimberly and Phyllis went about the business of making sure that the dancing went no further than an R rating, Rebecca continued to watch Kevin. His back greeted her as he danced with Tracy. Snow White did her best hoochie moves, backing her apple bottom up against him. Tracy caught sight of Rebecca when she turned around. She wrapped her arms around Kevin's neck, flashing a wicked smile.

Rebecca grew hot with anger. She marched over to Kevin and grabbed him by the arm. "What are you doing?" she demanded.

Confusion spread across Kevin's face. "What's the matter with you? I'm only dancing."

"Why do you need to dance with her? I'm here- aren't I?"

"So you don't want me to dance with other girls?" Kevin flashed his charming smile as he followed her to the riser.

"Not like that."

"Okay, then." Kevin shrugged. "I won't."

He kept his word, not dancing with anyone else during the party. Rebecca thought that he was being very sweet and respectful of her wishes.

Many songs and an almost depleted snack and refreshment supply later, Kimberly pulled Rebecca aside. Rebecca could tell that her friend felt distressed as they passed through the swinging doors that separated the dining room and the kitchen.

"I don't want to make you mad, Rebecca. But, I should never have invited Kevin and his buddies."

"What's wrong?"

"I think those jerks are drinking. That's what's wrong."

"Drinking?" Rebecca's eyebrows crept skyward. "Kevin's not drinking. I've been with him most of the party."

"You weren't with him long enough to keep him from grinding with that slut Tracy."

Instead of answering, Rebecca stared at Kimberly with a facial expression that demanded to know why she was being so mean.

"Sorry," Kimberly grumbled, her eyes descending to the pristine hardwood floor. She lifted them a moment later. "Maybe Kevin's not drinking. But I think his friends are. And he brought them here. They keep passing around a soda bottle. I mean – who brings their own soda to a party? And when have you ever seen guys drinking out of the same soda bottle? Plus, they're starting to be a little rowdy. This is just what I need. I'm lucky my mom hasn't come downstairs yet. If this starts to go bad, she might not let me have another party for a long time."

Rebecca's eyes widened like an owl's. "Well, what are you going to do?"

Kimberly shrugged, pacing back and forth. "I don't know. I don't know what to do."

Rebecca thought for a second. "I know," she declared. "You go up to one of them and act like you want some of whatever they're drinking. When they give it to you, run away and pour it out."

Kimberly's eyes danced with mischief. "Won't that make them mad?"

"Do you care?"

"Hell no! I only invited those guys because of you."

"And I only asked you to because of Kevin."

Phyllis came pushing through the doors. The look on her face screamed disgust.

"Not cool. You two have a girl's moment and don't invite me."

"Sorry," Kimberly said. "We were just discussing how we're going to stop Kevin's jock buddies from drinking."

Phyllis looked Rebecca square in the eyes. "You got other concerns, girl. I don't see Kevin or that slut Tracy out there."

Without a word, Rebecca rushed through the swinging doors. She checked Kimberly's living and dining rooms, moving at a frantic pace. Just as Phyllis said, there was no sign of Kevin or his admirer.

It's probably nothing, she told herself, trying to deny her worst suspicion. *Kevin wouldn't do that to me.*

She convinced herself that she would feel much better once she caught up with him.

Her eyes fell on the sliding doors that led from the living room to Kimberly's spacious backyard. She stepped through them onto the patio, heading down the stone steps at its foot. She heard giggling from the left side of the house as she rushed past the tarp covered pool. She rounded a corner and saw Kevin and Tracy fondling and tongue kissing each other.

They stood on a small walking path - amid a flower garden in the process of wilting with the season. Rebecca leaned back against the wall of the house, surrounded by tall shrubs. Kevin's back faced her. Tracy cooed and giggled as Kevin's hands, mouth, and tongue explored with enthusiasm. Their costumed bodies pressed together like canned sardines.

Rebecca considered that the visual of Snow White making out with a police officer would be hilarious in different circumstances. Something snapped in her a second later. She rushed toward the two canoodlers, not bothering to spare any flowers in her path. She shrieked like a harpy, her fist raining punches. Blind rage kept her from processing who her blows fell upon as obscenities gushed from her mouth.

A pair of strong hands gripped her waist. Realizing that those hands belonged to her betraying boyfriend, she twisted her torso in a wild attempt to break his grip. "Don't ever touch me again!" she screamed. She dissolved into a mess of tears as she rushed past a crowd of onlookers that included Mrs. Meisner. She soldiered on through Kimberly's house and out the front door.

Rebecca continued down the long front walkway, moving as fast as she could without running. She heard footfalls behind her, accompanied by the pleading yells of Kimberly and Phyllis.

Her tears flowed unabated as her friends drew closer. She slowed and turned as they reached her. "Sorry, I ruined your party," she said to Kimberly.

Kimberly cocooned Rebecca in her arms. "It's not your fault," she said. "It's that asshole's."

III

Kevin waited by the bike rack outside of school, sans his usual entourage. Desperation covered his handsome face.

Anger enveloped Rebecca at the sight of him. "Excuse me, girls," she said, smirking as she stepped away from Kimberly and Phyllis. "I have to get my bike."

She shot Kevin a death glare before casting her eyes away from him. Stepping around him, she removed her bike from the rack. Hands on hips, Kimberly and Phyllis moved to the edge of the school courtyard. They glared at Kevin as the scene unfolded, set to spring into action like two-thirds of Charlie's Angels.

Kevin turned and grasped one of the bike's handlebars. "Why are you touching my bike?" Rebecca said, sneering at him.

"Why are you avoiding me?" Kevin used his best put upon voice. That voice combined with the puppy dog expression on his face would have made him irresistible had he not betrayed her. "I called you like twenty times yesterday."

"Yeah." Rebecca nodded. "I almost got in trouble with my grandmother because of that. You think that's going to help you get back on my good side?"

"What will help me get back on your good side?"

Though she burned with anger, Rebecca took pains to keep her voice low. There were still students leaving through the front entrance and she had no intention of creating a spectacle at Mackenzie. "Nothing," she said. "Nothing will help you get back on my good side. I'm not just hurt about what you did. I don't like you anymore. Not even a little bit."

Kevin's eyes changed then, going from wounded to intense. He let go of the bike. "You sure about that?"

"I'm absolutely certain," Rebecca said, taking a step back while steadying the bike. "Now, please leave me alone."

"I don't think I can."

Rebecca's voice took a bold leap. "You'd better. You'd better leave me alone."

An odd smile emerged on Kevin's face. "I do what I want," he declared. "And you're stupid if you think you can just cut me off."

Rebecca eyes widened before she giggled. "Omigod. You're a far worst asshole than I thought you were. Why don't you go find your little slut from the party? I'm sure she'll have you."

Rebecca climbed on her bike then, letting it drift to a stop in front of her friends.

High fives and calls of "you showed that jerk" abounded as Kevin stormed off. Rebecca felt proud of herself, thinking that her dealings with him were done.

IV

Rebecca saw very little of Kevin during the next few days. She felt relieved, believing that he had gotten the message. Basketball season was only weeks away, so she figured that he'd thrown himself into getting ready for it. She assumed that Tracy Caldwell occupied his spare time.

Rebecca hoped that Kevin was having a good time with that slut. What kind of girl would make out with someone else's boyfriend at the same party with them? And what kind of pig would be on the other end of such an encounter?

Kimberly called Rebecca the day after the party and told her that other Mackenzie girls felt very supportive of her. Rebecca soon realized her friend was right. On several occasions, girls approached her and murmured encouragement. It was always some variation of "Don't even worry about jerks like that," or "I used to have a big crush on that guy, but now I know he's just a pig."

The support of her peers brought Rebecca a smorgasbord of satisfaction. Kevin deserved to have his name trashed by those who used to adore him.

Rebecca went to Kimberly's house after school that Thursday. She was doing some online research for her history class when an instant message window opened at the bottom of the screen. Curiosity caused her to open it.

SuperKev the BoyWonder: Hi, Rebecca. If you won't talk to me, can we at least IM each other?

Rebecca's face warmed with anger as she pounded a response on Kimberly's keyboard.

Rebee S: I've got an IM for you. Fuck off, asshole!

SuperKev the BoyWonder: Why do you have to be so hateful?

Rebee S: Because I hate you! Now, leave me alone. Shouldn't you be at basketball practice or something?

SuperKev the BoyWonder: I just got home from it. I didn't even shower before I started IMing you.

Rebee S: So, what do you want? A prize?

SuperKev the BoyWonder: Yeah. You're the prize I want.

Rebecca chuckled. Kimberly looked up from her bed, where she lay on her stomach with her biology textbook spread open in front of her. "What are you laughing at?"

"Nothing." Rebecca kept her eyes glued to the screen.

Rebee S: I would have fallen for that sweet talk once. But not anymore.

SuperKev the BoyWonder: It's not just talk. It's how I feel.

Rebee S: And how did Tracy Caldwell's tongue feel? How did it feel when you felt her up, knowing that I was close by?

Kevin's next response appeared after a long delay.

SuperKev the BoyWonder: I'm sorry about that. It was a big mistake. This whole situation sucks. You know half the girls at school hate me now.

Rebee S: Aww, poor baby!!! Am I supposed to care about that? Why don't you go screw that slut Tracy Caldwell?

"You find any good articles yet?" Kimberly asked, her tone impatient as she awaited the use of her computer.

"No!" Rebecca shrieked. "I'm too busy IMing my asshole ex-boyfriend!"

"What?" Kimberly popped off the bed and crossed the room to her computer desk. As she looked over Rebecca's shoulder, another message popped up on the screen.

SuperKev the BoyWonder: At least Tracy Caldwell will put out. Maybe it never would have happened if you had done the same. You can't expect a guy like me to be satisfied with blowjobs.

Rebecca's fingers blurred as she typed her response.

Rebee S: You are a real piece of shit! If I had known how you really are, I would've never gotten involved with you. I never want to communicate with you again! Not even through IMs. I mean it, you fucking asshole!

SuperKev the BoyWonder: I know you're mad, but I've had enough of you cursing at me. You really should be nicer.

"Aaargh!" Rebecca groaned, unleashing another flurry of speed typing.

Rebee S: I hope your balls fall off, you incredible asshole. I wish I was some big, tough guy right now, just so I could beat the shit out of you. Never contact me again! I mean that!!!!

She closed out the IM window before Kevin could respond. Her hands gripped the edge of the computer desk as her breathing grew shallow. Kimberly leaned in and hugged her.

"You set him straight," Kimberly said, laughing. "I think that jerk got the message."

"He did- didn't he?" A chuckle dissipated Rebecca's angry visage.

"Hell, yes. There's something really wrong with him if he bothers you after that."

Chapter 15 - Finding John Rainbird

Rebecca sat at one of the Bay Corner library's half dozen computers, surfing the web with no particular purpose. Having unfettered access to Kimberly's computer while they hung out had kept her from coming here in weeks.

Kimberly and her mother went to visit relatives this weekend. Rebecca intended to take a day trip to visit her own mother, but her mother's boss asked her to work a double at the last minute.

"I'm sorry, baby," Emma sighed over the phone. "But I can't afford to turn down a chance at extra cash. You know I'm saving up to get a little place when I leave the halfway house."

Rebecca told her mother not to worry about it. She just hoped that Emma was telling the truth about the whole thing. Although her mother now treated her far better than she ever had, Rebecca often felt like nothing more than a pleasant diversion to the woman. She preferred that to having no relationship at all.

Rebecca plugged a pair of headphones into the computer and cued up an Alicia Keys video on BET.com. She bobbed her head to the music as John Rainbird Jeffries walked in.

He looked much less ragged than the last time Rebecca saw him. His long black hair hung like a lion's mane. His unzipped gray jacket revealed a Led Zeppelin t-shirt. Plain black jeans complemented black leather boots that sported yellow laces. He seemed to have grown two or three inches taller.

Rebecca sat ramrod straight, not knowing how to respond to his presence as his dark eyes fell on her. She felt a flutter of relief as his lips curled into a small smile. Butterflies danced in her stomach as he sauntered over and sat down in the carrel next to hers.

"Hey, Rebecca." The small smile bloomed into a grin. "I was hoping that was your bike I saw outside."

Rebecca clicked the video off and removed the headphones from her ears. "Hi, John Rainbird. I'm surprised you didn't see my bike outside and turn the other way."

He laughed. "Yeah. I was pissed at you for a while."

"You 'were' pissed?"

"Yeah. Past tense. Let's go outside and talk, okay?"

They stood in front of the library moments later, ignoring the windy November weather. John pointed in the direction of the library's bike rack. "That's my new bike, next to yours."

Rebecca's eyes fell on a beautiful silver and red Schwinn. She recognized it as one of the company's New Bike Path models. "That's an awesome bike," she said.

John grinned. "Yup. Now, we both have fancy new bikes."

"I'm glad for you," Rebecca said. Her smile changed into a frown as she looked away for a moment.

"I'm sorry I didn't show up last time," she said, finding the courage to seek out John's eyes. "I had to work on a school project with a friend. I would have called you if I had a way to."

John shrugged. "It's not your fault I didn't have a phone. Anyway, I was kind of hoping you'd blow me off. It was like I was looking for an excuse to stop being friends with you. I guess I was jealous."

Rebecca cocked an eyebrow. "Jealous? Of what?"

John's dark pupils bore into her. "Think about my life at the time, Rebecca.

Just like I was the only friend you had last summer, you were also the only real friend I had. I had hoped that we would end up at the same school together. But then you wound up at Mackenzie. Meanwhile, I had to go to Havre de Grace High with a legion of cretins, not knowing anybody there and being the first Indian anyone at the school had really been around. My poor and bummy looking appearance didn't help things."

He shook his head. "Then I had my grandfather giving me a hard time about going to an 'Anglo' school in the first place. Yeah, I was jealous of you. Jealous of you and mad at the world. The first time you disappointed me, I took it as an opportunity to cut you out of my life. I guess I figured it would be better that way. Lately, though- things have been going a little better for me. So, I started thinking that being so hard on you wasn't fair. I've been hoping to run into you and now I finally have."

Rebecca nodded. "I'm just glad to see you now. So, how have things gotten better for you?"

John sprouted a Cheshire grin before beginning his tale.

One overcast morning, he loaded his worn out old bike onto the rack at the rear of the massive school bus as he always did. Always one of the first to board the bus, he sat in his preferred seat across from the bus driver in the second row. He'd discovered that not many kids sat near the front, resulting in him being pretty much left alone. A group of girls at the rear of the bus were the only passengers who boarded before him. Sometimes, he wondered if he wasn't the subject of their laughing and snickering.

So be it, he thought. *As long as they don't try to mess with me.*

The bus made its' third stop at the southern edge of Havre de Grace. At first, John paid no attention to the trio of kids that boarded and seated themselves in two of the rows opposing him. "Hey, kid," a shrill voice soon called across the aisle to him.

John turned to behold a plump faced boy with rosy cheeks and a faux Mohawk.

The crest of the fauxhawk was died blue. Yellow hair on the closely cropped right side contrasted orange hair on the closely cropped left. "I'm Rooster," the boy said, looking John over.

With a flourish of his hand, he indicated his friends in the row behind him. "This lovely young lady is Brittany." A thin, pale brunette with earnest eyes smiled at John. She was a frail kind of pretty, as if she should wear a label that says, "Fragile, handle with care."

"And this bright young intellectual is Oswald." A pasty faced boy with sandy brown hair gave John a nod. He and Rooster could form a 10 if they stood beside each other, with him being the 1. John noticed that all three dressed in clothing that could only be described as skateboard Goth. "We prefer Ozzie. It sounds much cooler. Like Sabbath- you know? There's more to that old guy than the T.V. show."

The bus driver turned up the country music he'd been listening to, eliciting groans from the rear of the bus. "Then y'all need to stop talking so loud," he chided. His strained voice spoke of decades of heavy smoking.

Rooster snickered as he slid over to the window seat. "Come sit with us so the bus driver doesn't have to turn that crap up any louder." He patted the spot he'd just vacated. "We don't bite. Well, Brittany might if she likes you enough."

"You can bite me," Brittany said, frowning.

"I'd prefer to bite your hunky older brother. I just love a military man."

"In your dreams, fatty."

Smiling at their exchange, John sat with them as requested. It was the beginning of him becoming the fourth of a quartet. He found out that though Brittany and Ozzy were accomplished skaters, Rooster wouldn't dare engage in such physical exertion. He just thought the clothes were cool.

"Your eyes get all dreamy when you talk about Brittany," Rebecca observed.

John's smiled turned goofy.

"Aww. Is she your girlfriend?"

"I guess you could say that."

They stood in silence for a while, just looking at each other. "Does she treat you well?"

John nodded.

Rebecca touched his arm. "I'm happy for you. I had a boyfriend for a while. But, he turned out to be a sick jerk."

She told John all about Kevin then, except for the part when she used her mouth on him.

"What a creep," John said, scowling. "Want me to kick his ass for you?" His clenched fists alerted Rebecca that he was serious about the offer.

"Easy, big boy," she said, hugging him. "I don't want you getting into trouble just for me."

For the first time, she thought of John as someone suited to carry out violence. He was tall, rangy, and wiry strong. She allowed herself a brief fantasy of him punching Kevin's lights out.

"You sure?" he said. "Cause I'll be glad to do it for you."

Rebecca laughed. "When did you get to be such a fighter?"

"All Maupai are taught how to fight at a young age." He placed one hand at knee level. "We first start wrestling when we're this tall."

"Well, it would hardly seem fair to use all that fighting experience against one unsuspecting jerk," Rebecca smiled, punching his arm.

John summoned a mock scowl. "You better watch who you're hitting on before I have to use all of my fighting experience against you."

Rebecca put her fists in front of her, doing her best approximation of a fighter's stance. "Come on, big guy." She bobbed in place. "I'm ready for ya."

John burst out laughing. "I see you still have your same sense of humor. Listen, Rebecca- other things have changed in my life besides making new friends."

Rebecca grew serious. "Good things, I hope."

John smiled. "Really good things."

He detailed a life changing conversation with his grandfather that followed a suspension for fighting in gym class.

"It wasn't my fault," he explained to his grandfather. "I was changing out of my clothes in the locker room when this jerk Jason Tilden started messing with me. He's a football jock, short and muscular. Anyway, I was minding my own business when the guy starting ragging on me. Going on about when was I going to get a gym uniform and stop wearing Daisy Dukes to class? I asked him when he was going to stop letting sh-excrement spew unabated from his idiot mouth. His buddies started egging him on then, saying stuff like 'Man, you 'gon let Hiawatha talk to you like that?' He walked up close to me, then – so I punched him in the face. Next thing I know, I'm rolling around in the locker room getting beat up by him and his buddies. I was nice and bloody by the time the gym teachers came to break it up." He laughed.

Wise Eyes stared hard at his grandson before shaking his head. "I knew that sending you to an Anglo school was not wise."

"Grandfather, please."

"Please, nothing. You are so determined to immerse yourself in their world. Well, tell me- does it seem they will accept you? You are the one bruised and bloodied, yet you received the punishment of the aggressor. The white man's justice is perverse, even in his schools."

"Grandfather, this isn't even in the same neighborhood as the Trail of Tears," John Rainbird said. "Everyone gets five days for fighting at that school."

He took a deep breath, corralling the courage to express himself. "And, if I wasn't wearing Salvation Army clothes all the time it might have never happened. Father of my Father- why do I always have to dress this way? Could you please spend some of the social security benefit I get on some decent clothes for me?"

"Keep a respectful tongue with me, John Rainbird," Wise Eyes said.

"Forgive me, Grandfather." John Rainbird softened his voice as he looked away. "But I really need them."

"To the Maupai, clothing is for covering. It is not for glory."

"I know that," John Rainbird said. "And I understand not having expensive clothes. But could I not look ragged, at least? Do you think my parents would want me to look so ragged if they were alive?"

"Ragged by Anglo standards."

"Ragged by your standards as well, Father of my Father," John said. His convictions overcame his anxiety about being disciplined for his temerity. "You wear better clothing than mine when you're not working. Also, the Anglo world is where I will make my life, Grandfather. Just because you want to live like people did 100 years ago doesn't mean I should have to."

Wise Eyes stared at his grandson for a long time. "I should punish you for speaking to me so."

"There is plenty of punishment in my life as it is," John Rainbird said. "What are you doing with the money, anyway? You don't seem to be spending it on yourself or anything for Blessed Earth."

Wise Eyes regarded his charge with a grave countenance. He instructed John Rainbird to sit as he walked to his room. He held a stack of papers when he returned.

"Perhaps I have deprived you of many material things," he said. "But, it is only thinking of your ultimate well-being that has led me to do so. That and honoring your parents' wishes. If they were still alive, they'd want nothing more than to know that you have a bright future ahead of you, whether that includes college or not. Try as I have to get you to embrace the Maupai ways, I see that you are of a new breed like your father was. You are nearly a man by tribe standards, anyway. It is time for me to accept that you will never content yourself with life at our simple commune."

Rebecca's eyes remained riveted on John as he continued. "He handed me the papers, telling me that he had saved most of the money from the monthly death benefit checks, so that I could use it for college or however else I saw fit once I turned eighteen. I almost jumped out of my shoes! There was more than $25,000 in the account he opened for me. When he showed me that, I felt like I had a brand new life. All that money means I'm still going to college, even if my chances of getting a scholarship are hurt by not attending an elite high school. Ever since I found that out, I've been a lot happier."

Rebecca's lower jaw made a grand effort to unhinge itself from the rest of her face. "$25,000? Omigod, John. Are you serious?"

He grinned and nodded. "Yes. Isn't that wonderful?"

She threw her arms around him. "It is wonderful! I'm so happy for you."

John returned her embrace with his long arms. "Thanks. Anyway, I've been able to convince my grandfather to let me have a little spending money. Hence, my awesome new bike and improved wardrobe, obtained in the luxury clothing aisles of such high end stores as JC Penney and Wal-Mart. Oh- I got a prepaid cell phone, too." He pulled the unglamorous model from his pocket, showing it off. "So, my friends and I can actually call each other, although I try not to have very long conversations. I like to make the minutes last for a while, 'cause Wise Eyes doesn't give me much. Anyway, this baby really makes me feel like I'm part of the 21st Century."

He stepped back, regarding Rebecca as if she were a new discovery. "I hope we can be friends again, Rebecca, especially now that we no longer have to use smoke signals to stay in contact."

Rebecca held her right hand up for a high five, smiling when he slapped her palm. "We never really stopped being friends, John Rainbird. We just haven't seen each other for a while."

Chapter 16- Kevin's Revenge

I

Rebecca first realized that something was wrong on the second Monday of November.

While she and Kimberly walked from one class to another, two girls she didn't know glanced in her direction and began whispering. She assumed that they were still talking about her having told Kevin off at the Halloween party. She felt surprised that the incident had such a long shelf life.

It wasn't until lunch time that she suspected something more significant was going on. She and Kimberly passed Michael Ealy and Ryan Jennings on the way to the cafeteria.

The boys smirked a greeting to Kimberly before focusing their attention on Rebecca. "Wassup, Wonder Jaws?" they chirped in unison.

Rebecca frowned. "What the hell does that mean?"

Kevin's cronies laughed. "Oh, so you don't know yet?" Michael asked. "I guess that explains why you haven't gone into hiding."

"What are you talking about, jerk?"

"You'll find out soon enough," Ryan said, grinning like the Devil after convincing a pious man to sell his soul.

Kimberly intervened on her friend's behalf. "Whatever. You jerks can go to hell."

Ryan chuckled. "Gladly, if your friend will be there to keep us company."

Michael treated Kimberly to a lewd sneer. "I wonder if you're as good at it as she as."

Kimberly sighed and hooked Rebecca's arm. "Forget about these idiots, Rebecca. Let's get to the cafeteria."

There was more of the same when they sat down to eat. Many of the kids who shared their lunch period seemed to be snickering and whispering about Rebecca.

"What the hell is going on?" Rebecca wondered, ignoring the tray of food in front of her. "Why does everyone seem to be looking at me and whispering about me?"

Memories of her outcast days at Bay Corner School welled up, causing her to feel the first rumblings of fear.

"I don't know." Kimberly shrugged from across the table. "You know that it takes a little longer for the primo gossip to get to us because we're in AIA. If there's anything worth sweating, Phyllis'll give us the scoop at the end of the day."

Rebecca drummed her fingers on the table. "But, there's no reason for anyone to gossip about me."

Kimberly smiled kindly. "Don't worry, Rebecca. It's probably just some bullshit to do with Kevin. You know a jerk like that isn't just going to let you dump him free and clear, even if you did catch him red handed making out with some slut. He's probably started some trouble to try to heal his bruised ego. But, how bad could it be?"

They met Phyllis in front of the school at the end of the day. A stricken expression plastered the tall girl's face.

"Damn, dark and lovely," Kimberly said. "What's eating you?"

Phyllis did not respond right away. As she waited for an answer; Rebecca noticed that many of the exiting students looked in her direction and snickered. A pimple faced blond boy looked at her and pantomimed a blowjob.

"In your dreams, pizza face," Rebecca said, sneering and flipping him off. She scanned her surroundings to be sure that no school staff had seen the gesture. "What the hell is going on with everyone today?"

"I have something to tell you, Rebecca," Phyllis said, speaking in a depressed tone that Rebecca had never heard from her as her eyes sought a spot on the ground.

"What is it?" Rebecca asked, feeling a shiver travel up her spine.

Phyllis moved in close, wrapping an arm around each of her friend's shoulders before whispering the terrible news. Upon hearing it, Rebecca staggered backward as if someone had slugged her in the face. She clutched her chest as her heart began a series of wind sprints. Her stomach kept pace with its' own palpitations, threatening to geyser forth the lunch she had forced down.

Kimberly reached for her. "Are you okay, Rebecca?"

"No, I'm not okay! I'm not even close to okay." Rebecca rushed to her bike in a haze of emotions, manhandling it from the rack.

"Rebecca! Maybe you should come to my house so we can talk about how to deal with this."

"I just want to be alone!" Rebecca shrieked, keeping her back to her friends. She started peddling as she voiced the sentiment. A multitude of tears spilled as her legs churned away, only slowing a few times during the four mile trek home. Her lungs seared as she careened to a stop on her front lawn. She let the bike fall to the ground before stumbling inside and collapsing on her bed.

Rebecca had thought that her days of being tormented and embarrassed ended for good when she left eighth grade behind. She spilled salty tears onto her pillow, now realizing that she was about to face a new kind of humiliation.

II

Kimberly and Phyllis called on three-way that evening. Rebecca felt no desire to talk to them, but she figured that Grandma Rose would suspect that something was bothering her if she didn't. She wasn't ready to share what had happened with her guardian. She hoped that she would never have to.

"Are you okay, girl?" Phyllis asked.

"No, I'm not." Rebecca closed her bedroom door and turned up the relic of a portable stereo/cassette player that sat on her nightstand, mindful that the walls of the rancher were thin. "I'm totally humiliated. How will I ever live this down?"

"I feel so bad for you," Kimberly said. "I mean I knew the guy was a jerk, but his asshole-ness must have evolved since I dealt with him. I wish you would've never gotten involved with him."

"I wish I hadn't, either. I should have listened to you guys."

"Don't you dare beat yourself up over this, girl," Phyllis said. "This is all on him, not you. I hear he's got it fixed up so that no one can tell who's with you on the video. Sick motherfucker."

"He probably got some geek techie to doctor it," Kimberly said. "Mr. Popular can get people to do all kinds of shit for him. This is really bad, Rebecca. I just can't figure out how he could tape you without you knowing it."

Rebecca considered Kimberly's last comment. "The teddy bears! It was probably the teddy bears. That fucking monster."

"What?" Phyllis and Rebecca queried in unison.

Rebecca explained about the teddy bears that were in Kevin's quarters.

"Yeah," Kimberly agreed. "They're probably like those nanny cams people use. He is such a horrible person."

"I feel so stupid," Rebecca said. "When I saw them I thought it was the cutest thing in the world. I thought it was really sweet and quirky- him having stuffed animals and all. I wish there was something I could do about this. Can you guys think of anything?"

"I don't know, girl," Phyllis said. "Kimberly and I can stick up for you- do some IMing and texting about how sick it is that Kevin set you up like that. We should at least be able to keep some of the girls at school from giving you a hard time. After all, all you did was blow your boyfriend. That just about comes with the territory now days. He's the sick bastard that made it into a public spectacle."

"That's true," Kimberly agreed. "I really wish you would have listened to me." She sighed. "I just hope school administration doesn't find out about this. If they do, they'll probably kick you out due to the morals clause."

"Shit!" Rebecca slapped her bedroom wall, struck by the horrible astuteness of Kimberly's assertion. She was sure to get kicked out of Mackenzie if the administration ever found out about the blowjob video. Getting kicked out of Mackenzie would be a million times worse than being snickered at and referred to as Wonder Jaws. It would result in her being shipped to Havre de Grace High- where the likes of Pamela Lawson and her cronies waited. Of course, John Rainbird would also be there. But, John Rainbird couldn't save her from such harpies, especially if they had a new scandal to torment her with. Falling back into their clutches would be a far more miserable and wretched experience now that she'd been free of them for what she thought was for good.

Rebecca ended the three way phone call after she heard all the words of sympathy and support she could stomach. The phone rang again a few minutes later. John Rainbird's cellular phone number flashed on the Caller ID display.

"Hey, John Rainbird," she answered.

"Hi, Rebecca. What's the matter? You sound kind of sad."

"I'm not feeling too well, John."

"That sucks. I'll let you go, then. Talk to you tomorrow, maybe."

"Maybe."

"I hope so."

After the call ended, Rebecca reflected that John didn't know anything about what she was now involved in. He didn't have to find out, either. Living down on the Maupai commune and having no connection to Mackenzie meant that he might never hear of it.

She felt relieved about the prospect of his ignorance. She thought about the time when she tried to use her mouth on him at the river, about how John told her she didn't have to do that to be his friend.

She realized that John was a much better person than Kevin. Kevin pretended to be a nice guy to try and get what he wanted from her. John was a real nice guy. He wanted nothing more than to be her friend.

Rebecca hadn't met John's girlfriend, Brittany, yet. She hoped that Brittany realized how lucky she was. Rebecca sighed as she lay on her bed, thinking that if she hadn't gotten all caught up with the Mackenzie School and gone swooning over Kevin, John might've become her boyfriend.

I guess I'm lucky just to have him as a friend, she thought. *As stupid as I am, I'm lucky to have any friends at all.*

III

Rebecca suffered ceaseless torment during the next few days. Unfamiliar boys pantomimed blowjobs or mouthed "Wonder Jaws" when they crossed her path. An equal number of girls snickered or shook their heads when they saw her.

The few students who tried to be nice to Rebecca added unintentional fuel to the fire of her humiliation. She would rather have been invisible than have people offer their condolences about the harsh treatment she received. A tall, pretty blond upperclassman patted her on the shoulder while she moved through the hallway on one such occasion, smiling and telling her not to worry about the "pigs" who'd done this to her. "Just give it some time. People will forget about it as soon as the next interesting thing happens."

"That girl's right, you know," Kimberly said, as the girl walked away. "It'll all die down sooner or later."

Rebecca scowled, poised outside of their next classroom. "Like the whole Knife Lady's Daughter thing died down?"

"That was a different time and place, Rebecca. I told you half of the girls who know about this are on your side."

"Somehow, that doesn't make me feel any better."

Rebecca and Phyllis went to Kimberly's house after school that Thursday.

They were all hanging out in Kimberly's room when Rebecca blurted a question. "Have you guys seen the video?"

Her friends' silence served as a resounding yes. Rebecca's eyes smoldered. "You have seen it? How? What-was it sent to your cell phone cameras?"

Kimberly and Phyllis looked away, their eyes fleeing their friend's angry stare. Their reaction only egged Rebecca on.

"Why won't you guys answer me? You know what? I want to see it. I want to see the video!" She stalked over to Kimberly and snatched her handbag away.

Kimberly sprang from the perch of her bed. "Hey!"

"I want to see the video," Rebecca said, turning away as Kimberly tried to grab the bag from her. Rebecca opened it and removed her friend's cell phone. "Is it on here? I know you've seen it!"

"Stop that!" Phyllis screamed, moving into Rebecca's path. "Stop it, Rebecca."

Rebecca stared into Phyllis's eyes. "I want to see the video," she spoke slowly. "I want to see what everyone is talking about."

Phyllis looked past Rebecca, to Kimberly. "I guess we'd better show her."

Kimberly nodded and walked past Rebecca to take a seat at her computer desk.

She logged onto the internet and turned to face her distraught friend. "Come on and check it out." She crooked an index finger as her eyes became blue pools of sadness. Rebecca settled into her seat as she departed, looking at the search results on screen.

"Click on the one that says "Wonder Jaws" video," Kimberly said.

Rebecca did as she said, opening up to a web page that was unadorned save for the title "Wonder Jaws" in a huge flashing blue font. A warning of sexually explicit content stood beneath the flashing letters. A play video icon waited at the bottom of the page.

"You sure you want to do that?" Phyllis asked, standing over her shoulder.

Rebecca sighed. "I need to see. I have to see."

She clicked on the icon. A video feed of her on her knees came to life. The image of the lucky guy was blurred save for his legs and erect penis. A robotic male voice moaned and urged her on, saying things like, "Yeah, Rebecca. Yeah. That is so good." There was no way that anyone could identify the voice or body as belonging to Kevin.

Rebecca pounded the computer desk as Kimberly placed comforting hands on her raised shoulders.

"You should turn it off," Phyllis said, moving to do so.

"No!" Rebecca protested. "I should see this. I need to see this!"

After what seemed like an eternity, the throbbing penis on the video released its' load. Rebecca watched as her video counterpart took it all in the face. The video ended on that vulgar and (for her) horrible note.

Rebecca exploded from the chair, throwing a surprised Kimberly off balance. "So, that's what everyone's been watching?" She screamed. "So, that's what everyone's been watching?"

"We're sorry, Rebecca." Phyllis extended her arms in an attempt at comfort.

"Yeah. We're really sorry." Kimberly hugged Rebecca, too. Cocooned in her friend's arms, Rebecca disintegrated into a storm of chest heaving sobs.

IV

That Friday, Rebecca saw Kevin for the first time since the video became the talk of the school. She and Kimberly stood at their lockers after dismissal from their last period class.

"Hey, ladies," Kevin called from behind.

Rebecca turned to see her tormentor and Ryan Jennings strolling toward her. They wore blue and gold basketball uniforms and satanic smiles.

"Stay away from us," Kimberly growled. "We have nothing to say to you."

"Maybe you don't have anything to say to me," Kevin said, sneering. "But I think Rebecca might." His eyes cast a malevolent gleam as he stepped close to his ex-girlfriend. "I mean, after all, she doesn't have anything in her mouth to keep her from talking."

An unseen force swept Rebecca from her own body, leaving her to watch someone in her spitting image turn hellcat. Her consciousness had front row seats as the biracial girl rushed a tall, sinewy, blond boy and tried to claw his face. The girl screeched like some raging animal, kneeing her target between the legs when he grabbed her hands. As the recipient of her rage slumped to his knees, his taller friend tried to grab her. She stepped back and slapped the intervening friend's face hard enough to turn his cheek. Spittle flew along with obscenities as the girl moved in to kick the blond boy. Her own friend tried to intervene and earned a shove against a locker for her efforts.

Two school staff members seized the girl and held her fast. Watching the girl scream and struggle to twist free, it occurred to Rebecca that one of the men restraining her was the school's principal. She realized that the girl she now watched was in huge trouble.

Chapter 17- Losing Mackenzie

I

Rebecca sat in Mr. Halloran's office a short while after attacking Kevin, her out of body experience having come to a merciful end. Mr. Halloran regarded her with a woeful expression, as one might regard an ailing relative on their deathbed. Rebecca couldn't think of another time that she'd seen him in that state.

"I need to know what got into you a short while ago, Rebecca," he said.

"I can't tell you."

"What do you mean you can't tell me?" Mr. Halloran kept his voice neutral. Frustration flashed in his eyes, telling Rebecca that the circumstance was difficult for him. "Rebecca, you have to tell me something about what happened in that hallway. Otherwise, I'll have to assume you lost your mind. Do you want me to assume that, Rebecca?"

Rebecca shrugged, making firm eye contact with him. "I mean- you probably think that, anyway. You know about my mother and all. Maybe you think I'm just taking after her."

Mr. Halloran's lips spread into a kind smile. "That's not what I think at all, Rebecca. If I had to speculate, I'd say that perhaps Kevin did something to provoke you into violence. I know that you and he were seeing each other until you caught him making out with Tracy Caldwell at Kimberly's Halloween party."

Rebecca's jaw dropped as her eyes leaped for the stratosphere. "You kn- knew about that?"

Mr. Halloran nodded, drumming his long ebony fingers on his dark brown desk.

"I try to keep my ear to the grindstone. It's part of being a good principal."

Rebecca frowned. "Then you should already know exactly what that little scene was about."

Mr. Halloran shook his head. "I can't catch everything that happens. It's not like I have paid informants or anything." He leaned forward, a determined expression on his face. "No. I need you to explain what that was all about. I'm hoping that once I know the circumstances, I'll have reason to be lenient in disciplining you. But first, I need the information."

Rebecca shifted in her seat as she pondered Mr. Halloran's words. He was a good principal who really cared about kids, just like his brother. She knew that as well as she knew that he would love to cut her a break. But she also knew that being videotaped giving a guy a blow job and getting her face come on was about as serious a violation of Mackenzie's morality clause as possible. The fact that the video was posted on the internet made matters much worse.

As an institution, Mackenzie High placed as much importance on reputation as achievement. As kind as Mr. Halloran was, he wouldn't keep Rebecca as a student if he ever found about the video. She had no choice but to lie.

"Kevin's been harassing me," She said, thinking that at least there was some truth in the statement. "Teasing me and sending me nasty IMs and e-mails. Bragging about all the new girls he's been with since we broke up. Telling all his friends that he got bored with me because I'm such a prude." She paused to trail her hands down her face. "They've all been teasing me- him and his jock buddies. He was teasing me today, too. I guess I just lost it."

Mr. Halloran rubbed his palms together as a knowing gleam came into his eyes.

"That wasn't that hard, now, was it? It seems that young Mr. Anderson's ego is growing faster than his body. I'll deal with him. Meanwhile, I will have to send you home pending a rules violation hearing. You know we don't abide fighting at this school. Not for any reason."

"Are you going to kick me out of school?"

Mr. Halloran laughed. "A wonderful young lady like you? I wouldn't dream of it." He grew serious. "But, the board will have to come up with a suitable punishment. One that will discourage other students from thinking that there's ever a good enough reason to physically attack their classmates." He motioned toward his desk phone. "I guess you should try to reach your grandmother now."

II

Rebecca had to tell Grandma Rose the same story she told Mr. Halloran. That meant having to admit that she'd snuck around to have a boyfriend. Shocked at having been deceived for so long, the matriarch slapped her granddaughter across the face as soon as they arrived home.

"I won't have you end up like your mother," Grandma Rose said, her voice trembling. "If I have to keep you under lock and key, I won't have that! That would hurt far worse than the pain I feel now. Now get to your room!"

Rebecca did as she was told, collapsing into a sea of sobs on her pillow. It wasn't the slap that caused her tears. She cried because she had made her grandmother feel ashamed. She cried because her grandmother could now get sick with the fear that she'd end up like her mother.

She felt disgusted about putting her grandmother through this. What had gotten into her? Why had she been so determined to sneak around? How had she gotten into this mess?

She supposed a lot of it was hormones. Adults always blamed the dumb stuff that teenagers did on hormones.

No, she admitted to herself. *There has to be more to it than that.*

Trying to stem the tide of tears, she reminded herself that at least Mr. Halloran and Grandma didn't know the whole story. Things would be much worse if the adults involved in her life learned about the video.

III

"So, that's why I'm grounded," Rebecca said, having just omitted the same facts from Emma that she omitted from Grandma Rose and Mr. Halloran. She didn't feel bad about the deception anymore. What was the alternative? Admitting that she'd been videotaped sucking dick and uploaded to the internet?

"Aw, Rebee," Emma's voice oozed sympathy. "You're at that age now, I suppose. You'll just have to be smart about guys, smarter than I was at least. Try not to let them get you into trouble or distract you from what you need to do in life. Are you sexually active?"

"No, Mom," Rebecca giggled, thinking, *only if blowjobs count.* "God, that's so embarrassing."

"Well, I'd be a terrible mother if I didn't ask. I've had enough of being a terrible mother to you, Rebecca. I'm trying to do better, nowadays. Even though I don't have custody of you."

"You are doing better," Rebecca said, wondering why it was always her job to ease her mother's guilty conscience. If Emma had been a better mother to her, she might not have been so quick to blow Kevin in the first place.

No. She stemmed the tide of her bitterness. *I won't think like that.*

No matter how her mother failed her when she was younger, her own choices had thrust her into this predicament. Her grandmother warned her about how teenaged boys were. Kimberly and Phyllis gave her numerous warnings about Kevin.

I was the one who chose not to listen, she thought, *even sneaking over to his house. I was the one who chose to use my mouth on him.*

She told herself that she had to do better and be smarter than that. She believed that her entire future depended on her continuing as a Mackenzie student.

That night, Rebecca knelt by her bed and prayed for God to forgive her folly and not punish her too harshly. She promised the heavenly father that if he worked things out so that she could continue at her dream school, she wouldn't have anything else to do with guys like Kevin Anderson.

Please, God, she pleaded. *Please don't take my future away from me.*

IV

Rebecca heard the phone ring on Tuesday evening, four days after her incident with Kevin. Forbidden to answer it herself, she listened in on Grandma Rose from her room.

"I'm doing alright, considering," Grandma Rose said. "Do you have any news about my darling granddaughter?"

Grandma Rose fell silent as she listened to the caller's response. Rebecca wondered if it was Mr. Halloran or some other school official on the other end. She hoped that whoever it was gave her grandmother the okay for her to return to school.

"Alright," Grandma Rose responded to whatever had just been said. "We'll see you then. You have a nice evening, Mr. Halloran. Thank you."

It was Mr. Halloran, Rebecca thought as Grandma Rose's footsteps padded toward her bedroom door. The door creaked open as Grandma Rose turned the knob.

She stood there for a moment, hands on hips. Her face wore a grim expression. "You were listening in, weren't you?"

Rebecca smiled, trying to be charming. "I can't help it if the walls are thin in here."

Grandma Rose's face contorted, struggling to suppress a smile. "Don't try to be cute right now, Rebecca. You'll be very fortunate to get out of this situation without a severe punishment."

Rebecca nodded. "I know, Gran."

"You better know." Grandma Rose scowled and wagged an index finger. "I'm not going to lecture you anymore, but you know how I feel about what you did."

"Yes."

Grandma Rose's eyes softened. "Anyway, we have an appointment to see Mr. Halloran, tomorrow at 4:00. We'll find out what they've chosen to do with you then. You better hope they let you off easy."

"I don't even care if they let me off easy, so long as they let me back in," Rebecca said, springing off her bed. "I'll do anything they want, pull janitor duty- landscape the school grounds- anything!" She smiled and held out her arms.

Grandma Rose couldn't resist returning the smile and accepting Rebecca's hug. "What am I going to do with you, girl?" she sighed.

V

Rebecca and Grandma Rose sat across from Mr. Halloran in his office. The look in his eyes was one of mourning.

He drew in a deep breath before delivering the boom. "I know about the video, Rebecca." The sadness in his voice complemented his grave countenance.

Salty tears burst forth from Rebecca's eyes. Her right hand shielded the expanse between her eyes and bottom lip. Mr. Halloran stood from his chair. "I'll give you some time to discuss it with your grandmother." Two long strides carried him from the office.

"Wait. Where are you going?" Grandma Rose demanded. "What have you said to upset my granddaughter so much? How could you do that?"

Mr. Halloran responded from outside his office door. "I haven't done anything that I had a choice in, Mrs. Saulters. I'll leave it to Rebecca to explain things to you."

Rebecca gulped in a deep breath as Mr. Halloran closed the door. She used some Kleenex from the box on his desk to wipe her face and blow her nose. The expression of dread on her grandmother's face made her wish that she could somehow make this all go away, but she knew that she couldn't. She composed herself long enough to explain every lurid detail of her current ordeal, girding herself for another slap to the face as she did so.

I deserve a slap and worse, she thought. *I deserve to have my name cursed and maybe be disowned for the shame I've caused. Maybe I really am becoming just like my mother. Maybe I need a shrink and some medication, too.*

Grandma Rose surprised Rebecca by sweeping from her seat, engulfing her in a vise grip of a hug and peppering her cheeks with kisses. "You poor baby," she murmured. "Oh- you poor, poor baby."

Her compassion reduced Rebecca to tears again. "That's alright," Grandma Rose said, still holding her. "That's alright."

"Ready to invite the kind man back into his office?" Grandma Rose asked after Rebecca managed to regain her composure.

They nodded in agreement and offered apologies as Mr. Halloran went on about how sorry he was to lose a student of Rebecca's caliber. Instead of walking behind his desk to seat himself, he rested his rear on the edge of its surface.

"I know that teenagers often make huge mistakes," he sighed. "And I know that teenage boys will go to huge lengths to take advantage of their female counterparts. I am aware of young Mr. Anderson's reputation. If there were any proof, I would gladly expel him from this school. And not for one second have I considered the notion that this one deed defines Rebecca. Still, the morality clause allows for no leeway in such situations."

"It's not your fault, Mr. Halloran," Rebecca said, wearing a weak smile. "I appreciate everything you've done for me during my short time at this wonderful school."

"Oh, Rebecca." Mr. Halloran stood erect, holding out his long arms for her to wade into. "I'm so sad to lose you." Releasing her, he titled her chin up with one large hand. "Learn from this, okay? Learn from this. Don't let this beat you! You can still achieve all the success you seek in life, with or without Patrick F. Mackenzie High!"

"Yes, Sir." Rebecca nodded in agreement.

Her agreement was not sincere. She didn't believe a word of the platitude that Mr. Halloran left her with. A stifling combination of hopelessness and self-disgust besieged her as she and Grandma Rose drove home in silence. She wondered how Mr. Halloran had found out about the video. Maybe Kevin had spilled the beans when Mr. Halloran confronted him about the hallway incident. When she gave her account of what was going on between them, Rebecca assumed that Kevin wouldn't talk about the tape. In her anger and short sightedness, it didn't occur to her that Kevin would be quite safe in talking about the video. After all, it had been doctored so that his face and voice weren't on it. Telling Mr. Halloran that Rebecca had snapped on him because he'd given her a hard time after seeing the recording would serve as a simple excuse.

More tears salted Rebecca's eyes as she struggled to restrain herself from punching the door panel on her side of the Harvester. She wiped them away in disgust, thinking that becoming a damn cry baby wouldn't help it.

I'm fucked, she thought. *I've ruined the best chance I had at being viewed as something other than a freak and leaving this shit town behind.*

VI

As John Rainbird's disorientation subsided, he realized that he remained in a study room at the University library, holding his Chemistry book open to pages 432 and 433. The opposing pages were damp with sweat from his hands. He rested the book on the table in front of him before checking his wristwatch. It read 3:23. He'd been zoned out for more than an hour.

No, zoned out isn't an accurate description, he thought. *I've been far more than that. I've been on an express trip through Rebecca's memories.*

He had remembered things just as Rebecca might have experienced them- meeting Kevin and liking him only later to have a falling out- then him ruining her life. He didn't need to have any visions about how the rest of it had played out. He knew all too well.

As he often did, John Rainbird wondered if Rebecca would have fallen for Kevin if he hadn't abandoned their friendship for a time.

Not yet knowing about the death of Gregory Rollins or the impending death of Kevin Anderson, John shrugged off his wild imaginings about Rebecca as the offspring of an overactive mind and guilt riddled consciousness. He got up to buy a soda from a nearby vending machine before returning to his studies.

John's dream of the horrifying demise of Kevin Anderson came two nights later. Less than 48 hours after that dream, he found himself at Blessed Earth, about to participate in his second Celebration of Return within a three week period.

Chapter 18 - The Indian Friend

As the Celebration of Return ceremony began at Blessed Earth, Mrs. Anderson finished telling Detective Tremblehorn and his partner what she knew about what happened between her son and Rebecca Saulters. Her account did not offer the firsthand details of John's visions. Instead, it was a mix of the injured family's claims and the truth she knew of her own son. She remained clear eyed and composed as she recounted the sordid tale.

"Kevin never admitted that he was responsible for that videotape, but I knew he had done it. He's like his father in that he can be cruel when he doesn't get his way. I guess Anson and I are both responsible for that. We've indulged our children far too much."

She drew in a deep breath. "That poor girl committed suicide sometime after." She looked from one detective to the next. "Kevin wasn't himself for a long time after that. Oh, he tried to act like he was fine, but he wasn't. He became very distant, brooding even. He lost about ten pounds, wasn't playing sports as well, lost interest in his social life. I'm not telling you this because I want you to feel sorry for my son, Detectives. After all, he survived that whole mess and the poor girl didn't. I'm telling you this so that you know that the only people who might hate my son still live right here in Bay Corner. The poor girl's family and- and her Indian friend."

"Indian friend?" The detectives asked in unison.

Mrs. Anderson nodded. "Yes." She made eye contact with Detective Tremblehorn. "No offense."

"None taken. Tell us about this 'Indian friend'."

Chapter 19 - The Ceremony of Return

Leather tassels hung from the chest and tail of John Rainbird's deerskin jacket. Deerskin pants and a pair of leather moccasins completed his ensemble. His mane of hair rested in two thick braids. Red paint covered his face.

The paint symbolized the crimson pallor of a crying baby. The practice was part of the belief system embodied by the Celebration of Return ceremony. Any tribesman returning home after an extended time away was considered to be "reborn" to the land. Those welcoming the returning tribesman decorated themselves as the elder spirits, or guardians of the land.

In accordance with those beliefs, John Rainbird sat on a huge quilt in the center of Blessed Earth, a large clearing that was the Maupai equivalent of a town square. He folded his legs and craned his head toward the cold ground. As he did so, every female member of the tribe formed a line to his left, the foremost of them about five paces beyond the quilt. Their faces were painted solid brown, symbolizing Mother Earth.

The males formed a line equidistant from John, on his right. Their dress was identical to John's. Their faces were painted gold, symbolizing Father Sun.

Each line stretched like that of a popular ride at an amusement park. Both groups stood in order from oldest to youngest.

Father Trotting Fox stood at the front of the men. John wasn't sure how old the supposed shaman was, but the man's skin bore wrinkles to match an elephant's hide.

Maybe the old guy should change his name to Strolling Fox, John thought, thinking of the deliberate pace at which the elder always moved.

Wise Eyes seemed youthful in comparison to his cousin, the elder. A cold wind began to whistle as Trotting Fox clapped his ancient hands. A low warbling

174

began deep in his throat, growing progressively louder, as did his clapping. Soon, every man and boy mimicked him.

When the chorus of sounds reached a crescendo, Trotting Fox danced toward the quilt, using his hands to pantomime pulling a rope. John performed his part in the ceremony by jerking to his feet, portraying a child being snatched from the womb. As the others continued to warble and clap, the just short of toothless old man caught John in his arms. John felt the elder's chest heave as his drew in a powerful breath. He bellowed in the Maupai language: "I, Father Sun, welcome you back to the land, my child!"

John replied in his own strained version of his tribal tongue, "I, Son of the Land, thank you for your welcome, Great Father."

The old man's bellow brought Sminga, the eldest woman in the tribe, to life. She warbled deep in her throat and clapped like Trotting Fox. The other females mimicked her. John pivoted as the old woman danced toward him, pantomiming the tug of a rope as her counterpart had. Her brittle arms gripped John with all her might as she drew in a deep breath. "I, Mother Earth welcome you back to the land, my child!"

John replied, "I, Son of the Land, thank you for your welcome, Great Mother."

The ceremony continued with each line moving in order of descending age. Each greeter repeated the same movements and cries that Trotting Fox and Sminga had. John's sole job was to pivot into each greeter's embrace and speak his thanks, but there were so many of them that he soon felt fatigued. Wise Eyes was the fourth male to welcome him. He hugged John with a strength and intensity unmatched by any who preceded or followed him.

The wind grew from whistling to howling by the time the lines reached those who were a bit younger than John. But John was not cold, for all of the movement had heated his body. He smiled as Susan Bright Eyes, a chubby girl of perhaps fifteen, embraced him and cried the refrain of Mother Earth. The tremble he felt confirmed her nervousness. He shouted his thanks, sneaking a glance at the remainder of those assembled.

Soon, he would be welcomed by smaller children. Then those who were little more than babies would be carried forth by parents of the same sex, struggling to repeat the lines and hugging John as best as their little arms could. John recalled struggling to suppress his laughter when a 4 year old mangled the lines to him during the ceremony that was held when he returned to Blessed Earth for Thanksgiving break.

John did not get another chance to test his composure against what he perceived as pure silliness. He stumbled as Evan Moon Dancer, a boy of perhaps 14, danced toward him, mimicking the pulling of a rope as so many others had. The wind screamed like a banshee. Its' great breath blew the part of the quilt that was no longer supported by John's weight skyward. His stumbling feet kept the rest of the quilt joined to the earth, causing it to whip about from the struggle between the two forces.

At first, John felt that he had grown light headed from the duration and intensity of the ceremony. He collapsed to the ground before he had time to realize there was something altogether different going on.

John opened his eyes an indeterminable amount of time later. He discovered that they no longer belonged to him, just as his thoughts were no longer his own thoughts.

Chapter 20-The Knife Lady and Her Daughter

I

Wild eyed and clutching a bottle of Chivas Regal that held only a few swallows, Emma Saulters crashed her daughter's bedroom door open.

"Ra-beck-a," she slurred, leaning against the near wall. "Ra-beck-a! Wake up!"

Rebecca stopped pretending to sleep and sat up. "Yes, Mom?" she asked.

"It ain't right," Emma said, swooning. "It ain't right what did that to you bastard!"

"What?"

"I-it ain't right what that bas-tard did to you. You know what the fuck I meant!"

"I told you he never did anything to me." Rebecca maintained her well practiced lie.

"And I tooold you I don't bleve your fuckin' lies!" Emma's shaky free hand became a shaky fist. "I shoed beat your fuckin' ass."

Rebecca scrambled free of her covers, preparing to make a run for it or dive under the bed.

Emma snorted, spittle flying from her drunken lips. She cackled, becoming a two-legged hyena. "I ain't do that gone to, you stupid little bitch. I'm going to fix that motherfucker instead. Fix that good motherfucker!"

Emma turned away from the bedroom, tossing her head back to finish the liquor. When no more of the dark liquid swam into her mouth, she hurled the empty bottle. It sailed down the hall and shattered against the far living room wall.

"Fix that motherfucker," she cackled again, managing not to invert her words as she headed for the dowdy apartment's kitchenette.

Now fearful for the man her mother spoke of instead of herself, Rebecca followed. Her fright turned to absolute terror when Emma grabbed a chef's knife from the rack.

"What are you doing, Mom?"

An astounded expression sprouted on Emma's face. "What did I just say, you little retard? I'm gone to fix that motherfucker once and for all! Teach him bow been a pervert."

"You can't do that, Mom," Rebecca said, moving toward her. "If you do that, you'll go to jail."

Emma used her free hand to grab Rebecca by the collar and sling her to the floor. Rebecca bumped her left arm against the metal bar that jutted from the bottom of the stove as she fell. Pain coursed through the offended limb. As her mother manhandled her, the hand holding the knife almost lost its' grip and sent the steel blade into her ten year old body.

"Shut the fuck up!" Emma screamed. "I'm doing this for you, you little cunt. You little whore. Get in my way again, so I'll break your fuckin' jaw then!"

Rebecca said nothing, only crying and rubbing her pained arm as her mother stuffed the knife into a purse and stormed out into the cold December night.

Rebecca felt frantic, thinking that although she was just a little girl, she had to do something. After all, whatever happened tonight would be all her fault, no matter if she was only ten.

If her mother hadn't caught her watching nasty movies months earlier, none of this would be happening. Uncle Gregory warned her again and again, not to tell anyone out about the movies he showed her or the things he taught her. "Especially not your mother or your grandmother," he said. "This is something so special between us- that- that they just wouldn't understand."

"Do you think they'd be mad?" she once asked, huddled in his lap as she stared at him with the kind of adoration that only little girls can muster for a father figure.

Rebecca never forgot the look of alarm on his face, nor did she forget the shakiness of his voice when he answered. "They'd be awful mad, Angel. They'd be awful mad."

She would always be his "Angel". To everyone else, Rebecca was Rebee or Becky. But to Uncle Gregory, she was Angel.

Well, his Angel had let him down. She hadn't meant to. It was just that she was so bored and restless. He went out one night to "supplement his income", as he liked to put it. Rebecca's mother had been comatose for days, stuck in the grip of one of her sad spells. Thinking that Emma wouldn't stir, Rebecca rooted through the big tool box that Uncle Gregory kept in the hall closet. She knew that he kept dirty movies in the bottom of it.

She inserted a DVD devoted to the fine art of blowjobs into the DVD player. She sauntered into the kitchen, grabbing a banana before settling onto the tattered living room couch. She peeled back the banana's skin and began to mimic the skilled suction demonstrated by the "actress" onscreen.

Rebecca heard Emma rise from her creaking bed and walk across her creaking bedroom floor a few minutes later. She turned off the TV and dropped to all fours in front of the couch. Her mother might never have known anything was amiss if Rebecca had remembered to close her own bedroom door. She felt helpless as she heard Emma's footfalls approach the open room. She knew that Emma would not be happy to find her bed empty at that late hour.

Within moments, Rebecca was caught and sent off to her room with some foul words and a flurry of stinging slaps to her bottom. A few minutes later, her mother appeared in her doorway, jarring her eyes by flicking on the light. Rebecca gasped. Her volatile mother glowered in the doorway, holding the DVD in one hand and the banana in the other.

"That fucking pervert teach you about this shit?" Emma screeched. "Is that why you guys are so fucking close? And you- you little whore! You've been going right along with it."

Rebecca burst into tears, her lips quivering. "Mama, I…"

"Shut the fuck up!" Emma screeched. "And stay put. I'll fix your fucking "Uncle" when he gets home."

That fixing consisted of assailing him with curses and threats as soon as he darkened the doorstep. It culminated with him receiving his walking papers. That had been months earlier. Her mother had spoken little of her ex-boyfriend since then, although Rebecca sometimes heard her crying and cursing his name in the middle of the night. Rebecca cried sometimes, too. She missed Uncle Gregory and knew that he'd still be around if she hadn't gotten caught.

Tonight, she cried because her mother had gone off to kill the closest person to a father she ever knew. It was all her fault and she didn't know what to do about it. A light bulb flashed in her head, giving her a bit of hope.

The police! I can call the police! They probably have Uncle Gregory's address. I'll tell them about everything Mom said and the knife she took! They can get some officers out to Uncle Gregory's address and keep anything from happening!

Rebecca was about to dial 911 when someone beat a staccato rhythm on the front door. "Open up, it's the police," a gruff voice followed the knocking. Her heart leapt as she stood on tiptoe and looked through the key hole. She saw two cops in full uniform, one tall with pale and pasty skin- the other stocky with skin the color of honey. Standing with them was Mr. Stanifslaufsky, an elderly neighbor.

Rebecca swung the door open and grabbed a frantic handful of the taller officer's uniform.

"Please, officers. You guys have to help!" She spilled the tale of her mother's exit at light speed, struggling to be as coherent as possible while omitting any references to her "special times" with Uncle Gregory. The honey colored officer did not hesitate in calling her claim in on his police radio.

"We have to go," he said, bending to her eye level and placing an assuring hand on her head. "I promise we'll do everything within our power to make sure that no one gets hurt."

Rebecca ended up staying with Mr. Stanifslaufsky until her grandmother arrived. "I only called the cops 'cause I thought your daughter might be beating on this little girl here," he said. "Sounded like all hell broke loose in here."

Grandma Rose fixed him with an intense stare as he stood in the doorway. "I can assure you; my daughter would never hurt my granddaughter."

The old man's weathered lips curled into a smirk. "I hope you're right. And I hope no one gets hurt where she ran off to." He turned and stepped into the hall, grumbling, "Young people are so crazy these days."

Rebecca clung to her grandmother like an infant, hoping for the same thing the old man hoped for with a desperation he could not have felt. Her grandmother clung to her, murmuring assurances that everything would be alright. Rebecca wished that she could believe her, but she knew what her mother was capable of.

Rebecca said a silent prayer as she sobbed in her grandmother's arms.

Uncle Gregory is a good man, God. My Uncle Gregory is a good man. No one's ever treated me any better than him. Please don't let my mother kill him. Please, God, don't let my mother kill him.

Terror and helplessness consumed her, along with the knowledge that praying and waiting were all that she could do.

II

"I guess you got a right to hear firsthand why your mother's locked up," Grandma Rose said. "It's bound to all be in the news anyway."

She and Rebecca sat at the kitchen table of Grandma Rose's two-bedroom rancher on Einhurst Road. After three days, Rebecca still couldn't get her head around the fact that she now lived in the residence she'd so often visited.

Such thoughts evaporated as Grandma Rose recounted the details of her mother's crimes in painstaking fashion. As her grandmother talked, Rebecca visualized the events as if she were watching a movie.

The film began with a close shot of Uncle Gregory curled up in sleep with his new girlfriend, at his new apartment. The apartment was similar to Rebecca's mother's apartment in size and furnishing. Uncle Gregory's new girlfriend was as pretty as Emma, maybe more so since she kept up her appearance better. The new girlfriend and Uncle Gregory dozed in peace, until some rude person mashed a thumb against their doorbell and kept it depressed.

"What the hell is that?" the pretty new girlfriend grumbled, still as much asleep as awake.

"You mean, 'who the hell is that'?" Uncle Gregory growled, climbing from the bed. "Who's the asshole who's lost his fucking mind?" He kissed her. "Don't worry, babe. I'm going to straighten this bullshit out right now."

His body tensed with anger as he stomped down the long stairwell that led from his second floor apartment to the foyer. *Someone's getting cussed the fuck out and maybe a fist in the gut*, he thought.

He felt surprised to see Emma. He looked her over, drinking in the fact that she was disheveled, droopy eyed, and drunk to the point of staggering.

He cracked the front door, keeping the inside chain latched. "What are you doing here?" he asked.

"I w-want to talk," she slurred.

Uncle Gregory's eyes widened. "Talk about what? Emma, you're the one who drove me off. You made it clear that you didn't want me near you or Rebecca ever again." His eyes narrowed as he looked her over once more. "How did you even get this address?

Emma shrugged. "Public rec- ord. Its puhhhh-blic record."

Uncle Gregory forced a smile. "You're drunk, Em.

"I had to get drunk jusa talk to you!"

Not wanting to have to explain Emma's presence, or who she even was, to his new girlfriend, Uncle Gregory undid the chain and stepped outside, softly closing the front door behind him.

"What is it, Em?"

"Iiiiive been thinkin' a lot since I ran you off, and I guess maybe it wasn't quite right." She smiled in a silly manner that only a drunk can manage, swaying in place.

Uncle Gregory cleared his throat and shrugged. "That's water under the bridge. I think the fact that it ended like it did proves that maybe it wasn't meant to be."

Emma's alcohol dilated pupils pulled off the magic trick of widening even further. "Soooo, you've moved on, then?"

Uncle Gregory shrugged. "I guess so, Em. It ain't like you gave me a choice, accusing me and all. I guess I'm doing the best I can."

"Well, I'm not." Her drunken eyes performed another transformation, shrinking from the wide orbs of surprise to the narrow slits of a stalking predator. "I'm not because I can't move on. You bastard!"

Emma reached into her purse with a dexterity that defied her blood alcohol content. She stabbed Uncle Gregory once in the right side of his chest before he even realized that she held a knife. Blood pooled his tank top as she raised the knife for another strike.

He stumbled against the doorway, suffering a merciless slash to his left hand when he raised it to shield more vital targets. "What are you doing?" he screeched as he scrambled along the porch.

"I'm ridddinng the world of one sick bastard!" Emma's third strike buried the knife in Uncle Gregory's left shoulder. A rabid sneer painted her face as she ripped it free, causing a crimson shower from his wound.

She was moving in for the kill when Uncle Gregory's girlfriend ran screaming onto the front porch and struggled for the weapon. Her reward was a slash to the face, followed by two short jabs to the gut. Uncle Gregory rallied then, grabbing Emma's knife hand in an attempt to return his girlfriend's life-saving effort.

Police sirens and the sounds of tires screeching onto the gravel path drowned out the grunts of their struggles. Never losing focus of her murderous goal, Emma swung a vicious knee into her ex-boyfriend's crotch. Blue and red light illuminated the porch as Uncle Gregory sank to his knees. The frantic voice of an officer commanded, "Drop the knife, Ma'am! Drop the knife!"

Emma paused for perhaps two seconds before bringing the knife up over her head. Cops or no cops, she was determined to finish the job.

"No!" Uncle Gregory screamed, making a pitiful attempt to ward off the knife with his outstretched arms. His girlfriend lay sprawled just to his left. Blood leaked from her perforated abdomen as she moaned in agony.

Shots rang out. Emma screamed and clutched her now mangled right hand as the knife went clattering. The footfalls of two officers ascended upon the porch. Emma managed to leap onto Uncle Gregory and bite his ear before they reached her.

"Let him go!" one of the officers demanded. "Let him go or we'll have to use pepper spray."

Emma responded by shaking her head back and forth, like an enraged pit bull trying to rip its opponent's flesh free in the midst of a dog fight. Her victim screamed like a condemned soul on a spit in hell, begging the officers to get her off him. They did not hesitate to give her an eyeful of what they'd promised.

Emma released Uncle Gregory's mangled ear, alternating between groping at her blinded eyes and uncorking blind swings at the policemen. After subduing her and waiting for paramedics to arrive, the officers hauled her off to the county lock-up.

Grandma Rose sighed, shifting in her seat as she concluded the tale. "She'll remain at the Women's Detention Center until trial," she said. "All we can do is pray for your mother, you know?"

Rebecca nodded. Her grandmother continued. "I hate to say this about her but she never has been quite right. I guess you know that being her daughter, even if you don't have the words for it because you're so young. Hell, I don't have the words for it myself, old as I am. Even when she was a young girl like you, your mother never was quite right. But I never dreamed she would do anything like this."

That's because you don't know what I did, Rebecca thought. *You don't know what she found out about.*

Rebecca couldn't shake the belief that she was responsible for everything that happened. She felt so terrible that she couldn't imagine things getting any worse than they were at that moment. She soon became educated about that misconception.

III

Emma's lawyer negotiated a plea deal for twin counts of aggravated assault and assault with a deadly weapon, as opposed to the twin counts of attempted murder Emma would have faced at trial. She made no reference of what she suspected of Uncle Gregory as a defense. Instead, she admitted to suffering strange spells all her life and claimed that her worst ever led to the attack. A psychiatrist examined her and diagnosed her with bipolar disorder. The presiding judge showed leniency in sentencing her to five years in a minimum security prison, with the caveat that she take prescribed medications and attend therapy sessions for her now confirmed condition.

The "Harford County Aegis" hummed with details of the event and its resolution. The same was true of the tiny "Bay Corner Press". Incidents of such violence were a rarity in the little town seated on the headwaters of the Chesapeake. There had only been six murders in Bay Corner's entire history, four of which were committed back in '81 by the lunatic Charlie Cassidy. An occasional drunken Saturday night fistfight was the normal extent of violence in Bay Corner.

While Emma Saulters joined Charlie Cassidy as something of an urban legend, her young daughter became a pariah. For weeks, the tension simmered around her at school.

Girls Rebecca knew as friends - such as Pamela Lawson and Shanae Edwards - turned cold shoulders to her. Staff members looked at her in a weird way or talked to her as if her feelings were porcelain. When she sat at a lunch table, all the other kids moved away.

The tension boiled over one afternoon in mid-January while Rebecca presented a report on local demographics to her fifth grade Social Studies class. She rattled off information (obtained mostly from the U.S. Census website) as she displayed a pretty poster chart she made.

"According to the government census that was conducted this past summer, Bay Corner has a population of 2,731 permanent residents. Of those 2,731 permanent residents, 833 were identified as Black or African-American, including 34 first or second generation Nigerian Americans. 1,208 were Caucasian, predominantly of Anglo-Saxon or German origin. 281 residents were identified as non-white Hispanics - a majority of whom were Mexican-American. 79 residents were Asian-Americans, 64 were Indian-American (as in the country India), 214 residents were Native Americans of the Maupai tribe, and 52 were first or second generation Arab Americans. Of the total of 2,731 residents, 129 people were categorized as multi-racial, including me. The information that I have gathered leads me to conclude that Bay Corner is one of the most ethnically diverse small towns in the United States."

"Thank you, Rebecca." Mr. Handley clapped, prompting most of her classmates to follow suit. "That was a well prepared and well -presented report."

"Yeah, but she forgot one thing, Mr. Handley," a boy's voice came from the back of the room.

Robert Bailey. Oh, God, Rebecca thought.

She'd noticed him sneering at her often during the past few weeks. She couldn't imagine what he might have against her.

Mr. Handley sighed. "What did she forget, Robert?"

"She forgot to mention that Bay Corner also has its very own crazy slasher!" Robert shrieked. The rest of the class buzzed in shock.

"Robert!" Mr. Handley barked, wagging his finger as he strode toward the boy. "That remark is completely unacceptable!"

Robert's face flushed a hateful crimson as he sprang from his seat. His hazel eyes glowed feral with intensity. "Fuck you, Handley! This little freak's mother nearly killed my aunt." He pronounced aunt as ant.

"Now I'm supposed to sit in class with her like nothing happened?" He ran across the room and grabbed Rebecca by her shoulder length mane of hair. She screamed, trying to fight him off. As they rolled into the floor, he hooked his hands deeper into the thick brown strands. The entire class burst into an uproar.

As tears streamed from the pain of the enraged boy yanking at her roots, Rebecca raked her fingernails down his cheeks. Robert released her with a scream, his hands shooting to his wounded face. Mr. Handley reached him then, grabbing him around the waist from behind and carrying him from the room. As he was hauled away, Robert screamed, "See! It runs in the family. You didn't even need a knife to cut me, Knife Lady's Daughter!"

To Rebecca's horror, about half of her classmates laughed at that last remark. Feeling like a bawling fit was coming on, she ran from the room.

Because Rebecca felt too distraught to finish the school day, her grandmother left work early to pick her up. Rebecca thought that she should have known that her mother's actions had affected some of her schoolmates. After all, Bay Corner was a small town.

Robert was switched to the other fifth grade class when he returned to school from his suspension. He and Rebecca were also subjected to conflict resolution with the school psychologist. After much prodding, Robert admitted that Rebecca had nothing to do with her mother's actions. He stopped sneering at her whenever they crossed paths. But as far as the rest of her peers were concerned, the damage was irreversible.

Rebecca got a strong taste of that damage as she walked home from school a few days after the classroom incident. "There she is, everyone," Pamela Lawson called from behind, her voice shrill and cruel. Pam Lawson who had been her friend before all the trouble started.

"Rebecca, we have a song we made up just for you!" she chirped, eliciting a chorus of laughter from the pack of kids who accompanied her. Rebecca didn't have to look back to know that Shanae Edwards walked lockstep with her new tormentor. Rebecca had once formed the third of that triumvirate. "Come on, everyone. Let's sing the song."

Eight or nine youthful voices sounded as one. "Knife Lady's Daughter." The male and female voices blended as if they had spent hours practicing. "Knife Lady's Daughter. She knows how to slaughter, because her mother taught her. Knife Lady's Daughter. Knife Lady's Daughter. She knows how to slice and dice and she will take your life. She will take your life. You'd better stay away from the Knife Lady's Daughter. Knife Lady's Daughter. Knife Lady's Daughter. She knows how to slaughter, because her mother taught her. Knife Lady's Daughter.

Knife Lady's Daughter. She knows how to slice and dice and she will take your life. She will take your life. You'd better stay away from the Knife Lady's Daughter."

Once she recovered from the initial paralysis that their cruelty caused, Rebecca ran with the desperation of a zebra pursued by hungry lions on the plains of the Serengeti. The refrain repeated beyond enumeration as her feet streaked along the pavement. The sound of the cruel singing faded as she pushed herself to maintain the quickest speed possible. Rebecca didn't stop running until she reached her front walk. Her breath came in ragged bursts as she walked to the front steps and collapsed into a heap of tears.

Chapter 21- A Visit From Wise Eyes

John's vision of Rebecca in elementary school faded as she cried. His mind began the gradual swim towards self-awareness, like a deep sea diver climbing towards the surface of the ocean. As it reached its' destination, he heard a faint voice. He tried to focus his awakening ears.

"….to us now," he heard. "I think he's coming back to us now."

John's eyes fluttered, then popped open. He lay on a plain pallet, covered with several blankets. Trotting Fox sat in a hand fashioned wooden chair before him. Wise Eyes stood behind the ancient man. A weathered hand touched John's concealed right shoulder.

"Yes, you have come back to us, my child," Trotting Fox said, his voice rattling like an old radiator when the heat is first switched on. "Rest easy. You have been gone for some time."

White moonlight shone through the window overlooking the pallet, contrasting the golden glow from a candle that stood on a wooden stool a few steps away. John realized that he lay in Trotting Fox's lodging, not Wise Eyes's.

"Why am I here?" He attempted to sit up, only to be wrestled back into place by the chieftain for his trouble.

"Be still, Son of my Son," Wise Eyes said. "Be still. You must come back to yourself slowly."

Trotting Fox returned with a cup of hot tea in hand. John had not noticed the old man leaving his side.

"Sit up slowly," Trotting Fox said. John did as he was told, swinging his legs over the edge of the pallet. He realized that he still wore his ceremonial outfit.

Trotting Fox reached the cup out to him. "Take it with care."

John was glad to find his hands steady as he did so. The tea heartened him, warming his bones. An image of collapsing upon the giant quilt floated to the surface of his memory.

"Allow me to speak with the Son of my Son, Elder Trotting Fox," Wise Eyes said.

Trotting Fox nodded. "I will tell the others he has come back to us."

A happy murmur arose from outside the hut a few moments later, informing John that many of his tribesmen had waited outside in their concern for him. It was good to know that so many cared about his well-being.

Wise Eyes made a throat clearing noise before speaking. John felt sure that it was because of nervousness, not cold.

Wise Eyes chuckled. "You had quite the spell, grandson," he said. "You caused quite the uproar among the Commune. Some feared that the Elder Spirits came to take you early. Many small children wept and many women clutched their breast. They will rejoice to know that you are alright."

"I'm glad to be okay, too."

Wise Eyes took Trotting Fox's former seat. He leaned toward John, the candlelight illuminating the intense scrutiny etched on his face. "I'm not so sure you are 'okay', Son of My Son."

John drained the last of his tea, keeping his right hand on the empty cup as he sat it on the pallet. "What's that supposed to mean, Grandfather?"

Wise Eyes leaned back into an upright position. "You would have me believe that your spell came from overexcitement? From the ceremony- perhaps?"

"I suppose so."

Wise Eyes chuckled and shook his head. "When you returned for Thanksgiving weekend, we had the very same ceremony. Yet, you endured no such spell."

John nodded. "No. No, I didn't."

"You do not know it, but you have slept for more than seven hours. It is now close to midnight."

Fuck, John thought. *Brittany probably called me back and I missed it. She's probably worried sick about me.* "Where's my cell phone?"

"Your cell phone? That's a strange thing to ask for at a time like this."

"I was waiting for a call from Brittany."

Wise Eyes smiled. "Yes. Your Anglo girlfriend. I suppose your cell phone is back with the clothes you wore home. I have been here since you fell."

"Could you get it for me?"

"I will get it for you shortly. First, you and I must finish our discussion."

John swallowed his desire to say, "I didn't realize we were having a discussion, Grandfather." He knew that verbalizing the thought would only delay receiving his cell phone. He hoped it still held some battery charge. "Okay," he said.

Wise Eyes took a deep breath. "Alright. According to Maupai legend, falling the way you did indicates contact with the spirit world."

John laughed. "And what spirit would that be, Grandfather? Something other than the mix of two hundred or so Mother Earths and Father Suns who welcomed me?"

Wise Eyes shook his head. "No, that is only ceremony. There is only one Mother Earth and one Father Sun. But, you know that there are far more spirits than those."

"I know that you believe there are far more spirits than those."

Wise Eyes stood and leaned over his grandson, resting a gentle hand on John's forearm. "I don't wish to upset you when you have just come back to us, but the spirits of balance are believed to visit fainting spells upon one whom they charge with a task."

John sighed. "That's a lot to swallow, Grandfather."

"Swallow it you may have to, even if it's against your nature to believe in such things. You had no peace in your slumber. You murmured things, made sounds that could not be understood. If the spirits have charged you with a task, more spells will visit you. Did you see anything in your sleep?"

John shook his head, lying without hesitation. "No. Not that I remember."

Wise Eyes returned to his seat. He watched John in silence, long enough to cause discomfort. "Well, that is good to know," he said. "Perhaps the spirits are not charging you with a task. Perhaps you were overwhelmed by the ceremony, just as you say. But you should know that if it happens again, it must be the spirits and they will not leave you be until you have done what is required of you."

Chapter 22- John and Brittany

After listening to what he thought of as Wise Eyes's mumbo jumbo, John recovered his almost dead cell phone and dialed Brittany. He made a profuse apology for missing her calls.

"You don't have to keep apologizing," Brittany said. "I'm just glad you're okay. Now get your ass over here."

"I have to go, Father of my Father," John said to Wise Eyes as he prepared to leave.

Wise Eyes waved his grandson away. "Go. I suppose you need time with your 'girlfriend'. But know that we have another serious matter to discuss."

"Yes, grandfather," John said, assuming that the old man referred to more mumbo jumbo. He dismissed Wise Eyes's words as he rushed to get his motor scooter from Blessed Earth's tented storage area.

John Rainbird shared an edited account of what befell him during the Celebration of Return upon arrival at Brittany's house. He told his girlfriend that he had gotten dizzy and fainted but omitted his visions of Rebecca. He refused to burden Brittany with haunting images of the lost friend that now tormented him, feeling that she had shown more than her fair share of patience and understanding about his feelings for Rebecca when Rebecca died.

Brittany perched on her boyfriend's lap in the sitting area of her parent's basement. Her hands formed a tent around the back of his neck as her head rested on his shoulder. Her raven hair smelled of jasmine and honeysuckle. Although her natural hair color was black, it wasn't as striking or ethereal as the shade that the fresh dye job supplied. The gloss on Brittany's lips matched her hair, as did her form fitting blouse and snug jeans. John Rainbird wondered if his girlfriend of four years would ever let go of the Goth thing. He decided that he didn't care as long as she remained a sexy Goth, the evolution of the skateboard Goth look she favored when they met as high school freshmen.

John Rainbird wished that he didn't hear Brittany's parents moving about upstairs. If they hadn't been at home-then- well it had been since Thanksgiving Break. He had one hell of an itch to scratch and he was all set for the occasion, having bought a pack of Trojans before he left campus. As if reading his mind, Brittany giggled, craning her neck to whisper into his ear. "Don't worry. The old folks won't be up much longer. They're already way past their bedtime."

John smiled. "You are so mean."

"But, I won't be mean to you." She trailed one hand along his torso. "I'm going to make widdle Johnny feel all better."

Once they were certain her parents turned in, Brittany pulled out the sofa bed and did just as she promised. Afterward, as he lay next to her, John thought nothing of the visions he'd been having. The fainting spell he suffered during the Celebration of Return also ceased to trouble him.

"You just keep coming up with new tricks, don't you, girl?" He rested his left hand on her bare back as she lay on his bare chest. "Where do you learn that stuff?"

She giggled. "My other lovers teach me."

"Very funny."

"Just kidding." She lifted her head to kiss him on the cheek. "You know you're the only guy I've ever been with. And I'd like to keep it that way, so I always want to learn different ways to satisfy you."

John knew that Brittany told the truth. She was the second girl he'd been with. His only other sexual dalliance had come under extraordinary circumstances.

Brittany sighed. "You know, I could get a lot wilder if we weren't always worried about my parents."

John knew just where the conversation was headed. "Do we have to talk about that now, Brit? Can't we just enjoy lying here for a while?"

Brittany sprang off him and slipped her black lace underwear back on. Her eyes blazed with intensity. Although he knew the glare was a sign of displeasure, John found it even sexier than her lithe body. He hoped for round two once the impending argument ended.

Brittany's thin lips trembled. "No, we can't, John. We can't fully enjoy that because I have to worry about my parents barging in on us."

John propped himself up on his elbows. "Why would they do that?"

Brittany stood in front of the sofa bed with her hands on her hips. "I don't know, John. But here's the thing- they don't need a reason. They don't need a reason because it's their house. And they can go anywhere in it, or do anything with it, as they please. Just as your grandfather can do anything within his home that he pleases. If that means having no electricity or other modern amenities, that's his right! It's his right because it's his house. You and I don't have those kinds of rights because we live in other people's houses. And I'm tired of living like that, John. I'm tired of there being limits on what you and I can do together. I'm also tired of hearing about you having to do weird Indian stuff that you really don't believe in. But, I guess you're not that tired yet, John. Either you're not that tired or you're too scared to do something about it."

John didn't reply at first, only sitting there and watching her glower at him. He smiled after a few moments- a huge, radiant smile that he knew she had trouble resisting. "It makes me feel great that you're so passionate about being with me, Brit."

"About living with you," Brittany corrected. The hard look in her eyes and the matching set of her mouth softened just a little. "I'm passionate about living with you. I just want to live with you and love you and share my body with you freely."

She set her gaze upon a corner wall. John knew that she avoided looking at him out of fear that his smile would snuff what remained of her ebbing anger.

John sat all the way up, swinging his legs over the edge of the mattress. "I want that too, Brit. Please come here."

Brittany's chest heaved as she sighed before wading into her boyfriend's outstretched arms. "I just want to really, really be with you," she said. "We'll have enough money to be okay."

"I know," he said, resting his head on her shoulder. He did know. Though he didn't have a job at the moment, he'd accumulated quite a windfall from the death benefit he'd received from Social Security until he turned 18. $600 a month for ten years had been nothing to sneeze at, even if his grandfather had used a third of it to provide help with basic expenses. Other than that, it was all saved up for John to have a nest egg for college. John Rainbird still remembered the confrontation he had with Wise Eyes when he was 14, the one that led to the old man revealing just how much savings he'd amassed for his grandson. What was more than $25,000 almost doubled during John's high school years. Wise Eyes agreed to give John a little more of the money to spend on leisure as a result of the argument, but there would be no fancy designer clothes or hundred dollar pairs of shoes. The bulk of the money was to serve as his college fund, a condition that was not negotiable.

Receiving a full academic scholarship to the University of Delaware meant that John Rainbird didn't have to touch those savings to further his education. He continued to be frugal after he turned 18, even with all that money at his disposal.

Although his grandfather no longer forced that frugality, the habits were hard formed. John worked as a Chesapeake Bay excursion tour guide each spring and summer after he turned 15, using the money he earned to buy a few prized possessions (including his laptop and a newer cell phone). He also used money from work to finance expenses for his senior prom, although he turned 18 six weeks before it and therefore had access to the savings.

John Rainbird only touched the savings twice. The first time was to obtain a lawyer for a legal matter he faced in ninth grade. The second occasion was the nearly seven thousand he spent on his and her Vespa motor scooters for he and Brittany, leaving him with just over 38,000 in the account his grandfather set up. Restraint even governed him when buying the scooters, causing him to forego the option to purchase more expensive models that could reach exceed 60 Mph, instead of the ones he opted for that topped out at 40 Mph.

Although a halfway decent one bedroom apartment in Harford County ran about $800 a month (not to mention utilities), Brittany was right. With his savings and her working 40 hours a week at the Bay Corner Diner while enrolled at Harford County Community College, they had enough money. He'd also be working the Chesapeake Bay excursions come the end of spring. Plus, after getting used to living with modern amenities at UD, he found the Luddite accommodations of Blessed Earth even less tolerable He also wanted to be as free with Brittany as she wanted to be with him. Years of sneaking around her parents to have sex stripped sneaking around her parents to have sex of its charm.

What then, was his hesitation? As he held Brittany in his arms, he admitted to himself that it could only be fear of the unknown.

Screw that, he thought. *Fear of the unknown kept everyone at Blessed Earth in a 19ᵗʰ century time warp. I'm not ever going to be like that. My parents wouldn't want me to live like that for one second.*

He squeezed Brittany tighter, enjoying her pleasant smell and the feel of her thin but supple body. He nibbled her left earlobe. "I need to stop being so silly, Brit. You're right. It's time we get an apartment together."

"Do you mean it?" she squealed, clapping and jumping up and down. The only other time he'd gotten such an unrestrained and typical feminine reaction from her was when he bought her Vespa. She tried to convince him to take the Vespa back at first, but he knew there'd be no talk of taking back what he just said.

"Yeah. We can start looking while I'm home from school, but I don't want to rush into getting any shitty place. I mean, any place with electricity and a real bathroom would be an improvement for me, but I want you to be really comfortable."

Brittany pressed her hands against John's chest, forcing him back first onto the mattress. She lay on top of him, grabbing the sides of his face and feeding him her wonderfully adroit tongue. "I really appreciate you being so considerate, John Rainbird. I really appreciate that, but I'll be comfortable anywhere so long as I'm with you."

As they engaged in foreplay that led to their second sexual romp of the night, John tried not to think about the way Brittany had just cooed his name. "John Rainbird." Brittany had always called him John or Johnny to show affection. The person who made habit of referring to him as John Rainbird- coming just short of singing it the same as Brittany just did- had been dead for years.

Chapter 23- John and the Detectives

I

John Rainbird's cell phone buzzed like a swarm of angry bees, interrupting his peaceful slumber. Brittany stirred in her sleep and mumbled something unintelligible as he snatched it up, her nude body entwined with his. The young Maupai's groggy eyes recognized the number as that of the pay phone that stood just beyond the northern extremes of Blessed Earth. The time on the phone's display read 5:17 am. He placed the phone to his ear and pressed the talk button.

"Hello?" he grumbled.

"While you slept, Son of my Son," Wise Eyes began, "while you slept, policemen came here for you."

"Wha-," John Rainbird sat up on the edge of the mattress, pushing Brittany's arm away. She mumbled and turned over in her sleep. "Grandfather, what are you saying?"

"When you had your spell, we took you to Trotting Fox's home as you remember waking there. While you were resting, policemen came, wanting to see you. I told them they were not welcome on Maupai land, but they did not heed. They said that they believe you might have information about a possible murder."

Those words jolted John wide awake. "Grandfather- did you say 'murder'?"

"Your ears do not deceive you, Son of My Son. They were from downstate-Prince George's County. One of them was Maupai, from the Eastern Shore. He called himself Tremblehorn. I said to him, 'Tremblehorn- were you not raised to learn that treading on our ground without permission is an insult?' He said that he meant not to insult me, but that he was duty bound to speak with you. I brought him into Trotting Fox's home, to show him what condition you were in. The other one had to wait outside. He said that they would come back tomorrow, see if you felt better. He left a cell phone number that you may reach him on. That is what I want you to do, Son of My Son. Now that you are feeling better and had time to romp with your Anglo girlfriend- I want you to call this Detective Tremblehorn. I want you to speak with them, so that they have no reason to set foot on Blessed Earth again."

"Yes, Grandfather. Grandfather- you do know that I don't know anything about any murder?"

"I am not the one you need to convince, Son of My Son."

John punched Detective Tremblehorn's number into his cell phone as Wise Eyes read it to him. Confusion assailed him as he ended the call. He saved the detective's number before turning the phone off and sliding it away.

"What's going on, John?" Brittany asked, her voice full of sleep. "Who are you talking to this time of morning?"

He rolled back on to the mattress, turning to face her. "You caught me. You know what- I can't live with this secret any longer. That was my other girlfriend."

Lying there in the dark, he could just make out a bemused smile on her face.

"Yeah, right. Now tell me what the real secret is."

He brushed his lips against hers. "You want to know the real secret?"

"Yup."

"That was my crazy ass grandfather. He's worried because I rushed off to see you. I guess he thinks I should have rested more, considering what happened to me yesterday afternoon."

"Aww," Brittany said. "That's not crazy, John. That's sweet. He's worried about his widdle grandson."

John Rainbird frowned. "Well, he needn't worry so much. I'm fine."

202

Brittany giggled. "Think I don't know that after the time we just had? Believe me, I know."

She panted a lazy smooch on him, entwining her body with his again. "Now, take your handsome self back to sleep, lover boy."

"Alright," John Rainbird said. "Let's go back to sleep."

But he did not go back to sleep, not right away. Instead, the wheels of worry turned, sweeping him along a route of slumber murdering dread.

The University of Maryland is in Prince George's County, he thought. *The University of Maryland College Park. No! It couldn't be. It can't be!*

But, he knew that it was, just as he knew his impending conversation with the detectives would confirm his fears. There'd be no denying that the dreams- the things he'd been "seeing"- were not figments of his imagination at all. They were forecasts of the actions of something he unleashed upon the world. The things he "saw" foretold real horrors to come.

II

Brittany kissed her boyfriend awake at 8 am, ignoring his morning breath as her tongue explored the recesses of his mouth. John Rainbird would have loved having another romp for the road, but she rushed him along. "You should go before the old folks upstairs start to get ready for church."

"Do I have to?" he sighed, cupping her bottom and pressing himself against her.

She giggled and kissed him again. "Yes. See, this won't be a problem when we get our own place." She ground her pelvis against him, her smile mischievous. "We'll be able to have each other anytime we want- no interruptions."

John's crotch swelled as he returned her smile. "We'll start looking next week." Brittany kissed him once more. "I can't wait."

He maneuvered his Vespa a short while later, the mid-December chill clinging to his body as he rode. His trip ended at the Bay Corner Diner, where he washed down a breakfast of bacon, eggs, toast, and grits with two glasses of orange juice. Valerie, his waitress, treated him like royalty. The veteran waitress had taken a liking to Brittany, so he figured it was only natural that she thought well of him. He wolfed the food down, his heavy mind keeping him from enjoying it as much as usual. He paid the tab and left a tip that would do nothing to damage Valerie's opinion of him- then headed outside to face the inevitable.

Astride his stationary scooter, John scanned the diner's parking lot to confirm that no one passed within earshot. He dialed Detective Tremblehorn's number, coiling into a bundle of nerves as the call rang through.

The detective's voice remained cordial and neutral as they arranged a meeting outside the Super 8 Motel in Havre de Grace.

"You're looking much better than when I last saw you," Tremblehorn said, as John Rainbird parked the Vespa.

"Well, I haven't seen you before, so I can't make any comparative statements about your appearance," John said, climbing off his transport.

Carpenter smirked. "Cute. You mind talking in the car?"

Tremblehorn soon sat next to John in the backseat of the detectives' sedan. Carpenter turned to face John from the driver's seat.

Tremblehorn regarded John with a bemused expression. "You and I are from the same tribe, kid. You know that?"

John nodded. "My Grandfather told me that one of the policeman who came to Blessed Earth was Maupai." He looked Tremblehorn over. "He didn't mention that you were a half breed, like me."

Tremblehorn chuckled. "No, I don't suppose a Traditionalist like him would.

So, which of your parents was Anglo?"

"My mother."

"Same here. My father left the commune in Wicomico County forty years ago. Started off as a dishwasher for the original Phillips, sharing a flea bag apartment with three other guys. He didn't care, was willing to do anything to join the modern world. All the time there, he studied the cooks, learned how to prepare the food. By the time he met my mother, he'd become a cook for a competing restaurant. He eventually went from a successful cook to co-owner of a seafood restaurant. Ever heard of 'Shorebirds'?"

John shook his head.

"Guess you never been out Ocean City before. Anyway, I share all this autobiographical information with you to tell you I never lived the commune life. I've visited a few times, but I never considered living that way of life. I feel like a real fish out of water when I'm around that, you know?"

John nodded. "It isn't a life for forward thinking people. If my parents hadn't died, I would never have had to live at Blessed Earth. I'm going to get an apartment with my girlfriend soon, though. No more of that primitive shit for me."

Tremblehorn laughed and patted John on the knee. "You seem like a decent enough kid, John Rainbird. You've had trouble before in the past though- haven't you?"

John swallowed hard, all too aware of what Tremblehorn referred to.

"Only one time. And that was expunged from my record when I turned eighteen."

"Oh, it was expunged from public record," Carpenter said. "But, it wasn't expunged from the memory of the people you had the run in with. We talked with the lady of that household yesterday."

John scowled. "You had no reason to talk about me with anyone. You had no reason to even know I exist."

"Oh, believe me," Carpenter said, "we had never heard of you before our conversation with Mrs. Anderson and we definitely did not come here from PG County to look for you."

"Yet our conversation with her led us to you," Tremblehorn said. "Perhaps this is a case of the universe restoring balance, as our people believe."

Carpenter's dark eyes narrowed into slits. "You want to tell us about what happened during that incident?"

"Why should I tell you that?"

Carpenter chuckled as Tremblehorn answered the question. "You should tell us because the kid you threatened all those years ago is now dead. He's dead and by all appearances, he was murdered."

John's pupils widened. "Murdered? So you think I did it? Because of something that happened when I was in ninth grade?"

"We didn't say you were a suspect."

"Not yet, anyway," Carpenter said.

"But if you had nothing to do with Kevin Anderson's death," Tremblehorn said, "there's really no reason for you not to talk about that incident in ninth grade, is there?"

John hesitated before answering. "No," he said. "No, I guess there isn't."

III

The great tide of anger that had been rising within John Rainbird massed into a tsunami of pure rage. He could no longer tolerate knowing that his friend lay in the ground while the tormentor who was responsible for her death went unpunished.

"I wish I could make them all pay," Rebecca said the last time he saw her alive. "Everyone who's done this to me. I wish I could make them all pay."

John Rainbird couldn't bring all who had wronged her to task any more than she could. But he could give the main culprit a well-deserved beating. The sun yawned and squinted at the horizon on this Sunday morning, meaning that he was sure to catch his quarry at home.

Gloved hands and a cheap hooded sweatsuit protected John from the swirling February winds as he rushed toward his destination. His legs pumped at Tour De France speed, causing his new Schwinn to whistle a work song as he neared Mackenzie Hill. The ritzy and secluded neighborhood stood at the opposite extreme of Blessed Earth, in matters of architecture and culture. John reached the western extreme of the main road that led to it in no time, turning left into a hilly road that was much narrower than its predecessor. The bare trunks of juniper trees lined the second road.

The juniper trees disappeared as John Rainbird climbed the incline. A large sign that read, "Mackenzie Hill, a Community of Distinction, Established 1986", stood just beyond the trees. John slowed his bike to a trot as he approached the gated estates. His lips curled into a sneer when he saw the wrought iron letters of Anderson Manor.

The young Maupai climbed off his bike and walked up to the gate, which had an intercom to buzz visitors in. He assessed the height of the structure, estimating it at about eight feet. He scaled it without hesitation, his movement as fluid as a squirrel scampering up a tree. His hood swept from his head as he did so, exposing his long black pony tail. He heard no alarm as he dropped to the ground inside the property.

The main house stood on an incline, about fifty yards beyond the gate. But the main house was not what John Rainbird's destination. He headed for the pool beyond its backside, knowing just where the person he sought resided. He stood outside his destination within moments, having relied on Rebecca's description to guide him there.

John Rainbird felt no doubt that the bastard was in there. He wouldn't have been surprised if he had another unwitting girl sharing his bed at the moment. What kind of family let a 14 year old pretty much have their own apartment, anyway? Wise Eyes would regard such a circumstance as a shining example of Anglo madness. The young Maupai's anger was so powerful that he did not consider the madness in his intended actions for even a moment. That anger had festered within him for weeks, spreading like a malignant tumor. It metastasized now, obliterating any thoughts he might have had about consequence and causing complete surrender to his violent compulsion.

He drew back his arm, throwing his shoulder into each blow as he pounded on the door of the pool house. "Kevin Anderson," he bellowed, raining blow after blow. "Kevin Anderson! Come on out here! Come out, Kevin Anderson. You come out now!"

The door creaked open, moments later. A matinee handsome blond kid regarded John with confused oceanic eyes. "Who the fuck….." John Rainbird decked him with an overhand right before he could finish the question. "I'll fucking kill you," John Rainbird howled, leaping onto the boy's prone form. "I'll kill you for what you did to her!"

He managed to bloody Kevin's nose before two strong hands snatched him backward, out of the pool house. His hands scrabbled on the tiled poolside surface as he tried to get to his feet. A vicious kick to his ribs sapped the vigor from his efforts. He felt one of them collapse inward, the excruciating pain leaving no doubt that it was broken.

This was not the way I planned things, he thought.

He tried to haul his wounded body upright, but was shoved back down. He became aware of a man's voice taunting him. "Teach you to sneak onto my property, attack my fucking son."

John Rainbird's world swam before him in a gray haze of pain. He looked in the direction of the taunting voice and was just able to make out a tall, blond man who looked an awful lot like the boy he throttled moments earlier.

I must have been out of my fucking mind to come here, he thought, trying to crawl away.

"Hit him one, son," the man urged, sounding to John Rainbird as if his voice came from a great distance.

"But Dad, shouldn't we call the police?"

"You're an Anderson, boy. You'd better bloody this Indian like he bloodied you. Do it!"

That was the last thing John Rainbird remembered before a clubbing blow to the side of his head shoved him into darkness.

IV

"My grandfather used some of the money from my college fund to pay for my defense," John Rainbird said. "He got me a good lawyer from Baltimore. The guy was able to get me probation. The fact that they broke two of my ribs and gave me a concussion had a lot to do with that. Also, I'd never been in any kind of trouble before."

"You're lucky they didn't kill you," Carpenter said. "Breaking onto someone's property like that."

"What do you think you would've done if the father hadn't stopped you?" Tremblehorn asked. "Would you have killed him?"

John Rainbird snickered. "Killed him? I would've beaten the shit out of him, but murder never crossed my mind. I just wanted the guy to feel some real pain, considering all the pain he caused."

"You say that…but…"

"But look at how you acted that day," Carpenter finished the thought. "You went to a rich family's property first thing in the morning, scaled their fence and assaulted their son, with no thoughts of the consequences you might suffer. Now, you expect us to believe you would have stopped short of murder?"

John Rainbird leaned forward, fixing his eyes upon Detective Carpenter. "You know what, detective? Maybe I wouldn't have stopped. Maybe I would've beaten that bastard to death or into a coma. I was out of my mind with grief and anger- and he certainly deserved no better. But the fact is -I was stopped. I was stopped and I suffered worse injuries than I gave. Plus, that was going on four years ago. I haven't been near that guy or in any other trouble since. If I had, my record wouldn't have been expunged. Would it have?"

Carpenter smiled, folding his large hands together over the back of the driver's seat. "Hell of an argument. Have you been practicing it?"

John Rainbird scowled. "Practicing? I know you guys aren't trying to suggest that I had anything to do with how Kevin Anderson died."

"Well, you certainly had reason. Unless you expect us to believe that you really forgave and forgot."

"To be quite honest with you, I did not forgive him. And I definitely haven't forgotten. I just realized it wasn't up to me to punish him for his deeds." John

Rainbird turned toward Tremblehorn. "You're familiar with what our people say about balance, brethren?"

Tremblehorn nodded. "The spirits always restore it if the people do not."

"So you think what happened to Kevin Anderson is 'balance'?" Carpenter made air quotes.

John relaxed against the upholstery of the squad car. "Detective, I don't even know what happened to him. I only know that he was found dead because you guys told me. I also know that he was found in Prince George's County because that's where you guys come from. That means that I couldn't possibly have done it, because the closest I've ever been to there is driving past on a charter bus to D.C. during my senior class trip."

The two detectives did not offer an immediate response to John's last statement, regarding each other in silence instead. After a few seconds, Detective Carpenter returned his attention to their interviewee.

"So, you were nowhere near PG County last week?"

"I told you- I've never been there."

"Can you prove that?"

"You can ask my roommate or the professors who taught my fall courses, if necessary. All I did last week was take my exams at UD."

"We'll start with the roommate. You got a contact number?"

John Rainbird fished out his cell phone. "He's back home in North Carolina, but I got his cell phone number saved into my phone." He opened his electronic contacts list and read the number off, knowing that Earl would provide him with a rock solid alibi.

"Is there anything else, detectives?" He said, placing a hand on the closest door latch.

"Not for now," Carpenter said, waving a dismissal. "Don't worry- we'll be in contact if we need you again."

John Rainbird nodded, opened the door and started to exit the vehicle before sitting back down. His eyes scanned the two detectives as he summoned the courage to satisfy his curiosity. "How did Kevin die?"

"You don't know?" Tremblehorn asked.

"How could I know? I told you guys I had nothing to do with it. And even if you think I'm lying, telling me exactly how he died wouldn't make a difference, would it?"

The detectives looked at each other for a few moments before Carpenter nodded at Tremblehorn. "He was found in his dorm room," the half-Maupai detective said. "His lungs were filled with water."

John Rainbird's eyes widened. "You mean…"

"He was drowned," Tremblehorn said. "Kevin Anderson was somehow drowned before being placed on his own bed in his own dorm room."

"Oh, God," John Rainbird groaned. He hoped the detectives credited his reaction to the unfathomable nature of what Tremblehorn told him. In actuality, it was caused by knowing how Kevin had come to be found in that state. Not long after being arrested for trespassing on the Anderson's estate and assaulting Kevin, he'd done everything within his power to create such a vile punishment for the bastard. But, that had been four years past and nothing had come of it. Now that his long abandoned wishes had been fulfilled, he wished it had remained a malicious fantasy.

The nature of Kevin's death confirmed that John had succeeded in calling upon the spirit world. Dread filled him, accompanying the realization that he could not control what he'd unleashed.

Chapter 24 - The Rabbit Hole Deepens

I

"Looks like the kid told the truth," Detective Carpenter said, flipping his cell phone closed. "The roommate backed up his alibi." He shrugged. "I guess it could have been rehearsed."

"I doubt that," Tremblehorn spoke from the passenger seat of the departmental sedan. They were still in the parking lot of the Super 8. "The kid just left here five minutes ago. That's not enough time to rehearse a story. Besides, did he seem like he was lying to you?"

Carpenter shook his head. "If he was, he's the most convincing liar I've seen in 14 years of dealing with the lowest of the low. But if he didn't do it- who did?"

Tremblehorn rested a hand on his chin. "You think maybe the victim's mother was wrong?"

"About what?"

"About the thing with the girl being the only major conflict her son was ever involved in. I think a kid like that- who gets off on humiliating people- has to have done it more than once."

Carpenter clapped his hands. "You're right, partner. An arrogant, spoiled rich kid like that? Of course he got off on embarrassing others. The thing with the girl was probably the only time that 'mommy' couldn't deny what he did. And if he's humiliated others like he humiliated that poor girl..."

"There might be quite a few people out there who had a reason to get back at him."

"Damn straight!" Carpenter pounded on the steering wheel. "Sometimes having you as a partner is alright, Red. I say we head back to PG and start a two-pronged attack, come tomorrow. We'll get the Harford County Police to investigate any bad blood the victim might have had locally. Meanwhile, we try to find out if he was into any darker shit at College Park. His roommate already told us he was a real party guy- so who knows? He could have been into some real seedy shit under that All-American boy façade."

Carpenter shifted the car into reverse and backed out of the parking space. Tremblehorn placed a hand on his partner's right shoulder just after he maneuvered the car into the light Sunday morning traffic. "I have one caveat to your plan."

"What's that?"

"We need to stop off at that awesome diner again before we head back."

Carpenter laughed. "I thought that went without saying."

II

Detective Ballinger felt frustration to the point of despondence. It had been six days since he'd pulled the case of Gregory Rollins. Six days without anything in the neighborhood of a legitimate lead. He replayed the fruitless efforts of his investigation as he drove toward his home precinct.

Emma Saulters was the only person he knew to have a pressing reason for wanting Rollins dead. But the Emma Saulters he interviewed seemed almost Zen like, far too peaceful to have been capable of murder, even of a man who she believed to have molested her young daughter. She seemed to be a strong example of someone reforming herself in prison. Also, her alibi for the time of Rollins's death proved legitimate. Plus, prison built fitness or not, she was still a small boned woman.

Male or female, it would have taken either a behemoth or a group to overpower a grown man and drown him in the Snake River, haul his corpse from the water, drag him back to his apartment, and place him in his bed. Doing all of that without being seen constituted an even neater trick.

Ballinger took small comfort in arriving at a scientific explanation for the orgasm Rollins had at his time of death. He chalked it up to the dying body engaging in an involuntary function, having heard that such release was common in men who were hanged. He wished he had an explanation for the other aspects of the case that seemed to be science fiction, but the orgasm explanation exhausted his faculties in that department

Ballinger questioned several of Rollins's old cronies, none of who had a beef with him or knew anyone who did. They all claimed that Rollins had been as straight up a guy as a small time criminal could be.

Feelings of futility taunted Ballinger as he marched into the precinct. He plopped down at his clutter free desk, reviewing the case file until Captain McCafferty appeared over his shoulder.

"I take it you're still getting nowhere with that case."

Ballinger looked up. "Well, it's not exactly a cakewalk."

"I know it," McCafferty said, nodding his huge head. He had a linebacker's neck and the frame to match it. The fabric of his dress shirt strained to contain the mass of his flesh. One of his bear paws came to rest on Ballinger's shoulder. "Listen, you're not going to work this case by yourself, anymore. I'm giving you Hargrove."

Ballinger spun around in his chair. "Hargrove? Captain, you know I hate being paired up. That means I got to check in with somebody else anytime I wanna make a move. It slows me down- you know?"

McCafferty smirked. "Seems like you couldn't get any slower with this one."

"That newbie won't make it any better. He's only been with major case for four months."

"That's true. But, he's been a cop for four years, which means he made it to this squad in one less year of service than you did."

"Captain, I…"

McCafferty held a hand palm forward. "This is not open to debate, Ballinger. And I'm not going to listen to you bitch about it. After we're done here, you will fill Hargrove in on the particulars of the case."

Ballinger shrugged. "So, we're not done already?"

The captain's barrel chest heaved as he unleashed a belly laugh. "I just have to love you sometimes, Ballinger." He composed himself. "No, we're not done here. But the other thing I'm about to tell you might actually lift your spirits a little." He paused. "I took a call from the Prince George's County police department about twenty minutes ago. You've probably been too busy investigating your own case to hear of it, but a reserve on the University of Maryland basketball team was found dead in his dorm room this weekend. It's been on all the news channels, but as far as the press knows, the kid's cause of death was undetermined. Thing is, that's just a crock of shit. The kid was drowned just like your victim was."

Ballinger's eyes attempted to somersault from their sockets. McCafferty nodded and continued talking. "The victim was in identical condition to yours. The orgasm…the urination. And he was a local kid- Kevin Anderson. Rich kid, was a huge sports star at Mackenzie High. Way better at baseball than basketball. Was expected to be a big time player for Maryland's baseball team come springtime."

"Oh, my God…"

"Not only that, but the water in his lungs was tested, too."

Ballinger rose from his seat, marveling that his throat could feel so dry. "Don't tell me. The water was from Snake River?"

McCafferty shrugged. "Ok, I won't tell you. But, that doesn't make it not true."

Ballinger placed a hand on his forehead. He took a deep breath, collected himself. "Damn, Captain. How deep do you think this rabbit hole goes?"

McCafferty shrugged again. "That's for you, Hargrove, and the PG County detectives you'll be working with to find out."

III

John Rainbird sat at a computer in the Bay Corner library, reading the daily edition of "Gazette. Net." Typing PG County newspaper as a search had brought him to the URL for the online newspaper that covered the top news in Montgomery, Prince George's, and Frederick counties. He surveyed all of the headlines for Prince George's County. His eyes fell on one that read, "Blue Chip Athlete Found Dead in College Park Dorm Room." He clicked on it and read the text.

"On Saturday morning, December 13th, University of Maryland, College Park student Jason Hanson attempted to wake his roommate, Kevin Anderson. While doing so, he discovered that Mr. Anderson was not breathing.

Both Hanson and Anderson were prized freshman baseball prospects for the Maryland Terrapins. Anderson was also a reserve guard on the Terrapin's basketball team. As of press time, the cause of Kevin Anderson's death has not yet been determined.

A full investigation will be conducted by the PG County police department."

The police had lied to the press about knowing the cause of Kevin's death, but John's dream about it had not lied to him. Perhaps the dream about Gregory

Rollins was also true. John fought back his sense of dread to venture to the "Harford County Aegis" website. He scanned the boldface article headings, seeing one that read, "Mysterious Circumstances Surround Man Found Dead in Abingdon Apartment."

The body of the article began underneath the article heading. "Gregory Rollins, age 37, was found dead in his Abingdon apartment on Tuesday afternoon. Police have not yet been able to identify a cause of death."

John clicked on the word "more" after the last word in the text. "To Get the Rest of The Story, Current Subscribers Click Here," greeted him. Underneath that message was a link for new subscribers to sign up.

John Rainbird decided that he didn't need to read the rest of the article. He felt certain that Gregory Rollins and Kevin Anderson had met identical fates. That meant that Rebecca had returned to punish those who had wronged her, just as John Rainbird wished for almost four years ago. Now that the fruits of his hateful labor were manifest, he wished for a way to undo them.

Chapter 25 - Veronica

Veronica Myers couldn't understand why almost four years after the poor girl's death, she couldn't get Rebecca Saulters out of head. Her only reaction at the time had been to say, "Oh, man. That's messed up." She felt a little guilty about having picked on the girl so much, but she didn't come close to feeling responsible for what Rebecca did. It wasn't like she and her friends forced the girl to kill herself.

All they'd done in the time leading up to the suicide was egg Rebecca's house and spray "A Cock Sucking Slut Lives here" on its' sides, in blood red paint. It had all been Pamela Lawson's idea. That's how things always went when sticking it to Rebecca or any of their other targets. Pamela or Shanae Edwards supplied the ideas. Veronica and a loose association of second string flunkies carried them out. Most of the time, it was just Veronica. Rebecca had been their favorite target for years. Going back to fifth grade, she took whatever they dished out without resisting as general practice. She knew that Veronica would kick her ass if she didn't.

Rebecca had to know that being a whipping girl was her rightful place in the world. After all, having a lunatic mom who was all in the news for attempting to stab two people to death was social suicide. Veronica recalled her elation when Robert Bailey went off in Mr. Handley's class, ushering in the age of tormenting Rebecca. Before that, Veronica had always harbored secret jealousy of her smart, pretty, goody two shoes ass. She felt like slapping Rebecca's face every time the girl gave a right answer or drew praise from a teacher.

Before harassing Rebecca became a favorite pastime, girls like Pamela Lawson and Shanae Edwards had very little to do with Veronica. They recruited

Veronica into their circle only after Rebecca's status as whipping girl was set. Veronica felt pleased as pie to back up their verbal cruelty with her intimidating girth.

Rebecca didn't stand up to Pamela until the last few weeks of eighth grade. Veronica remembered the occasion like it was yesterday. They were all in Mr. Niedemeyer's class.

Student seats in Mr. Niedemeyer's classroom were arranged into four spaced rows. Closest to the blackboard, the first row spanned six chairs. The trio of rows descending from it spanned five chairs each. A space of three, maybe four feet separated each seat in a row.

Rebecca sat at the left end of the third row. Pamela Lawson sat to her right. Veronica sat in her usual seat at the left end of the fourth row. Veronica loved to sit in the back in all of her classes. She found that it was easier for teachers to forget about her back there. She hated being called on to answer questions in class. She gave the wrong answer half the time it happened.

Veronica struggled with the last Social Studies test of the year, as she had struggled with most of the ones before it. She rolled her pencil on the desktop, trying to recall enough information to get at least some of the questions right. Her eyes wandered, settling upon Rebecca. She got a good look at the rich chocolate brown hair that rested on Rebecca's shoulders. The Knife Lady's Daughter wore a loose fitting t-shirt and knee length mesh shorts to school. Rebecca had a nice shape by eighth grade, though she didn't wear anything to show it off. Veronica figured that the girl probably wore C-cups now, something that Veronica only matched because she was so overweight. Rebecca had started wearing looser clothes during the course of the school year. Pamela led her clique in responding to that development by spreading rumors that Rebecca was a lesbian. Veronica contributed some choice restroom graffiti as her part of the effort. One stall bore the lovely platitude: "Rebecca Sallters loves knives and pussies ekwilly", scrawled in magic marker.

Half breed bitch, Veronica thought, watching Rebecca take long pauses between writing answers on her test paper.

Veronica knew that Rebecca could have finished the test much faster if she wanted to, but she didn't want to seem like a know it all.

Well, she is a know it all, Veronica thought. *Fucking nerd. She can be as nerdy and pretty as she wants, though. She'll still always be the Knife Lady's Daughter.*

Veronica's eyes left Rebecca to seek out Mr. Niedemeyer. The chubby, balding, bespectacled man busied himself with marking papers. Mr. Niedemeyer was one of those teachers who never seemed to take a moment to relax. He always found something school related to do, even during independent classwork and testing time. Veronica thought about throwing something at Rebecca to take her mind off her own frustration with the test, thinking that Mr. Niedemeyer might not catch her with his head buried in the pile of papers on his desk. She reminded herself that whenever something against the rules occurred in his classroom, he always seemed to know who did it. Even if his blind little eyes weren't looking, he was always able to identify the guilty party. Veronica didn't know how he did it, but just knowing that he could stifled her impulse. She could always take her frustration out on Rebecca later, in the hallway.

Veronica could knock Rebecca's books out of her hands, as Shanae had done a few days earlier. "What are you going to do about it, KND?" Shanae sneered. "Stab me?" Pamela had goaded Shanae into doing what she did, but Veronica didn't need any prompting to do the same. Of course, Rebecca only got red in the face and picked up her books when Shanae challenged her. There was nothing she could do, even though she was taller and thicker than skinny Shanae. Rebecca was smart enough to know that coming back at Shanae would only give Veronica a reason to jump on her. Veronica wished that Rebecca would give her a real reason to kick her pretty, smart ass. Until that day came, knocking her books from her hand would have to satisfy. She could kick them up the hall for good measure.

Veronica returned her attention to her test paper and tried to pull some correct answers from the dark recesses of her inattentive mind. She bore no illusions about escaping summer school courses. That she'd have to trudge through six hot weeks of Summer Math before being allowed to move on to high school was a foregone conclusion. Still, she stood on the border line for passing or failing Social Studies for the year. Passing this last test could make or break her. Most of the questions on the test were multiple choice, so she had at least a guesser's chance.

Veronica had just started to remember information she didn't think she could remember when Pamela yelled. "Leave me a-lonnnne!"

Mr. Niedemeyer perked up right away, dropping the assignment he'd been grading. "What is the matter, Miss Lawson?" He tilted his glasses so that he could peer over them, ambling his squat frame around his desk.

"Knife gi-Rebecca keeps trying to look on my paper!" Pamela continued her performance, her pale skin turned beet red. Muffled giggles and murmured "oohs" floated through the classroom. Veronica didn't have to glance at any of her classmates to know that they had all forgotten about their tests for the time being. They were now set to witness the sort of incident that would be big hallway talk, at least for a day. Veronica hoped that Pamela would perform well enough to cause the Knife Lady's Daughter another crushing embarrassment.

Mr. Niedemeyer didn't buy what Pamela was selling. "Oh, I seriously doubt that, Miss Lawson," he said, speaking in his usual monotone.

His contradiction only added more fire to Pamela's performance. "What are you saying, Mr. Niedemeyer? Are you saying that I'm lying?"

Mr. Niedemeyer cleared his throat. "I'm saying that Rebecca hardly has any need to look to your paper for answers. She has consistently posted the highest grades in this class, all year."

Pamela started to cry then, really turning on the waterworks. "So what!" She sobbed. "That doesn't mean I'm lying, Mr. Niedemeyer. Maybe geek girl forgot to study this time!"

Rebecca sprang from her seat and got in Pamela's face. "Who are you calling 'geek girl'?" she said, glowering. "I'm sick of you calling me everything other than my real name."

"You'd better get out of my friend's face!" Veronica bellowed, popping up like a six foot tall jack in the box. Mr. Niedemeyer turned his attention to her, eyeing her bulky frame with alarm.

"Get to the office, right now, Miss Myers, or I'll call school security." He somehow managed to infuse his monotone with authority.

"Fine." Veronica stormed out, elaborate braids shaking as her ebony hands gesticulated. She paused in the doorway to utter a threat. "But, Knife Girl better watch how she talks to my friends!"

Veronica plotted to kick Rebecca's ass as she waited in Mr. Halloran's office. The principal threatened to suspend her for the rest of the year if she did anything, but she wasn't too worried about that. She just had to get Rebecca off school grounds. She didn't think that Rebecca would tell. She never told about anything else. Rebecca knew her place was to take whatever Veronica dished out. She might have forgotten herself for a few seconds, but a little ass whipping would be a good reminder.

Once Veronica found out what happened in Mr. Niedemeyer's class after she was sent to the office, she decided to give Rebecca more than a "little" ass whipping. Other kids said that Pamela had stopped crying and stared Rebecca down. "You don't like Knife Girl?" she sneered. "How about Knife Lady's Daughter? You're used to that one."

The rest of the students in the class laughed at that. That's what always happened. Pamela and her bunch picked on Rebecca and all the other kids laughed like a pack of hyenas. Rebecca played her part by doing nothing to defend herself.

This time Rebecca surprised everyone by tossing the script away, grabbing Pamela around the neck and wrestling her to the floor. She hissed, "I'm sick of it, you hateful bitch. I'm sick of you fucking with me. I'm sick of all of you!"

Other kids told Veronica that Mr. Niedemeyer looked like he was about to have a heart attack as he broke the fight up. After it was over, Mr. Halloran assigned both Veronica and Pamela to two days of in school suspension. Veronica had to serve hers before Pamela. Mr. Halloran was smart in not wanting them to be together all day.

Separating the two friends couldn't keep Veronica from kicking Rebecca's ass, though. Rebecca was given a one day suspension for fighting. That was the school minimum. Veronica knew that she would have received a much longer suspension if she'd done that. But then she wasn't a known goody two shoes among teachers. Man, she couldn't wait to get her hands on that bitch!

Veronica met up with Pamela and Shanae after school on the first day of her ISS. She walked between them as they all headed home. Tara Andrews walked with Crystal Ritchie behind the three of them. Veronica entertained the other girls with promises of what she would do to Rebecca when she got her hands on her. They were close to a mile from school when Veronica saw Rebecca speeding toward them on her rickety old bike. Veronica took a moment to process that she wasn't dreaming before bellowing, "There you are. You little bitch!"

Veronica exploded toward Rebecca like an angry rhino. The other members of the quintet egged her on, yelling, "Get her! Beat her ass!" Rebecca surprised Veronca by jumping off the bike, allowing the careworn conveyance to clatter to the curb.

As Veronica closed in on her, Rebecca put up her guards in a cursory attempt at defense. She never stood a chance. The first blow from Veronica's big fist struck just under her left ear, knocking her off balance. Rebecca went down, folding herself into a ball while struggling to shield her face.

"Got you now, you dumb little bitch," Veronica growled, kicking at her prone victim. "Touch my fuckin' friend. You should've stayed your freaky fuckin' ass in the house!"

The kicks landed on Rebecca's arms and thighs, causing her to groan in pain. When Veronica drew back her thick leg for another, Rebecca rolled just enough to avoid it. She attempted to recover to a standing position, but Veronica shoved her back down.

The big girl climbed atop her then, her massive weight pressing Rebecca's back into the unforgiving concrete. The other girls laughed and screamed profane taunts as Veronica rained slap after slap upon Rebecca, pressing her weight down even further. Veronica's fisted right hand pistoned through Rebecca's vain attempt to protect her face, loosing a red trickle from Rebecca's left nostril.

The sight of blood satisfied Veronica. "That good enough for you, Pam?" she asked.

Pam giggled. "Yeah. I think the little freak has learned her lesson about touching me."

They were all about to leave when Tara Andrews spoke to Pam in her shrill voice. "I think you should hit the dirty freak a few times yourself." A chorus of meanness followed her suggestion. "Hell, yeah! Hit that bitch! Hit that bitch! Hit 'er!"

Veronica grabbed Rebecca's wrists and pinned her arms to the ground. "Come hit this bitch," she growled, staring at Rebecca with contempt. Tears trickled from Rebecca's eyes as she looked anywhere but at Veronica. Mucus joined the blood that continued to trickle from her nose.

Pamela smiled, looking down at the helpless girl. "No," she said. "Look at how pathetic she is. The little freak is actually crying. Ha-ha! There's snot and everything. Let her up, Ronnie."

Veronica's voice rose in a mixture of surprise and disappointment. "You sure?"

"Yeah," Pamela said, giggling. "We'll let the pathetic little bitch off easy, this time. Besides, you need to get home and wash her filth off you. I hope you don't catch ringworm or something. Come on girls, let's get out of here."

As they walked away, Veronica stopped to hoist Rebecca's bike and toss it into the street.

"Good one," Shanae chortled as they continued on their way. "Remember the time w…remember the time somebody slashed her tires?"

Veronica laughed, thinking that the tire slashing had been fun. She fell in line with the other girls, confident that Rebecca had been beaten back into her proper place and would never try to rise from it again. She stood about a hundred yards away when she turned and saw Rebecca sitting on the sidewalk. Small groups of kids snickered as they passed her, reenacting the beating they witnessed. "Oh and you better not snitch!" Veronica bellowed, her voice carrying down the street. "Snitch and you'll get more of what I just gave you!"

Change came at breakneck speed after Veronica administered that beating. The last few weeks of eighth grade sped by, ending in a graduation ceremony that Veronica was allowed to participate in even though she had to complete summer school courses in Math and Social Studies.

Rebecca looked prettier than any other girl at graduation. Watching her erstwhile whipping girl be flooded by whistles and catcalls from admiring boys as she walked across the stage, Veronica felt that her time for tormenting Rebecca had ended. In spite of her crazed mother and lack of fashionable clothes, the Knife Lady's Daughter was beautiful and smart. You couldn't keep a combination like that down and Rebecca would get a fresh start in high school.

Rebecca was sure to attend a high school for smart kids, like Mackenzie High or Harford Technical. She would have the chance to live down being the Knife Lady's Daughter, something that just couldn't happen at Bay Corner School. It was the only public school in the town, spanning grades K-8. At Bay Corner, kids had pretty much the same classmates year after year. Plus, the school was small. There were only two eighth grade classes during Rebecca and her tormentor's eighth grade year. Each of those classes consisted of twenty-one students. From grades K through 8, there were maybe 300 students total. Such close packed and unchanging conditions were fine for kids who fit in, but they made school a daily hell for outcasts like Rebecca.

Veronica knew that all of that was over when Rebecca walked across the graduation stage, looking like a young princess. Rebecca would go on to bigger and better things soon enough, while Veronica would be stuck right where she was. She figured she'd have to find someone else to pick on at Havre de Grace high school, where she was sure to share classes with the dumbest of the dumb. Veronica felt certain that the beating she had given Rebecca was her last real chance to torment her.

Veronica didn't cross Rebecca's path again until the following fall. By that time, Veronica had been struggling with high school course work for the first month or so of school. She didn't see how she could ever get any better at school work. Even when she tried very hard, she never felt like she was doing well. Worse than her struggles was the fact that her grandmother was having her evaluated for Special Education Services. Being classified as some sort of retard to go along with being a fat giant was just what she needed. Even worse, Pamela and Shanae seemed to have less and less time for her. Unlike at Bay Corner, they did not have the same classes. Plus, Pamela and Shanae were pretty girls; they were conventional. It was only natural that they start to make conventional friends. Knowing that she could never truly fit in with regular girly girls, Veronica sensed that her friendship with the other girls was fading away.

She, Pamela, and Shanae walked together on an infrequent Saturday occasion when they saw Rebecca headed towards the Bay Corner library, accompanied by Kimberly Meisner of all people. Kimberly Meisner hadn't done anything to indicate that she knew Rebecca existed during the previous few years, but they must have become friends at MacKenzie High. Veronica now thought of what followed often, for what followed hastened the end of her friendship with Pamela and Shanae.

Pamela pointed the pair out to the others, saying, "Look, there's KND. Omigod, I think she's with Kimberly Meisner. I never thought I'd see that, but screw it. Let's mess with her for old time's sake."

None of the threesome was prepared for the passion with which Kimberly leapt to Rebecca's defense. They didn't expect her to threaten to sic her father, the Town Councilman, on them if they tried to do anything to Rebecca.

The things Kimberly said about Pamela and Shanae only keeping Veronica around to do their dirty work was the worst part of that confrontation. That spoken truth struck Veronica much harder than the realization that she no longer had a free pass to bully Rebecca. Pamela and Shanae's vehement denials did nothing to dull the harsh sting of truth.

By the time Rebecca's video scandal started, Veronica and the other two girls had drifted apart, talking little outside of shared bus rides to Havre De Grace High. Veronica always felt like a third wheel during those daily encounters. She felt relieved when Shanae and Pamela stopped riding the bus, figuring that Shane's older brother must be taking them to school.

Rather than seeking new friends, Veronica brooded alone.

She took to cigarette smoking and drinking beer whenever she could filch one from her father or convince some adult to buy her some. She had an IEP and her schoolwork had been dumbed down to the point where she could manage it. She considered it to be dummy's work for a dummy.

Veronica leapt at Pamela's plan to spray paint Rebecca's house, more out of boredom than enjoyment. She made peace with the fact that sharing the plan was the most Pamela had talked to her in weeks. She went to the house on Einhurst Road well after nightfall. Pamela and Shanae kept watch, prepared to whistle a warning if anyone stirred while Veronica did the deed.

Veronica imagined Rebecca bursting into tears at the sight of her handiwork. The image of the Knife Lady's Daughter crying didn't bring her as much enjoyment as it used to.

Veronica didn't imagine that Rebecca would do much more than cry, but the girl killed herself soon after that. Once that happened, Veronica and the others stopped talking altogether. Veronica fell in with a group of kids who were way into motorcycle culture.

These guys and girls were all as rough as Veronica. They all loved leather jackets and big black boots. Most of them had at least a few tattoos. Veronica soon dressed like her new friends. Some of the older ones already had their own bikes. They taught her how to ride.

When she was 16, Veronica began working part time in the warehouse of Cute Tykes Toy Company. She knew how it went in Bay Corner. People who were local, had a good work ethic, and were not very smart or talented could always find honest work with Bay Corner's largest employer. You started out part-time in the warehouse and then moved up to full-time on the assembly line, after you proved to be a good worker. Veronica started out that way, hoping to have full- time work when she graduated high school.

As her luck would have it, the national economy bottomed out in the time between her first day of work at Cute Tykes and her high school graduation this past June. People now spent far less money on toys and other recreational items. Because of that, the company instituted a hiring freeze and allowed only their most senior employees to work full time. Veronica did not make that cut.

She planned to have her own apartment by now. Instead, she was stuck in her daddy's shitty old basement. She had enough problems without thinking about some chick dying four years ago. Yet, she couldn't shake her thoughts of Rebecca. It annoyed the hell out of her that she should feel so guilty about the things she'd done to that girl. Shit, she'd only been a kid. Plus, Kevin Anderson had done much worse. He was the one who ruined Rebecca's life.

Veronica broke free from her reverie long enough to hop on her Yamaha and head to the liquor store. Though she was only 18, she'd been buying her own alcohol unquestioned for almost a year now. She knew that her intimidating physical appearance did the trick. She wore her dark hair in an unruly afro. Tattoos adorned her neck and the backs of her hands. She was a little heavier than she'd been in high school and her lips formed a perpetual scowl. One good look at her was enough for a store clerk to decide that ringing her up and sending her on her way was a lot smarter than risking confrontation by asking for ID. She wouldn't start any shit if they denied her, but they didn't need to know that.

More often than not, Veronica joined up with her fellow bikers after she scored some alcohol.

She and the others were a loose association, not a gang, though Veronica didn't mind if some people thought they were. It only added to her intimidation factor. Bitches like Pamela Lawson and Shanae Edwards would turn tail and fly if they saw her now, not that she had the least interest in prissy little bitches like that.

Veronica didn't meet up with her biker buddies on this occasion. Instead, she took a half pint of Jack Daniel's back to her basement room. She blasted Avenged Sevenfold from her stereo as she drank straight from the bottle, loving the way the JD burned on the way down. The head swimming effects of the alcohol teamed with her recent lack of sleep to make her drowsy. Although it was only mid-afternoon and she sat in the one chair she owned as opposed to lying in her bed, her eyes collapsed shut.

Chapter 26- The Proposal

John Rainbird began Tuesday, December 16 by telling his grandfather that he intended to find an apartment with Brittany. He ended that day by doing something he hadn't imagined.

The revelation to his grandfather came just as the morning sun awakened, before the old man set out to do a hauling job. Wise Eyes gazed at John Rainbird from his seat next to him on the couch, remaining silent for a long time. "Will you not marry her?" he asked.

John Rainbird blinked. "What?"

Wise Eyes chuckled and patted his grandson on the shoulder. "Son of my Son, you have much of your father in you, may he walk in beauty. Life at Blessed Earth was too slow for him, not enough luxury. He joined the Anglo's army just so he could be part of their world. He also chose himself a white woman, your mother...."

"Grandfather, I already know all of this."

Wise Eyes frowned. "You interrupt your grandfather? That is not the Maupai way."

John Rainbird looked away. "I apologize, Grandfather. Please forgive me."

Wise Eyes sighed. "I forgive you, Son of my Son. I speak of your parents to tell you that although your father was drawn to the Anglo world as you are, he honored the Maupai ways when it came to his woman. When he came to know she was the one he sought, he did not lower himself by 'shacking up' as so many of the Anglos do. He did what was right by the spirits and made her his wife."

John Rainbird rose to his feet. "Grandfather- I'm only eighteen years old. Surely you can't expect me to get married."

Wise Eyes joined John Rainbird in standing. He poked a gnarled index finger into his grandson's chest. "So, you are not too young to lay with a young woman each night? But, you are too young to marry her? Your father was just a bit older than you are now when he married. It is the Maupai way to marry young. Perhaps you don't love this girl as much as you profess, or are you waiting to see if someone better comes along? Are you choosing not to buy the cow because you can get the milk for free, as the Anglos say?"

Those words struck a resonant chord within the young tribesman. He sat down on the couch and thought long and hard after Wise Eyes left. He considered the pros and cons of the thing, pouring over them again and again. Brittany had made no secret about wanting to marry him someday. He reckoned that living with a girlfriend was a lot like being married already. Waking up and sleeping in the same bed every day required a serious commitment. He didn't think he could love any other girl like he loved Brittany. Brittany was as unanchored to Bay Corner as he was. When he graduated from college, she would follow him anywhere in the world to start fresh, regarding wherever they went as setting out on a grand adventure.

Another pro was the fact that due to his savings, they wouldn't have to start out dirt poor.

The only possible negative John Rainbird could think of was that they were so young. He decided to view their youth as a blessing. There were people who went through their entire lives without finding someone to love as he loved Brittany. His lips parted into a Jack-O Lantern grin as he decided that Wise Eyes was right. He and Brittany should marry.

He wolfed down some dried venison before washing himself in the freezing facsimile of a shower. He dressed himself and zipped off on his Vespa, headed for the Harford Mall. His excitement kept him from considering that the mall didn't open until 10 am. He paced outside for more than twenty minutes before the doors opened and he rushed to Kay Jewelers, on a mission to pick out an engagement ring.

He told the cute salesgirl that his spending limit was $2,000. After perusing a few rings within his price rage, he settled on what he thought was a nice one. The 14 karat gold band was shaped to approximate the silhouette of a bird in flight. The 1 carat marquis cut center diamond was offset by rows of tiny diamond accents on each side. The salesgirl's smile radiated as she went on about how beautiful the ring was. John Rainbird paid for it with his bank card, knowing that Brittany would love it.

He dropped in on Brittany during her lunch break at the Bay Corner Diner. They sat together in a corner booth. "Fries and a salad?" he pointed to the plate in front of her. "That's halfway to a nutritious meal."

Brittany rolled her eyes. "Oh, God. I hope you're not going to try to tell me how to eat once we move in together. Even my father doesn't do that."

John Rainbird smiled. "I do lots of things your father wouldn't do."

Brittany giggled. "That is so sick, John."

"I can't help it. Even in your waitress uniform, you fill me with bad thoughts." He reached across the table and placed his hands over hers. "But seriously, I have something to tell you later."

Brittany raised her eyebrows. "Why can't you tell me now?"

John Rainbird looked around. "It's private. Very, very private."

Brittany pulled her hands back. "Jesus, John. You really make me sick sometimes. You don't do that to a person! Now, I'm going to spend all day wondering what it is."

"Good." John grinned. "That'll help your day go faster."

That evening, Brittany let him in through the outside door that led to her parents' basement, just like usual.

"So, did your day fly by?" he asked.

"Ha-ha. Very funny." She pinched his arm.

"Ouch." John Rainbird rubbed the offended spot. "What's your problem?"

Brittany scowled. "You'll get more of that if you don't spill it."

"Alright," he said. "Alright. You know how we're going to find an apartment together?"

"What of it?"

"Well, I've been thinking." He stood from the sofa and reached for the winter jacket he'd hung over a chair. "I know we're young and all, but if we're ready to make that commitment…" He pulled a gold gift bag emblazoned with "Kay" from one of the deep jacket pockets. "…There's no commitment we can't make to each other."

Brittany slumped against the sofa as he reached inside the bag and handed a gold wrapped box, decorated with a shiny gold bow, to her.

"Omigod," she whimpered, nearly dropping the box with her right hand as she pressed her left hand against her chest. "Oh, God. This can't be what I think it is."

John smiled, standing in front of her. "Open it."

Her hands trembled as she did so. John dropped to one knee as her eyes fell to the ring. "Will you marry me, Brittany?"

Tears filled Brittany's eyes as she reached out and helped him to his feet.

"Of course I will," she said. "There's nothing I want more."

Brittany convinced John to pay for a hotel to celebrate the life changing occasion. "Just this once," she pleaded. "I want to be unrestrained to celebrate this. I don't want to have to worry about trying to keep quiet on account of my parents."

Unrestrained was what Brittany proved to be. John felt dead tired when they finished ravaging each other. The unmistakable scent of sex permeated the hotel room. One of Brittany's arms reached across him, resting on his left shoulder. Her head lay on his chest.

Thoughts of the deaths of Gregory Rollins and Kevin Anderson kept John Rainbird from sharing sound sleep with his fiancé. He couldn't think of any explanation for what happened to them, other than Rebecca's spirit returning to take vengeance on them. He'd seen them die in his dreams and those PG County detectives confirmed that Kevin's cause of death was just what he imagined. No, imagine wasn't the right word for it. He foresaw it.

His past actions had caused it. The horror of that knowledge paled in comparison to his certainty that others would fall to the creature he had summoned.

Although John Rainbird held Kevin Anderson responsible for ruining Rebecca's life, he bore his own burden for not saving her. She all but confessed her intentions to him, but he failed to decipher the message.

Chapter 27- John and Rebecca

I

John Rainbird viewed Rebecca contacting him of her own volition with optimism, thinking that she might be feeling a little less depressed. They rode in silence until they reached their familiar destination, placing their bikes within a grove of trees that overlooked the bank of Snake River.

"I'm glad you finally called me," he said, staring into Rebecca's brilliant brown eyes. "Saved me from having to drag you outside again."

She shrugged. "I figured I'd make it easy for you, since you obviously aren't going to leave me alone."

John Rainbird called her and/or visited her daily, determined to help her bear the cruel burden of her pariah status. Rebecca's grandmother now entrusted him with convincing her to eat, a task he undertook with varying levels of success.

"I can't leave you alone," John Rainbird said, chuckling. "You were my friend when I had no friends."

Rebecca turned from him and walked toward a cluster of sitting rocks that rested at the northern end of the grove. She sat down on the one in the center, patting a spot next to her. John Rainbird settled onto it. Rebecca rested her head on his left shoulder and reached her opposite arm across his waist. Her body radiated enticing heat, along with a pleasant fragrance. Even her hair smelled good. John Rainbird noticed that it looked more lustrous than it had in some time. Butterflies beat their wings in his stomach. The valves of his heart began to churn faster.

"You were my friend when I had no friends, too. And you're still my friend, now that I'm a laughing stock again."

"You'll never be a laughing stock to me, Rebecca."

"Aww." She straightened up to smack his cheek with her moist, luscious lips. "You're such a great guy, John Rainbird. Brittany's lucky to have you."

John Rainbird sighed. "Speaking of Brittany," he said, "she asked about you the other day."

"Really?" Rebecca's eyebrows shot toward the late afternoon sky before returning to their natural habitat. "What did she say?"

"She wanted to know why you never come to hang out with us anymore."

Rebecca snickered. "Yeah, right. Like that worked out the last time we tried it."

The Saturday Rebecca referred to began in a pleasant fashion. John Rainbird had ridden his bike over to Rebecca's house, hoping to meet her grandmother's approval.

Rebecca warned him that Grandma Rose was sure to give him a thorough grilling, especially in light of the Kevin Anderson debacle. She couldn't have been more right.

Once John Rainbird passed Grandma Rose's interrogation, he led Rebecca on a bike ride to Havre de Grace. They met Brittany, Ozzie, and Rooster there. John introduced Rebecca to the others before they all rode off to the Havre de Grace Marina together. The outing went well, until Brittany and company made the mistake of complaining about how much Havre de Grace High sucked.

Rebecca flipped out, screaming, "At least you guys can go to school! Maybe you should appreciate that, instead of complaining so fucking much! You could be like me!"

She climbed on her bike and sprinted away. John left his other friends to check on her. She calmed down when he caught up to her, apologizing about ruining the gathering as he escorted her home.

"I told you, they don't care about that kind of stuff," John Rainbird said. "They don't blame you for flipping out after what you've been through."

Rebecca trailed a gentle hand down John's cheek. "I bet Brittany would blame me for wanting you for myself."

John's eyes widened as the valves of his heart once more picked up the pace. "Rebecca, I…"

"Don't worry," she giggled. Her eyes performed an impossible dance of mischief and sadness. "I'm not going to try to suck your dick again." She returned to her previous position of head resting upon his left shoulder, opposite arm across his waist. John's heart beat triple time as his crotch began to stir. "Remember that?"

"Of course I do."

"I'm glad I didn't scare you off for good with that. Remember when we first met?"

John wrapped his left arm around her shoulder, pulling her body against his. "How could I forget?"

II

John Rainbird first saw Rebecca as he rode along the Nissum Trail on a hot June day. She sat astride the only bike he'd ever seen that was as ancient and creaky as his, about a hundred yards ahead of him.

The tired wheels of his conveyance sang a song of protest as he increased his speed, closing the distance between them. She slowed her own pace and eased to her left, allowing him to pull alongside her.

"Hello," he said.

"Hi," she said in a flat tone, inspecting him with wary eyes.

She beheld thick, jet black hair amassed into a single long braid, sharp, dark eyes, and an aquiline nose that looked like the beak of a large bird. He had high cheekbones, thin lips, and almost pale skin offset by a reddish sheen. He wore cheap, raggedy clothes and was far from the cleanest boy in the world.

When John Rainbird looked at Rebecca, he saw a pretty face and a road map of supple curves that promised to expand in the future. She had skin the color of sandpaper, skin that was flawless save for the fresh bruises sprouting on its surface. Rich, voluminous brown hair was tied into a ponytail. Her clothes and shoes were as generic as his, no doubt bought from K-Mart or Wal-Mart. At least her cheap clothes seemed to be new, unlike his tattered gear. Wondering how she had gotten the bruises, he probed, "It looks like you had some trouble."

"What's it to you?" she said, sneering at him.

"Just don't like to see anyone hurt, that's all."

She sighed. "I'm sorry. I have no reason to be mean to you."

"It's okay." John Rainbird risked a grin. "I guess I wouldn't be in such a friendly mood if I was in your condition either."

She laughed, the sound as full and pretty as her face. "I need a rest," she said, slowing her peddling to a crawl. "Mind if we stop for a minute?"

John shook his head. "No. I don't mind at all."

They laid their bikes alongside the trail, hunkering down on a huge rock that sat at the edge of the woods that the Nissum stretched past.

"What's your name?" She asked. No sooner had she done so than a trickle of blood escaped her nostril. Mortification consumed her face as she clapped a hand over it. "Oh, God. I look completely disgusting, don't I? What a way to look when meeting someone."

"My name is John." He pulled a cloth from the pocket of his beat up jeans. "And there's no need to be embarrassed by what someone else has done to you."

She took the cloth and blew into it, unleashing a tiny stream of blood. She blew into it again. No more blood came.

She looked her new acquaintance over. "I guess you're right. Hey...I don't mean any offense... but John, that's not a Maupai name. Is it? Aren't you one of them?"

John banged his fist against his knee in mock anger. "Damn it! I've got to get a better disguise." A cheesy grin decorated his face.

She giggled. "You're funny."

"I try to be."

"So, about that name?"

"Yes, you are correct. John is an 'Anglo' name, as my grandfather would say. My father gave it to me because he didn't want me limited by a traditional name. My second name is traditional though. Rainbird. John Rainbird Jeffries. That's me."

John Rainbird's new friend smiled and ran her hands through her hair. "I like 'Rainbird'. That's very pretty."

John's face flushed a deep crimson. "Thank you."

"I'm Rebecca." The girl extended a dainty right hand.

John gave it a quick shake. "Nice to meet you, Rebecca."

"Nice to meet you, too." She fidgeted with her hair again. "How old are you?"

"13."

"I'm 13, too. Are you in the eighth grade?"

A sad expression came over John's face as he nodded.

"Well-how come…"

"You've never seen me at Bay Corner School?" he finished her question. "My grandfather wouldn't allow me to go. I've been home schooled for the past four years."

Rebecca's eyes widened. "Home schooling? That must be weird."

John frowned. "Home schooling sucks. My parents would never have made me do that." He paused, his Adam's apple bobbing as he swallowed hard. "But, now there's only my grandfather to take care of me. Crazy old guy tries to make my whole life be about Blessed Earth. That's the name of the commune we all live on. My grandfather doesn't want to admit that the traditional Native American way of life was lost long ago. I pray that he'll someday wake up to the reality of the twenty-first century, but he hasn't yet."

Rebecca nodded. "So, you live out by the Bay-right?"

John Rainbird nodded.

"I don't get home schooling. I mean – are you smart and all?"

John Rainbird chuckled. "I'm very smart. I have a 138 I.Q. I could do very well in regular school if my grandfather would let me go."

"You seem like a nice kid," Rebecca said, smiling. "If you had a chance to go to regular school- you and I might have been friends already. I don't really have any friends."

John Rainbird smiled. "Well, there's no reason we can't be friends now, even if I don't go to your school. Besides, my grandfather promised to allow me to attend a public high school. I swore that if he didn't let me, I'd run away. He looked into my eyes and saw that I meant it. He always says that the eyes are the guardians of a person's soul. As such, they hold a person's essence and my essence told him that I had every intention of doing as I said."

Rebecca giggled. "The eyes are the guardians of a person's soul? Your grandfather talks that way?"

"All the time."

"I don't mean to sound stereotypical- but is your grandfather like a- a shaman?"

John Rainbird stood from the rock, doubling over in laughter. "Maybe in his own mind." He sat back down. "So what about you, Rebecca? Are you 'smart and all'?"

Rebecca laughed her full laugh again. "When it comes to books, I'm plenty smart. I can't figure any way not to be a social outcast, though, hence this afternoon's beating. Man, I really hope I get a scholarship to Mackenzie High so I won't have to deal with this crap in high school."

"You're trying to get one of those, too? I really hope I get one."

Rebecca's eyes widened. "You're trying to get one, too? I hope…" She clapped her hands. "I hope we both get one!"

John Rainbird smiled. "That would be real nice." They sat there for a few moments, aiming cheesy grins at each other.

Rebecca glanced at the tattered Mickey Mouse watch on her wrist. "It was nice talking with you, John Rainbird."

John Rainbird nodded. "But, you have to get home."

"Yup. I'll see you around."

"Okay." John Rainbird's eyes dropped to the ground. "Do you really want to? See me around- I mean."

"Yes," Rebecca said, birthing a shy smile. "I hope we can be friends."

"I hope so, too," John Rainbird said. "I'd give you my phone number if we had one, but we don't even have electricity at Blessed Earth. But I bike this trail lots of afternoons."

"I hardly ever ride this way," Rebecca said, not seeming the least bit surprised about the electricity revelation. "I'm more into riding along Snake River."

"Not me. My people have too many spooky tales about that river for me to hang out there. I steer far clear of that place."

"Well, maybe you'll feel better about riding out there if you're with a friend."

"Maybe." John winked. "I'll ride with you until you get off the trail. Okay, Rebecca?"

She blushed, winking back at him. "I'd like that, John Rainbird."

"This is where I get off," she said, climbing off her bike once they reached the part of the trail that branched off into the woods beyond her neighborhood. She took a step toward the slope that functioned as the Nissum Trail equivalent of a highway exit. "I'll be seeing you, John Rainbird," she said, turning to treat her new acquaintance to a beaming smile.

"I'll see you, Rebecca." The brightness of his smile matched hers. He took off on his bike, continuing down the trail.

Though he was attracted to Rebecca in a way he couldn't yet put into words, John Rainbird was about as innocent and sheltered as a 13 year old could be in the 21st century. He thought that she was pretty, but he had no basis for thinking of Rebecca in an outright sexual fashion. When they next crossed paths, she showed him that his innocence far surpassed hers.

III

Rebecca found John peddling along the Nissum Trail almost a week after their first encounter.

"Hello, again, John Rainbird," she said, smiling as she sped up to pull even with him. Now that her bruises had faded, she seemed even prettier than when he first saw her. Her clothes and conveyance, however, still rivaled the meager condition of his.

"Hello, Rebecca," John said, returning her smile as he slowed just a hair. "Fancy meeting you here."

"Not really." Her beige face flushed pink. "I came here looking for you."

"You did?" John Rainbird's voice cracked in surprise.

"Yup."

"Well, it took you long enough."

John followed suit when Rebecca braked and climbed off her bike. They walked their bikes along the trail.

"I've been keeping a low profile." She pointed to her fading bruises before returning both hands to the bike. "Figured it would be best to stay to myself for a while."

A troubled look emerged on John's face. "Hey- you never told me about that."

Rebecca waved a dismissive hand. "It's no big deal. Let's just say you haven't missed a whole lot by being home schooled the past couple of years."

"I think I have," John said. "Remember, I've only been home schooled since my grandfather got custody of me. After my parents were killed."

Rebecca fell silent, bit her lip and looked away. "Sorry to bring up bad memories."

"No biggie." John placed a reassuring hand on her shoulder. "I can handle talking about them now. I don't even mind telling you how they died."

They came to the rock they sat upon during their first meeting. John laid his bike at the edge of the road and settled in. "Come sit with me." He patted the rock's surface next to him. "I'll tell you all about it."

A mortified expression dawned on Rebecca's face. "Umm, no offense- John Rainbird- but I don't know if that's such a good conversation to have."

"Sure it is!" a sing-song lilt colored his voice. "If we're going to be friends, we need to know important stuff about each other. And you wouldn't have come looking for me if you didn't want to be my friend. Now, come on."

"Okay," she muttered, laying her bike next to his and settling down. John Rainbird cleared his throat and began his tale.

It began with his father, Robert Lightfoot Jeffries. Robert was christened Light of Foot by his father, but he took an Anglo name upon reaching legal age. Like his son after him, young Robert found the ways of Blessed Earth antiquated, impractical, and far too limiting to produce fulfillment. He wanted to experience modernity and the world at large, joining the army just to get away. He surprised himself by becoming a great soldier, feeling more at home in the military than he ever felt at Blessed Earth. He met John Rainbird's mother at a bar in Havre de Grace while home on a furlough.

She was a leggy, flirty blonde with striking blue eyes. He bought her a drink, learning that her name was Jessica. She told him she never had the pleasure of meeting a real live Indian before. He told her that he never had the pleasure of setting eyes on a woman so beautiful.

They were married eight months after they met. The new bride birthed John Rainbird four months after the wedding.

Robert ascended the military ranks as his family life bloomed, becoming a field lieutenant in time for the first invasion of Iraq. His son was less than eighteen months old when he led troops in Desert Storm. While he was off protecting national interests, Jessica cared for the boy in their army provided home at the Aberdeen Proving Ground.

Robert's wanderlust stayed with him long after his combat duty obligations ended. He became an Army Recruiter at his beautiful wife's urging, but he never felt content to sit still and do it in one place.

He worked out of military installations in New Jersey, Virginia, and South Carolina. Tragedy struck in South Carolina, when John was only eight years old.

Robert drove south on I-95, on a balmy Friday evening, headed to Hilton Head Beach for some much needed rest and relaxation. He, his wife and their young son road tripped, eating up the highway without a care in the world. The pleasant occasion became a nightmare when a large sedan appeared, hurtling toward them.

Robert swerved just enough to avoid a head on collision at 70 miles per hour. Still, the other car broadsided his vehicle with pulverizing force. John Rainbird later learned that the other driver had been so drunk that he drove through a gap in the median barrier that divided northbound and southbound traffic.

Neither of John Rainbird's parents survived the wreck, though he was pulled unscathed from the wreckage. People said his survival was a miracle. John Rainbird thought the miracle wasn't big enough, considering that he lost his parents.

After that, Wise Eyes became John Rainbird's guardian. The young Indian went from army schools and a ton of travel to the stagnant life of Blessed Earth. Life at Blessed Earth meant being home schooled and no new friends outside of the Maupai. Life at Blessed Earth also meant living like a primitive, never having a proper shower, and boredom, boredom, boredom.

"I haven't had any real friends since I started living at Blessed Earth," he told Rebecca. "I can't bother with the other Maupai kids. They all think they're extras for a remake of Dances with Wolves or something."

He patted her knee. "When I saw you - all bruised and peddling a beat up bike like mine, wearing dumpy clothes like mine, I said to myself 'John Rainbird Jeffries, she's a kindred spirit if you ever saw one."

Rebecca smiled and arched an eyebrow.

"Ha-ha!" John Rainbird laughed. "Kindred spirit. Maybe some of Grandpa's Old Indian mumbo jumbo has seeped into my head." He shrugged. "Mumbo jumbo or not, I can't think of a better phrase to describe what I thought about you."

Rebecca nodded. "Yeah, we definitely have some things in common."

"So, what's your story? How come kids want to beat you up?"

Rebecca hesitated before answering. "You ever hear of that lady who went crazy a few years ago? Showed up at her ex-boyfriend's place and stabbed him and his girlfriend. Almost killed the girlfriend?"

"Yeah. My grandfather talked about it some. Said it was another case of an Anglo's corrupt soul becoming fertile ground for evil spirits."

Rebecca giggled. "Your grandfather sure does talk funny!"

John Rainbird laughed. "The sad thing is he doesn't even know how funny it is."

Rebecca sighed. "That crazy lady is my mother."

John Rainbird said nothing, taking care to keep his face impassive.

"That's why other kids pick on me. They call me the Knife Lady's Daughter and Knife Girl. Having been stuck at the same school with them all these years, I never get a chance to live it down."

"Well, I'm not other kids," John Rainbird said. "I don't care about what your mother did. I think you're a really nice girl."

Rebecca blushed. "Thank you. You want to hear any more about my mother?"

"Sure, if you want to talk about it. You listened to my tale of woe."

"Thanks. Well, while my mother was on trial, some doctors diagnosed her. They said she was bipolar. Said that her illness had never been diagnosed and treated- that the attack was the result of a manic episode. Because of that, the judge gave her a lighter sentence and ordered that she receive proper medical care while she was locked up. I just found out that she's getting out early for good behavior in a couple of weeks."

John Rainbird's eyes widened. "Is she coming to live with you?"

"She has to stay at a halfway house first. After that, I don't know."

Rebecca sprang to her feet, holding her hands out to her new friend. He hesitated before standing to take them in his.

"I just can't wait to visit her!" She released his hands and hugged him, resting her chin on his shoulder. He responded with a two handed pat on the back.

She stepped back, a bemused glint in her eyes. "You act like you've never hugged a girl before."

"Whatever," he grumbled.

Rebecca walked away from him and gathered her bike. "When do you have to be home?"

"Not for two hours yet."

"Good! Let's pedal out to Snake River."

"I told you," John Rainbird protested, "I don't ride out there."

Rebecca rolled her eyes and taunted him with a smile. "I know you're not going to let a girl be braver than you? Come on. It'll be fun."

John sighed as he stared at her. "Ok, I'll go," he said. "It's awfully far, though."

"It's not even two miles away." Rebecca swung her bike around so that it faced the direction of their destination. "See if you can keep up." She sped off, her coltish legs moving the bike with precision.

They sped to the head of the Nissum Trail before heading west and passing through a tree lined residential area that preceded the path that led to the river. They ended at a span of trees that overlooked the river, climbing off their bikes and walking down to the rocky shore.

"It's beautiful, isn't it?" Rebecca said, looking down at the winding body of water.

John Rainbird nodded. "Look at how it undulates. It really is like a snake."

Rebecca laughed and punched his arm. "Undulates? You really do have a high I.Q, don't you?"

"Whatever. You probably use fancier words than that, Miss Mackenzie scholarship candidate."

"Whatever. You're a candidate, too."

John Rainbird laughed. "More Indian mumbo jumbo," he muttered.

"What?"

"It's just that sometimes I think all the stories my grandfather tells affect me more than I realize. I was just thinking that this river was alive."

"Oh, but it is," Rebecca said. "You should know that. There's a lot of life in this water. All kinds of fish and turtles. Maybe you ought to listen to your Granddad sometimes."

John shook his head. "He isn't talking about wildlife when he says it. He means alive like full of spirits."

"Spirits?"

"Yes." John Rainbird's eyes explored the great aquatic serpent. He saw a blue heron swoop down upriver. "Look at that," he said, pointing at it.

"That is so cool." Rebecca grabbed her new friend around the shoulders and squeezed. John Rainbird felt his face flush scarlet. "Blue herons are so cool. So what were you saying about spirits?"

"Let's sit down here for a second," John Rainbird said. "I have another story to tell you."

They sat, letting their feet dangle off the edge of the riverbank.

"Are you going to tell me stories all the time? Is that like an Indian thing?"

John smirked. "Well, I can keep it to myself, if you prefer."

"I was just kidding." Rebecca pressed her hands together as if in prayer. "Please regale me with your tale, dear Bard."

John chuckled. "Regale?"

"That's right."

"What a pair of nerds we are. Anyway- the reason why I didn't want to come here, silly as it may sound- is because of an old Maupai legend."

A huge smile illuminated Rebecca's face as she clapped her hands. "Ooooh, a legend. Please tell me all about it."

John Rainbird cocked his head to the right. "I hope you're not being a smart ass."

Rebecca sighed. "I wouldn't be a smart ass about that, John Rainbird. Now, tell me."

Chapter 28 - The Legend of Charging Bear

I

Long before Christopher Columbus's errant navigation opened the flood gates of European conquest, The Maupai numbered in the thousands along what is now Harford County. The chief of the Maupai at that time was known as Charging Bear. As his name implied, Charging Bear was a man of great physical strength and agility.

His younger brother, Quiet Eyes could not match his fierce physicality. But Quiet Eyes did possess more cunning than perhaps any Maupai ever born.

Quiet Eyes burned to become chieftain, but their father granted the honor to his older brother before dying of the yellow sickness. For eight years, Quiet Eyes stewed in silence while Charging Bear led the tribe as he saw fit. He led them through war and conflict with other tribes, through feast and famine. Quiet Eyes's jealousy plotted with his certainty that he could do better, poisoning his soul.

Quiet Eyes decided to kill Charging Bear, just as sure as Cain decided to kill Abel. Once he made the decision he bided his time, waiting for an opportunity to present itself. That time came during a wild boar hunt, during which the best hunters of the tribe always split into pairs. Charging Bear and Quiet Eyes partnered on this occasion.

Charging Bear felt delighted to hunt alongside Quiet Eyes. He hadn't the slightest suspicion that his brother hated him. This was because Quiet Eyes never showed his true feelings, always pretending to be content with his life and station within the tribe.

Hearing the boar snorting in the brush, Charging Bear smiled and whispered, "I shall flush him out, brother. Then you shall have the pleasure of placing an arrow in his hide." He clapped Quiet Eyes on the shoulder. "Aim true, brother."

"I shall not miss," Quiet Eyes replied.

He was true to his word. His arrow pierced Charging Bear's back, the iron head tearing through his heart. The great chief fell dead without a single gasp. Quiet Eyes dissolved into hysterics, tugging at the arrow that protruded from his fallen brother's blood splattered wound.

"My brother," he wailed. "My brother. Forgive me, Great Spirits. I have killed my brother!"

Quiet Eyes then collapsed into a catatonic state. Several members of the hunting party carried him back to the village, while others carried their dead chieftain.

Quiet Eyes remained in a severe depression for many moons after that. It was not an act, for now that he had murdered his brother, he loved him as he had not before. He ate only a tiny amount of food and spent most days lying about his hut. His appearance grew haggard and his strong body wasted away.

The care of his tribesmen and the passage of much time brought Quiet Eyes back to health. He faced judgment before The Council of Elders a short time after he was determined to be of sound mind and body. They absolved him of responsibility for his brother's death. The misfortune had been ordained by the spirits. After all, it was not the first time that a Maupai warrior had fallen during a hunt.

Within a year, Quiet Eyes seemed as sharp of mind as he had always been. He also regained much of his lost weight. Although his spirit remained full of sorrow for what became of his brother, The Council of Elders decided that he should become the new chieftain. At first he refused, but their persistent urging convinced him that it was now his duty to lead the tribe. So it was that Quiet Eyes achieved his deepest desire.

One member of The Council did not believe that Quiet Eyes was as he appeared to be. Cloud Walker was the tribe's shaman, or medicine man. As such, he was thought to know the way of the spirits better than any other Maupai.

Cloud Walker never revealed that he knew people at least as well as he did spirits. The shaman had always been aware of Quiet Eyes's ambitious and cunning nature. He felt no doubt that the man had murdered his own brother. In his eyes, Quiet Eyes's illness and contrition had been one magnificent and vile extended performance. Cloud Walker didn't share his belief with anyone, having the foresight to know that the other elders would make Quiet Eyes chief with or without his consent. If he had dissented, Quiet Eyes would have seen him as a threat and disposed of him.

Cloud Walker knew of a way to insure that Quiet Eyes was punished for his murder and deception that would not require direct confrontation. "It is time to discover if the old legends are true," he muttered to himself. In the dead of a cold autumn night, he dug Charging Bear's body out of its place in the sacred Maupai burial ground. He draped the reeking carcass across his horse and rode out to the edge of Snake River.

There he performed a ghastly ceremony, praying that the spirits of the river give Charging Bear new life, just long enough to avenge his own murder. He tore away the coins pasted to Charging Bear's eyes so that the fallen chieftain could enjoy the long sleep. He removed the tufts of fur that were embedded in Charging Bear's ears so that he could hear no evil. He promised the river spirits that they could take him five years earlier, if they punished Quiet Eyes. He cut himself and dripped blood into the great man's corpse. Then, he pushed what remained of his fallen leader into the river.

II

"Nothing happened for three years after that," John said, watching the rapt expression on Rebecca's face. "Cloud Walker began to believe that maybe Quiet Eyes hadn't intentionally murdered his brother, since the spirits had not yet punished him. He began to worry that the spirits would punish him for needlessly desecrating the grave of a great chieftain."

"Then one autumn night, a terrible commotion came from Quiet Eyes's lodging. There was much screaming and rushing about. The screaming was Quiet Eyes's wife, crying to the ancestral spirits for mercy. Quiet Eyes lay dead in his tent, with no eyes and no tongue. Also, someone, or something, had snatched his heart from his chest."

Rebecca gasped.

"Quiet Eyes's wife lay bed ridden and mute in her terror for days afterward. When she was able to speak again, she swore that he had been slaughtered by his brother, returned from the dead- returned from Snake River." John Rainbird sighed before smiling sheepishly. "I don't like coming here because of that story."

"I can see why," Rebecca said, pulling him closer and resting her head on his shoulder. "You don't believe it, do you?"

He shook his head. "I guess not. It's still spooky just to think about, though."

Rebecca swung her feet back onto solid ground and walked toward the grove of trees where their bikes waited.

"Where are you going?" John asked.

She winked, crooking a finger at him. "Come here."

As they stood among the trees, she cupped her arms around his neck as if they were slow dancing at a prom. She brought her face close to his.

John blushed. His hands froze at his sides, not quite knowing what to do.

"Have you ever kissed anyone before, John?"

"N-no," he stammered. "Have you?"

A sad look emerged on Rebecca's face. It disappeared a moment later, replaced by a warm smile. "Yes. But, I never kissed you. And I want to."

"Okay," was all that John Rainbird could manage. He stood paralyzed until her lips touched his. They felt soft and warm as they applied cautious pressure.

John Rainbird remained paralyzed for a few more beats before reciprocating. Rebecca's lips parted then. His lips followed. Her tongue slid into his mouth, engaging in polite exploration.

John Rainbird returned the favor. Rebecca pressed her body tight against his. A tremendous stiffening sprouted within his jean shorts and pressed against her leg. He threw his arms around her. Her breasts crushed against him as her lips and tongue abandoned all caution and modesty, working at a blitzkrieg pace.

Breathing quickened and face flushed scarlet, Rebecca pulled away.

She stared into his eyes. "I really like you, John Rainbird."

She reached for his shorts and unzipped them, crouching to the brittle ground.

"Wh-what are you doing?" he asked, pushing her hands away.

"You don't want me to?" Rebecca stood in shock. "I thought all guys liked to."

"No, I would not like that!" John Rainbird seethed. "I would not like that at all!"

Rebecca's jaw fled from the rest of her face. Her head bowed to give it some company. She began crying, huge teething baby's tears. "Oh, God, John," she said, burying her face in her hands. "I'm so sorry. I feel so fucking stupid. I just wanted to do something you'd like. I just wanted to treat you nice because you're my friend."

John Rainbird hugged her hard, almost lifting her from the ground. "You don't have to do that to be my friend, Rebecca. That's just like- I don't know what to think of that." He let go, standing back to take a good look at her. "I think I'd better go."

"Wait," she pleaded, her voice anguished.

John Rainbird shook his head as he climbed onto his bike. "I'll see you around, Rebecca."

Chapter 29- Losing Rebecca

I

Although Rebecca often hugged John Rainbird or pecked him on the cheek as their friendship blossomed, she made no more attempts to seduce him.

Her behavior remained modest when they reunited in the wake of Kevin Anderson scandalizing her.

John Rainbird supported and encouraged her as much as he could during that black time, but the constant humiliation and alienation kept her in a state of despair. Rebecca's mood reached her darkest just before Christmas.

On Friday morning, December 22, Rebecca called John Rainbird on his cell phone, cajoling him to come to her house. John Rainbird didn't have school because it was the first day of Christmas break. He rushed through the chores his grandfather left him, then hopped on his bike and peddled over.

Although that day was a work day, John Rainbird felt surprised by Grandma Rose's absence. He hadn't expected Rebecca to invite him over without adult supervision.

After Rebecca assured him that it was okay to come in, they sat and watched cartoons on the living room couch. She scooted close to him, resting her head on his shoulder. He wasn't sure what fragrance she wore, but it sure smelled good.

"You really are the only true friend I've ever had," she said. "Kimberly and Phyllis dropped me like a bad habit once I got kicked out of school. I guess they can't bare to be associated with anyone outside of Mackenzie High."

"Screw those bitches," John Rainbird said. "You didn't need them anyway."

"I n-eeeed a new life," Rebecca said, following her words with a sigh. "But, I'll never have it."

John Rainbird leaned his head against hers. "Rebecca, don't talk that way."

"Why not? It's the truth. My life is completely ruined. You have to know that. What's worse is that my mother is having a harder time getting readjusted now."

She told John Rainbird about how her grandmother forced her to come clean with her mother after she was kicked out of school. Her mother had blamed herself, thinking that if she had been a better example to Rebecca things wouldn't have gone that way. Rebecca omitted the detail about her mother feeling guilty about leaving her at Gregory Rollins's mercy when she was a young girl. John Rainbird would have no inkling of that detail until a vision told him close to four years later.

"Even worse than that, my grandmother is also fucked because of me," Rebecca said.

"What do you mean by that?"

"You think being the guardian of the town slut makes her life easier?"

She told John about the spray painting incident and the even worse occasion when one of her grandmother's co-workers escalated an argument by claiming that her family's bloodline must be cursed, seeing as how it could only birth nut jobs and skanky whores. Grandma Rose lost her temper and blackened the other lady's eye.

Her consequence from Cute Tykes was retirement with a full pension, taken eighteen months earlier than she had planned. Her social consequence was having women she palled around with for decades disassociate themselves with the ease of pulling a plug.

"I'm so tired of all this," Rebecca said, sobbing. "I'm so tired. I just want to get away from all this."

She straightened up, tears falling as she looked into John's eyes. "I just want to get away from this. I just want everyone who's tormented my grandmother and me to pay for what they've done."

John Rainbird lacked the words to comfort his friend, so he kissed her instead. She flinched before surrendering the soft fullness of her lips to his. The kiss began with cautious restraint, like an untrusting diner tasting unfamiliar fare. Soon they began to devour each other, like famished wolves upon a fallen moose. John Rainbird's heart became a jackhammer, ripping chunks of asphalt from a defenseless street. A ravenous beast awakened, straining against the cage of his jeans. Rebecca hoisted herself onto his lap, the passion of her exploring hands matching her lips. Her breathing became that of a jogger at the end of a several mile stretch. Her chest heaved, causing her breasts to jiggle.

John Rainbird's hands ran amuck, exploring every delicious curve of Rebecca's body. Rebecca's tears salted his face as they continued to consume each other's kisses. The beast beneath his waist smashed against her panted thigh. She slid her left hand down to its housing, treading a gentle trail over its length. The knowing hand paused before moving up to work at his zipper.

Rebecca massaged John Rainbird's exposed erection, giving him pleasure he could not have imagined. She released his length to pull off his jacket. He responded by doing the same to her top. Their pants followed their tops in tumbling to the carpet. Rebecca took her friend's hand and pulled him from the couch, walking backwards as she led him into her room.

A look of apprehension dawned on his face before she leapt back into his arms. They rolled around on the bed, underwear clad crotches pressing against each other as they kissed and fondled. Rebecca rolled to her side before grabbing John

Rainbird's boxers and tugging them off. She slid her panties off as his eyes widened.

She hoisted herself on top of him then, trying to push and angle his masthead inside. "Wait," he groaned, pushing her hips back.

"What is it?" she asked, faced flushed and breasts engorged.

"We don't have a condom."

Rebecca sighed. "We don't need it. But, I have some if it'll make you feel better."

John Rainbird nodded. "It would."

Rebecca smiled, climbing off him and removing a foil package from the top drawer of her bureau. She assailed her lover's naked body with kisses before dressing him with the prophylactic. That task out of the way, she rolled onto her back, spread her legs and crooked her finger at him.

They fumbled around for a few moments before John Rainbird gained entry to what he thought of as a little slice of heaven. Rebecca sighed, lifting her hips and placing her hands on the small of his back.

A great pressure built within the young Maupai as he pumped away. Rebecca moaned and squeezed the surface of his back as she moved in concert. John Rainbird felt overcome as a milky tidal wave exploded into the condom. He collapsed on top of Rebecca, wondering if he hadn't died.

Rebecca hugged him, joining him in silence as they lay still for a few moments. John Rainbird was the first to break the silence. "I guess we'd better put our clothes back on."

Rebecca snuggled into his arms after doing so. "That was just as nice as I imagined," she whispered.

"You planned that?" John asked.

Rebecca hesitated, taking a deep breath before answering. "I was hoping you might want me, if we were alone. I hope you don't feel like I tricked you."

"Well, you kind of did," John Rainbird spoke into the top of her head.

"Please, don't be mad at me," Rebecca pleaded. "With all that I've been going through lately, I just wanted something special. I wanted something that no one could take away from me. I just- I thought that nothing could be more special than my first time being with you."

John Rainbird coughed. "Your first time?"

Rebecca giggled, lifting her head from his chest to look at him. "Blowjobs and intercourse aren't exactly the same thing, you know."

John Rainbird's voice cracked. "So you and Kevin never…"

Rebecca shook her head. "No. I had planned to save that for marriage. That's what I wanted to do before everything got ruined."

They fell silent until John Rainbird said, "Well, I'm glad it was special for you. You know it was my first time, too."

Rebecca returned her head to his chest. "I'm glad. Now, you'll always have something to remember me by, even when you're an old man."

John Rainbird smiled for a moment, before his face took on a quizzical expression. "Hey, why did you say we didn't need a condom?"

"Because I know I can't get pregnant.

"How can you be so sure?"

"Just trust me, John Rainbird. There's no way I would've gotten pregnant, even if we hadn't used a condom."

"Alright," he relented. "But I don't see how you figure that."

Rebecca lifted her head and initiated a long tongue kiss. "Just trust me, you silly Indian," she said, after coming up for air. "Hey- did it feel good to you?"

"Didn't it seem like it?"

Her voice acquired a playful lilt. "It's hard to say. I mean it was over so quickly."

She trailed her hand along the crotch of his shorts, causing immediate arousal. "That's okay. I'm ready to give you a second chance. This time slow down when you feel like she's ready to blow."

John did just that, lasting much longer on the second go round. Their bodies were slick with sweat by the time he spilled his load into another condom.

"That was much better," Rebecca said, kissing him on the forehead. "I hope you'll never forget this day."

II

Rebecca's grandmother awakened to find her missing on Christmas Eve, two mornings after her sexual romp with John Rainbird. A neatly printed note lay on Rebecca's bed, expressing the sentiment that she couldn't stomach the hell that her life had become any longer. Her body was found floating in the near frozen Snake River the day after Christmas, a horrible yuletide tragedy. John Rainbird's immediate response was to seek revenge at the Anderson's residence, resulting in a hospital stay that caused him to miss Rebecca's funeral. He held Kevin Anderson most responsible for the circumstances that led to Rebecca's suicide, but plenty of others tormented or abandoned her along the way.

John Rainbird blamed himself for failing to absorb the meaning of Rebecca's ominous words. "Now, you'll always have something to remember me by, even when you're an old man," followed by, "I hope you'll never forget this day." Those were the words of someone who didn't intend to be around much longer, as was the expressed confidence that she would not have gotten pregnant even if they hadn't used the condom. If only he had understood the meaning behind her words, John Rainbird might have kept her from killing herself.

John Rainbird couldn't bring Rebecca back, but he hoped to make all who had wronged her pay. Her wish that they all be punished germinated within him, becoming a virus of undiluted hatred. He found himself unable to shake the tale of Charging Bear's return that he shared with Rebecca in better days. Some unknowable force gnawed at him, arguing that it would be delicious if Rebecca could somehow return to punish her tormentors as Charging Bear had punished his brother. John's grief stricken, resentful state rendered him powerless to resist the unseen imp's silver tongued exhortations.

Chapter 30- The Ceremony of Dead Reckoning

I

The voice in John Rainbird's head sounded dulcet, reasonable, and seductive. It batted away all reservations about its urgings, dismissing them like the idiot ramblings of a town drunk.

"You could bring her back, just like Quiet Eyes brought Charging Bear back", the voice repeated what had become its mantra. John Rainbird replied that he couldn't do that, for he was no shaman and did not know the shaman's arts. "How difficult could it be?" the voice countered. "According to the legend it seems a very simple task. You could probably learn all you need to know through research."

John Rainbird argued that Rebecca deserved to rest in peace. "She will rest in peace only after those who wronged her face retribution for what they've done," the voice said. John Rainbird argued that he'd only heard of Maupai being brought back from the void. "Her closeness with you connects her to our clan," the voice asserted.

John Rainbird argued that he would have to unearth Rebecca's grave in order to perform the necessary ceremony. "Surely you can accomplish that," the voice countered. "You know where she is buried. Just take your time and plan it well before you execute it. Far less intelligent people than you have accomplished that feat."

John Rainbird argued that perhaps he could manage to unearth Rebecca's grave, but he couldn't drag her body all the way to Snake River to complete the task. "Surely you don't need the entire body," the voice assured him. "You just need something of her essence. A lock of hair would do just fine."

The relentless urging ground John Rainbird's resistance into coffee beans, ready for percolation. When his ribs healed well enough to allow a comfortable range of motion and his concussion subsided, he began the due diligence needed for the upcoming task.

He spent countless hours perusing books, print and internet articles about Native American folklore that centered on communing with spirits and raising the dead.

He learned that many tribes had passed along such tales. In most of them, the Ceremony for Dead Reckoning was described as very similar to the one described in the tale of Charging Bear. A shaman had but to commit the body of the wronged to a place of strong spiritual influence (such as Snake River), trickle three drops of their own blood onto the body of the intended, and promise a grave personal sacrifice to the spiritual gateway.

While reading such accounts, John Rainbird again considered that he wasn't a shaman and that he would not be able to transport Rebecca's entire body to the river. Once again, the persuasive voice in his head convinced him that such worries were inconsequential.

"It is the spirit of the ceremony that matters," the voice argued, "not following it to the letter. You do want the bastards who wronged Rebecca to pay, don't you? Her death may have been ruled a suicide, but you know it was really murder, don't you? That bastard Kevin and everyone else who ever fucked with her drove her to take her own life. They drove her to her death, and the so called justice system of this realm offers them no consequence for doing so. You would be a pitiful excuse for a friend if you did not try to make them pay."

John Rainbird took care not to let anyone know what he was doing. He never asked for any assistance while doing his research, relying only on his own search capabilities. In front of family and friends, he projected the image of trying to be strong in his grief.

It was not a difficult task to accomplish with Wise Eyes, who was the strong and silent type anyway. From time to time, the old man asked his grandson if he felt alright. John Rainbird always nodded, saying that he guessed he felt about as well as could be expected. Without variation, Wise Eyes stared his grandson down before nodding acceptance of the answer. John Rainbird knew full well what his grandfather looked for. Weight loss, beady, bloodshot, or dilated eyes, unusual unkemptness- any signs that John Rainbird might not be eating right or abusing substances. There were no such signs and John Rainbird's grades did not suffer. There were also no more incidents like the one that landed the youth in the hospital, so the old man assumed that his grandson was not crippled by his loss.

Brittany felt more attuned to her boyfriend's spirit than Wise Eyes did. She knew the depths of the wounds that Rebecca's death caused him, so she did her best to comfort him. He was kind enough to pretend to be comforted whenever she held him in her arms and promised that he would get through it. She could never know that true comfort came from the silvery voice in his head, the one that promised a comeuppance for every bitch and bastard who had desecrated Rebecca's life.

Research about the Ceremony of Dead Reckoning was not the only kind John Rainbird conducted. He also read countless internet articles about corpse exhumation and grave robbing.

John Rainbird learned that in addition to a sturdy shovel, it would be best to bring a spade to easier penetrate the soil's initial resistance. He would need a length of rope to pull the coffin out of its earthen pit so that he could open it. He would do well to case the graveyard before undertaking the grisly task, learning entry and exit points and gauging the soil around the grave to calculate the difficulty in penetrating it.

John Rainbird found out that the cheapest method of protecting a coffin was with sectional burial liners. They were nothing more than thin concrete panels reinforced with thin chicken wire. John Rainbird knew that Rebecca's grandmother was far from wealthy, so he felt safe in assuming that sectional burial lining was the method used on Rebecca's coffin.

John Rainbird began visiting Rebecca's grave once a week, his visits serving a dual purpose. The first purpose was to look on the resting place of his lost friend, shed tears, and lay flowers at the base of a humble tombstone that read, "Here lies Rebecca. A bright flame too soon extinguished."

John Rainbird couldn't imagine a more appropriate epitaph. The cruel little world of Bay Corner had snuffed out the bright flame of promise of his one true friend. If his grisly undertaking somehow proved successful, some of the populace of that cruel little world would pay.

John Rainbird's second purpose was to learn the lay of his future crime scene. He wanted to be as smart as possible about carrying out his intentions. After what happened at the Anderson residence, he'd get far more than a slap on the wrist if the authorities caught him committing another act of trespassing. That would be bad enough without adding the consequence of being caught desecrating a grave. If he wasn't sent to a youth detention center, he'd spend some time in a psych ward, or both. While he was incarcerated, the people who had violated Rebecca would continue to go unpunished, enjoying their cruel little lives.

John Rainbird couldn't tolerate failing in his task, so, he took obsessive care in his preparation. He tested the soil around the tombstone with his foot, finding it pliant instead of hard packed. He observed the iron fencing that surrounded the graveyard. He felt pleased to find that though it stood perhaps nine feet high, the rungs at the top of it were not spiked or jagged. That meant that he could sling his tools over and climb it, should he arrive and find the gate locked. He could unearth the grave, pry open the tombstone, cut locks from Rebecca's hair, place everything back and leave the same way he entered. The only other factor to investigate was whether there was a night watchman or alarm system that would sound when the gate was touched at an unwelcome hour.

John Rainbird made that determination by sneaking away from Blessed Earth in the middle of the night and doing a trial run. He rode his Schwinn over to the side road that coiled into the Southwestern edge of town. Upon arriving at the moonlit, secluded setting, it occurred to him that the Anderson residence was less than a mile and a half north. A crazed desire to peddle his bike up to their "manor" for round two seized him, screaming to have its itch scratched. He resisted the urge, recognizing it as a distraction from the far more important task at hand.

The rear of the cemetery faced a wooded area. John Rainbird peddled around and laid his bike on the ground there. He walked up to the tall black fence and grasped a vertical bar with each hand. He looked through the opening between the bars, searching for any sign of activity. No human or animal stirred. No light shone other than the moon.

John Rainbird stood there for a long time, ignoring the torpid January wind that his hooded jacket protected him from. He grew confident that there was no watchman or alarm system, walking around to the part of the gate that faced the secluded road. John Rainbird couldn't imagine why anyone would drive through this area in the middle of a cold winter night, but anyone who did would be alarmed by the presence of his hooded figure.

John Rainbird turned 360 degrees, scanning the cemetery and its vicinity. No cars passed by and the nearest houses stood half a mile up the road. Satisfied that he would be unseen, he tried the gate. Finding it locked did not surprise him.

No matter, he thought. *I'll just climb it when the time comes.*

John Rainbird walked the circumference of the cemetery's perimeter, heading back to his bike. He had just stood the conveyance up when an impulse to scale the fence seized him.

The vengeful young trespasser laid the Schwinn back down before attempting the feat. It wasn't an easy task, for there were no real footholds on the elusive surface. After slipping off half a dozen times, John Rainbird realized he had to shimmy to the top, like a reverse version of a fireman sliding down a pole. His heart thudded as he did so. It would be just his luck to attract unwanted attention while stuck near the top of the nine foot high fence.

The young Maupai soldiered on, figuring that he had come too far to stop. One lanky leg swung over the top side of the fence, leaving his balls in a precarious perch above it. He knew that they would suffer excruciating pain for any misstep. He swung his rear leg over and pitched to the rough turf. A shockwave traversed his nervous system upon impact.

I'll have to land better the next time I try that, he thought, rubbing his legs.

The cemetery proper seemed many times larger by moonlight than it did in the daytime. Pale light glinted off a legion of tombstones and mausoleums. The place and its surrounding area remained entombed in silence, the kind of silence that portended disaster. Not even an owl hooted to provide John Rainbird a soundtrack.

Rebecca's tombstone stood a few hundred yards beyond where John Rainbird crashed to the earth. He walked over to it, keeping his head on a swivel and his ears peeled for any sight or sound of approach. The determined young man saw nothing but markers of eternal rest and heard nothing save the pounding of his own heart. He realized that he sweated despite the cold weather.

The moon cast a shadow over the stone carved words of Rebecca's epitaph. John Rainbird crouched before the headstone, wondering if her soul rested as the body six feet beneath him did. Maybe he should walk away right now, leave well enough alone. The universe would produce consequences for those who terrorized her in time. Maybe it was just plain bonkers for him to be crouching in front of his best friend's grave, planning the desecration of it in hopes of obtaining some supernatural vengeance that was straight out of a horror movie.

"You want to back out now, do you?" A familiar voice spoke inside its head.

"Have you lost the stomach to do right by your friend? I would've thought she meant more to you than that."

Though the words were challenging, even mocking, the tone was as dulcet and even toned as it had been since the first time John Rainbird heard it. John Rainbird offered the weak argument that it would be better to allow Rebecca's soul to rest. The little voice refuted that sentiment with ease, swearing that Rebecca's soul would never rest until those who victimized her were punished.

"Until then, she shall wander the borderlands between this realm and the next," the voice said. "Would you have that on your conscience? Would you have her lead an afterlife of misery because you've lost the stomach to complete your duty? Would you leave the jackals who hounded her to this very grave without consequence?"

Tears filled John Rainbird's eyes as he cried out, "No, I will not! No, I will not let them get away with it!" The winter wind carried his voice through the darkness as he fell forward from his crouch, wrapping his arms around Rebecca's tombstone and kissing it as if it were her actual flesh. "I'll make them pay, Rebecca," he sobbed. "You and I together will make them all pay."

II

As January moved aside for February, John Rainbird made numerous trips to home improvement/hardware stores after his trial run. His first such trip was to the Home Depot in Aberdeen, where he purchased a shovel and one of the huge flashlights that Anglo hunters used to jack light deer. He placed the flashlight in a basket attachment that rested in front of the bike's handlebars. The shovel lay in a huge duffel bag that he slung over his shoulder.

He made his second trip to that Home Depot about a week later. This time, he purchased a sheet of felt and some extra batteries for the flashlight. He purchased a spade from the Lowe's in Abingdon next; not wanting to buy everything from the same store for fear someone might remember him. He completed his purchases with a length of rope and an Exact-o knife from a hardware store in Havre de Grace. There were several hardware stores in Bay Corner that he could have purchased any of the needed supplies from, but he knew the town shopkeepers would surely remember an Indian boy buying such items. Worse yet, Wise Eyes and some of the other working men of the tribe purchased supplies in those stores. It was a real possibility that the other Maupai would figure out what he had planned if they found out about his purchases.

John Rainbird hid the items that he purchased in the woods beyond Blessed Earth, until he felt confident that he could perform the necessary ceremony.

The night that he took action seemed far more foreboding than that of his trial run. The crescent moon shone muted light as the late night wind roared its discontent.

John Rainbird zipped up his winter jacket and eased out of his lodgings with the stealth of a great cat, taking care not to stir his grandfather. He walked alongside his bike, using its gleaming handlebars to guide it to the place where he kept his grisly tools hidden. He removed them from their sanctuary, stuffing the shovel, spade, and coiled rope into the huge duffel bag. The flashlight, extra batteries, and felt were bagged and mounted in the bike's basket attachment. The retractable Exact-o knife hid in a jacket pocket.

It was past 1 a.m. when the young tribesman began his jaunt from the woods beyond Blessed Earth to the cemetery. He had the roads of Bay Corner all to himself. The cold blasted his hooded face, but his body and gloved hands were warm from exertion by the time he reached his destination. He trudged the circumference of the great resting place, seeking the woods bordered rear. He laid his bike among the bushes as he had during his practice run. His breath became vapor before him.

The night was as black as he could remember any night being. He looked through the black fencing and beheld a landscape that appeared to have been scrawled in grey and black ink. A feeling that he was about to do something terrible nagged him. Before it could mount a strong argument, the voice that had replaced Rebecca as his fondest friend struck it down. "There is no reason to back out of this," it said. "Rebecca would do the same for you. She wouldn't let anyone get away with hurting you like she was hurt. If someone killed you, she wouldn't let them go because she was scared of doing what needed to be done."

John Rainbird took a deep breath, gathered the duffel bag from his side and heaved it over the fence. A dull thump sounded as it joined the dark, inky landscape on the other side. He placed the shoulder strap of the bag that held the flashlight over his left shoulder before shimmying up the fencing as he had done before. He took great care once he reached the top, positioning his body so that he could shimmy down the inside of the fence instead of crashing to the earth as he had before. He felt relieved when he reconnected with terra firma, glad not to have fallen or damaged the flashlight that would be his only significant illumination.

He slung the duffel bag over his right shoulder and ambled to Rebecca's tombstone. He unburdened himself of both bags, kneeling before the grey stone marker and kissing it. "If there is a God in heaven or spirits in the Cross World, your flame will light once more," he spoke aloud, having read her epitaph again. He removed the contents of each bag and set about his grisly task.

The first thing John Rainbird did was cut a square of felt to cover the huge lens of the flashlight. He affixed the covering so that the colossal beam that the flashlight emitted shrunk to Hobbit size. He used the now tamed source of light to scan for signs of activity. There were none.

It was then time to put the shovel and spade to work. John Rainbird used the heel of his foot to drive the spade into the still pliant soil that surrounded the headstone. Once he had a wheelbarrow's worth of soil removed, he switched to the shovel. As he worked, the flashlight sat facing him a few feet away, lighting his actions with its sedated beam.

Sweat began to pour from John Rainbird even though the night air bordered on freezing and the soil didn't offer much resistance. He unzipped his jacket and removed his hood before continuing.

John Rainbird threw all the dirt he removed to the left of the grave. Soon he stood within a rectangular gap, giving no thought to the ghastliness of his deed or location. He toiled without pause, until the shovel gritted across a hard surface. He set the shovel down, climbing out of the grave to grab the flashlight. He shone it into the gap, revealing the top of the burial liner. It was the sectional kind, just as he had hoped.

John Rainbird set the flashlight down and uncoiled the rope, climbing back into the grave to thread its fibrous body through the iron rings on half of the segmented top. He climbed out of the grave again, wrapped the ends of the rope around his gloved hands and lay on the ground at the grave's edge. He tensed every muscle of his body and yanked as hard as he could.

The chicken wired segments of concrete danced loose as the end swung up with ease. John Rainbird repeated the process with the other side of the grave liner, leaving the entire coffin exposed. He climbed in next to it, staring at its wooden surface. He groped without looking, for one of the digging tools he'd laid aside. His hands came to rest on the spade. He gained a secure grip on its base before bringing its business end down in an axe chopping blow.

The coffin latch splintered. John Rainbird tossed the spade aside.

For the first time since his grisly task began, the young Maupai became aware of the smell of raw earth. He thought to reach for the flashlight before deciding that he didn't want a good look at what remained of Rebecca's corporeal form. He lifted the wooden lid, trying his best to ignore the creaking sound it made. The wind grew even more hostile, kicking some of the unearthed soil into a cloud to announce its fury.

John Rainbird reached into his right jacket pocket and pulled out a sheathed pair of scissors. He uncovered them and trailed his free hand along the coffin until he reached the head end. Without looking, he reached inside and clutched a handful of Rebecca's hair. She had always had such beautiful hair. The contents of his stomach performed somersaults of protest as he used the scissors to cut some of it.

Shame accompanied his revulsion. He could not deny that he was desecrating her body. He turned away and vomited into the unearthed grave.

"Too late to turn back now," the dulcet voice hummed to him. "It will be more than worth it in the end. You'll see."

John Rainbird stilled himself, cutting off another clump. He sheathed the scissors and returned them to his pocket along with the clipped hair. He closed the coffin lid before forcing what was left of the burial liner back over it. He climbed out of the rectangular pit and looked at his wristwatch. It was 2:44 a.m. It had taken a good hour and a half to accomplish all that he'd done. He pushed his body, returning everything he had disturbed to the closest possible semblance of its previous state before leaving the same way he came.

He checked his watch again before setting his bike into motion. It was now 3:47 a.m.

It was time to return his supplies to their hiding place and go home. He did not worry about being discovered, knowing that Wise Eyes always rose at 6 a.m., though he used no alarm or clock of any sort. Since the next day was a school day, John Rainbird would subject himself to the cruelty of the shower chamber at 5:30. Enduring the tepid water and the winter cold that penetrated its sheathing would be worth ridding himself of the cemetery dirt that now coated his body. He resolved himself to somehow make it through the coming school day without rest, maybe spending some time with Brittany afterward.

He planned to go to bed early the next evening. If Wise Eyes asked him what was wrong, he would say that something he ate at school didn't agree with him. He had no doubt that the old man would react by shaking his head and saying something to the effect of, "I have told you times without number about eating the Anglo's filth. Perhaps this will teach that lesson." Once he finished taunting his grandson, he would bring some hot tea to help settle what he thought was an ailing stomach.

As John Rainbird approached the woods that surrounded Blessed Earth, he reflected that the grunt work of his task was done. He would now wait until all was still during the next night. When it was, he would ride out to Snake River and perform the Ceremony of Dead Reckoning.

III

Five thirty a.m. came too soon for John Rainbird's liking. After subjecting himself to the shower chamber, he wrapped himself in heavy clothes and the winter jacket that he had well cleaned.

Wise Eyes rose at 6 a.m., just as sure as the sun sets in the west each evening. "A new day to you, Son of My Son," he grumbled, wiping sleep from his eyes.

"A new day to you, Grandfather," John Rainbird replied. As usual, he had rekindled the fireplace and fed the woodstove. The smell of warming venison and potatoes now permeated the simple lodging.

They said a blessing and shared the unadorned meal after Wise Eyes returned from his own adventure with the outdoor shower. John Rainbird appreciated the nourishment, even if it would have tasted better with some kind of condiment. He noticed his grandfather staring at him between forkfuls.

"Are you alright?" Wise Eyes asked.

"I am fine, Grandfather. You ask me that very often lately."

Wise Eyes arched an eyebrow. "With good reason – don't you think? You have suffered a terrible wound."

John Rainbird sighed. "Yes I have. But I'm not going to fall apart. I've lost people close to me, before, remember?"

Wise Eyes glowered, wagging a calloused pointer finger. "How dare you ask me if I remember! You have no right to say that to me. I lost my son at the same time you lost your father. You do not speak to the Father of Your Father that way. That may be how your Anglo friends speak to their elders, but you are still among the Maupai."

Yeah. Until I'm 18. Then I'm out of here. John kept that sentiment internal.

"I apologize for that, Grandfather."

Wise Eyes's face softened as much as its leathery texture allowed. "I accept your apology, Son of My Son. Yes, I know you've lost people close to you before. But, that does not mean that you will heal from a new loss any better."

He placed a coarse hand on John's forearm. "I just don't want you to let your grief make you into something less than your true essence. I have always been pleased with your clean spirit, even if you do have too many Anglo ways for my liking."

John Rainbird thanked his grandfather for the kind words, thinking that he didn't deserve them because there was nothing clean about his spirit anymore. It was now soiled by his vengeful obsession. He could not wait for the ensuing day and evening to pass so that he could slink off in the black of night and perform the Ceremony of Dead Reckoning.

Brittany huddled with John Rainbird during the bus ride home after a school day that consisted of him struggling to stay awake in class. Ozzie and Rooster joked that they should get a room. John Rainbird felt relieved when his girlfriend and friends exited the yellow vehicle at the southernmost stop in Havre de Grace. Now he could cease being social and start focusing on the task that awaited him.

Two black girls and one white girl sat with each other at the rear of the bus, talking loudly and sneaking glances at him. One of the black girls was the largest female he'd ever seen.

John Rainbird had seen the trio ever since he started busing to and from the high school. He never paid much attention to them before, since it had been his custom to turn and isolate himself in a window seat before Rooster made the introduction that prevented him from remaining a total loner. In more than four months of riding the bus with him, none of the girls in the back had ever uttered a word to him. John Rainbird knew that it was because they thought he was creepy. He didn't mind that circumstance at all.

Other than the small clique of girls, there were four other unassuming students on the bus. John ignored that quartet, stealing glances at the trio of girls who stole glances at him. He found himself wondering if they had ever done anything to Rebecca. Logic dictated that if they lived in Bay Corner, they had gone to Bay Corner School before attending Havre de Grace. That meant there was a very good chance that they harassed Rebecca in the past. Maybe they were even responsible for Rebecca's condition on the day he met her. He reconsidered the other four kids on the bus, thinking that they too might have picked on Rebecca or at least laughed at her torment.

Everyone who's harmed her will pay, he thought, removing his bike from the rear of the bus and beginning the mile trek home from his stop.

He stayed to himself when he made it home, ignoring the younglings whom implored him to play ball games. He washed some of he and his grandfather's clothes in the basin next to the shower chamber, scrubbing them many times over with homemade soap. He had just rinsed the laundry and hung it on the line when he turned to see Trotting Fox standing in his path. "Good afternoon, young John Rainbird," the raspy voiced elder said.

"Good afternoon, Father Trotting Fox," John Rainbird replied with the customary honorific given to Maupai elders, casting his eyes away in a proper Maupai show of respect. John Rainbird didn't need to look directly at Trotting Fox to be aware of the crenellated, bas relief quality of his skin or to know that his rheumy eyes projected an ocean of concern. He waited for the elderly shaman to announce the intentions of this visit.

"I thought of all you through the night," Trotting Fox said, his voice a knife sharpened on a whetstone. "They were not good thoughts."

As was the custom for Maupai youth with their elders (and all Maupai when being addressed by a chieftain or shaman), John Rainbird stood silent. He would not speak unless queried or otherwise prompted to do so.

"I am greatly concerned about you, young John Rainbird. I know that your heart is still stricken from your loss. Beyond that, you harbor great anger. The kind of anger that could lead to foolish action."

"May I speak, Father Trotting Fox?"

"You may speak, John Rainbird."

"I am very angry, Father Trotting Fox. I hate what was done to my friend. I can't stand that those who hurt her have not been punished. But, I will not do anything like I did before. I know that Rebecca would not want me to ruin my life and I know that it is not left to me to punish those who wronged her."

Trotting Fox steadied himself on his cane as he stepped closer, moving to within an arm's length of John. "Perhaps my thoughts did not tell me true, then. I am a very old man, young John Rainbird. Some would say ancient. Perhaps in the lengthening of my years, my powers of foresight have declined. Perhaps this was not a case of foresight at all. Perhaps it was only my concern for you manifesting as I slept."

A bolt of fear struck John Rainbird, traveling through his entire body. He felt certain that the old man was about to lay withered hands upon him, to try to read him as only a shaman could. If he did that- then he might 'see' what John was up to.

"Think of something else," the inner voice that had guided John's dark plans urged. "Focus on something else. Form a barrier so that he can't sense your true intentions. Quickly! He's about to grab you now."

John erected a mental wall of his future hopes- of traveling the world as a biologist or environmentalist, of living far, far away from Blessed Earth and Bay Corner.

He visualized globe-trotting adventures with Brittany, who would grow up to be an offbeat, but well known, visual artist and renowned designer of dark themed couture. He envisioned seasonal visits to the Commune, where he would regale those who would hear him with his tales of adventure. He envisioned convincing his people to embrace at least some of what the outside world had to offer. Electricity and proper showers would be a start.

Trotting Fox stepped forward in the next instant, moving with a quickness that defied the cane in his right hand. He allowed the cane to clatter to the ground, seizing John Rainbird's hands with his own aged mitts. John Rainbird blinked as an almanac of wrinkles pressed against the smoothness of his young palms. A great surge rushed through his mind and body as Trotting Fox probed him. John concentrated harder on his hopes for the future.

Trotting Fox released his hold after a few seconds, staggering a bit. John Rainbird started to get the shaman's cane for him, only to be waved off. "I am fine," Trotting Fox said, his voice tremulous as he stooped to pick up the wooden helper. John Rainbird glanced at him and saw that his brow trickled sweat.

"More importantly, it seems you speak the truth," Trotting Fox continued, "I saw only thoughts of your future when I read you. If there was something else there, I could not reach it." He grinned, revealing a rare concession to 'Anglo' ingenuity -a mouth full of fresh dentures. "The older I get, the more my arts seem to fail me. If I live long enough, perhaps I will not be a shaman at all. It is an eternal shame that I seem to have no successor in the arts. Your grandfather was the last at Blessed Earth to show the talent, but a chieftain cannot also be shaman. The spirits do not approve of such imbalance."

"Perhaps one of the younglings will show themselves to have such talent," John Rainbird said.

Trotting Fox nodded. "I can only hope that they reveal themselves soon. I will not draw breath forever to teach them. I will leave you now, John Rainbird, son of the Maupai and grandson of its chieftain."

"Until next time, Father Trotting Fox."

John Rainbird breathed a sigh of relief as the shaman pivoted on his cane and ambled away. He had no doubt that Trotting Fox would've broken through the wall of distraction he constructed if Trotting Fox were younger and used the shaman's arts more often. John Rainbird decided that his success in fooling the elder meant that the Great Spirits wished the ceremony to be conducted.

Great Spirits indeed, John Rainbird thought.

He chuckled as he headed inside, considering that he'd never placed much stock in all that Indian hokum. Now that such beliefs served his purposes, he had no problem placing his faith in them. He guessed that fourteen wasn't too young an age for hypocrisy. He knew it wasn't too young an age to be poisoned by the kind of bitterness that wouldn't release him until he did something to avenge his departed friend.

The rest of the day passed with all the speed of a mud turtle attempting to cross a divided highway. John Rainbird tried but failed to get some sleep before the wee hours arrived.

IV

John Rainbird peddled toward Snake River at breakneck speed, bearing no bags of tools during this trip. His only cargo was the clumps of hair, X-Acto knife, and scrawled paper in his jacket pockets. As his legs churned, he thought about the times he and Rebecca had raced to his destination. He thought about the sex they shared the last time that he saw her. She had been such a beautiful person, inside and out. A crying jag sought to overtake him, but he fought back the urge. He meant to do something far more useful than dissolve into tears.

The cruel winter air penetrated the young Maupai's jacket, crystallizing the perspiration that his furious peddling birthed. He slowed as he approached the part of the riverbank where he and Rebecca most often hung out. His mouth felt dry and he was short of breath. His heart raced from more than just his cycling effort.

The young traveler propped his bike against a tree that stood half a basketball court's length from the riverbank. He walked to the edge of the riverbank and looked down at the water. At night, the serpentine body seemed far more intimidating, far more sinister than during the day. The moonlight glinted off its black, undulating surface. It seemed to pulse with dark energy, to beat like a great aquatic heart. It seemed to wait for him, to hurry him to complete the task he'd committed himself to. If he had not felt sure before, he felt sure now. The river lived. It was a great, dark serpent hungry for prey.

John Rainbird understood how Rebecca had been seduced into its murky depths. He would not have been surprised to find that it had no bottom. His fear of the great body before him caused him to reconsider performing the ceremony. If there was a spirit world, the river had to be a portal to it. Such a place must be populated by beings he could not hope to have any understanding of or control over. Perhaps he should let well enough alone, lest he unleash some force that would do as it pleased instead of granting the wishes of a sad and angry teenaged boy.

"No!" An angry voice shrieked within him. "You will not back out of this!" The voice lost its anger a moment later, returning to its familiar dulcet, insistent quality. "You will not let fear of the unknown stop you. The river is not evil. The spirit realm is not evil. Do not think of the awesome sight before you. Think of your friend instead. Think of those locks of hair in your jacket. Will you abandon her now that you've come this far? If you do not go through with it, you will have desecrated her grave for nothing. Are you a desecrator? Or are you a true friend? I thought that you would stop at nothing to do right by your friend."

"I will stop at nothing to do right by my friend," John Rainbird replied.

"Then do it," the voice urged. "You've come this far, now take the final step. Chant the words, spill your blood. Cast her remains into the river. Free her to take her vengeance, so that her spirit may rest. If you do not finish your task, her soul will wander the borderlands between this realm and next. She deserves better than that, John Rainbird Jeffries. After all that's happened to her, her soul deserves to rest."

As usual, John Rainbird just couldn't argue with the voice's logic. He pulled the clumps of Rebecca's hair from his jacket pocket. The scrawled paper in his opposite pocket followed. He studied the paper for a few moments, making sure that he had the wording right.

Satisfied, John looked skyward, staring at the crescent moon and summoning his mechanical command of the Maupai language as he chanted, "Spirits of the River, O Spirits of the Great River, I humbly beseech thee. Oh, Spirits. Great Spirits, Great Spirits who walk beyond this realm, I have but one request. I beseech you to deliver vengeance to those who have harmed the body I hold." He held Rebecca's hair skyward. "I ask that you breathe new life into her expired shell, Great Spirits. Grant her breath long enough to take vengeance on all who have destroyed her, Great Spirits. Allow her to have vengeance in this realm before returning to your infinite bosom."

John Rainbird stuffed the paper back into a pocket and removed the X-Acto knife. He curled the four fingers of his opposite hand around the mass of hair they held and pointed his thumb toward the moon. The X-Acto knife sliced the pad of the digit, causing him to wince as crimson streaks leapt from the perforation. He pressed the wounded digit into Rebecca's hair, causing warm blood to coat its tangled darkness.

The untrained shaman thrust the bloody mass skyward, screaming in his tribal tongue, "Great Spirits! Oh, Great Spirits, I beseech your to grant Rebecca her vengeance before returning her to the great belly of your realm. I offer you my blood as a token of the sacrifice I will grant thee for this Great Spirits! Great Spirits, I swear to deliver myself to you three years earlier than the time you have appointed to me if you grant me this boon, Great Spirits!"

He flung the bloody mass of hair into the water. No splash or ripple along the surface confirmed its landing. No bolt of lightning or crackle of thunder served as fanfare. John Rainbird bound his thumb with some cloth he'd brought along before heading home at a much slower pace than he came.

John Rainbird shook his head at his own foolishness as he peddled. He had desecrated his friend's grave and remains for nothing. The Ceremony of Dead Reckoning was pure Indian hokum, primitive mystical bullshit just like all other Indian legends and superstitions.

I must really be out of my mind with grief to have gotten caught up in such nonsense, he thought.

John Rainbird neared the end of the road that gave way to the woods around Blessed Earth when he noticed a solitary crow flying overhead. He smirked, thinking that like him, the crow was the only one of its kind foolish enough to be out and about on such a cold winter night.

Chapter 31- Rainbird's Burden

I

Brittany stirred for a few moments, murmuring and kissing John Rainbird on the cheek before returning to her peaceful slumber. John Rainbird turned his head to read 6:18 a.m. on the red digits of the hotel alarm clock. Thoughts of the past had kept him up all night. He watched his girlfriend's blissful sleep, fearing that he might never sleep that well again.

John Rainbird realized that he'd been a damn fool after Rebecca died. A grief stricken, headstrong, fourteen your old fool who had trifled with forces he couldn't understand. He waited a long time for something to happen in the aftermath of the ceremony. When nothing did, he came to believe that things were better that way. As time passed, he stopped thinking about what he'd done at all, though he never abandoned Rebecca's memory. Her absence was a void that could never be filled.

Until he found out about the deaths of Gregory Rollins and that asshole Kevin Anderson, he believed that her soul had gone on to a better realm, despite his macabre machinations. Now, he knew that wasn't so. The ceremony had worked in a delayed fashion, just like in the tale of Charging Bear.

Rebecca (or some hideous force that inhabited her) had taken two victims already. John Rainbird cringed, thinking that he had wished for all who caused her suffering to be punished. He realized that he had no idea how many people that might be.

II

Two pairs of detectives sat across a booth from each other in the Bay Corner Diner.

It was not quite 8:30 a.m. on Wednesday. Detective Mark Ballinger downed coffee at a pace that suggested he'd feel content to inject the caffeine into his veins with a syringe, if that were an option.

"I guess you PG boys are early risers," he said, smirking.

"Not really." Detective Lonnie Carpenter faced his new colleague. "But since we got a long drive back, we figured we'd better start early today."

Ballinger slurped more of his coffee. "What's it? Ninety minutes tops? That's not so bad."

"Easy for you to say when you don't have to do it."

"Yeah, well- I guess it's my good fortune that my hometown is the epicenter of the sci-fi shit we have to investigate. So, there's no need for me to go anywhere- is there?"

Detective Mike Hargrove put a hand on his temporary partner's shoulder.

"Don't mind Detective Ballinger, guys. He's just not used to this much collaboration with others."

Detective Tremblehorn grinned. "Like to fly solo- do you?"

"That's my preference," Ballinger said.

"Yeah?" Carpenter said, sneering. "Yeah? Well, our preference is to stay in district when we conduct an investigation. Our preference is to work cases whose circumstances do not appear to be paranormal. So, I guess none of us are getting our preference right now."

Ballinger nodded. "Amen to that. So whoever killed our two victims had the same M.O., Correct?"

"That's right," the two PG County detectives answered in unison.

"Let's spell it out for each other, then. Every single detail- any tiny fact that might have something to do with each case."

They did just that over breakfast. The flow of information resulted in Rebecca Saulters being identified as a common thread among the two victims. Rebecca's mother asserted that Gregory Rollins molested her daughter. Kevin Anderson's mother admitted that her departed son reduced the poor girl's life to a living hell, fueling and igniting the chain of events that led to her suicide.

Mrs. Anderson also revealed that John Rainbird Jeffries swore to make Kevin pay for what he did. He went so far as to scale the Anderson's security fence, bringing the fight to them at home.

"We've checked him out," Tremblehorn said. "He hasn't been within a sniff of trouble since then, but that doesn't mean he hasn't been biding his time. The boy is Maupai. We are a very patient people."

Ballinger arched one ginger eyebrow. "Patient enough to nurse a grudge for four years before taking action?"

Tremblehorn smiled. "Patient enough to nurse a grudge for far longer than that."

Ballinger thrummed his fingers on the table. "Well, then- I say we pay up and find this kid again. Maybe this case won't be as tough a nut to crack as we thought."

III

"Wow," Ballinger said. "So, you grew up in a place like this?"

The four detectives stood on an earthen path that bisected parallel copses of naked trees. The leaf covered path stretched about as wide as a basketball court is long. A group of what could be best described as large huts sprouted several hundred yards down its length. The December sun glinted through the trees, giving the wooded landscape a golden glow.

"Hell, no," Tremblehorn answered. "My father left the commune in Wicomico County long before I was born. I grew up in Ocean City."

"But, you know something of their ways?" Hargrove asked.

"I know enough to get by. Better let me do the talking like I did the first time Carpenter and I came here."

Ballinger stepped with great care as they sauntered along the path, hoping not to get too much dirt on his expensive shoes. The other detectives were more concerned with startling the Maupai.

A wiry young man appeared fifty yards from them, passing a home that looked like a large, wooden shed. The young man kept an upright gait and intense, unwavering eyes as he bore down on them. He wore a shingled leather jacket over a chambray shirt. A leather hat, blue jeans, and brown work boots completed the rustic ensemble. Despite the determined set of his jaw, he looked to be about 15 years old, 16 at the most.

"What are you men doing here?" he asked, his voice a growl.

"We are policemen." Tremblehorn showed his badge, taking care not to make sustained eye contact. "We request an audience with your Chieftain."

"I know that you are policeman." The young Maupai's gaze roamed from Tremblehorn to Carpenter. "The two of you have already had audience with Chief Wise Eyes."

Tremblehorn nodded. "Yes. But, now we have need to seek his audience again."

"The Maupai have no matters that should concern Anglo policemen- or even one of our brothers who has chosen to walk among them. Nor any black skin who would align himself so. The Maupai tend to our own."

Carpenter covered his mouth at the "black skin" comment. He wondered if the situation wasn't too absurd to be reality. He stifled an urge to pinch himself as a bullfrog's croak split the forest air.

"Leave your quarrel, Billy Moon Child." A slight, white haired man used an ornate wooden cane to ambulate the path. An eagle's head carved with startling accuracy formed the top of the cane. His leathery skin bore rings to rival a two hundred year old redwood. "I will speak with them."

"Yes, Father Trotting Fox," the boy said, seeming to shrink before his elder. "I will take my leave now."

"My pardon for him," The old man said, watching the youth depart with milky eyes. "I am Trotting Fox, the eldest living member of my tribe, cousin and advisor to Chief Wise Eyes. The Chieftain is off on a roofing job." He pointed a gnarled finger. "Young Billy Moon Child will be off to meet him now that he's finished his morning lessons. We home school most of our youth here. We have a long standing arrangement with the Calvert School."

"Was John Rainbird home schooled?" Tremblehorn's voice rose in wonder.

"Only until he began what the Anglos call 'high school'. His spirit was far too hungry to remain chained to Blessed Earth. Wise Eyes told me that you detectives sought him two days past. It is he whom you still seek."

"You are prescient, Trotting Fox the Elder."

"I thank you for the compliment, my distant brethren, as I thank you for respecting the greetings of our tribe. But, neither Chief Wise Eyes nor the Son of his Son are here. Is there some assistance that I may offer you?"

Tremblehorn reached into his wallet and pulled out a contact card. He held it out for Trotting Fox to take, being careful not to thrust it into the elder's palm. "If you could be so kind to make sure that the grandson of the Chieftain receives that card. We have given him one already, but this is just in case he no longer has it. It is of vital importance that he contacts us again."

Trotting Fox's eyes contracted as the polite croak of his voice shifted into a suspicious tone. "Of what sort is this matter of 'vital importance', Detective Tremblehorn?"

Tremblehorn found the eyes of each of his cohorts in silence, communicating that he had to tell the old man something to insure his cooperation. Each of them responded with a slight nod. Tremblehorn avoided direct eye contact with the old man as he shared important details of the case.

Trotting Fox said nothing for a long time, his rheumy eyes seeming to look beyond all who stood before him. "I am sure that young John Rainbird has nothing to do with the events you speak of," he said. "Still, I will see to it that he contacts you. There is one thing I request of you in return."

Instead of asking what the request was, Tremblehorn waited for the old man to continue. Trotting Fox broke with Maupai practice, staring into Tremblehorn's eyes. Tremblehorn received the hostile message as if it were shouted into a bullhorn. "Do not bring these others to our lands again. Twice they have been here in the past few days. You know that Maupai do not take kindly to the uninvited."

Tremblehorn nodded his agreement as Trotting Fox made a production of sizing up the other three officers. His weathered lips twisted into a sneer as he did so. "If you should need to speak with anyone at Blessed Earth again, come alone. The others can hear of our encounter from your lips."

Tremblehorn nodded again, casting his eyes away from the old man. "I will do as you ask, Trotting Fox the Elder. I hope not to have to call upon you or Chief Wise Eyes again. I'm sure that I'll soon be satisfied that John Rainbird had nothing to do with the matter I'm investigating."

Trotting Fox nodded. "I am also sure of that, Detective Tremblehorn."

Tremblehorn's cohorts followed him in walking away, heading to their parked cars at the head of the road that ended at the woods. Carpenter broke in to laughter at the end of their stroll. "Black skin?" he said. "Wow. Let me find out that all the complaining civil groups have done about the Washington Redskins' name has been misdirected. The team was probably named by your tribe."

Tremblehorn shrugged and smirked at the same time. "Hey, you can't blame the old guy, Lonnie. You're probably the darkest thing he's ever seen in those woods, besides maybe a skunk."

Concern darkened Ballinger's face. "You guys are joking around, but I hope that kid doesn't turn out to be behind these killings. If we have to arrest him, we might need a riot squad just to pry him away from his people."

"Let's not put the cart before the horse," Hargrove said, drawing a reproachful look from his partner. He ignored it and finished his thought. "Let's find out for sure whether we like the kid for this first."

"Let's find out for sure whether we like the kid first." Ballinger did a pitch perfect imitation of his partner's husky voice. "Who writes your dialogue- Steven Bochco?"

Carpenter opened the passenger side door of his and Tremblehorn's car. "If you two are about to have a lover's quarrel," he began, "I suggest you do it while getting away from this creepy area." He and Tremblehorn got into the car.

As the two teams of detectives drove away, Trotting Fox stepped inside his home. He sat down in a hard carved wooden chair, in the Maupai equivalent of a living room. The elder had not been angry with the policemen, though he had been far from kind to them. Trotting Fox's anger was with himself, for an error he made years earlier. He had proved blind at the time, not considering all that he should have.

He knew there was something amiss in John Rainbird Jeffries, had sensed it just as deer sense an approaching storm. Yet, he laid his hands upon the boy for but a few moments, feeling relieved when he did not sense any malicious intentions. He should have pressed harder, should have burned tea leaves with sulphur and spoke his enchantments. More care should have been taken in consulting the guardian spirits.

But Trotting Fox had felt very tired and a bit self-absorbed, rife with sorrow about his declining eyesight and increasing need for a cane. He was also out of practice because the need for true shamanism had become a rarity considering the static conditions of Blessed Earth.

No! He would not allow himself excuses. It was not the Maupai way. It was not the way of a revered elder and Shaman, one who could have been chieftain if he so desired. The fact was that he underestimated young John Rainbird those years ago. Worse than that, he had failed to recognize the influence of malevolent spirits upon the boy.

When Trotting Fox attempted to sense the boy's thoughts, he only sought to see if John Rainbird intended to commit violence against those who tormented his fallen friend. He didn't imagine that John Rainbird knew enough to call upon the spirit world to do his bidding, or rather have it call upon him.

IV

Brittany held her fiancé around his waist as he piloted the Vespa. Her helmet strapped chin rested on his left shoulder. "Damn, you're going slow," she complained, combating the puttering engine by speaking several octaves higher than usual. "You know I have to change for work. Are you trying to make me late?"

"Sorry." John Rainbird matched his passenger's volume. "I'm just a little tired. I had trouble sleeping."

"Yeah, I can tell from your bloodshot eyes. You should have slept like a baby after what we did last night."

"Well, maybe I didn't enjoy it as much as you did."

Brittany chuckled. "Liar. I was there, remember? It felt so good to you that you almost cried."

"I did not almost cry."

"I'm sorry. Maybe you were imitating a dying animal."

They arrived at Brittany's house a few minutes later. "Here you are," John said, adjusting his helmet as she climbed off. "Home sweet home."

She removed her helmet to plant a lingering kiss on his lips. "Not for much longer. Soon my home will be with you, my fiancé."

"Fiancé," John Rainbird said. "I like the sound of that."

"You should." Brittany flashed a radiant smile. "It was your idea. Best one you've had so far." She hugged him and planted another enthusiastic kiss. "I'll see you later, fiancée," she chortled, turning toward the house she grew up in. She rubbed her engagement ring as she sauntered up the walkway.

John Rainbird watched her go, thinking of how much he loved her and how glad he felt to make her happy. He wished to share her unfettered joy about the engagement, but the horrible burden he bore made that impossible. He kick started the Vespa and headed for Blessed Earth, not knowing that a confrontation awaited him there.

V

The afternoon sun burned bright as John Rainbird approached Trotting Fox's hut.

The youngling who delivered the elder's summons asked John Rainbird if he would be arrested by the Anglo policeman, reinforcing his certainty of what Trotting Fox sought him for.

Trotting Fox appeared in the doorway before John Rainbird could knock or call out to him.

They exchanged the customary greetings before the old man invited the young man inside. Trotting Fox motioned for John Rainbird to sit in one of the old wooden chairs he used as furniture. The old man then took a seat next to him.

As per Maupai habit, the old man avoided eye contact. "I must speak with your grandfather about you," he said, his familiar croak seeming more dry and strained than usual.

"Why must you speak with my..."

"Be silent, Young John Rainbird," Trotting Fox growled. "I will speak with Chief Wise Eyes about you. I will crush the leaves and burn the sulphur. I will do all of those things, then I will send for you."

He used his cane to climb to his feet, steadying himself before letting it drop. His cadaverous hands seized the still seated John Rainbird by the cheeks, forming claw hooks and digging into them.

A flash of warmth accompanied the pain that shot through John Rainbird. Trotting Fox released the young man within seconds of seizing him.

"Yes, I must crush the leaves and burn the sulphur." Labored breathing now accompanied the old shaman's croaking voice. "I will speak with the Father of Your Father. Then I shall send for you. You may leave now."

John Rainbird stood, rubbing his offended cheeks. "Father Trotting Fox, I...."

Trotting Fox waved him away. "You may leave, now."

John Rainbird spent most of the next six hours brooding, thinking about the evil that he had unleashed and wondering how his grandfather and Father Trotting Fox would approach him when the time came. It occurred to him that they might have discovered what he had done, but he used his still formidable powers of denial to convince himself otherwise.

D-Day came in the fading light of evening. The youngling Alex Redfoot grinned as he informed John Rainbird that Trotting Fox and Wise Eyes would see him now. John considered the fact that Wise Eyes had not looked in on him, though the old man had to have returned to Blessed Earth from work hours ago.

Adults and younglings milled about between the simple structures of Blessed Earth as John Rainbird began his second far too short walk to the shaman's hut. The rudimentary door again opened before his knuckles found wood. Wise Eyes took rough hold of his arm and ushered him inside. The chieftain's eyes were a wildfire, burning unabated.

"What have you done, boy?" he howled, manhandling John Rainbird into a wooden chair.

The younger man's eyes became those of an owl. "What do you mean?"

Wise Eyes did not answer as he closed the door.

"You cannot hide it from me any longer," Trotting Fox spoke from his seat next to the young man. "Because of my weakness, I allowed you to hide it from me before. But, I have crushed leaves and burned sulfur. I have communed with the guardian spirits as I should have years ago. I now know what you have done."

John Rainbird swallowed hard, his throat too dry to issue words of protest.

"The Ceremony of Dead Reckoning," Trotting Fox continued. "I had no idea you even knew the story. After all, you spent the first part of your life away from the Commune, raised by a father who preferred the ways of whites to the ways of the people, a father who hardly even spoke the language of our people to you, making you clumsy in our tongue to this very day. And you have learned only the least of our customs since the Father of Your Father took you in."

John Rainbird kept silent the sentiment that he knew more of the Maupai ways than the old man thought, even if he chose not to embrace them. Instead, he offered, "I've heard the story a few times."

"You've heard the 'story' a few times," Wise Eyes growled. "You've heard the story a few times- but have you learned its' lesson?"

"I'm not sure what you mean."

Wise Eyes closed the distance between them, lips twisted into a feral sneer, clay skin bubbling with fury. John Rainbird thought that his grandfather was about to strike him before Wise Eyes smacked his own palm. "Of course you don't know what I 'mean'. You are ignorant and untrained. That is why you have unleashed this evil among us."

Trotting Fox glanced at the young Maupai, holding his eyes for a moment. Wise Eyes shrank away, much to John Rainbird's relief. He had feared having to take a beating from his grandfather. If Wise Eyes had hit him, he would not have fought back- even though he thought he could take the old man down if he tried. He would have shielded himself as best he could, but out of respect, he would not have fought back.

"Tell me everything that you did involving the ceremony, including how the idea sprouted in your mind," Trotting Fox said. "Leave nothing out."

John Rainbird did as requested, describing everything, down to the constant urgings of the little voice that spurred him on. Trotting Fox said nothing for a few moments after the tale ended. Wise Eyes stood against the wall nearest the rudimentary front door. The fury that had painted his face was long dissipated. A combination of abject misery and worry replaced it.

Trotting Fox sighed, pressing his careworn hands together. It occurred to John Rainbird that the situation was worse than he had thought- and he had thought it downright horrible. He had never seen Wise Eyes or Trotting Fox so stricken with worry. "It is far worse than I thought," Trotting Fox said.

The elder went on to explain that John's Rainbird recollection of the tale of Charging Bear was far from accurate. The young man had recalled it as a revenge tale, a lesson that acts of evil like the one Quiet Eyes committed would be punished by the spirit realm. That was because he had not heard it often enough or perhaps not internalized it as anything more than an entertaining story. The true purpose of the legend was to serve as a warning of the sinister powers of the spirits that inhabited the Snake River. The heinous acts of the reanimated Charging Bear did not cease with what was done to Quiet Eyes.

In the tale that Trotting Fox now told, the wraith that inhabited Charging Bear's remains returned several more times, carrying off his former wife and child into uninhabited reaches of the forest, forcing her to become his lover. The shaman who raised him from the dead had to engage the creature in its cavernous lair at the foot of the river. The shaman escaped death by a hair's breadth before managing to drive the spirit from Charging Bear's body. He and the band of warriors who accompanied him in battling the creature then burned Charging Bear's remains. Even that was not the end of the horror, for Charging Bear's wife had become pregnant by his reincarnation. She went mad from being his captive, developing some hellish version of Stockholm syndrome. The madness of her young son matched her own. He behaved more like a feral beast than a boy. The warriors were forced to kill them both. They cut out the unborn fetus when they were done, burning it along with its mother and would be sibling. Though the wraith held Charging Bear's wife captive for just a few weeks, the fetus was as developed as one perhaps halfway through pregnancy.

"I did not remember that part of the story," John Rainbird said, hanging his head.

"Perhaps, or perhaps one of the spirits of the river forced those details from your mind," Trotting Fox responded. "Your biggest mistake was venturing there at all. Your second biggest mistake was performing the ritual untrained and incorrectly. You called upon the spirits while only offering a small part of your friend's body. Her hair. That means that whatever abomination that has escaped the realm that the river conceals is nearly all hatred, feeding off all of her bad memories. It is certain that only a tiny portion of her spirit remains within the vessel, far smaller than what remained of Charging Bear. The creature that drives her surely has a stronger hold in this realm than the one that drove Charging Bear. It may never stop its slaughter. It may seek to avenge any cross word that was ever said to your friend."

"What can we do?" John Rainbird howled, tears sliding down his cheeks.

"You can stop your useless crying and think, try to recall anyone else who might have wronged your friend in even the smallest way. Once you have done that, we must try to contact them- warn them all. What we all must do is track this foul spirit. We must track it and confront it, cast it back to the watery depths from which it emerged. We must send it back or give our lives in the attempt."

Wise Eyes chimed in. "What about the matter of the Anglo policemen?"

Trotting Fox jutted his chin toward John Rainbird. "He will tell them the truth and hope that they believe it."

Alarm sounded in Wise Eye's voice. "Father Trotting Fox, they will never believe him. They will think him a mad Indian and lock him in an Anglo jail!"

Trotting Fox used his cane to hoist himself from his seat. "I have already thought of that, Chief Wise Eyes. If they arrest him, they will soon be compelled to let him go."

Chapter 32- Ronnie and the Shade

I

"Buy you another beer?" Big Harold said, shaking Veronica from her reverie. The gigantic biker dwarfed even her, standing a good 6-8 in boots. His bullish, leather jacketed frame carried more than three hundred pounds. Inked renditions of figures from the Sistine Chapel decorated his massive neck. A blue bandanna covered his bald head, a grinning skull and crossbones peeking out from his left temple.

Save for his extraordinary size, Harold didn't look much different from the average patron at "Throttle". Bodies bursting with tattoos lined every corner of the well named biker's bar on this night. All of them seemed to be having a grand time, except Veronica.

"Sure," she said.

Harold held up two gargantuan fingers that peeked out of fingerless leather gloves. "Yuengling," he said to the bartender. He looked Veronica over before breaking into a huge, gap toothed grin. "Damn, Ronnie. You're even more tight lipped than usual, tonight. Something wrong?"

Veronica shook her head to punctuate the lie she told. "I just feel like bein' quiet, Big Harold. That's all. Don't you ever feel like bein' quiet?"

"I guess I do, sometimes," the bull elephant spoke as if realizing the truth about himself for the first time. He seized the twelve ounce bottle before him in one massive hand, nodding toward its twin that stood in front of Veronica. "That's the great thing about beer. You don't have to talk to drink it."

Drink without talking they did. Veronica drifted into her own thoughts as she downed the suds. The steady beat of her mind drowned out the sounds of the bar, even the constant fusillade of hard rock that piped from the jukebox.

December 17th, Veronica thought. *Christmas'll be here in eight days.*

She predicted another boring, depressing holiday that would end with her passed out from boozing in her basement room after her father did so upstairs. Her father had a falling out with most of his relatives when Veronica was a young girl. The master mechanic wasn't cut from the same cloth as they were, wasn't even measured by the same tailor. Most of them were the wine and cheese type, wouldn't be caught dead with engine oil on their hands. Hell, they wouldn't be caught dead changing their own flat tire.

The rift never came close to being patched as Veronica grew up, resulting in most of her relatives being strangers to her. She knew that they wouldn't want to see her at Christmas now, if they ever had. One look at her looming size, prominent tattoos, and ever present biker gear would lead to the conclusion that she was a bull dyke- or maybe even a hermaphrodite. Those prim and proper people would be damned uncomfortable with her at the Yuletide dinner table. Thing was, she wasn't a bull dyke, hermaphrodite, or transsexual. She was a straight woman- one who lacked even an ounce of femininity.

Her manliness placed severe limits on her romantic options. None of the biker guys she hung out with would ever give her a sniff, not even if they were shit faced drunk. Biker dudes could dig hanging out with a big, mannish chick like Veronica, but they preferred girly girls (albeit girly girls with tattoos) when it came to the bedroom. Also, most of the bikers she knew were white. They didn't seem the least bit prejudiced, but she'd never seen a black girl on any of their arms. She supposed that if any of them ever did take to a black girl, it wouldn't be a huge, menacing one like her.

Veronica hadn't been screwed in close to a year, had only ever been screwed by two guys in fact. They were both fat, hairy things, as ugly for guys as she was for a girl. They both dropped her like a bad habit at the first chance to nab women of normal comportment. Veronica didn't feel the least bit surprised. Even the ugliest of Goliaths like Harold had an itty, bitty wife.

Veronica was only eighteen, but she already felt certain that no guy would want to be with her the way that she was. The rub was that she loved herself in her current state. She didn't want to slim down, and she damn well couldn't imagine herself in make up or some top that served her huge boobs on a platter.

The hell with it, she thought.

She didn't need men for sexual satisfaction, that's what her special toys were for. It would be nice to know some love other than the kind her drunken father had for her, though. Oh, well. What was she going to do- kill herself like Rebecca Saulters? She was much too strong for that. She'd continue with the status quo, riding her bike, hanging out with other bikers when she felt like it, drinking her fill, working her bullshit job, and fucking herself with a toy when she got good and horny.

Veronica had to admit that thought it was far from satisfying, her life could be much worse. She might not have love, but she didn't think love compared to the nervous dance of square people's eyes when they crossed her path. Nobody fucked with her, ever. That wasn't a bad deal.

She downed a few more Yuenglings with Harold, then patted him on the back and took her leave. "You alright to ride, girl?" he asked. She laughed, the snort of an amused bison, reminding him that she'd downed far more alcohol than that before hopping on her bike.

Reverence washed over her as she rode past the Harley Davidson Store that stood like a beacon, its expansive lot right next to the drinking hole she'd just departed. She meant to have her own Harley one day, if she ever scraped enough money together.

The Yamaha would have to do for now. She opened it up on the just short of deserted Route 40, speed limit be damned. She enjoyed the winter current beating against her as she zoomed the twenty miles or so from Middle River to the Bay Corner Junction. She decelerated from her 90 mph clip as she merged onto town roads, but the exhilaration from going so fast accompanied her for the remainder of her trip home.

The familiar sight of her passed out dad greeted her from the living room couch. The remains of a dispatched twelve pack lay about his feet and the upholstery. Veronica shook her head, thinking that there was a perfectly good table three feet in front of him. He also might have used a trash bag, instead of opting to be a total pig. Then again, doing something like that would mean that he was a different person. She wondered if he had been different before her mother died. It seemed to her that he had been, but then she only had the memories of a five year old to consult about the matter. She wondered if she also might have been different if her mother had lived to take part in raising her.

Veronica chided herself for thinking that hypothetical, pussy-ass, sensitive bullshit, stooping to clean up the cans. Despite their sloppy arrangement, not a drop of beer had spilled on the shag carpet or the couch. The esteemed George Myers always drained every drop. She learned very well from him.

He did not stir as Veronica moved around him. His bearish snoring complemented his bearish body. Veronica teased a hand over his Old Testament beard, feeling a mixture of love and pity. She removed a blanket from his disaster of a bedroom and covered him with it.

"Goodnight, Dad," she muttered. He shifted to his right side and resumed his thunderous snoring.

Veronica headed down to her room, changing into the tattered grey sweatsuit she wore as pajamas. She reached into her bureau and pulled out a pint of Jack Daniels. She began her late night ritual, attacking the contents of the bottle without distraction, not stopping until she passed out in her seat. She never imagined that she might be drinking herself to sleep for the last time.

II

John Rainbird Jeffries found himself snatched into the consciousness of a huge black girl. The girl's forearms matched the width of a normal woman's thighs. Tattoos stood in relief on them, as well as on her wide neck. Her coarse black hair was tied into a ponytail. She stood on a landscape that was barren, save for a queen sized bed in dire need of retirement.

John Rainbird sensed that the large girl felt as confused as she felt cold. Fog the thickness of a hearty soup enveloped her, eliminating visibility. "Where the fuck am I?" she growled, teeth chattering. He realized her identity at that moment.

Veronica Myers was her name. She'd been one of Rebecca's chief tormentors at Bay Corner School, giving John Rainbird's departed friend a beating just before he met her.

After Rebecca was humiliated and ruined by Kevin Anderson's video, Pamela Lawson and Shanae Edwards had goaded the big beast into spray painting horrible graffiti on Rebecca's home. It read, "A Cock Sucking Slut Lives Here"- a billboard in red on both sides of the house. When it came to matters of tormenting Rebecca, Pamela Lawson and Shanae Edwards were the masterminds of cruelty. Veronica was their giant, pliant tool.

The vandalism was but the last of many vile things the trio of girls did to Rebecca. John Rainbird imagined Veronica a bit smaller and without the numerous tattoos. He realized that he had often seen her in the halls of Havre de Grace High.

A tide of anger about all the girl had done swept through the young Maupai. He attempted to banish it as soon as it emerged; hoping that doing so might somehow prevent the inevitable.

"Fight me now," a robotic voice croaked from the midst of the fog, informing John Rainbird that his hope would not be actualized. "Fight me now, you fat fucking dyke."

Veronica whirled around, balling her meaty hands into fists and assuming a boxing stance. "Who the fuck said that?" she bellowed. "Who called me that?"

"What does it matter who speaks the truth?" the croaking robot answered. "The fact is- you are a fat fucking dyke."

"I am not a dyke," Veronica protested. "I like guys just fine."

A hyena cackle tore at the opaque air. "Then why do you never have a boyfriend? Oh, that's right." The voice changed on the second statement, becoming dulcet, airy even. John Rainbird could never forget that voice. It belonged to Rebecca.

"You're a fat, fucking, miserable bitch, just as miserable as your alcoholic father," it said, unleashing a sing-song of hatred.

John Rainbird felt Veronica recoil at the words. The voice belonged to Rebecca, but not the cruelty. The Rebecca he knew had never been mean enough to say things like that. The Rebecca he knew had no cruelty in her.

That Rebecca appeared, looking as pretty and unassuming as John Rainbird remembered. She wore a knee length denim skirt and a pea green sweater buttoned over a blouse. Her straightened long hair laid about her shoulders. Not a single blemish marked her flawless taupe skin. He felt as if she had never left him, until he looked again.

The Rebecca who stood in this barren, fog shrouded landscape wore the vacant eyes of the dead, eyes that looked no more real than glass ones. Claw like nails protruded from the toes of her bare feet. Faded black scars marred her wrists. John Rainbird's fear for Veronica increased tenfold when he saw this. Though he used Veronica's eyes, she did not seem to see what he saw.

"Once you knew I was an outcast, you decided I was the perfect victim. When your bitch friends started picking on me, you provided the muscle." The creature that looked like Rebecca threw its pretty head back and emitted another hyena cackle. "Where are you friends now- you fat ugly bitch? Anywhere but near you, that's where. They tossed you aside when they were done with you, and who could blame them. Who wants to hang out with Queen Kong all the way through high school? No, they left you alone and now that's how you'll die- alone. But don't worry. Those bitches will get theirs, too."

The creature that looked like Rebecca snarled, revealing the fangs of a great cat. "I promise you, those bitches will get theirs, too." The creature cackled once more, licking its dead lips in anticipation. "But you first."

For just a flash, Veronica saw the creature as John Rainbird did. She gasped as the image dissolved; leaving the Rebecca she had known before. The big girl's eyes became saucers before she made a Herculean effort to narrow them. She managed to force some dry words past her quivering lips. "You can't take me, you little bitch. You couldn't take me then, and you can't take me now."

She charged across the blank surface of the dreamscape, intent on obliterating the fifteen yard distance that separated her from her adversary. The Rebecca creature disappeared from Veronica's path as she reached the spot where it had stood. A powerful force seized the big girl from behind and spun her around. She found herself trapped in a crushing bear hug. Veronica felt more shocked than scared. She had never been overpowered in her life, just as she had never believed in people returning from the dead.

"I got to stop drinking myself to sleep," Veronica groaned. "This is some fucked up dream."

The creature that looked and sounded like Rebecca smiled, the arch of the expression as pleasant as it was cruel, its fangs having disappeared. Veronica realized that her adversary smelled of river water - river water and sodden leaves.

"I'll bet you don't really want to fight me, Ronnie," the Rebecca thing cooed. "I think you really are a lesbian, because you look like you want nothing more than to kiss me."

Veronica looked into the creature's fish eyes and realized she wanted to do just as it said. She parted her lips, inviting the cold, wormlike tongue that shoved itself through the opening. A great tide of water rushed in behind the ghoulish proboscis.

Chapter 33 - Rainbird Wears Orange

I

John Rainbird awoke in a frigid sweat. Brittany slept like a log next to him. John felt pleased that he had not cried out and awakened her.

The clock on Brittany's nightstand read 4:37 am. Her fiancé had come through the basement door late in the evening, as per their nightly ritual. Once all was still with her parents upstairs, they had at each other. She reached into her mini-fridge after they finished, warming hamburger and onion rings from the diner.

They snuggled and talked for a while before falling asleep. John Rainbird kept the talk small, not speaking of his visions or trouble with the police. Nor did he tell Brittany about the conversation with his grandfather and Father Trotting Fox. He didn't think she could accept any of that as truth without hard proof. The young Maupai didn't want to accept any of it himself, although he now knew it to be reality.

If denying the circumstances could make them disappear, John Rainbird would have done so without hesitation. But denial wouldn't help, so he had no choice but to confront the macabre circumstances. When logic leaves but one possible explanation, that explanation must be true, no matter how unlikely. He thought he'd read something like that in a book once. Maybe he didn't have the wording exactly right, but he understood the sentiment. Logically thinking, he'd performed an arcane ceremony nearly four years ago, spilling his own blood and desecrating his friend's grave to do so.

The blood of the shaman swam through his veins due to his relation to Wise Eyes and Trotting Fox, even if he had not been trained in those arts. He and his shaman's blood called upon forces beyond the understanding of any grief stricken fourteen year old, or perhaps it was as Trotting Fox said. Perhaps those forces called upon him.

Whether he had controlled or been controlled, John Rainbird's wish that everyone who had harmed Rebecca pay retribution was well on its way to fruition. If his latest vision were correct, then Veronica Myers had just become the thing that used to be Rebecca's third victim.

He had no idea how many more victims the wraith would now take, or how many people would be found to have wronged Rebecca. He did know that Pamela Lawson and Shanae Edwards would be targets because of what he'd seen while inhabiting Veronica's consciousness. Still, there could be countless others who he didn't know about.

Before his vision of Gregory Rollins, John Rainbird had no idea that the man even existed. Yet, the molester was found dead soon after John Rainbird's vision of his demise. The same held true for that bastard Kevin Anderson.

Now a vision of Veronica meeting her comeuppance at the hands of the creature plagued him. John Rainbird held slippery memories of Rebecca describing a big girl who used to bully her in eighth grade. He didn't know the girl's name until he "dreamed" of her. That knowledge was now useless because she was sure to be dead. As Trotting Fox said, John Rainbird would have to somehow anticipate who else the creature might attack. If he couldn't do that, an untold number of people might die. Even if he could, there might be no stopping the evil he had released.

John Rainbird took great care to be quiet as he gathered his clothes from the foot of Brittany's bed, not wanting his departure to wake her.

He tore a page out of the composition book she kept in her knapsack. He fished the knapsack's pockets for a pen, using it to scrawl a note that explained he had to leave early to run some errands for Wise Eyes. It was an outright lie, but the truth would only make him seem crazy.

John Rainbird slipped out of the basement door after he finished writing. He walked his scooter out of Brittany's yard, lugging it a full block in the cold night air before climbing aboard. The effort of lugging it was worth not having to deal with an awakened Brittany.

John Rainbird killed the Vespa's engine as he approached Blessed Earth, not wanting to awaken any Maupai other than his grandfather.

He found the wizened chieftain sitting on the couch, a candle lighting their modest approximation of a living room. Wise Eyes's hands rested on his knees. His eyes seemed as distant as the horizon.

John Rainbird sat down next to his grandfather, clearing his throat as he searched for something to say. "You're up early," he ventured.

"Early?" Wise Eye's voice sounded as distant as his eyes looked. He shifted in his seat. "Yes. I suppose I am up early. But, then I haven't truly slept."

A tremor of guilt rocked John's consciousness. "It's because of me that you haven't slept, Father of My Father. I have brought tribulation upon you."

"No!" Wise Eyes roared. Intensity lit his eyes as he looked at his grandson.

"Never say that, John Rainbird. What you did was not the doing of man. What you did was the doing of evil spirits. The spirits of that river have always haunted the Maupai. They are carnivorous creatures, feeding on the darkest parts of a man's soul. They feed on those parts while planting the germ of something far worse than what was already there. I am far more to blame than you are, Son of my Son. When your father died, I became your guardian. I found you to be so much like him that it exasperated me."

He stood and walked to the lone window of their tiny residence. He looked out of it for a moment, before returning to his seat.

"Your father was never much for the ways of Blessed Earth- and neither were you. In fact, you were even worse because your father only knew the ways of the Anglo world as fantasy growing up. It was wanderlust that led him away from here as soon as he considered himself a man. You, on the other hand, knew Blessed Earth only through rare visits. You were like a trout out of water when you came to live here, for what child could embrace the humble ways of the Maupai after becoming accustomed to the white man's amenities?"

Wise Eyes, chuckled- a dry sound devoid of humor. "I taught you the ways of the Maupai that were necessary for you to live here. I knew that you had not come to stay. Our simple ways appeal to less and less of our youth. The day will come when none choose the life of Blessed Earth. We shall all be scattered amidst the white man's world, as so many tribes have scattered before us. Since you did not come here to stay, I did not bother you with what I knew you would only think of as Indian hokum. I told you to stay away from Snake River, but I never explained why."

Wise Eyes bowed his head and leaned toward his grandson, placing his hands on the young man's forearms. John Rainbird fell still with surprise as his grandfather performed their tribe's gesture of supplication.

The old man's voice quavered when he spoke again. "I must plead your forgiveness, Son of My Son. Truth be told, I had a less honorable reason for holding back on my teachings. Every time that I looked at you, I saw your father. I saw your father and my heart filled with bitterness of how he thought less of the way of life he was brought up in. I have always kept a distance between us because of that. Perhaps if I had not done so, you might have truly understood the story of

Charging Bear. Perhaps if I had not done so, you might not have unleashed this force we must now contend with."

John Rainbird grasped the old man's arms, easing him into an upright position. When John Rainbird did so, he saw tears stream down Wise Eyes's face. The young man buried his hands in the old man's tears before dragging their salty refuse down his own cheeks. He leaned forward, arching his neck to place his chin against Wise Eyes's forehead. Up close like this, he smelled the hand rolled cigarettes that the chieftain favored.

"I forgive you, Father of My Father," John Rainbird said. He then copied the pose of supplication that Wise Eyes had just used. "Will you forgive me for my youthful foolishness? For sneaking about and unleashing this evil force upon the world?"

Wise Eyes reciprocated all of his grandson's previous motions, concluding with a chin rub against John Rainbird's forehead. "I forgave you the moment I discovered the truth."

They sat silent for a while - their conciliatory idle unbroken until John Rainbird told his grandfather about his vision of Veronica Myers.

"Perhaps we can find her," he said, not believing his own words. "Find her and warn her."

Wise Eyes sighed. "You know as well as I do that it is already too late for the one you speak of."

John Rainbird started to argue before making a final confession to himself. This was no time for delusion or wishful thinking. "So, what do we do now?"

Wise Eyes pulled one of his hand rolled specials from the pocket of his chambray shirt. A lighter exited the same location, bringing flame to the small pleasure. The chieftain took a long, slow drag from the cigarette as his grandson tried his best to ignore the acrid smell of smoke.

"We wake Father Trotting Fox," Wise Eyes said. "We wake Father Trotting Fox. Then we alert the Anglo police and wait."

II

John Rainbird couldn't get any reception on his cell phone, so he walked to the phone booths that stood beyond Blessed Earth to call Brittany. He reached her just before she left for work. She was furious with him, saying that waking up to find him gone had been quite a shock and that she'd tried to call his "stupid" cell phone. He apologized, saying that she looked so peaceful that he couldn't bear to wake her.

John Rainbird walked back to the phone booth around mid-day and called Brittany on her lunch break. It was a long walk, but his cell phone still wasn't getting good reception. He didn't feel like having a conversation where he could only make out every other word or that dropped forty five seconds in. Besides, walking passed the anxiety ridden time of waiting for the policemen.

When John Rainbird spoke with Brittany during her lunch break, she told him that she couldn't wait to see him that night. "You'd better not run out on me like that again, either," she scolded him. "That's no way to treat a fiancée. Leaving a note doesn't make it okay."

"I won't run out on you again, Brit," John Rainbird said, omitting his certainty that he wouldn't see her at all. He had little doubt of how he would spend that evening.

The wait ended soon after that phone call, when Detectives Tremblehorn and Carpenter arrived at the outskirts of the Commune. John Rainbird, Wise Eyes, and

Trotting Fox walked to meet them after Wise Eyes advised all who signified to stay put.

The quintet walked to the same phone booths that John Rainbird called Brittany from. Tremblehorn and Carpenter's vehicle waited there.

Two white detectives stood outside of the car behind the first vehicle. One of them wore fresh trimmed red hair and perhaps the neatest red mustache on the planet. The other stood a few inches shorter and wore a shaggy brown goatee.

Tremblehorn acted as the mouthpiece for the detectives, introducing the second pair and sketching their involvement with the ongoing investigation. He apologized to Trotting Fox for not coming alone, insisting that police procedure gave him no latitude. Wise Eyes interrupted him when he began to share details of Veronica Myers's death.

"We know why you are all here," he said. "Young Veronica Myers is dead and you've discovered that she once tormented my grandson's deceased friend."

Wise Eyes ignored the widened octet of the detective's eyes. "You are aware that the Son of My Son once promised revenge on all who tormented his friend and since all three of the dead did so without question, you think that he has set about upholding that promise."

The old man's eyes danced over Tremblehorn's. "Am I correct so far?"

Tremblehorn coughed and nodded. "Yes. You are."

"You are correct in concluding that the Son of My Son is connected to these deaths," Wise Eyes said. He grabbed John Rainbird's hands and held them aloft.

"However, it is wrong for you to assume that his mortal hands performed those deeds. I know that you did not grow up on a commune or reservation, just as John Rainbird did not spend his early years at Blessed Earth. So, perhaps you will not believe what he is about to say. Surely, all of your comrades will assume it to be crazed Indian ranting."

Wise Eyes glanced at John Rainbird. "But, The Son of My Son will tell the tale just the same."

III

John Rainbird told it all- the story of how he robbed Rebecca's grave and performed the vengeance ceremony, the flashbacks he experienced that could only be Rebecca's memories, and his visions of her victims meeting supernatural demise.

When he finished his tale, the detectives slapped handcuffs on him, just as he and his elders expected. None of the three Maupai resisted or argued as the lawmen hauled John Rainbird away.

Each of the Maupai viewed the arrest as a necessary step in an urgent dance. They knew that John Rainbird would be released from the Harford County Detention Center after the wraith took its next unfortunate victim.

The detectives transported John Rainbird to the sheriff's office, where they interrogated him in a hot and cramped interview room. Wise Eyes and Trotting Fox waited outside in Wise Eyes's truck while the detectives employed everything but the kitchen sink in an effort to trip John Rainbird up.

The detectives worked on the young Maupai in tandem. They worked on him alone. They launched simultaneous verbal assaults, trying to make him fold under pressure. They talked fast. They talked without pause. They fell silent, staring at him for what seemed like forever. They cozied up to him.

When none of that worked, the detectives screamed in his face. They said things that John Rainbird knew to be misrepresentations or outright lies. They promised him that things would go much easier if he confessed. The detectives assured him that if he tried telling any of the cockamamie Indian hokum he told them to a jury, he'd spend the rest of his life in prison.

They told him that most Bay Corner citizens would think him guilty just because they resented the Maupai occupying land that the town could use for better, more profitable purposes. They took turns telling him that going to trial would be the worst possible course of action.

When John Rainbird had borne all the psychological assault he cared for, he locked eyes with the black detective and swore that there was nothing that any of them could do to make him confess because he had not killed anyone.

He growled that they might as well take him to the Harford County Detention Center because they would not get another word from him. After more than an hour of sustained silence on John Rainbird's behalf, the detectives did just that. Wise Eyes and Trotting Fox followed behind them once they led him out of the station. Not trusting Anglo authority, they wanted to be sure that their fellow tribesmen had not been beaten.

Booked into the Harford County Detention Center, John Rainbird sat as still a stone, on a concrete slab in a holding cell. Three others shared his temporary digs, including a fat white man and a black man with matted cornrows. The third detainee was a skinny and shirtless white boy of John Rainbird's approximate age.

The shirtless young man paced the cell like a caged panther, shouting through the bars that it was "fucking freezing" in there. The guards who made a circuit outside of the cells only snickered at his whining. A female guard once yelled for him to "shut the fuck up". He did so for all of thirty seconds before starting up again.

A guard escorted John Rainbird from his cell after an interminable amount of time, granting his allotted phone call. He placed the collect call to Brittany's cell phone.

"Omigod!" she screeched, having been told by the operator that the call came from the Harford County Detention Center. "What are you doing in jail?"

John Rainbird sighed. "I can't tell you that right now, Brit," he said "I can only explain it to you after I get out. For now, I can only say that I'm innocent."

A long silence passed before Brittany spoke again. "Innocent? But, then why…"

"Brittany- don't you know me? Don't you know that I'm too decent and have too much going for me to have actually committed a crime?"

"Yes," Brittany answered without hesitation. "Yes. I do know that."

"That's my girl. Now believe me, I'll be out of here before long. I'll explain the entire crazy story to you then."

"Okay." Brittany's choked voice told her fiancé that she was crying. "Okay. Does your grandfather know you're locked up?"

"Yes. That's why I'll be out soon. Anyway, I just called you so you wouldn't think I stood you up. I wish you would stop crying."

"What do you expect, John? My fiancé- the love of my young life is in jail. How can you expect me not to cry?"

"I guess I can't," John Rainbird said, looking over his shoulder at the guard. The guard pointed at his wristwatch. "Anyway, I'll be out soon. I love you, Brit."

"I love you too, John."

John Rainbird wished that he had asked Brittany what time it was as the guard led him back to his holding cell. He had no way of knowing since the authorities took all of his property save for his clothes and shoes. That included his shoe strings and belt, in case he had any ideas of hanging himself.

John Rainbird couldn't measure how much time had passed, but he was certain that it had passed at a snail's pace.

He wondered if Pamela Lawson or Shanae Edwards would be next, or if the creature would kill someone whom hadn't occurred to him yet. He flinched at his own selfishness, thinking that the sooner the wraith struck again, the sooner he would have to be released. John reconciled the horror of that sentiment with the notion that the sooner he got out, the sooner he and his elders could try to save at least some of the creature's intended victims.

IV

John Rainbird didn't find his stay at the Harford County Detention Center to be altogether unpleasant. The food was disgusting and he wasn't too fond of the orange jumpsuit that read HCDC across the back, but at least no one bothered him. He felt certain that being Indian helped him in that department. He assumed that most of his fellow prisoners had never seen a real life Native American before, let alone a tall and brooding one like him.

John Rainbird's cellmate was a small man with thinning brown hair and a sallow, blotchy complexion. John Rainbird speculated that the man awaited trial for embezzlement or some perversion. The guy said little, except to be polite. John Rainbird sensed the fear pouring from him. The tribesman was honest with himself, admitting that inspiring such unease was far more pleasant than feeling it.

During the course of his incarceration, John Rainbird learned that the HCDC was divided into two tiers. The bottom tier housed inmates serving out sentences of eighteen months or less. An overwhelming majority of them had been convicted of nonviolent offenses.

The second tier of HCDC housed prisoners whom awaited trial. The species in this human menagerie ranged from petty thieves and drug dealers to accused murderers like John Rainbird. Maybe the fact that he was an accused killer had as much to with other prisoners beating a wide path as being an Indian did. Whatever the reason or reasons, he was glad to be more or less left alone.

While in captivity, John Rainbird eschewed the exercise yard, opting to perform endless sets of push-ups and dips within his cell instead. He only left the iron cage to eat and make phone calls. He was allowed one supervised call per day now that he had been processed into the system.

On his second day there, he called Brittany and explained why he was incarcerated. He told her that the cops suspected him of killing all those people because of their connection to Rebecca and his four year old vow of revenge. He did not mention that some demonic incarnation of Rebecca committed the murders, feeling that Brittany wasn't ready to digest such a terrible truth.

John Rainbird swallowed hard when Brittany stopped crying long enough to ask him if the accusations were true. "Don't you know me?" he asked. "Don't you know that I could never do something like that?"

Brittany dissolved into hysterics, begging his forgiveness for even questioning him. She then asked if there was anything she could do to help him.

"Yes," John Rainbird answered. "Yes, there is."

V

Brittany parked her Vespa in a white lined parking space outside of a huge architectural rectangle in Edgewood. The block letters on the building face read, "Harford County Sheriff's Office, Southern Precinct." She bounded up the high stairs leading to the glass entry doors, anxious to carry out the mission her fiancé had given her.

Minutes after speaking to the front desk clerk, Brittany found herself in an interview room with two detectives. One was tall and well dressed with immaculate red hair. The other dressed just as well, but wore a scraggly brown goatee and a nasty bit of five o'clock shadow.

The redhead proved to be the one Brittany spoke to on the phone- Detective Ballinger. The smug, would be ginger model now sat across the table from her.

No matter, Brittany thought, *makes no difference if the cop I give this information to is a nice guy or a smug jerk. I'm only here to help John Rainbird.*

"So," Detective Ballinger began. "Brittany- is it?"

"Yes." Brittany nodded, annoyed at his pretense.

As if my name is so hard to remember, she thought. *As if someone in his profession can afford to have trouble remembering names.*

"You are John Jeffries's fiancée?"

"John Rainbird Jeffries."

Detective Ballinger smirked. "My apologies. John Rainbird Jeffries. You're John Rainbird Jeffries's fiancée?"

"Yes, I am. I told you that on the phone. I wish you wouldn't be so smug. I didn't have to come here, you know."

"You're right," the detective with scruffy facial hair- Detective Hargrove chimed in. "You don't have to be here. You'll have to excuse my partner, Ms. Taylor. He doesn't mean to be so irritating. It's just his nature."

Brittany waved a dismissal. "It's alright. Maybe I'm being too sensitive. It's just that – my fiancée is locked up for murder and I know he hasn't killed anyone."

"How can you be so sure?"

"Well- for one thing- the other night when that girl Veronica was killed- he was with me. He couldn't have done that."

322

"Strange." Hargrove shifted in his seat. "John Rainbird didn't name you as an alibi when we arrested him. We would have spoken to you much sooner if he had."

"He was probably trying to keep me out of it," Brittany said, feeling unsurprised because John Rainbird had already made that revelation to her. "He's protective that way."

Hargrove arched an eyebrow. "Yet, he wants you involved now?"

"Only because he wants to help you guys stop the killings. That's why I'm here"

"You're here to help us stop the killings?"

"Yes. And whether you believe it or not- he was with me that night."

"He was with you all night?"

Brittany nodded. "Yes. We fell asleep together."

"What time do you think that was?" Ballinger jumped in.

Hargrove gave his partner a look that said he would handle the matter, then caught Brittany's eye. "What time do you think that was, Brittany?"

"I probably fell asleep a little after midnight."

"And when you woke up- was he with you?"

Brittany's face flooded crimson as she fell silent.

"You see," Hargrove said, nodding. "That's where we have a huge problem, Ms. Taylor. Even if your fiancé had been next to you when you awakened, that wouldn't preclude the possibility that he snuck away and eliminated the victim while you slept. Harford County is a very small place- is it not? We're not completely convinced of his alibis for the other two murders either. And your boyfriend is half-Maupai, having spent his formative years on a tribal commune."

"I don't see what that has to do with…"

"Ritualistic aspects of killings. The Maupai are a very ritualistic people."

323

Brittany sighed. "I know that, but John never bought into that tribal crap. He hated that everyone on his commune seemed stuck in a time warp. That's why he was in college. He wanted to complete his education and become a great man. Become a great man and influence other members of his tribe to forsake what he called 'primitive' ways."

Hargrove nodded. "I believe he told you all that. Maybe his actions even made it seem true. But my line of work has taught me that it is quite ordinary for people to be other than what they seem. Especially to those who love them the most."

Tears brimmed in Brittany's eyes, smudging her dark mascara. "John hasn't killed anyone."

Hargrove shrugged. "I'd like to believe that. He seems to be a really nice kid. Been a model citizen his entire life, save for the time he broke onto the Anderson's property in broad daylight and tried to take a piece of the young mister's hide. Oh- and the promise he made to repay everyone who ever harmed Rebecca Saulters."

Hargrove removed a handkerchief from his pants pocket and handed it to Brittany.

She used it to wipe her tears and blot her make up. "That was four years ago." Her voice quavered. "That was four years ago and he was fourteen years old."

"That's true. You'd hope that a kid could get over the anger of such a tragic loss by now, but maybe he hasn't. Maybe it's festered within him for all those years leading to this."

Hargrove paused, relaxing in his seat. "But you didn't come here to debate with us. Did you- Ms. Taylor? This is not your fiance's trial and none of us are lawyers."

Memory sparked in Brittany's eyes. "You're right! I didn't come here to debate with you. I got so caught up in defending John that I almost forgot."

She reached into a pocket of her jacket and removed a folded piece up paper, sliding it across the table to Detective Hargrove.

Detective Hargrove unfolded the paper. "What's this?"

"A list of names of who might be killed next. John read them to me the last time we talked."

Detective Ballinger leapt to his feet, unable to keep quiet any longer. "And how would he know who'll be killed next?"

Brittany scowled. "He doesn't. He only knows enough to agree with you guys' assertion that someone is killing people who abused Rebecca Saulters. Since he's not doing it, then the real killer must still be out there. Those are the only names he could recall of people who did Rebecca a wrong turn. He said I should tell you to talk to the principals of her former schools to try and find out who else might have screwed with her. In the meantime, you should look into protecting these people."

Chapter 34 - To Protect and Serve John Rainbird's List

I

"So that's how it went," Hargrove said, having finished a recount of the encounter with Brittany. He, Ballinger, Tremblehorn, and Carpenter clustered around his desk on the main floor of the Special Investigations Unit.

Tremblehorn and Carpenter had returned from reviewing ME Chandrunkunel's findings in the death of Veronica Myers. The huge young woman drowned to death, just like the previous victims. She had somehow been drowned, yet found in her basement room, in the house she grew up in. The water in her lungs also came from Snake River. The only difference between the departed Miss Myers and the male victims was that there was no evidence of sex play before her death.

"I guess our guy only likes to get male victims off," Carpenter quipped after Chandrunkunnel finished filling him and his partner in.

Carpenter now looked over Tremblehorn's shoulder as they both eyed the list that the erstwhile tribesman held. There were six names on the list: Pamela Lawson, Shanae Edwards, Robert Bailey, Tara Andrews, Crystal Ritchie, and Principal Thomas Halloran (of Mackenzie High School).

"Principal Halloran still heads that fancy school," Ballinger said. "Being the only one of us from Bay Corner, I'm actually familiar with some of these kid's names. I know the Lawson's- they're pretty well off. Just a step down from Mackenzie Road money. I recall hearing of Robert Bailey joining the military right out of high school."

"You think anything that kid said held water?" Carpenter made an unintentional pun.

Ballinger cleared his throat. "Not the suggestion that the dead girl's spirit has returned from the grave to take revenge on those who harmed her. I just can't believe something like that. Still- I wonder…"

"You wonder how the hell a wiry kid like that could manage the physicality that would be required for him to have done it- right? I mean- Rollins was an out of shape stoner, but Kevin Anderson had a strong body- an athlete's body, and the girl had to be pushing three hundred pounds. So how does someone who's maybe one hundred seventy pounds on his best day manage to do all that?"

"Exactly." Ballinger's eyes lit up. "Also, there was no evidence of physical struggle on any of the victims. I don't see any rational explanation for that."

"You mean, we haven't discovered any rational explanation for that yet." Tremblehorn scowled, handing his partner the newspaper. His eyes scanned the close space, finding those of each of the other detectives. "I hope you detectives- you men of faith in strong evidence and rational deduction - aren't letting any of that Indian's ghost story color your thinking."

Ballinger locked eyes with his Maupai colleague. "I'm just saying - I've never seen anything like this. The things that have happened don't seem earthly possible."

"No, they don't," Tremblehorn agreed. "But, that doesn't mean some angry spirit is killing these people."

Hargrove stood up. "Spirit or not, the victims had all wronged Rebecca Saulters in some way. I think this list is legitimate."

Tremblehorn nodded. "Besides Principal Halloran and Robert Bailey, are any of these others still local?"

"Have to check into it," Ballinger said. "All of these kids are around Rainbird's age. Even if they're college students, they should be home for winter break, just like he was."

"Meaning that if they're all clustered about the county," Hargrove said, "they're sitting targets if our guy isn't actually the killer."

Carpenter nodded. "Let's split up this list and find out the exact whereabouts of everyone on it. Also, Tremblehorn and I can visit Rebecca Saulters's old grade school. You two take the high school. See if we can find out if this list needs to be any longer."

"Sounds like a plan," Ballinger said. "Although, I hope we got the right guy already. If we don't..."

"If we don't," Tremblehorn said, "then someone else will have to die to prove it."

II

The detectives only needed a few hours to account for the whereabouts of each name on John Rainbird's list.

PFC Robert Bailey was two thirds of the world away, serving a tour of duty in Afghanistan. His mother informed Detective Ballinger that the young man had departed for basic training one month after graduating from high school. Ballinger figured that whoever or whatever had killed Gregory Rollins, Kevin Anderson, and Veronica Myers couldn't touch him in the war torn lands of Central Asia. All Bailey needed to worry about was getting his ass shot off or blown to smithereens.

Principal Thomas Halloran could be found at Patrick F. Mackenzie High from 7 am until well into the evening. When he did go home, it was to a big colonial just a few minutes from the water in Havre de Grace.

Pamela Lawson was home for winter break from Bowie State University, a college close to Tremblehorn and Carpenter's neck of the woods. She spent her time off in the house she grew up in. "That is when she's not out partying or running around God knows where," her mother groused to Detective Hargrove.

Shanae Edwards was also home for winter break from Bowie State. She and Pamela were still close friends, a fact that seemed to be a significant factor in Pamela attending a historically black college. Shanae often accompanied Pamela to go "partying or running around God knows where."

Tara Andrews lived with her tattoo heavy, long haired boyfriend. Judging by his weathered mug, he was at least thirty. The scar tissue on his knuckles confessed to many fights. The faded bruises on Tara's cheeks confessed that some of those fights had been with her. The battered young woman had fallen far from her days of filling out the quintet of mean girls headed by Pamela, Shanae, and Veronica.

Crystal Ritchie, the other member of the quintet, had become a different sort of fallen woman. Young Miss Ritchie was a known prostitute in Eastern Baltimore County. She operated out of the seedy motels that dotted the stretch of 40 East between Rosedale and Middle River. Her pimp used Craigslist and supposed online "dating" services to attract clientele. She shared an Essex residence and heroin habit with three other lost young women.

After tracking down each of the potential victims, the detectives arranged protective surveillance for each of them. The Maryland State Police and Baltimore County Police felt pleased to alternate vigil outside of the Essex residence. They had been after Crystal's pimp, a smarmy and clever young predator named Steven Connor, for quite some time. The guise of protecting Crystal from a possible killer was just added justification for them to study his den of whores.

Carpenter and Tremblehorn did the honors of camping outside of Mr. Halloran's home and office. They found him to be ebullient, charming, and positive to the point of irrepressibility. They hated wiping the pearly smile off his face by apprising him of what was going on. He said that he still felt bad about kicking Rebecca out of Mackenzie School, but that school policy had left him no latitude. Rebecca had been one of his favorite students in the truncated time he knew her.

"I often think that I could have done a sight better by her," he said. "But, I can't imagine someone wanting to kill me because I followed school policy."

Once the two detectives parked outside of his home, Halloran returned to his usual good spirits. He brought them coffee and fresh buttered rolls during their first night of surveillance. Halloran even offered to put them up in his guest quarters.

"I have plenty of room," he smiled. "I am a notorious bachelor. Being devoted to one's work can make it difficult to maintain romantic companionship."

The detectives politely declined the offer. "Don't wan't to get too cozy," Carpenter said. "Being uncomfortable makes us more alert."

Carpenter and Tremblehorn stayed in the car, bundled against the winter cold and napping in shifts. They cranked up the cruiser's engine and heat at regular intervals throughout the night.

At 6:30 the next morning, the kind principal brought his guardians a tray of piping hot sausage and egg biscuits and pleasant smelling home brewed coffee.

"I intend to keep you gents well-nourished so long as you keep watch over me." Halloran's smile shone at 2,000 megawatts even as the sun struggled against the fading darkness. "I must be off to work, now. I've got a prestigious school to run."

He turned and headed toward his own vehicle, a late model blue Volvo.

While the PG County detectives watched over the gracious principal, their Harford County counterparts kept tabs outside of the grungy residence Tara shared with her cradle robbing, woman beating boyfriend. They were very happy to inform the brute that they would be posted up outside for a while. Beating Tara's ass wouldn't be an option for him, at least not for a few days. Tara was safe from her boyfriend for now. Whether she was safe from facing cruel vengeance for tormenting Rebecca Saulters remained to be seen.

The Harford County Sheriff's office assigned a blue and white to watch the respective residences of Pamela Lawson and Shanae Edwards. Once each of the names on John Rainbird's list was assigned a babysitter, there was nothing to do but wait. The first two nights of coordinated surveillance were uneventful to the point of boredom, making the entire operation seem like a foolish pursuit. The third night was a creature of far more vicious temperament.

III

John Rainbird granted himself no mercy in his honesty, crafting no delusion about the fact that he was waiting for someone to die a horrible death. He wondered if this was what military leaders felt like when they sent unfortunate troops off to certain demise, those chosen serving as sacrificial lambs for the greater good. He didn't know how people who made such decisions slept at night. He struggled to sleep in his time at the Harford County Detention Center, surprising himself by praying to the divergent gods his father and grandfather introduced to him as a child- his father's Jesus and his grandfather's Great Spirits.

John Rainbird couldn't decide which belief system felt more plausible during his adolescent years, so he never embraced either. Except for his vengeful wishes and machinations after Rebecca died, he never granted too much credence to the possibility of an afterlife or spirit realm. Even the attempt to raise Rebecca from the dead was nothing more than a manifestation of his grieving, young heart acting out. He hadn't believed that Rebecca would walk the Earth in any form- at least he now thought he hadn't. But Rebecca did now walk the Earth- in the form of a wrathful apparition. Now faced with empirical evidence that there are other worlds than these, the young Maupai had no problem praying to the higher powers of both Christian and Maupai belief.

Like Christians, the Maupai held faith as a crucial part of prayer. If that shared belief were correct, then John Rainbird's prayers didn't have a chance. He had no faith that his impassioned pleas would stop whatever had become of Rebecca from taking its next victim. The only question was which of the six names that appeared to him in a trance state would be next.

John Rainbird bided his time, knowing that sooner or later the creature would appear to him in a horrific vision of the destruction of its next target.

When that time came, he would be released from the human menagerie he now inhabited.

Wise Eyes and Trotting Fox would then set about the task of helping him expel the demon. John Rainbird wondered who the sacrificial lamb that ensured his freedom would be, shivering at the clinical nature of his speculation.

IV

Pamela Lawson did the drunk's shuffle to her front door, fished her keys out of her pocket in an effort akin to searching for buried treasure, then turned and waved to her friend Shanae. "Alright, girl!" she yelled. "I'll see you tomorrow."

Shanae beeped the horn of her Nissan Sentra XE, flicked her left turn signal, and did a quick turnabout, bringing her car within a few feet of the blue and white parked across the street from Pamela's house. She beeped her horn at the young officers inside, chortling a good night before heading for her home four blocks away.

"That's my girl!" Pamela yelled, not caring at all that it was nearly 3 am as she delighted in her own obnoxiousness. Her dislike of cops babysitting her had intensified now that she'd plied herself with five or six drinks. She was three years too young to be served alcohol according to the law, but the bartenders at Club Choice's down in Baltimore City never checked her for ID. Why should they? When she and Shanae gussied themselves up and put on their club clothes, they both looked to be at least 21.

Pamela giggled as she let herself into the dark house, thinking about how comfortable she felt in black nightclubs. She was often one of the few white patrons in such places, but she didn't give a damn. Pamela's best friend was black and Pamela "loved" black guys. That was why she felt so comfortable attending Bowie State. Her mother's befuddlement at that aspect of her only encouraged Pamela to embrace black people more. She loved her mother, but the lady needed to stop clutching to the antiquated belief that people should stick to their own kind.

Pamela pulled the front door shut and tried to hang her jacket on the coat rack to the left of it. She missed and left the jacket in the floor. She giggled, knowing her mom wouldn't be happy to find it in the morning. She reconsidered, thinking that she didn't want to be awakened bright and early to argue about it.

There'd already been enough arguing since Pamela came back from Bowie. Her mother acted like she was supposed to just sit in the house and twiddle her thumbs for the entire semester break.

Fuck that, Pamela thought.

Her mother had her fun in college and Pamela intended to do the same. Just because Brenda was now engaged to a church deacon didn't mean Pamela had to act like a different person. Her mom was such a hypocrite, trying to push that holy junk Deacon Davis spouted on her now grown daughter.

At least I don't do one night stands, no matter how drunk I get, Pamela thought. *And I won't be having any unplanned children.*

Pamela checked the contents of the stainless steel refrigerator, knowing that the fancy machine wouldn't contain what she really wanted. Her mother used to keep the bottom shelf stocked with wine and wine coolers, but that was BDD-before Deacon Davis. Pamela settled for a Coke Zero. She sat down at the kitchen island and lapped from the can, like a thirsty dog from a water dish.

As tense as things had been in the ten days she'd been home from school, they'd been much worse in the past few. The police had come around, dredging the specter of Rebecca Saulters. They believed that someone was killing people who wronged the poor girl, said that Pamela had been known to be quite the nemesis. Sure, that was true, but only through eighth grade- the whole knife lady's daughter thing.

Pamela had nothing to do with that blowjob video. In fact, she only crossed Rebecca's path once after eighth grade graduation. Rebecca and her new bosom buddy Kimberly Meisner got the best of that encounter.

Pamela and Shanae did goad Big Ronnie into spray painting Rebecca's house after the dick sucking video came out, but they were never credited with it. That could have been anybody. The video was the biggest joke among kids in their neck of Harford County- at least until Rebecca killed herself. Pamela felt horrible after that happened, but she didn't feel the least bit responsible for it.

She didn't deny that she'd been a cruel kid, but she was among the least of Rebecca's tormentors when the poor girl died. Besides, that had been four years ago. No matter how hysterical her mother became about the policeman's claims,

Pamela didn't imagine that anyone looking to avenge Rebecca's death would come after her.

Pamela knew that Kevin Anderson had died under mysterious circumstances, but that was while he was away at college and she hadn't heard of any official confirmation that someone murdered him.

He could have killed himself, too, she thought. *I don't think he did, but you never know what people might do.*

The red haired detective's revelation that someone murdered Big Ronnie was far more disturbing than learning about Kevin, but Ronnie never grew out of liking a fight and had even become a biker chick. There was no shortage of people who led that sort of lifestyle being killed.

After learning that they would be placed under police watch whether they liked it or not, Pamela and Shanae agreed to do their best to ignore the patrol cars parked outside of each of their houses. They also pledged not to worry, even if their respective parents were terrified for them.

"It's just a coincidence," Shanae asserted during the brief time they spent discussing the circumstances. "Besides, if anyone made that girl kill herself, it was Kevin Anderson. Why would someone come after us? And if there was anybody like that- why would they wait four years?"

"Amen to that," Pamela chortled, thinking of that conversation. She gulped down the rest of her soda before shuffling off to her bedroom. She was just about to plop onto her bed when a tsunami of pressure threatened to explode from her bladder. She raced to the bathroom next to her bedroom, just reaching the toilet in time.

"I almost pissed on myself," she muttered, sitting on the throne of relief. "I am really dru-unk!"

Pamela assured herself that being in such a state was quite alright since Shanae had pulled driving duty tonight. She'd needed the good time more than usual, with all the shit that was going on around her.

The drunken young woman plopped onto her bed and dozed off, not bothering to remove her tight fitting blouse or snug jeans. She had no idea that she was about to come face to face with the girl she tormented so long ago.

V

Sleep came as the crushing coils of a python. John Rainbird was its doomed prey. The more he struggled to stay awake, the more his consciousness strangled. Despite his awareness of this, he couldn't stop struggling.

A sense of foreboding filled him as he tossed and turned on his bunk, in a futile effort to stave off the inevitable. His cellmate slept below him in tranquility, as if he did not know he was incarcerated. The sound of his snoring was so faint that it was almost polite. John Rainbird did not want to join his fellow inmate, because he knew that his own sleep would serve as a path into the spirit realm. In that realm, a malevolent spirit that he knew all too well would take revenge on another who had wronged its host. John Rainbird did not want to witness the horrible truth of that realm, but he had no choice.

Soon he lost all consciousness, his pupils rolling back to reveal only the whites of his eyes. Just as the prey of a boa is bound to suffocate once the snake's muscled body takes hold, so the tribesman lost his struggle. He was thrust into a dreamscape beyond dreams, a theatre of the mind that broadcasted a live and uncensored documentary. John Rainbird was about to witness more of what his younger, grief-stricken self once wanted. He wished he could reach into the past and throttle that misguided idiot for the horror he unleashed.

VI

Michelle Lawson embraced the gospel of turnabout as fair play, making a beeline to her slumbering daughter's room. If Pamela could disrupt her sleep in the middle of the night by entering the house in a ruckus, then it was right and just that she jolt Pamela from her sure to be drunken slumber now that morning was here.

Michelle's lips curled into a cruel smile as she crashed through the door. She approached the foot of Pamela's bed, all set to shake her awake. Michelle did a double take, hoping that her eyes had deceived her on first glance. Pamela slept on her back, a position her mother had never found her in when going to awaken her. This development was far more significant than a new sleeping habit, for her chest remained motionless, failing to rise and fall in the rhythm of breathing. Her left arm dangled from the edge of her mattress, more limp noodle than human appendage.

Michelle thrust aside the hard shell she so often presented since her daughter began the tumultuous, authority challenging journey through adolescence. She became the mother of a toddler again, a helpless young child. Michelle searched her helpless child for a pulse, but found none.

"Oh, God!" she wailed, a banshee in the morning. "No! Please, God noooo!"

Tears splattered Michelle's face as she pulled her cell phone from the pocket of her slacks. She dialed 911 because that's what people do in such situations. She knew that the EMTs who arrived could do nothing but confirm her daughter's death.

Chapter 35- Free to Fight

I

John Rainbird didn't feel surprised or excited upon his release from the detention center, knowing that Pamela Lawson's death had precipitated it. At least now he could intervene before her killer took more victims. The price for that opportunity was watching Pamela die.

He awakened screaming from the horrific vision in the middle of the night, causing such a ruckus that another prisoner on his tier yelled, "Man, someone shut that crazy Indian up."

Two guards spoke to John Rainbird from outside his cell, trying to get him to settle down. They assured him that he was only having a bad dream, the manifestation of his mind messing with him in stir. "Happens to a lot of new fish," the older of the two guards said. "It'll pass."

The young Maupai recovered himself to nod his agreement to the guards, knowing that attempting to explain the truth of the situation to them would prove fruitless. He took small comfort in the knowledge that he'd be out soon. Now here he walked, in the bright of afternoon, passing through the exit doors of the modern dungeon that held him for more than three days.

Two of the detectives responsible for his incarceration waited for him on the front steps. "You guys should have believed me," John Rainbird groused.

Detective Ballinger frowned. Dark sunglasses obscured his eyes. "Who could believe something like that? You don't think your story was a bit fantastical?"

"I believe it sounded fantastical. That doesn't make it untrue."

Neither Ballinger nor Hargrove responded as they stared at their erstwhile suspect.

They looked unsure and uncomfortable to him, the polar opposites of the confident law men he'd turned himself into a few days earlier. John Rainbird supposed that being confronted with irrefutable evidence of the supernatural had that effect on even the staunchest of men. There was no debating that it had shaken his world.

"So, what happens now?" John Rainbird asked.

"Now we try to figure out how to stop whatever's doing this," Hargrove said, bloodshot eyes complementing his weary voice.

II

"I knew this was some sci-fi shit," Detective Carpenter said. He and the other detectives occupied both sides of a booth at the Bay Corner Diner. Plates of breakfast food and cups of coffee sat undisturbed before them.

"I knew it when we found that college kid drowned on his bed. I felt in my gut that no man could do all the physical evidence revealed. But then, being a detective, I fooled myself, trying to find a rational way to explain it. Well, there's no rational way to explain what just happened to that poor girl. We had two officers posted outside. They saw her stumble in from clubbing at nearly 3 am. Yet, her mother found her dead this morning, with her lungs full of water? That's definitely not humanly possible."

"No," Tremblehorn admitted. "It's not humanly possible. I've never believed in Maupai legends. I've always thought of them as nothing more than entertaining stories, thinking that actually believing in that kind of stuff is part of the reason that the small number of Native Americans left in this country can't do any better than they do. But after last night, I can no longer say that the spirit realm doesn't exist. Something beyond human understanding has taken the lives of our four victims."

Ballinger followed laughter with a scowl. "So, I'm supposed to tell my Captain that the case is taking a new turn now? That instead of trying to pin these crimes on a person- we're turning into the Ghostbusters? No way will any of our superiors buy that shit. I'm not sure I do."

"I'm not sure I do, either," Hargrove chimed in. "That's why we're not going to tell that to any of our superiors.

Ballinger snickered, turning to face his begrudged partner. "Well, then- what are we going to tell them- Smart Guy?"

"We're going to tell them that John Rainbird's not off the hook yet. That we think tailing him could lead us to the real killer or killers. That maybe Rainbird has a partner or several partners."

"You believe that?" Tremblehorn asked.

"Hell no! No human could do what was done last night. And I'm sure the water in the victim's lungs will be found to have come from the Snake River, just like with the others. I'm only suggesting that we tell our superiors that to buy time."

"Buy time to do what?" Ballinger asked.

"Buy time to visit the Maupai and find out if anything can be done to stop whatever's doing this."

III

"There is nothing any of you can do," Wise Eyes said, moving his leathery index finger left to right to indicate Detectives Carpenter, Ballinger, and Hargrove. "For the blood of the Maupai does not course through your veins."

The old man sneered at Tremblehorn. "Though you have not grown up within the tribe, your blood cannot be denied. You may be of use to us in this task."

The investigative quartet, John Rainbird, Wise Eyes, and Trotting Fox bunched together in Wise Eyes's tiny front room. John Rainbird and his two forebears pressed into the threadbare couch like sardines in a can.

The detectives sat across from them in rickety wooden chairs, two of which had been brought from the home of a neighbor. The afternoon sun struggled through the copse of trees that stood outside the structure. A sliver of it managed to pass through the lone window.

"What task do you speak of, Chief Wise Eyes?" Tremblehorn tried to honor the chieftain by mimicking his syntax.

Wise Eyes frowned. "I speak of sending this wicked spirit back to the void from which the Son of My Son foolishly summoned it. What other task would there be?"

"And how might he help?" Hargrove blurted, drawing a dirty look from his partner.

"You will help by remaining silent when it is not your place to speak!" Trotting Fox spoke for the first time, his voice like gravel in a landslide.

Ballinger smirked at his partner, as if bemoaning the folly of youth.

Hargrove bit his lip, swallowing a retort.

"Pardon my colleague, Father Trotting Fox," Tremblehorn said, looking in the shaman's direction, but avoiding his eyes. "He is not familiar with the ways of the Maupai."

"Nor are you," Wise Eyes sneered. "Not as familiar as you should be, with the people's blood running through your veins, my lost brother."

The chieftain grasped John Rainbird's forearm. "Neither is the Son of My Son. That is why he came to be deceived into unleashing the foul spirit that now wreaks havoc in the Anglo realm you've chosen to inhabit. I hold myself

341

responsible for not having taught him better. That is why I must help to vanquish this evil. Our culture believes that balance must always be restored when it is lost. Failure to do so brings doom upon those who ignore that responsibility."

Tremblehorn nodded. "How may I help with restoring that balance, Chief Wise Eyes?"

"You may help by adding your strength to our strength when the time comes. It will not be long."

IV

"I just can't believe this shit, John," Brittany shrieked. "I just can't believe any of this shit!"

The young couple sat at the edge of a dowdy motel room bed. John Rainbird made a cradle of his arms and scooped his fiancée into them. Brittany hitched and trembled as she sobbed, but John Rainbird held her fast.

"First you go to jail, suspected of murder of all things. Now you're telling me some spirit is the actual killer?" Brittany grew still, lifting her head enough to look into her fiancé 's eyes. Tears flowed down the reddened landscape of her face, streaking her familiar black mascara. "Some spirit that you raised from the dead? The spirit of a girl you probably loved more than you love me?"

She broke free from him, heading into the tiny bathroom before submitting to a crying jag. John Rainbird waited for her to cry herself out, deciding not to intervene. She seemed to go on forever, the blaring sound of her blowing her nose coming at regular intervals. The fit renewed its vigor each time he thought she might be done. The sounds of her misery subsided just as his patience did. She sauntered back to the bed and nestled herself in his arms again.

"I'm sorry." A wan smile unfurled on her now mascara free face. The matching lipstick she'd worn was also gone. John Rainbird thought she looked just as pretty without the adornment. "It wasn't fair for me to say you loved her more than you love me. I suppose you could have chosen her if you wanted to. Anyway, who cares about what happened when we were 14? It's just… I guess I can be as silly as any other girl." She laughed- a sound that did nothing to mask her anguish. "You sure know how to drop a bomb on a girl, you know? Calling me from jail was like Hiroshima and what you just told me was Nagasaki."

John Rainbird grinned. "Well, no more atomic bombs were dropped after Nagasaki."

"That's true. But, the after effects lasted for decades."

"That won't happen with us."

"How can you be so sure?"

"I can be so sure because I know grandfather and Trotting Fox will help me beat that thing, send it back to where it came from. Then we'll go on about our lives, doing everything we planned to do."

Brittany's eyes performed a joyful dance. "You mean getting married?"

John Rainbird kissed her on the forehead. "I mean getting married and getting the hell away from Bay Corner and all points Harford County."

Brittany squealed, clapping once before clasping her hands. "I can't wait." Her eyes darkened as sobriety gripped her. "You can't get hurt- can you?"

John Rainbird shook his head. "I don't think so. The spirit serves me because I called it forth. Now, I have to get rid of it."

A surprised expression colored Brittany's face. "You always said you didn't believe in that 'Indian mumbo jumbo'."

John Rainbird shrugged. "I didn't. Not really. I just did what I did because… I don't know."

"Because even though you've always been really smart, you could be as much of a bonehead as any other teenaged boy."

John Rainbird laughed. "You got me there. I'm not a boy anymore, though." He maneuvered himself to press his weight against his fiancée, ending up atop her on the mattress. "I'm a strapping young man. And I know how to do manly things."

Brittany giggled. "You are so silly. Okay, I'll play along. How bout you show me what kind of manly stuff you know how to do?"

"I thought you'd never ask," John Rainbird said, assaulting her with kisses.

Chapter 36- A Ghastly Correction

I

On the night of December 21st, Mother Nature abandoned the consistent 50 degree temperatures of recent days in favor of frigid conditions. The meteorological conditions of the first official night of winter were identical to those John Rainbird faced during his first unearthing of Rebecca's grave.

Just as it did on that occasion, the crescent moon flickered in the night sky like a dying light bulb. Just like before, the late night wind howled its fury.

John Rainbird zipped his winter jacket and bid farewell to his elders. Each of the old men blessed him in the Maupai fashion before he departed.

The young man gathered a replacement set of tools from his grandfather's woodshed, having long since rid himself of those used during the first disinterment. He stuffed a shovel, spade, and length of coiled rope into a massive duffel bag. A high powered flashlight, extra batteries, and felt became cargo for his knapsack. A new Exact-o knife hid in a pocket of his winter coat. He fixed the strap of the duffel bag upon his left shoulder and across his chest, joining it with the knapsack on his back.

Once again, John Rainbird began his jaunt to the cemetery in the dead of night. The wind conspired with the momentum of the Vespa to force a current of cold against his hooded face, but his coat teamed with leather gloves in keeping the rest of him warm. The young tribesman zipped through the deserted roads of Bay Corner, soon reaching the woods that bordered the rear of the resting place's circular body. He rested the scooter among the bushes, as he rested his trusty bicycle years ago.

John Rainbird breathed vapor as he looked through the black fencing to behold a landscape as bleak and devoid of light as he remembered.

John Rainbird wondered if Trotting Fox and Wise Eyes could be wrong- if completing the ceremony "correctly" might somehow strengthen the spirit that inhabited Rebecca. He pressed on, knowing that he didn't have any better ideas and he couldn't leave things as they were. He hoped that Trotting Fox and Wise Eyes were right in setting his course of action. If they weren't, there was nothing anyone could do but watch the wraith kill until it was satisfied. John Rainbird couldn't imagine living with himself if that happened.

The intended grave robber took a deep breath, pulled the duffel bag free of his torso and heaved it over the fence. He shimmied up the fencing as he did four winters previous, moving with slow caution at the top. He eased one leg over the graveyard side before following with the other, taking a relieved breath when his feet found earth without incident.

John Rainbird recovered the duffel bag and sought out Rebecca's tombstone. He placed the duffel bag and knapsack before the grey stone marker. "If there is a God in heaven or spirits in the Cross World, your flame will light once more," the young man spoke in response to his friend's epitaph. He removed the contents of each conveyance and set about his grim task.

John Rainbird cut a square of felt and affixed it to the flashlight's lens, releasing only enough light to illuminate the immediate area. That light guided him as he used the new shovel and spade to unearth Rebecca's grave. The spade tore into the still pliant soil that surrounded Rebecca's headstone, the heel of his foot driving it downward. He switched to the shovel once he expelled a satisfactory amount.

John Rainbird's exertion overcame the frigid night to lather him with sweat. He unzipped his coat and removed his hood before resuming his efforts.

The grave digger threw all the expelled dirt to the left as he worked. He soon stood within a rectangular gap, like before. Like before, he pressed on until his shovel scraped across a hard surface. He set the shovel aside and climbed from the grave to grab the flashlight. The reduced beam revealed the again unearthed burial liner.

John Rainbird uncoiled the rope and threaded it through the iron rings on half of the burial liner's segmented top. Like before, he wrapped both ends of the rope around his gloved hands, positioning himself on the ground at the grave's edge. The chicken wired segments of concrete offered no resistance, dancing loose after one strong tug.

John Rainbird repeated his actions with the other side of the grave liner, exposing the entire coffin. He climbed in next to it and lifted its wooden lid with ease. The latch he splintered during his first violation of Rebecca's grave offered no resistance.

He became aware of the smell of raw earth just as he had before. His hands scrabbled inside the musty wooden box, setting upon Rebecca's exposed bones. A chill that had nothing to do with the weather started at his spine and danced through his entire body. He retched inside the six foot pit, wiped his mouth, closed his eyes, and took deep breaths to keep from hyperventilating. He struggled to maintain his composure while dragging his dead friend's remains from her grave.

II

John Rainbird trudged backward through the graveyard, each hand hooked under what had once been Rebecca's armpits. The remains of his friend felt cold and clammy. The naked bones of the skeleton's feet scraped against the ground as he hauled it.

Revulsion and dread threatened to expel themselves from him in the form of vomit. He fought back the urge, tasting the acrid substance in the rear of his esophagus.

The mocking winter wind kicked up a few times as John dragged the skeleton toward the gate, causing the skull to swing forward and the jaw to chatter. The corpse's hair blew in his face, a cruel reminder of the voluminous mane Rebecca once had. The sack of bones was not as heavy as John Rainbird anticipated, but he still had a devil of a time reaching the fence with it. His muscles were acidic from excavating and reburying her grave. He stood at the doorstep of an anxiety attack. He glanced over his shoulder as he walked, serving the dual purpose of insuring that he didn't stumble and keeping his eyes off his morbid cargo.

After what seemed an eternity, the young tribesman reached the fence. He turned the skeleton so that the bones of its back pointed toward the structure. Squatting, he grabbed it by the torso and hoisted it overhead. Stretching his legs and arms to full extension, he draped his macabre prize atop the fence as a leopard might drag an antelope into a tree on the African savannah.

The moonlight mocked the sojourner as he climbed to join his prize, seeming to shine a spotlight on his ghoulish deeds. He found himself on the other side of the fence a few moments later, having kept the skeleton in mint form while escorting it back to the earth.

John Rainbird hauled his burden back near the bushes where his Vespa waited. The conveyance would have to wait a bit longer, because he needed to recover his bags from the graveyard. He did so with great anxiety, wondering how many times one could trespass there without getting caught.

After returning the duffel bag and knapsack to shelter, the young Maupai bent at the knees and took a few deep breaths. He wiped his forehead before venturing onto the road to signal his help.

III

"I think we all have to be crazy," Detective Carpenter grumbled, occupying the shotgun seat of Ballinger's Dodge Charger. An inauspicious leather jacket covered his Men's Warehouse quality suit and tie. Detective Hargrove sat behind him, dressed in similar fashion.

As always, the driver of the vehicle diverged from his colleagues, wearing a leather trench coat that would have been at home in a 70's crime flick. The clothes it covered were tailored by skilled hands.

John Rainbird sat behind Detective Ballinger, trying and failing to calm the anxiety that raged within him.

"We're not crazy," Ballinger said, idly turning the steering wheel. "We're only responding logically to the circumstances we're confronted with."

"By hauling a fucking skeleton in the trunk of your car? A skeleton that was robbed from its grave by a suspected murderer?"

"He's not a suspect, anymore," Hargrove said.

"He is to our superiors," Carpenter said.

"Fuck our superiors!" Ballinger bellowed, pulling the car to the side of the road. He turned to face his passenger. "And fuck you if you don't want to help. We're trying to save lives here. Now, no matter what our general belief systems are, we have been presented with irrefutable evidence that our killer is a supernatural being. I know you believe that Mr. 'I knew we were dealing with some sci-fi shit'. I know you still know that. So, don't try to back out just because what we're doing would seem crazy to anyone on the outside looking in. We're trying to save lives here, Carpenter."

The negativity on Carpenter's face shifted into a bemused grin. "Bravo," he said, clapping his ebony hands. "You should take a bow, Ballinger. You just presented an unbeatable argument."

"So, on with the show?" Hargrove asked.

"On with the show," Carpenter said.

A short time earlier, Hargrove helped John Rainbird carry Rebecca's remains from the wooded area behind the cemetery to Ballinger's waiting car. Carpenter kept watch for passersby while they did so. There were none in the middle of a cold winter night in quiet little Bay Corner, but those complicit in grave robbing could never be too careful.

Exhuming Rebecca's remains was just the first part of the Trotting Fox's plan. Now that Carpenter had been convinced to eat his reservations, it was time to move to the next grisly phase. It was time for John Rainbird to perform a ceremony he did once before. This time, he must perform it without error.

IV

John Rainbird Jeffries performed the Ceremony of Dead Reckoning without company during his first ill-fated attempt. This time, every male member of Blessed Earth of at least adolescent age surrounded him. David Tremblehorn stood in the midst of them. The traditional Maupai dress and face paint he wore indicated that he was no civil servant tonight. The 70 plus other Maupai males present were costumed in the same fashion.

Harsh blackness shrouded the ridge they clustered about. It received none of the pale moonlight that fell on the murky surface of Snake River below them. The great serpent seemed to slumber before them, but the Maupai assembled knew that it never slept. Tendrils of brine leapt from it, the smell burrowing into every nostril present.

Trotting Fox, Wise Eyes, and John Rainbird kept tomahawks laid at their feet, close to Rebecca's remains. Every other man and adolescent boy held a tomahawk or carried a quiver. Some bore both. Most of them embraced the prospect of the great battle their leaders promised them this night, their long suppressed warrior spirit rekindled by an imminent threat. A pleasant anxiety flowed through David Tremblehorn as he stood with his brethren. He submerged himself in the ways of the Maupai, ways no white man could fully understand, for the first time in his life.

Trotting Fox nodded at John Rainbird, the slight movement almost imperceptible in the darkness. He, John Rainbird, and Wise Eyes linked hands at the center of the circle.

Seventy plus brave men linked hands just beyond them, although it was not part of the ceremony. From the youngest to the oldest, they were all one tonight.

John Rainbird needed no scrawled paper to remember the wording of the ceremony this time. He repeated after his grandfather and the medicine man, who chanted in a wizened chorus of their tribal tongue.

"Great Spirits! Oh, Great Spirits."

"Great Spirits! Oh, Great Spirits!"

"I beseech you to grant Rebecca her vengeance before returning her to the vast belly of your eternal realm."

"I beseech you to grant Rebecca her vengeance before returning her to the vast belly of your eternal realm."

"I offer you my blood as a token of the sacrifice I will grant you for this, Great Spirits!"

"I offer you my blood as a token of the sacrifice I will grant you for this, Great Spirits!"

"Great Spirits, I swear to deliver myself to you three years earlier than the time you have appointed to me if you grant me this boon, Great Spirits!"

"Great Spirits, I swear to deliver myself to you three years earlier than the time you have appointed to me if you grant me this boon, Great Spirits!"

A traditional Maupai knife appeared in Trotting Fox's hand as if out of thin air. He dragged the small blade across the rough surface of his palm, handing it to John Rainbird when he finished. The principal of the ceremony winced as he did the same. Wise Eyes cut himself last, completing the circle.

The three men bent in unison, spilling their blood onto Rebecca's bones. They let the crimson streams flow for a ten count, then picked up the skeleton and tossed it into the river. The serpent hissed one grand splash before falling still again. All assembled knew that it would not be still for long. It would soon vomit forth something hideous and unwelcome. Then, a great and terrible battle would begin.

Chapter 37 - A Great and Terrible Battle

I

John Rainbird didn't underestimate the gravity of what he and his elders had done. They had each sacrificed three years of their lives to call a demon into physical form. Coupled with the time he promised in the first Ceremony of Dead Reckoning, John Rainbird had pledged a total of six years of his life span.

He supposed that didn't preclude him from living a long life in totality After all, he was only 18. His grandfather and Trotting Fox were a much different story. Wise Eyes was in his sixties and Trotting Fox- hell- John Rainbird had no idea exactly how old Trotting Fox was. He felt certain that the shaman was far too old to afford the loss of three years.

The young tribesman felt uncertain about defeating the wraith at all.

"Drawing power from two ceremonies will make it much stronger than it might have been," Trotting Fox explained, a few seconds after the ceremony concluded. "Our task will be far more difficult than defeating that which inhabited Charging Bear."

The spirit had traversed the In Between Land, the thin realm that separates temporal from eternal. It feasted on the essence of those John Rainbird marked there, no doubt growing more ravenous with each meal. Now, it would come forth in physical form, no longer needing the gateway of dreams to pursue its intended.

John Rainird considered these truths as he waited at his post, tomahawk in hand. He never learned to string a bow- to send its lethal projectile whistling into the vitals of an unsuspecting deer. His grandfather brought him along on a deer hunt during the fall of his eleventh year, but he could not persuade John Rainbird to take aim against the beautiful creatures.

John Rainbird's stance strengthened as he grew older. Many times Wise Eyes told his grandson that in the olden days, hunting wouldn't have been a choice. John Rainbird often stoked the old man's anger by pointing out that if it were the olden days- neither of them would have been born yet.

John Rainbird did have great skill with a tomahawk. He never used it to strike a living thing, but he enjoyed throwing it at trees and other still targets. During the years before high school, he and his tribal peers often passed time by seeing who could throw their tomahawk with more accuracy, making targets of objects in their natural environment.

Wise Eyes's grandson even competed in official contests during the "Medvurno" or tribal games- a sort of Maupai Olympics held each summer. He won third place during his best performance.

John Rainbird never imagined that he would one day hold one of the historical weapons with deadly intentions, just as he never truly believed that he could summon a vengeful spirit from the realm that housed it.

Before coming to the river to summon whatever foul spirit inhabited Rebecca, all of the Maupai men gathered at the headwaters of the Chesapeake Bay. Trotting Fox blessed John Rainbird's weapon in a ceremony there, along with the weapons of all the other assembled tribesmen.

The ceremony was a simple one. By turn, each warrior dipped his choice of arms into the headwaters of the Chesapeake. Trotting Fox plunged his hands into the water each time they did so, chanting words of blessing in the Maupai tongue. He chanted in such a rapid and quiet tone that John Rainbird could only make out half of what he said.

The young man gathered that the old man pleaded to the spirits of the Bay that their weapons strike their adversary true. The Maupai believed the Chesapeake to be a sacred body of water, a place that benevolent spirits smiled upon. Snake River was its polar opposite.

After the ceremony to call forth the spirit was complete, the assembled force splintered into half a dozen groups. John Rainbird, Wise Eyes, and Trotting Fox stood at the forefront of the group that remained at the ridge where the ceremony was performed. David Tremblehorn was among the nine others standing with them.

A second group was led by Herman Wolf, a young man John Rainbird's age. Herman Wolf's eyes ignited at the opportunity to demonstrate his prowess as a warrior. He would have felt at home 300 years ago, before the white man came, when there were frequent skirmishes between the Maupai and neighboring tribes. Herman Wolf's group stood vigil about a quarter of a mile down river. His predatory eyes scanned his surroundings without rest as he rubbed his hands together. The young Maupai itched to unload his quiver, sending a fusillade of arrows into a worthy target.

John Rainbird sensed Herman Wolf's excitement as Herman Wolf sensed John Rainbird's reluctance. All of the warriors, reluctant or eager, had entered into some sort of hive consciousness. Even David Tremblehorn's sentiments passed among the others. The erstwhile policeman felt as surprised as he felt determined, as delighted as he felt terrified. Standing at the river's edge poised to battle a hideous demon was the closest he'd ever felt to the ageless, indomitable heart of his tribe.

The other four troops of warriors spread out along the three mile length of the river. David Hawk, Samuel Trueheart, Travis Archer, and Joseph Prince each commanded a group. Each of these men was close to John Rainbird's father's age, if his father were still alive. David Hawk had no woman, but each of the other three leaders hoped that their womenfolk at home were safe. Samuel Trueheart and

Travis Archer worried about the adolescent sons who stood to fight with them. Their fear fueled a determination to fight as they had never fought before, to battle the coming evil until their last breaths.

Time was a mud turtle on dry land, crawling at a glacial pace. The whistling wind served as herald for the great serpent and its parallel shores. John Rainbird gripped the wooden shaft of the tomahawk with enough force to hurt his hand. His body became a transformer, conducting massive volts of anxiety.

He wondered if the creature that had once been Rebecca would even come tonight. After all, it had taken four winters for it to assume the form of the wraith that killed in dreams. The story of Charging Bear posited that it took several years for the great chieftain to claim his vengeance.

It will come tonight, Trotting Fox and Wise Eyes chorused in John Rainbird's head, still speaking in the Maupai tongue. Both men remained motionless, their eyes fixed upon the river. *It will come tonight because it is already here. It has already tasted. All you've done is make it whole.*

Beads of sweat formed on the young Maupai's forehead, defying the chilling wind. The message his forefathers had communicated, using what seemed to be telepathy, cemented the truth once and for all. He was not crazy. This was not some prolonged nightmare. This was reality, a reality in which John Rainbird stood at the banks of Snake River, prepared to face a nightmarish entity that wore the face of his dead friend.pt

"There!" Herman Wolf's words echoed through John Rainbird's consciousness. He saw what the strapping warrior saw- a moonlit figure emerging from the center of the river. The naked young woman floated amidst the coils of the aquatic serpent, a few hundred yards from its eastern edge.

The figure didn't look evil at all. It was Rebecca at John Rainbird's age, unclothed and possessing the radiant, coquettish beauty that young women in their prime possess. She made slow progress toward the shore, moving forward without rippling the water.

The enchantment of her beauty blossomed as she closed within fifty yards of Herman Wolf and his troop. Her soft brown eyes were those of a doe, those of one of God's Angels. Her smile was that of a gentle soul, of one whom brought magnificent tidings.

It is a mask, Trotting Fox and Wise Eyes sent a psychic scream into the night. *It is a mask, Herman Wolf! Use your true eyes!*

Herman Wolf blinked and shook his head. The silly grin that had parted his lips departed. He saw that the smile on the young woman's face was not that of a gentle soul, but the sneer of a ravenous carnivore. Its eyes did not twinkle with gentility. They were the eyes of a doll, devoid of love, compassion, or any other human emotion.

Herman Wolf strung a metal-tipped arrow and sent it whistling toward the creature. The creature's left arm shot forward, snatching the projectile from the air and tossing it aside. It repeated the trick with Herman Wolf's next two attempts.

"Step aside, brave men," it spoke in the hideous chorus that John Rainbird recalled from his visions. The dulcet voice of a young woman, the tinny voice of a small girl, and the droning vocalizations of a robot issued from one larynx. "I did not come for you. I came for those who have injured me."

The creature now stood in the shallows of the river, less than ten yards from the small band of Maupai.

Herman Wolf and his troops paused for a beat, seeming to consider its' words.

"You may not have come for us," the brave young warrior rejoined, "but, you have no claim to this realm at all. So, you may return to the abyss you were borne from or face us all."

He abandoned his arrows and removed his tomahawk from its strap.

The wraith threw its head back, erupting into laughter. Up close, Herman Wolf saw that it was lit from within, like a giant firefly. Its dead eyes sprang to celestial life, painted with Technicolor intensity. They locked onto Herman Wolf's gaze, making him their prisoner.

The brilliant spheres shifted colors, cycling from dark green, to dark blue, to deep brown, and back again. Herman Wolf and his band stood frozen, transfixed by the changing pupils. "I don't think you meant that," the ghastly chorus croaked, stepping onto the shore and walking right past them.

The wraith had moved 50 yards beyond Herman Wolf's troop when Trotting Fox pulled a tiny dagger from the belt of his garb and stabbed his left palm with it. A psychic shockwave of pain passed through John Rainbird and every other Maupai assembled.

Don't look into its eyes, Trotting Fox and Wise Eyes unleashed another screaming psychic chorus. *Do not look into its eyes!*

Herman Wolf notched another arrow and sent it flying at his prey's back. The wraith whirled at a speed that could only be achieved through supernatural means, just in time to avoid a direct hit. The arrow's metal head scraped the creature's right shoulder as it passed by.

A surprised look emerged on the creature's visage before the carnivorous sneer returned. It shook its head as the warriors rushed in, as if to say, "If you insist."

A flurry of arrows and tomahawks roared through the night air. The wraith moved in a blur, power beyond human understanding allowing it to dodge or deflect most of the weapons. A solitary tomahawk found its mark, turning over once in the air before slicing off the pinky, middle, and ring finger of the wraith's left hand.

A hideous cry pierced the night, sounding like the cry of a thousand cats mewling in unison. The creature's eyes ceased shifting colors, becoming blood red orbs without pupils. The interior light of the wraith dissipated, leaving it a moving shadow. The black blur descended upon Herman Wolf's troop, tearing a young man known as Osprey Feather's arm free from finger to elbow with one yank.

John Rainbird doubled over, clutching his own still intact appendage as psychic waves transmitted the bottomless nightmare of Osprey Feather's pain.

Every Maupai to Herman Wolf! The elders howled. *Every warrior to Herman Wolf!*

John Rainbird sprinted, his feet fast and sure, his breath endless. He sensed every Maupai not already engaged with the wraith running with him, the different troops bearing down upon their adversary in perfect concert. They felt every tear of flesh, every broken bone suffered by their brethren, yet they did not break stride.

Two members of Herman Wolf's troop stood alongside their young leader by the time the other warriors converged upon them. Nine other brave men lay with grave wounds. Osprey Feather met his end when the black creature snapped his neck after dismembering his arm.

Runnels of blood trailed along the ground, the harsh crimson masking the brown earth beneath it. The wraith wailed like something from the ninth circle of hell, red eyes pulsing with malevolence.

Arrows jutted from the creature's shoulders and breastbone, evidence that Herman Wolf's party did not fall without exacting a toll. A tomahawk burrowed into its right oblique.

The wraith tore the missiles free and tossed them with disdain. Miniature geysers of water spurted from the perforations in their wake.

Herman Wolf and his remaining warriors backpedaled into some nearby brush, making a desperate attempt to notch their few remaining arrows. The creature seemed to teleport through the night air, moving within ten yards of them without making a single footfall.

The 60 or so other tribesman clustered less than 50 yards from their enemy, standing still with uncertainty. They were reluctant to send their arrows flying, fearing that they might strike their comrades in such close, dark quarters.

Instinct guided John Rainbird to the head of the cadre. Trotting Fox had assured him that he would know what to do when the time came. The old man's words now proved prophetic.

"Rebecca!" he bellowed. "Rebecca, you must stop this!"

The wraith ceased its attack and turned to face him. The shadowy cast dissipated from its skin as it did so.

The burning coals that had been its eyes departed, replaced by the kind eyes of a girl John Rainbird once knew. The girl's full lips bloomed into a pleasant smile, one bereft of demonic craving.

"Hi, John Rainbird," the naked young woman spoke in a soft, sweet voice. Her voice was just as John Rainbird remembered it, with no small girl or robotic drone mixed in.

Herman Wolf notched an arrow as the two reunited friends regarded each other.

Wise Eyes waved crossing palms with vigor, a clear indication for the archer to hold off. The other Maupai joined Herman Wolf in waiting, standing poised to strike at the slightest provocation.

"You should stop this, Rebecca. It's wrong for you to do this."

Confusion spread across Rebecca's pretty face. "It's wrong for me to do this? You called for me, John Rainbird. You called for vengeance against everyone who's wronged me."

John Rainbird swallowed hard at her words, unable to deny the truth in them. "I – I didn't really believe that it would happen. I was just so angry. I was a mixed up kid. Just like you were a mixed up kid when you…"

A hint of malice glinted in Rebecca's eyes. "When I killed myself? No, I wouldn't say that I was mixed up at all. I was very certain that my life wasn't worth living anymore, that I'd never be anything more than a disgraced laughingstock. I couldn't live that way, so I found peace the only way I could. You couldn't leave me to that, though. You went messing around with forces you don't understand, violated my grave. You called me back." Her eyes shifted, losing their humanity and changing colors as they had before. As they cycled from dark green, to dark blue, to deep brown, and back again, John Rainbird realized that the changes mimicked the color of the river at various times of year.

The eerie chorus resumed when Rebecca spoke again. "You called me forth, so now I am here. I have a job to do, John Rainbird, and I will not stop until I have punished everyone who has it coming!"

"And who is everyone, Rebecca?"

Light shone from Rebecca's body again. She tossed her head back, emitting mechanized laughter. "Who is 'everyone'? If you must know, that bitch Shanae, that bastard Halloran, those betraying bitches Kimberly and Phyllis, Tara Andrews,

Crystal Ritchie. I'll get that little fucker Robert Bailey whenever he comes back here, and I'll save my miserable excuse for a mother for last." The creature laughed again. "Oh, it's going to be so much fun."

John Rainbird blinked, feeling as stunned as horrified. "Why would you kill your own mother, Rebecca? Don't you love her?"

"Ha! That crazy bitch needs to be put out of her misery. If it wasn't for her, none of that shit would have happened. She left me with that pervert Gregory. Well, I fixed him- didn't I? I'll fix her, too. I'll fix them all even better now that you've truly brought me back. Ha-ha! I'll fix them all, but I'll save that useless heap Emma for last. Going to take my time, too. I'm going to enjoy it so much."

John Rainbird scowled. "You are not Rebecca."

"What?"

"You are not Rebecca. The Rebecca I knew would never talk like that. The Rebecca I knew could never be full of so much hate.

The wraith sneered. "Maybe you didn't know that Rebecca as well as you think."

John Rainbird shook his head. "No. I knew her. I know her. Rebecca, don't do this. Don't let whatever has a hold on you do this. You can go back, Rebecca. You can rest in peace."

The light that shone from within the Rebecca entity fell away. The color of its eyes stopped shifting. For just a few seconds, Rebecca's true face looked upon her friend again. That face was as kind as he remembered. Then the vessel before him turned black, baring eyes of burning crimson as it had while fighting Herman Wolf's troop.

John Rainbird looped his tomahawk into his belt and walked toward the creature, feeling that he could still coax Rebecca from it. Herman Wolf stood ready to send an arrow piercing through the thing's back, but Trotting Fox again signaled for the young warrior to wait.

"You are not evil, Rebecca. Neither am I." John Rainbird held his hands out, palms up. "That creature who inhabits your body right now has taken advantage of us. It is from the river, from beyond the river. We should have stayed away, just as the legends of my people warned. I should have heeded those warnings."

John Rainbird stood within arm's length of the creature now. It dissipated, again leaving a nude Rebecca in its wake. "The creature- the thing that now fills you with hate- it somehow got into my head after you died. It was a whispering voice that never went away. Perhaps it whispered to you, too, causing you to do what you did. That thing is not the real you, Rebecca. You must break away from it. You must go and rest. I know the real you is in there somewhere and I know that your true spirit does not hold such hatred."

John Rainbird embraced his reanimated friend. Up close, the cloying scent of brine that emanated from her seared John's nostrils. Rebecca wrapped her arms around him in return, whispering in his ear, "Thank you, John Rainbird. Thank you. I love you."

She pecked him on the cheek, her lips a blast of frigidity. She collapsed into a heap the moment her lips left him. A swirling vapor floated from her body, climbing into the night sky. Every Maupai assembled relaxed as they watched its ascent. A cavalcade of weapons lowered.

John Rainbird smiled, knowing that the vapor was the departing spirit of his friend. His eyes, along with those of his fellow tribesman, remained riveted on its skyward progress. It floated free of the trees and continued its flight, intent on uniting with the moon.

John Rainbird sighed, content in his knowledge that Rebecca's spirit now knew the peaceful slumber of eternity. Rebecca's body was another matter.

The discarded carcass at John Rainbird's feet exploded into motion, seizing him with lightning quickness. It dragged him to the ground before he had a chance to draw his tomahawk.

II

Rebecca's soul had departed, leaving only the malevolent spirit that seduced John Rainbird into freeing it from its dark realm. No trace of humanity tempered the wraith's bloodlust as it attacked him. It was a black spot, a mud man with eyes of hellfire. Its vise like grip crushed the bones of the one who summoned it.

John Rainbird's brethren fell upon the fiend like hyenas on a wildebeest, pulling at its limbs and hacking with their blessed weapons. The creature released him and scurried away, its howls sending a hellish lament through the night. The force of Maupai fought without relent, determined to return the foul creature to the abyss from which it came.

The creature's efforts to regenerate its wounds could not keep pace with the Maupai blitzkrieg. Not a beat passed without the head of a tomahawk penetrating its shell. Each blow loosed a spout of brackish water, wetting the hard crusted winter soil. The creature staggered like a drunken man in a blindfold, not granted even a hair's breadth to gather itself.

John Rainbird struggled to his feet as his kin routed the creature. Towering tendrils of pain seized his right side, apprising him of his mangled ribs. The pain became a tsunami as he drew his tomahawk and ran toward the wraith. His adversary whirled to face him as he closed in, attempting to raise its monstrous arms. Tomahawk blows from Wise Eyes and Samuel Trueheart struck the creature in concert, each blade burrowing into a shoulder blade. The creature's nightmare eyes found John Rainbird's, hating him and accusing him of betraying their agreement.

John Rainbird ignored the pain that racked his body, gripping the haft of the blessed weapon with both hands and raising it over his head. "Back to the spirit realm!" His bellow preceded a mighty blow, the tomahawk burying itself in the creature's skull.

The creature's howls ceased as a blast of water escaped the fissure that John Rainbird's blow opened, spraying all who stood within ten yards. The thing from the river slumped to the ground and lay still.

Wise Eyes held his arms out at his sides, each palm directing the warriors to cease their attacks. Trotting Fox appeared next to John Rainbird, taking him by the crook of the arm and marching him to his felled foe.

"Now, you must finish it," the elder said.

John Rainbird did not have to ask what Trotting Fox meant. He grabbed the protruding haft of the tomahawk with both hands, wincing as he wrenched it free of the foul creature. He then methodically set about the task of dismembering the creature. A tomahawk was not within shouting distance of the ideal tool for such a task, but he knew that he could only use a traditional and blessed Maupai weapon. He also knew that it was left to the one who had called the creature forth to dispatch its body.

John Rainbird swung the tomahawk until he gasped for air and his arms became useless logs. His ribs screamed their fury the entire time. It occurred to him that an unseen force supplied the strength for him to fight through such agony. That unseen force came from someone who had once been his one true friend.

When the butchering of the wraith's body was complete, John Rainbird's fellow Maupai gathered the separated parts. Wise Eyes carried the creature's head in one hand, using the other to steady his grandson as they walked. The wraith's hellish eyes had winked out of existence, lending its head the lifeless appearance of a sculpted bust. The rent segments of the creature's remains were deflated balloons, no longer bearing the cursed water that once gave them weight.

Those who did not carry hacked off pieces of the wraith assisted the wounded members of Herman Wolf's troop. Herman Wolf himself carried his fallen comrade Osprey Feather over his shoulder.

The Maupai moved in unison as they walked the half mile back to the river's shore. Each tribesman who bore a body part placed it at the river's edge, arranging them in order from head to toe. As they did so, Wise Eyes positioned himself to John Rainbird's left. Trotting Fox moved to the young man's right.

The shaman lifted the husk of a head and chanted: "Great Spirits, O Great Spirits, we humbly beseech you to commit your lost kindred back into your bosom, for your kindred do not belong in this realm. We beseech you, Great Spirits, for it is the only way to restore balance for what has been wrought here. I gladly grant you three years of my lifespan if you grant this boon, great spirits."

He used his right bicep to press the severed head against his side as he produced the knife he had cut his palm with earlier, opening a neighboring wound without pause. He gathered the head in his left hand and pressed his wound against it, sealing his promise with blood.

Trotting Fox handed the head to Wise Eyes, who repeated the shaman's actions. Wise Eyes then handed the burden to John Rainbird, who did the same as his elders before tossing the dismembered part into the river. The three generations repeated the process with every rent portion of the creature, drops of blood reinforcing their promise.

Nine years, John Rainbird thought as the ceremony unfolded. *I've promised nine years of my life, altogether. Wise Eyes and Trotting Fox have each promised six.*

John Rainbird believed that he would by haunted by each of his elder's deaths, knowing that they sacrificed precious years because of his foolish actions.

No crackle of thunder or animal howl signified the end of the ceremony. Even the vociferous wind departed, leaving man and nature in mutual silence.

The Maupai fell into a long file, marching through the woods beyond the river into the western edge of Bay Corner proper. The sight of such a force of tribesman gathered would have caused great anxiety among town dwellers, but there was no one about to observe them during those black hours. They reached the Nissum Trail unseen, following its wooded course until it dumped out near the Eastern edge of town. John Rainbird looked in the direction of the trees that stood to the right of the trail when they had traveled three quarters through it, knowing that Rebecca's former home on Einhurst Road waited just beyond them.

David Tremblehorn's colleagues emerged from Detective Ballinger's Charger as the Maupai descended upon them at the outskirts of Blessed Earth. Detective Carpenter wasted no time in corralling his partner. "You alright, man?"

Tremblehorn nodded. He had not suffered any wounds from the creature, but he was forever changed. For the first time in his life, the spirit of his tribe had touched him. He now knew for a fact that there were worlds beyond the one he inhabited, that his people's belief in such worlds was more than a consequence of ignorant superstition.

"Is it finished?" Ballinger asked.

"It is finished," Wise Eyes said. "The price for my people was great, but it is finished. The vile spirit has been banished. There will be no more killing."

"Good," Hargrove said. "Now, I can go and get some fucking sleep."

"What will you tell your superiors?" John Rainbird wondered. "Won't they still expect you guys to arrest someone for the murders?"

Ballinger shrugged. "Who says we have to tell them anything? We'll all just go through the motions for a while, until it becomes a cold case. Won't be the first unsolved crimes in law enforcement history."

Carpenter chuckled. "Won't be the last, either."

Epilogue

I

Rose and Emma Saulters weren't the least bit surprised when a tall, careworn man knocked on the front door. They knew what brought him, having become accustomed to such visits in recent weeks.

People who tormented or had some connection to those who tormented Rebecca came to the house on Einhurst Road and humbled themselves before her mother and grandmother. They confessed their malice and begged for forgiveness, most breaking into tears as they unburdened themselves. Rose and Emma always forgave them, knowing that no matter how cruel or uncaring each of the confessors had been to Rebecca, none of them had killed her. The people mother and daughter christened "Rebecca's Pilgrims" might have believed they were responsible for her death, but Rose and Emma knew better.

They had met with Rebecca's Maupai friend and his forebears. The eldest of them, Trotting Fox, told them of his tribe's dread of Snake River, of their belief that it was a portal for wicked spirits. The young one, John Rainbird, detailed his compulsion to desecrate Rebecca's grave and summon a wraith that came to murder Rebecca's tormentors in their dreams. Trotting Fox told of forcing the wraith to take fleshly form and massing a great force of Maupai to face it with blessed weapons. He told of defeating the creature in a costly battle and watching Rebecca's essence ascend skyward. Trotting Fox assured Rose and Emma that Rebecca was at peace now.

Rose and Emma believed everything the Maupai said. It was easy to believe, because Rebecca visited them both in dreams, assuring them that she was free- that she was in a wonderful place now. They knew that no human authorities would catch the press christened "Drowning Killer" because the "Drowning Killer" had not been human.

Armed with all of that knowledge, Rose and Emma invited their caller in and waited for him to unburden himself. He sat down opposite the understated couch mother and daughter shared, on a matching loveseat. His fingers trembled as he held his hands out.

"I just want to apologize to you both," he managed. The scruffy blond beard he wore complemented the unkempt hair on his head. The two women were struck by his Nordic features, despite his poor grooming and haggardness from an obvious lack of sleep.

It was fitting that Mr. Anderson be the last of Rebecca's pilgrims, because he was the worst living offender. As he blathered in his confession, he raised his son to have disdain for females, to treat them as careless amusements. He also raised the departed Kevin to have the self-image of a minor God, to take his privileged birth as a sign of clear superiority over other kids.

"I taught him to treat his peers as a commodity at an early age," Mr. Anderson said, wiping tears away. "To manipulate people into doing his bidding, particularly young girls. I taught him about how pliable most of them were- that a boy of his known wealth, good looks, and inherent charm could have his pick of the litter. I also taught him to use them as playthings- that to do otherwise would cause him undue complications while trying to attain success in life."

The rich man bowed his head, covering his face with one large hand. "I even set him up in the pool house- against his mother's wishes. His own little bachelor pad- he was 12 years old when I gave it to him."

He fell silent for a few beats before looking at his hosts with earnest eyes. His thin lips bloomed into a bitter smile. "I knew he'd become sexually active at an early age- I guess I sort of wanted him to. I relentlessly beat the notion of using condoms into his head. I thought it would be great- having a young stud for a son. I knew he'd be a heartbreaker- but I didn't think it would be because of outright cruelty- purposely humiliating someone like he did Rebecca."

Red anger coursed through his face and balled fists, anger directed at himself. "But even after I found out what he'd done, I stood unconditionally in his corner. I goaded him on, telling him that it didn't matter if he posted that video so long as no one could prove it. I never once told him what he did was wrong. Some father I was. All I cared about was not getting any dirt stuck to the family name. I didn't lose any sleep at all in considering my son's terrible behavior. I brushed my poor wife's misgivings aside- telling her to stay out of it- telling her that I would guide the boy through this."

He sighed. "I did an outstanding job, too. An outstanding job of insuring that he didn't have to pay even a small penalty for his actions. I insured Principal Halloran that he would be facing a lawsuit if he took any disciplinary action against my son without proof."

Morose laughter escaped Mr. Anderson's throat. "I made it so that Kevin never experienced even the smallest of consequences for his cruel actions. I even made sure that Maupai boy got a good throttling when he broke onto our land. Then, I tried to have him locked away. The worst thing is- the worst thing is- I never lost sleep about anything I did, about the kind of father I was. I didn't even feel bad about it after Kevin was murdered. I saw the murder as a freak event, the actions of some crazy or pervert. I never considered that what happened might have been his comeuppance, even though I molded him into the kind of little prick to have it coming."

The confessor's bloodshot cobalt eyes widened and intensified. "But here lately- here lately I keep having these dreams. Your daughter visits me in these dreams. She takes me on a guided tour, showing me how cruel and selfish Kevin was, showing me how I molded him into that." He shifted in his seat. "These dreams- they seem so real. They are real. They're the truth. The truth is that I am greatly responsible for what my son did to your lost loved one. So I've come to apologize- to beg for your forgiveness, though I know I could never deserve you to grant it."

The guilty man watched the two women with pleading eyes as he fell silent, having said his earnest peace. Tears slalomed down his anguished face.

Mother and daughter glanced at each other, needing no words to express the shared sentiment that it was always this way. First a young man named Robert Bailey sent a letter all the way from Afghanistan, where he served in the military. The letter revealed that he'd been dreaming about Rebecca every night. The dreams made him confront the ramifications of his actions way back in fifth grade, when he christened her the "Knife Lady's Daughter." He had started her down a path of humiliation that didn't end until her death.

Shanae Thomas (who was the closest friend of the last of the *Drowning Killer's* victims), Tara Andrews, and Crystal Ritchie sought forgiveness in person. The three young ladies confessed harassing and bullying Rebecca from fifth until eighth grade. They were also complicit in vandalizing the very home they came to apologize in once the video scandal unfolded.

Nathan Halloran apologized for not doing more to keep Rebecca enrolled in Mackenzie High and for failing to level consequences against those who posted the damning video.

Kimberly Meisner and Phyllis Johnson apologized for deserting Rebecca at a time when she needed their friendship the most. A burly giant named Keith Myers came to apologize for raising a bullying lout of a daughter, the kind to take sadistic pleasure in picking on girls like Rebecca.

In exchange for promises to perform specific acts of kindness, the two Saulters women offered absolution to each of them. Just as they were sure of what Rebecca wanted from each party, they were also sure that each wish would be carried out once it was revealed.

For Principal Halloran, that meant galvanizing the establishment of a Mackenzie School scholarship in Rebecca's name and presenting her story to the student body as an example of what could happen when teenaged cruelty went too far. Kimberly and Phyllis were tasked with volunteering in soup kitchens on a regular basis, as Rebecca had. They were to do so in the towns they attended college in, as well as in Bay Corner while at home. Keith Myers had to sober up enough to volunteer some evenings as a counselor for a program that reached out to at risk youth. The price for Robert Bailey was to be an honorable soldier, never taking any action that the U.S. military could not disclose to the stateside public without fear of a disapproving outcry. Tara Andrews's price was to extricate herself from a life of whoring. Crystal Ritchie's task was to stop drifting through her post high school life without purpose- to pursue a path that would enable her to make a little money and help others. Working with the developmentally disabled seemed like a good start.

None of the "pilgrims" believed that what was asked of them was a great enough price to pay for their sins. None of them realized that their foul actions couldn't have driven Rebecca to suicide without being buttressed by an unseen evil. That evil traveled unchecked for a time- seducing Rebecca into believing that suicide was a far better choice than continuing to live the life of an outcast. That evil blinded Rebecca, preventing her from considering that her life might ever get better.

Rose and Emma waited for Rebecca's wealthiest pilgrim to gain his composure before revealing what was required of him. They felt no doubt that a man of his means and influence could get the job done.

II

Emma and Rose wore their finest Sunday pleasantry on this particular Saturday. They stood in the soup kitchen where Rebecca did her volunteer work. Mayor Ceasing, the surviving Anderson family, the Halloran brothers, and Rebecca's other "pilgrims" all clustered near. A dozen of the soup kitchen's volunteer staff joined the assembly. Many of them had worked with Rebecca before she died. More than fifty Bay Corner residents with direct connection to the person being honored were also present. Chief Wise Eyes was in attendance, along with John Rainbird Jeffries and his pretty fiancée.

Trotting Fox was not in attendance, having passed in his sleep during the Ides of March, two and a half weeks earlier. The death of such a vigorous man (even one as old as Trotting Fox had been) might have seemed mysterious to the uninitiated, but his people knew that his passing was the fulfillment of a grand sacrifice.

This was not a day to dwell on death or other losses. This was a day to commemorate a girl with a golden heart- a girl who showed kindness to others even when life was not kind to her.

Mr. Anderson's tireless lobbying efforts had made this occasion possible. As Vice President of Operations for the town's largest employer, he took full advantage of having the Mayor and Town Council's respective ears, insisting that

Bay Corner honor Rebecca for the selfless service she provided to the less fortunate.

Rose and Emma Saulters gave heartfelt speeches on Rebecca's behalf. Mayor Ceasing cut the ribbon, renaming the Bay Corner Soup Kitchen as the Rebecca Saulters Soup Kitchen. There was nothing left to do but serve food to the needy people assembled outside, as Rebecca herself had done many times.

III

The River waited, as it always had. Most of its ages of existence consisted of the same. It wasn't unusual for decades to go by before it found a suitable victim for its voracious clutches- but what are decades to that which is eternal? It had hoped to feast on the force of Maupai who dared to confront it, but they showed far more strength than expected. The one called Trotting Fox led them well. The river was not satisfied that the great man died a few weeks later (which was not even equal to the blink of an eye in its millennia old life). Nor would the river find satisfaction when the one called Wise Eyes and his offspring (the one called John Rainbird) passed from the land of men. The river would not be satisfied because the others would join Trotting Fox in an afterlife that men found pleasant, escaping being feasted upon by its hungry denizens.

The river lusted for new prey, unsuspecting victims that it could devour. The stigma it had acquired through local legend conspired with the pleasant reputations of the nearby Chesapeake Bay, Susquehanna River, and Bush River, reducing the amount of potential prey that wandered to its shore. But sooner or later, a wounded and malleable vessel like Rebecca Saulters would come. Then, the great serpent would feed again.

Coming Soon:

The Coming

A novel by

T.R. Braxton

MONTEBELLO BOOKS

October- 1975

I

Michael Foster's eyes fell on a breathtakingly pretty girl, distracting him from conversation with his jock buddies. The object of his admiration sat ignorant to her audience a few tables away, giggling with her friends. Prominent dimples complemented her cherubic smile. In a cafeteria full of teenaged beauties, she was the one to raise his pulse.

Michael figured that she had to be in the tenth grade or he would have known her already. In fact, if she had not been in the tenth grade there was a good chance he would have already had his way with her.

The girl smiled when she noticed Michael staring at her. It was a small and cautious smile, seeming to grant approval to test the water, but not to dive right in.

The smile Michael returned fell a hair short of goofy. He hadn't spoken one word to the girl yet, but he was already falling under her spell. His friend and teammate Hawkeye brought him back to earth by throwing a paper ball at his head.

"Damn, Cap'n," Hawkeye said, "What the hell you gawkin' at?"

Michael didn't bother to answer. Instead he picked up his lunch tray, unraveled all 78 inches of his wiry strong frame, and headed to the table where the girl sat.

A pair of the girl's friends choked squeals as they noticed him approaching. Michael thought that they were pretty cute, themselves- especially the one with the big titties. But he had come for the cream of the crop.

Looking at the girl with the big breasts, he spoke in his sonorous baritone, "You mind movin' down for me, baby?"

The large breasted girl blushed as she obliged him. Michael slid into the vacated space, directly across from his intended. He swept his long legs under the cafeteria table with the ease of one well practiced. Next, he fixed the girl with what he thought of as his sexy look.

"What's happenin', baby?" he asked, pitching his voice to sound even deeper than its natural state.

The girl rolled her eyes. "What's happening is I'm not your baby. My name is Marlena."

Michael chuckled, surprised by her sass. "I'm sorry." He smiled a charming smile. "What's happenin'- Marlena?"

"Nothing much." Marlena abandoned the mystery meat on her plate and bit into an apple.

"My name is Michael," he said, extending a sinewy right hand that could palm a basketball as if it were a cantaloupe.

Marlena hesitated before allowing her own normal sized hand to be engulfed in her admirer's. The brief contact before she pulled away caused a jolt of excitement to course through him.

"I already know who you are," she said. "You're Michael Foster-the captain of the basketball team. People say you're the best high school player in Baltimore since Skip Wise. Some people say you're the best ever."

"Yeah, that's me. I'm on the football team, too. Second team All-Metro wide receiver last year, an' football is only my second sport. I'm an all-around great athlete."

"I guess big things are in store for you," Marlena spoke with more than a hint of sarcasm.

"Maybe. You know most people are really impressed by that."

Marlena shrugged. "I'm not most people."

Michael burst into laughter. "No, you're definitely not most people. But, that's cool. I like your style. Mar-lee-nuh."

She couldn't help laughing at the silly way he said her name. The other girls seated at the table also laughed. Michael knew they would have done so even if they didn't think it was funny. Right around the time the *Baltimore Sun* started to write about him on a regular basis, his attempts at humor became unfailingly amusing to a large population of coat tail riders.

He felt sure that Marlena's laughter was genuine, though. He could tell that she wouldn't have faked a laugh for Christ himself.

During the next minute or so of conversation, Michael showed Marlena that he was more than just the Big Man on Campus, used to receiving the adoration that came with the role. He actually had a good personality. Still, she didn't give him her phone number until the next day.

The fact that Marlena didn't seem impressed only made Michael more determined to pursue her. He figured anything worthwhile in life would always be a challenge, that there is always a price to pay for getting what you want.

II

Marlena's mother wasted no time in interrogating Michael the first time he called her house. Ms. Atkins couldn't care less about how great of an athlete he was. She didn't care about the number of times his stats leapt from box scores in the High School sports section of the *Baltimore Sun*. She didn't care about how many colleges wanted him or that he led Patterson to a valiant loss in the state championship game during his first year on the varsity team. Ms. Atkins would not judge Michael on his athletic feats or his handsome looks. She told him all of this within a minute of answering the phone, the first time he called to speak with Marlena.

The remainder of the conversation consisted of Michael stating his case for why he should even be allowed to call Marlena. Once Ms. Atkins agreed, an emboldened Michael asked if he might take Marlena out some weekend. Ms. Atkins then demanded that he explain why her daughter should be allowed to go on her first date with the likes of him.

"Because I like her and I'll treat her with the respect a lady deserves," Michael said.

"My daughter *is* a lady," Ms. Atkins said. "I raised her that way. You really want to take her out sometime- you come on by the house and meet me tomorrow evening and I'll see how I feel about it after meeting you in person. I'll be home around 7, so I expect you here at 7:30. Marlena will give you the address. Now hold on while I call her to the phone. I won't have her talking to you all evening, either."

"Yes, ma'am," Michael said, realizing that things were bound to move slowly between he and Marlena with a roadblock like her mother in the path. A sly smile stretched across his face as he thought that he could afford to be patient. After all, he was getting plenty of sexual gratification elsewhere.

There were tons of chicks hoping to be his girlfriend or, better yet, the mother of his child. That way, they could use his future NBA money to give themselves the good life. Michael possessed a well-practiced knack for identifying girls who defined success as being taken care of by a well to do man. He called such girls his "victims". They didn't like for him to use rubbers, but his Uncle Clyde drilled him on the importance of being steadfast about that. "Bustin' a nut ain't worth givin' some hussy a free ride for the next 18 years," was one of Uncle Clyde's favorite expressions.

Michael had no intention of making Marlena a "victim". He wanted to be straight up with her, take her out on dates and treat her like a lady, just like he'd promised her mother. He needed to win Ms. Atkins's confidence before he could do any of those things.

III

Michael dragged Tito and Hawkeye to Old Town Mall (a strip of outdoor shops in East Baltimore) after football practice. Their initial protests of being tired from wind sprints, up downs, and drills were quieted by his promise to buy them each some wings and fries. Michael didn't love football nearly as much as he loved basketball, but that didn't stop him from being a formidable wide receiver. As a bonus, the football team's grueling conditioning program assured him of being in tip-top shape when basketball season started. Still, he had no intention of spending any time on the gridiron in college. Basketball was his future, as well as his true passion.

He parked his uncle's cobalt blue Electra 225 at a nearby parking lot before heading to the Diplomat shop. Once inside the popular men's clothing store, he peeled off a wad of bills that Russell Reed had given him.

The big time street hustler made a habit of giving Michael "some change" from time to time. Russell never asked for anything in return. He believed that "a big basketball star oughta keep some money in his pocket." Michael viewed Russell's generosity as one of the spoils of being a big time athlete.

Michael purchased a new dress shirt and pants to wear to Ms. Atkins's house. He hoped that his natty appearance would convince her that to behave as a gentleman with her daughter.

"Must be nice to be so rich," Tito ribbed Michael as he paid the cashier.

"Hell yeah! You keep bread like that an' you're still in high school?" Hawkeye joined in. "You sure you're not moonlighting for the Bullets?"

Hawkeye referred to Washington D.C.'s NBA team, which had left Baltimore three years earlier, but still played selected home dates at the Baltimore Civic Center.

Michael punched one of Hawkeye's heavily-muscled shoulders. "As long as I have money to buy y'all wings and fries- what do you clowns care?"

"Speaking of which," Tito said as they left the store. "It's time you pay up. I'm hungry like I got a damn tapeworm."

"You're always hungry." Hawkeye poked at his friend's slightly protruding stomach. "That's why you're gittin' a little belly."

"It might poke out a little but it's solid as a rock." Tito slapped the spot in question, producing a dull sound.

Michael grinned. "It's solid, alright," he said. "'Bout as solid as a bowl of Jell-O."

Within a few minutes, the three young athletes were greedily scarfing down the promised wings and fries in a carry-out just a few doors down from the Diplomat Shop. Michael's forever stretching frame overwhelmed the table they sat at much as it did the cafeteria tables at Patterson. His friend's bulky frames didn't fare much better.

Michael was the first to exit, carrying his new outfit hung safely inside a plastic covering. "Come on," he said, slinging his cargo over one shoulder and beckoning to his friends. "I got to git y'all home so I kin have time to change. I got to win Marlena's mother over tonight and that ain't goin' happen if I'm late."

"Man, you kin have any girl you want." Hawkeye shrugged as he fell in step. "Why you puttin' yourself through all this trouble over a sophmore?"

"I really like that 'sophmore'. Besides, we were sophmores just last year."

"Yeah," Tito said. "But, that was last year. Now, we're superstar athletes."

Michael grinned. "No, I'm a superstar athlete," he said. "Y'all are just in my shadow."

Tito scowled. "Forget you, man."

Hawkeye laughed. "Don't git offended, Tito. I'll be glad to stay in his shadow so long as I kin keep havin' his cast offs and rejects. I like bein' on the clean-up crew."

Tito frowned as Michael and Hawkeye slapped each other five.

Michael heard hooves clomp along the cobblestone pathway just then. The cry of: "Aeeeeeeee- rabb- bah! Aeeeeeeeee-rabb- bah here!" joined the hooves. Michael had heard some variation of that declaration many times, but never in such a pained, haunting tone. The eerie sound emanated from the old man who handled the reins of a small but determined horse that dragged a wooden cart stocked with fruits and vegetables.

Arabbers were a common sight in the inner city and downtown Baltimore. The moving vendors walked the streets alongside horse or pony-drawn carts of fruits and vegetables very much like the one that now approached Michael and his friends.

This particular arabber's skin looked ashen and leathery. Dark shades covering his eyes, belying the mild autumn sun. His strained voice sounded as if he spent a lifetime chain smoking unfiltered cigarettes. Something in that voice made Michael's skin crawl.

"Fresh frooots and vegetables! Fresh froooots and vegetables!" the arabber's chilling voice carried in the open air.

"Look, man." Tito chuckled and pointed as the man neared them. "That arabber's old as Methusaleh!"

"I think he *is* Methusaleh," Hawkeye added. "Even his damn pony looks old. His pony looks like a fossil."

"Shit, Hawk. That ain't no pony. That's a damn donkey."

Tito and Hawkeye nearly fell over laughing.

Michael scowled. "Y'all are just bein' ignorant," he said. "That's not funny-makin' fun of a man tryna earn an honest livin'."

"Damn, Cap'n," Hawkeye grumbled. "We were just jokin' around."

"Yeah? Well, your jokes ain't always funny."

The arabber drew within 20 feet of them, yet gave no indication that he'd heard the insults. Up close, Michael could see the creases and lines of a long, hard life in the old man's wizened skin. His horse looked just as careworn. Michael felt sorry for the old guy.

"How much for a cantaloupe?" Michael fell in step with the vendor, slowing his stride to keep his giraffe legs from outpacing the cart. He could've crawled and kept pace with the poor horse.

"Seventy-five cents." The death rattle voice nearly dropped into a whisper.

"I'll have two." Michael handed over a crisp five dollar bill.

The old man tugged at the pony's reins with calloused hands, it to stop its' labored movement. As the arabber felt around the cart for his requests, Michael realized that the poor guy was blind. The arabber placed the cantaloupes in a large brown bag before handing it to Michael. As the arabber reached in his pocket to make change, Michael waved him off. Feeling foolish, Michael reminded himself that the man couldn't see him.

"You kin keep the change, man."

"That's very kind of you, young man," the arabber said, smiling through dry, cracked lips. "But, I have to make an honest living even if I am old and blind. I'm far too proud to accept charity." He handed Michael three dollars bills and two quarters.

Michael wondered how a blind man could make change with such ease before their hands brushed during the exchange. A blurry image flashed through Michael's mind when they did. He almost dropped the money in surprise.

The old man recoiled at the same time, nearly losing his footing. "Oh, no," he gasped, cowering as if facing some terrifying entity. "Oh, please. No."

"What the hell just happened?" Michael asked.

"What's wrong, Cap'n?" Tito asked- as Hawkeye looked on in confusion.

The old man darted forward and seized Michael's wrist with a speed that belied his weathered appearance. As the old man held him, Michael's mind flooded with more blurred images, images that filled him with dread.

Michael made no effort to shed the arabber's grasp. Tito and Hawkeye yanked assailant away, just avoiding tumbling into the street with him. The arabber's shades fell from his face when they grabbed him. His eyes were seas of white, devoid of pupils.

"Oh my God!" Tito cried, releasing his hold. "This old bastard ain't got no eyeballs!"

Passersby gawked as the arabber stooped to recover his shades. A woman in a floral print dress grumbled to her friend about how youths today have no respect for their elders.

"Don't be disrespectful!" Michael heard himself speak, although he felt as if he were watching this scene unfold from far away. "Damn, y'all act like you don't have any granfolks! You got no business callin' him an 'old bastard'."

Tito hung his head. "You're right, man. I shouldn't have said that." He grew animated, pointing at the arabber. "But, he got no business grabbin' you like that!"

"Yeah, man," Hawkeye agreed. "Let's git away from this old ba…old man. He ain't right."

"Let your friends proceed on their way." The old man pointed a gnarled finger at Michael. "But I'll have words with you."

"Anything you got to say to Cap'n' you can say…," Tito began, only to be silenced by Michael's outstretched hand.

"Y'all start walkin' back toward my car," Michael said, his voice measured. "I'll be there in a minute."

"But…," Hawkeye grumbled.

"I'll be there in a *minute!*"

Tito and Hawkeye looked at each other in confusion as they did as told. Michael expected them to have plenty of questions when he rejoined them. Satisfied with the distance between himself and his friends, Michael fixed his eyes on the arabber. Having no idea why, he felt compelled to hear the old man out.

"You seem to be a kind young man." The arabber's gravelly voice made Michael uneasy. "It's a shame about your bloodline."

"My *what?*"

"Your bloodline. It's cursed, just as mine is. Though some would dare say mine is truly a blessing, I say it is a *curse.* No man should have to know the things I know."

Michael shrugged, his shoulders falling just short of caressing his ears. "I don't understand what you're talkin' about."

"You wouldn't. And I suppose that's not all that important, but what is important is this. You must father no children."

Michael laughed. "Of course I don't wanna have kids right now. I'm only 17. I'm still in high school."

"Yet you fornicate with many," the old man said.

"Shit, mister. That can't really be helped. The girls just throw it at me on account of me being a big basketball star. I always use rubbers, though."

The old man's laugh sounded as harsh as his speaking voice. "You would do well to take more precautions than that. You must not father any children."

"Yeah. I git it, man. I don't know what better 'precaution' there is than rubbers, though. The only other thing would be to trust the girl to use the pill. An' someone in my position would be stupid to trust that. There's plenty girls that

390

would love to git pregnant by me because they just know I'll be going pro after I graduate college. Shit, maybe sooner. The ABA drafted Moses Malone straight out of high school last year. You never know, I keep getting better…"

"You don't understand!" the old man screamed, removing his glasses.

Michael fell silent as he stared into the huge white orbs where pupils should have been.

"You must *never* father any children," the old man continued. "Not now. Not ever. If you do, you will bring only pain and suffering into the world. It is time for your cursed bloodline to end!"

"Alright, man. Alright." Michael decided that the old man was as crazy as his buddies thought. He figured that paying lip service to the crazy talk would help him get away sooner. "I got it. No children. *Ever.* Is there anything else?"

"Only that you would be a fool not to heed my warning." The old man put his sunglasses back on.

"I said I got you." Michael moved away, feeling as if a cloud had lifted. "Thanks for the cantaloupes. You have a good day, sir."

"I shall not rest until I know your fate."

It took a great deal of self-control for Michael to suppress what he felt was much deserved laughter. "Damn, man. If you wanna know my 'fate', jus' listen to sportscasts. Come the end of November, I'll be lightin' up every court I step on as usual. Until then, I might catch me a touchdown pass or two. Ain't nothin' more to my 'fate' than that."

Michael sauntered away, glad that the old man could not see the grin on his face. Back at the car, Tito and Hawkeye wanted to know what the hell the crazy old coot had said.

"Oh, nothin'," Michael lied. "I just reminded him of somebody he used to know."

"How the hell are you goin' remind him of somebody he used to know when he can't even see?" Tito asked.

"You's an ignorant fool sometimes, Tito. Did it ever occur to you that he might not've been blind his whole life?"

Hawkeye laughed, hiding the fact that he had shared the same narrow minded thought. "Yeah," he said. "I don't know what the hell goes through your mind sometimes, Tito."

As Michael drove away, the arabber remained where they'd parted, sheer terror coursing through every fiber of his aged being. He stroked his horse's mane, attempting to comfort himself as well as the animal.

"Please Lord, let him heed my warning," the arabber prayed. "Please Lord, let him heed."

Also Available from Montebello Books:

Dirty Hands

A novel by

T.R. Braxton

Terrell Hawkins, his closest cousin, and his best friend set out to have a good time on a Saturday night. Alcohol, marijuana, and immodest girls who like to partake in both are part of that pursuit. They don't expect the debauchery to end in tragedy, just as they don't expect their horrible response to embroil them in a struggle to avoid the authorities while growing increasingly distrusting of each other. Terrell and the others quickly learn that dirty hands can lead to desperate acts and that the worst of circumstances can cause even the best of friends to become enemies.

Available in paperback and e-book at Amazon.com, trbraxton.com, and everywhere books are sold.

Also Available from Montebello Books:

Sight

A novel by

T.R. Braxton

Young Nathan Walker performs feats with his mind that normal humans can't fathom, feats that drain his mind and body. His ability is instrumental in keeping his father, an early twentieth century civil rights activist, from harm. Tragedy strikes when Nathan's fear of his own power causes him to turn away from it. In the wake of that tragedy, Nathan focuses his vast and frightening capabilities on revenge. He will not stop until vengeance is his, even if he must sacrifice himself to obtain it.

Available in paperback and e-book at Amazon.com, trbraxton.com, and everywhere books are sold.

www.ingramcontent.com/pod-product-compliance
Lightning Source LLC
Chambersburg PA
CBHW021214260626
47172CB00002B/424